GRAHAMS TOWN.

SCALE
10 20   40   60   80   100 Miles

The Map Drawn & Engraved by J. Rapkin.

COMPANY OF SPEARS

COMPANY OF SPEARS

Allan Mallinson

BANTAM PRESS

LONDON • TORONTO • SYDNEY • AUCKLAND • JOHANNESBURG

TRANSWORLD PUBLISHERS
61–63 Uxbridge Road, London W5 5SA
a division of The Random House Group Ltd

RANDOM HOUSE AUSTRALIA (PTY) LTD
20 Alfred Street, Milsons Point, Sydney,
New South Wales 2061, Australia

RANDOM HOUSE NEW ZEALAND LTD
18 Poland Road, Glenfield, Auckland 10, New Zealand

RANDOM HOUSE SOUTH AFRICA (PTY) LTD
Isle of Houghton, Corner of Boundary and Carse O'Gowrie Roads,
Houghton 2198, South Africa

Published 2006 by Bantam Press
a division of Transworld Publishers

A catalogue record for this book is available from the British Library.
ISBN 9780593053416 (from Jan 07)
ISBN 0593053419

Typeset in 11/14.5pt Times by
Falcon Oast Graphic Art Ltd

Printed in Great Britain by
Clays Ltd, Bungay, Suffolk

1 3 5 7 9 10 8 6 4 2

Papers used by Transworld Publishers are natural, recyclable products made
from wood grown in sustainable forests. The manufacturing processes
conform to the environmental regulations of the country of origin.

FOREWORD

It is thirty-five years since publication of Correlli Barnett's *Britain and Her Army*, still probably the best military, political and social history of an institution uniquely reviled and yet revered. In a chapter called 'Decay and Reform' Barnett, who remains to this day the most trenchant critic of the mismanagement and mis-application of military force, describes the half-century after Waterloo in terms that have a contemporary ring: colonial fight-ing 'bred an emphasis on "regimental" qualities – discipline, personal bravery and boldness in combat – as the principal ingredients in military success, while on the other hand it led to a relative neglect of the intellectual requirements of the conduct of war.' He describes how 'thanks to their mercenary army' Britain as a whole 'would never feel the burden of world power in the Victorian age . . . The British could rage at military incompetence when the army they neglected (and never joined) suffered some disaster . . . they could presume to take pride in victories won despite their indifference. War became a noise far away.'

Matthew Hervey and the 6th Light Dragoons knew about noise far away: they had heard it well enough in India. But they also knew there could be noise at home – if not actual war then certainly something as repugnant, for in 1827 the Metropolitan Police Act was still two years off, and the magistrates therefore had early recourse to the army when civil disturbance threatened. There was Ireland too, restive in its condition of exploitative poverty and discriminatory legislation. There was, indeed, noise enough to disturb a good night's sleep from time to time, though never so much as to keep the country awake for too long.

So Hervey, thirty-six years old, and in the midst of that glorious metamorphosis from a regimental to a commanding officer, finds himself in noisy circumstances once again. And, naturally, he meets those who would put fingers in their ears rather than deal with the noise. For this is an age (Barnett's decay before the reform) when change is regarded as unnecessary, perhaps even injurious to those regimental qualities that had assured victory at Waterloo: discipline, personal bravery and boldness in combat. Meanwhile, in Prussia, a major general not very much older than Hervey – Carl von Clausewitz – who had fought the French that day in 1815, is putting the final touches to his penetrating study of war and its practice, so that if a Prussian army were again required to do its Kaiser's will it would do so with absolute efficiency. And at the other end of the technological spectrum, in southern Africa, an instinctive soldier, Shaka, King of the Zulu, is consolidating his astonishing military successes; for in truth Shaka and Clausewitz speak the same military language.

Last year, 2005, was of course the bicentenary of that other great battle in the Nation's struggle against Bonaparte: *Trafalgar*. Trafalgar and the name of Nelson are synonymous; and rightly so. But Nelson for all his genius and courage could not have won without good ships and good men. Indeed, the victory at Trafalgar was a victory for the *system* of the Royal Navy, whose foundations Pepys and others had so surely laid a century and a quarter before, and which continuing address and money had brought to a remarkable pitch of effectiveness by 1805. Last year was also the hundred and fiftieth anniversary of the Crimean winter which saw the near-destruction of a British army equipped, organized and trained as if for Waterloo: the ultimate decadence before reform. If the country could celebrate Trafalgar with such pride as last year, then she could also do well to ponder on the disasters of the Crimea, for the *habit* of success is no *guarantee* of success.

It is these uncompromising lessons that Matthew Hervey is realizing he must begin to learn – and painfully.

Rebuke the company of spearmen...
scatter thou the people that delight in war.

Psalm 68

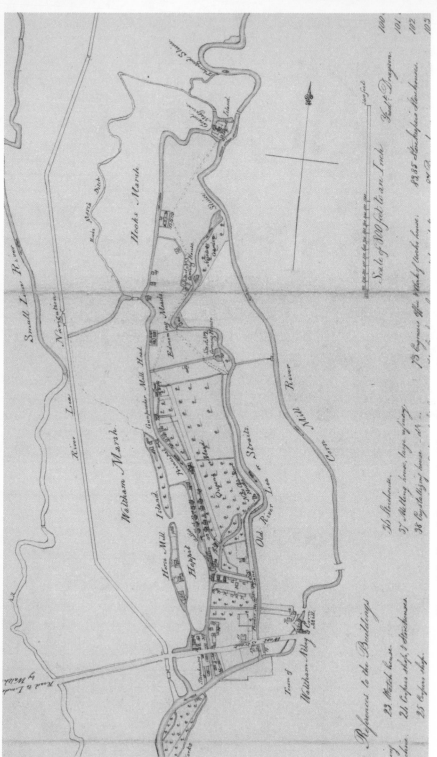

Plan of the Royal Gunpowder Manufactory at Waltham Abbey in 1830 by Frederick Drayson from his *A Treatise on Gunpowder*. The National Archive, ref. MFII 15/31

PART ONE
PATHS OF GLORY

England

CHAPTER ONE

MANOEUVRES

Hounslow Heath, 12 March 1827

Acting-Major Matthew Hervey nodded to the adjutant, and in as many seconds only as it took for him, the officer in temporary command of the 6th Light Dragoons, to rein round to face front again, the first section of the Chestnut Troop discharged a thunderous salvo. Gilbert, his battle-charger, and at rising fifteen years a seasoned campaigner, threw up his head but did not move a foot. Hervey let out the reins a little so that the iron grey gelding could play with the bit as reward.

He looked over his left shoulder, then his right. The lines were ragged. Troop horses had leapt forward, some had run back, others had reared and turned. Barely half the regiment stood as they had been dressed. Even his trumpeter's grey, a mare which should have known better, was showing a flank and bucking hard, determined to unseat her rider.

Hervey nodded again, the adjutant raised his arm, and the

Chestnuts' second section fired. As the smoke cleared, he could see the first section's men standing ready, guns reloaded, and second section's beginning the thirty fevered seconds of swabbing, ramming and tamping before the number one could shout 'On!' to tell his section officer that the gun was shotted and re-laid on its target.

Except that there was no shot or target. The Chestnut (more properly the *First*) Troop, Royal Horse Artillery, fired blank this morning. They did so to accustom the remounts – and recruits – of the 6th Light Dragoons to the noise of battle. It was not much by way of comparison with the real thing, Hervey knew (*by God,* how he knew!), but it was a good deal better than nothing; and certainly a good deal better than the usual method, the band's banging and crashing on the square. It was decent of the Chestnuts to oblige them thus, although the Sixth had paid for the powder; and in any case, Hervey thought there must be gain for the Chestnuts too, for there was nothing like the thrill of real powder instead of 'dry' drills on the parade ground – even if the gun jumped back not a fraction of what it would when shotted and full-charged. He would have each of them fire in turn now, six nine-pounders, to test the nerve of the horses which had been half petrified into docility by the two salvos. He nodded to the adjutant a third time.

Number one gun fired, and the remaining rooks in the distant elms took flight, so that Hervey imagined there was not a bird perched on any branch on Hounslow Heath.

'Rugged elms,' he mused. He liked elms. As a boy he had climbed them, about the churchyard in Horningsham, to test his courage or to see what the tall nests held. Or sometimes on the plain to gain a distant prospect. He loved the elm-lined lanes in high summer, dark leafy tunnels where he might catch sight of a roe deer at midday – still, secret places, a foreign land, far from the safe parsonage and yet within sound of the church bell. There were no elms in foreign lands, though. Or if there were, they were

4

poor specimens: he had seen none he could recall in France, or Belgium, none in the forests of the east – India, Ava – and certainly not in Spain and Portugal. Yet there *must* have been . . . but not the 'rugged elm'. He thought of his Wiltshire churchyard again, 'where heaves the turf in many a mould'ring heap'; beneath the tall elms, where 'the rude forefathers of the hamlet sleep'. Yes, the elm had a power to command attention, more so even than the oak. Elms were England's leafy witnesses – to village-Hampdens, mute inglorious Miltons and guiltless Cromwells, as well as to the great men themselves. What was it in that poem that could conjure a vision of his youth – his simpler, honest, *chaste* youth? Was it true that General Wolfe (as brave as any man to wear the King's uniform) had said before battle that he would rather have composed Gray's *Elegy written in a Country Churchyard* than take Quebec? Hervey did not suppose that Wolfe had meant it to be taken exactly literally, if he had said it at all; nevertheless there lay power in those words, power to invoke a visceral love of country. Was it not time for him, now, to return to the elms of Horningsham, to 'the blazing hearth', and to his makings? The question was pointless: behind him, albeit under his *temporary* orders, was his regiment – *his* regiment! This was what he had dreamed of for long years. There could never be a going back. Not, surely, without diminution? But was that not to pit himself against Gray's own injunction: 'Let not ambition mock their useful toil'? He must not allow himself conceit in this temporary command:

> The boast of heraldry, the pomp of pow'r,
> And all that beauty, all that wealth e'er gave,
> Awaits alike th' inevitable hour.

(He shuddered)

> The paths of glory lead but to the grave.

Number two gun fired. Gilbert snorted. Number four followed three with but a split second's interval. The last of the rooks, bravest of the brave, quit the furthest elms. Hervey glanced over his shoulder. The sight was no boast of heraldry, nor of anything else for that matter. He would have the Chestnut Troop blaze away until both ranks of the regiment, three squadrons in line, were dressed with a decent semblance of security (and he wondered if the Chestnuts would run out of powder before then). Then he would have his dragoons draw carbines, load and fire, return carbines, draw sabres and advance in line. They would not finish with a charge, however, as field days usually required: the heath was too broken to risk a gallop in regimental line – not, at least, with so many new men and horses.

Number five gun fired and a trooper from C Troop bolted, its rider, a seasoned dragoon, hauling on the reins for all he was worth but without effect. The Chestnuts' captain tried to stay number six gun, but it fired prematurely. The sponger was hurled a hundred yards still clutching the ramrod, and the ventsman was thrown to the ground beside the trail.

It oughtn't to happen, Hervey knew, but it did occasionally: all it took was a piece of wadding still glowing when the next charge was loaded. 'Insufficient sponging,' he said to himself. 'Poor devil.'

The Chestnuts' captain ordered his first section to continue the firing while the rest of the premature's crew doubled forward to recover the unfortunate gun number. They found him with not a mark on his face or hands, but motionless, his neck snapped. As they picked the man up, the runaway from C Troop found a rabbit hole and somersaulted twice, driving a shoe into the face of its floored rider. No one moved to his aid; no one would, not without the order of the officer commanding.

When neither horse nor rider rose, Hervey turned to the adjutant. 'Have C Troop bring in their man,' he said, sounding weary.

*

The Chestnuts thundered away for a full ten minutes more. Slowly the Sixth's lines began to straighten, and the troopers to stand quiet. Hervey was at last gratified. It had been barely a year since they had stood before the walls of the great fortress at Bhurtpore, where thirty times the number of guns had each thrown three times the weight of shot that horse artillery could dispose, and yet the regiment could not be called 'steady to fire'. It was not their fault, and certainly not his predecessor's in command, for the regiment had not brought those battle-hardened horses back from India with them, exchanging them instead (as required by the War Office for reasons of economy) with the outgoing regiment at Hounslow.

Predecessor in command: he ought to say *predecessors*, for there had been three officers with the privilege of commanding dragoons in the past twelve months or so. Hervey sighed. What a sorry procession it had been. Lieutenant-Colonel Sir Ivo Lankester, Bart, whose elder brother had been killed in temporary command of the regiment at Waterloo, had died at the head of his men in the storming of Bhurtpore, leaving a wife of but a year, and with child. Command had devolved without purchase therefore on the senior major, Eustace Joynson, a man much loved by all ranks for his devotion to duty, and facility with administration. But Joynson was a tired man and full of sadness (a wayward daughter – his 'life sentence' as he confessed to Hervey). He was ill-fitted to command, and he knew it, and so he had taken the windfall lieutenant-colonelcy to the regimental agents (it was said he would get fifteen thousand for it at least), and in the interim, while the commander-in-chief's staff considered the bids, so to speak, the Sixth had come under the orders of Hervey's old friend Major Benedict Strickland. Strickland had been senior to him by months only, but Hervey had looked forward nevertheless to rejoining the regiment after his ill-starred mission in Portugal. In all likelihood, Hervey reckoned, Strickland had been the first Catholic to have command of a regiment under a Hanoverian king, albeit temporary command, for the Test Act required that all holders of military office be

7

communicants of the Church of England (as well as taking the oaths of Allegiance and Supremacy, denying the doctrine of Transubstantiation). The Relief Act of 1793 had opened a door to Catholic officers, if a very small one, requiring a simple oath of loyalty rather than anything troubling to tender consciences; and Strickland had observed his religion discreetly. Even so, he had not always found things easy. When the Earl of Towcester – infamous memory! – had commanded, ten years past, 'damned papists' had been his taunt, but always protected by position, so that Strickland would have been on uncertain ground had he called him out.

Well, thought Hervey, watching C Troop's orderly corporal bringing the motionless dragoon to where the surgeon stood, Strickland had endured those years with commendable dignity. He had deserved his honour. It had been the cruellest fate that in three months he was dead too, killed in a smash with the Oxford mail as his chariot raced back to Hounslow along the foggy turnpike. Hervey had dined with him that very evening, and Strickland had taken him back to the United Service Club afterwards. Hervey's last words on bidding his old friend goodnight had been a promise to join him at Hounslow within the week.

And how he had looked forward to that. The Spanish business (or ought he to say Portuguese?) had left a bitter taste. He had gone to Lisbon full of hope. Kat – Lady Katherine Greville – the much younger wife of old, absentee Lieutenant-General Sir Peregrine Greville, and some years now Hervey's lover-patroness, had got him the commission through her influence with the Duke of Wellington. And then affairs had rapidly turned sour. He had fallen out with his commanding officer, Colonel Norris, over the best means of deploying the army of intervention (he could not feel much regret for that, since Norris was a tedious, pedantic, narrow-thinking artilleryman; though he *had* been his commanding officer), and although Hervey had been vindicated in his estimate of what was the best course for the army, he had paid a heavy price: he had never expected to see the fortress of Badajoz again,

8

and certainly not as a prisoner. He had escaped – not without bloodshed – but to the prospect of court martial. Had he not had friends, 'friends at court' (and Kat was, as ever, his most assiduous friend in that regard), he was sure he would have been finished.

A sudden hubbub to the left of the line made him turn, and testily, imagining another dragoon had involuntarily dismounted (such an unfortunate was always the butt of ribald advice, even if he were an officer – more so, indeed, for greater would be the sconce on return to barracks). He smiled, however: a big dog fox trotted parallel to the line not fifty yards off, stopping every so often and giving the ranks a glance, wary rather than timorous, then trotting on with an air of indifference. It was strange, thought Hervey, that he should break cover so close, when there was nothing before them but a mile and more of heath. Perhaps the sight of several hundred horses was not of itself alarming if they were not accompanied by hounds? Or perhaps here was one fox who had never been hunted, and therefore inclined to see a regiment of cavalry rather than a field of hunting men? He now halted directly to the front of where Hervey stood, as if one horse in advance of the rest deserved particular scrutiny. Hervey saluted him: he was a fine fellow, clean-coated, full-brushed – last year's cub, possibly. Many a time on Salisbury Plain with Daniel Coates he had observed the fox as close, and even in Spain, but he did not think he had seen a finer specimen. He could have sworn Reynard looked him straight in the eye. He took hold of his shako peak and bid him 'goodnight'.

Another of the Chestnuts' guns fired. The fox turned at once and ran left away from the line. Gilbert began dancing and pulling: there may have been no hounds, but a running fox surely spelled a chase. Horses the length of the line evidently thought the same, judging by the hallooing behind, until the cursing of the troop serjeant-majors brought back proper order. Spirits were high enough, reckoned Hervey; he could be content in that at least, even

9

if the greenness of so many horses and dragoons dismayed him. But then, was that not a part of the satisfaction of command, the drilling of a regiment? He might have them for a few months only – six, the regiment's colonel, Lord George Irvine, had thought likely – but that was sufficient time to drill them to a certain handiness; even to the satisfaction of the lieutenant-colonel who would in due course assume the substantive command. There might be no immediate prospect of active service (he thought it most unlikely there would be any reinforcement of the expeditionary force in Portugal, for there were five thousand redcoats there already, and the Duke of Wellington was most anxious to have them back), but – *fortis fortuna adiuvat* – opportunity there could come. The Greek war, for one, was unresolved; there was too the enduring promise – or threat – of aid to the civil power, and, of course, there was that combustible place Ireland. And if no one but he could be persuaded that the Sixth might have to draw sabres in earnest, there was the annual inspection in July: the major-general commanding the London District was known to be a man for the most exacting standards.

No, concluded Hervey, his six months' tenure would not be a sinecure. He was even beginning to wonder what chance he might have of seeing his people in Wiltshire, his daughter especially. Georgiana was ten, and he had scarce seen through one month with her. He left her in the willing care of his sister (at least, in the *dutiful* care), and by so doing he blighted what remained of Elizabeth's prospects, for she was closer now to forty than to thirty. Indeed, if there had been a silver lining in the black cloud of Badajoz it was the resolve that had grown out of his incarceration to put all this side of his affairs in order, to assume a decent responsibility for his daughter. It was hardly unusual to place a motherless child in the care of a guardian, but Georgiana was Henrietta's daughter: he dishonoured his late wife's memory, and their former love, by putting away their daughter thus. And so it was that he began to fret for leave to be with them – and, indeed, for the opportunity to press his suit (if he could put it as decidedly as that) with Sir Ivo Lankester's widow. He had met Lady Lankester but twice, first in Calcutta when she was in new mourning weeds, and then at dinner at Lord George Irvine's, but he had concluded that she would make him an admirable wife, and more especially an admirable mother to Georgiana, for she had an infant of her own. He could only hope that their differences in station, though in certain respects truly not great, and disparity of age (she was ten years his junior, perhaps more), would not incline her to set her face irrevocably against the notion.

Another gun fired, and a horse from F Troop bolted the ends of the line – towards the guns rather than away. Hervey groaned as he saw the wretched dragoon lying back almost flat in the saddle, reins at full length, while the trooper charged through the Chestnuts' limbers. Thank God they had been dismounted at the Duke of York's funeral! He could never have been confident of their steadiness otherwise. It was no surprise that Strickland had been so determined to return to Hounslow that night of the smash, to be ready for first parade. Foot drill was a not altogether alien practice for cavalry but it required very strict attention, especially when mustered with the Foot Guards under the eye of so many senior officers – the Duke of Wellington included. To dismount a regiment of cavalry had been an extraordinary rebuke to the nation, however. Everyone said so. The duke had been at the Horse Guards a month, now, insistent on withdrawing the troops from Portugal as soon as may be, for the dispatch of a mere five thousand men to Lisbon was these days a heavy drain on the disposable force of the country. Indeed it had been the cause of delay in the Duke of York's funeral arrangements: there had simply not been enough soldiers to bury a field marshal. Hervey could still barely credit it, for Waterloo had been but a dozen years before!

Strickland had not been the only casualty of the Duke of York's funeral. Hervey had been taken aback by the severity of the cold that night; the ceremonies were greatly delayed on the day itself, and the service had not finally got underway in St George's chapel until evening, by which time several dragoons had succumbed. They at least had been revived by the guardhouse braziers; several of the mourners, it was held, did not survive the week. The Duke of Wellington (so Lord John Howard, Hervey's 'friend at court', said) had been indisposed by the freezing air, and had not been able to attend the Horse Guards until two days following, so that there had been much industry in those first weeks, for the duke insisted always on the work of the day being done *in* the day. The accumulated work of several months could not be so quickly disposed of, however; not least the promotion lists which mounted by the day on the Military Secretary's desk. Hervey shook his head. It was the very devil of a business, for his stock stood never so low. The affair in Portugal had seen to that. And he needed his stock to be high, for he had lately applied for his majority. It was ironic that for so many years, when he had not had the means to purchase, the business of promotion had been merely actuarial, to be transacted between the regimental agents without reference to any other, and that now he had the money, the Horse Guards was scrutinizing every transaction. All because of the scandal over the Duke of York's mistress selling commissions. In truth, he assured himself, the scrutiny was but a formality, and he need not worry. What he ought to be addressing his thoughts to was the business of the lieutenant-colonelcy. There were always more buyers than sellers, in the cavalry especially, and the price would no doubt be hiked up improbably, beyond reach of but a few of the very richest peers. Except that if there truly were an Augean stream now flowing through the Horse Guards, it might be possible once more to have the lieutenant-colonelcy at regulation price. And since he was senior officer on full-pay duty . . . Though where he might find even the regulation price – £6,175 – was quite beyond him.

'Hervey?'

He woke from his troubled contemplation to see the Chestnut Troop's captain saluting. 'Dalbiac, you are finished?'

'There is one round left per gun. I would have them limber up and come into action again on that ridge yonder. Shall you charge?'

It was the usual way, and it would go hard with the dragoons if he said 'no', especially with the Chestnuts galloping half a mile to the ridge, but he was determined to work the regiment by degrees rather than give every trooper his head and then count the fallers. 'We shall not charge; we shall advance deliberately, with skirmishers out. Thank you for your support. How are your injured gunners?'

Captain Dalbiac frowned. 'The number seven's not long for this world, and the ventsman will likely lose his thumb.'

'Then I am sorry for them both.'

'The number seven occasioned his own misfortune, and if the ventsman *hadn't* burned his thumb to the bone there'd be the devil to pay!'

Hervey nodded. Fireworking was a hazardous affair, and it could only be done with the most faithful of drill. If the ventsman had not burned his thumb to the bone it would have proved he had not held it to the vent diligently. 'Very well. Perhaps you will let us occupy the ridge first and then join us for a final discharge?'

Captain Dalbiac saluted, reined about and cantered back to his guns.

Hervey glanced left and right. The line's dressing was good enough. 'The regiment will fire by half squadrons! Draw carbines!'

Four hundred right hands reached to the leather 'buckets' on the offside of the saddles to draw the short muskets – the cavalry carbines – just as Hervey had so often seen in the French war. There were not many veterans of those days now: the serjeants, for the most part, had been at Waterloo, and the majority of them were seasoned Peninsular men, though fewer than half had been at

Corunna. Of the corporals, there was but a handful who had clambered into the boats at 'Groyne' that day. It had been almost twenty years ago; what else did he expect? *The old order changeth.*

Except that in too many respects the old order did not change fast enough. Here they were with the exact same weapon their fathers – even grandfathers – would have been handy with, dependent on a piece of flint to spark loose powder in the pan. The primitives who had lived on Salisbury Plain had worked flints; as a boy he himself had played in the pits. It did not seem to him that the techniques of war had advanced with the despatch possible. He had lately returned from Portugal in a ship whose power came from steam as much as from the wind, and he knew there were locomotives which derived all their traction from that source. Why, therefore, could science not serve the soldier better? The answer was – and he knew it – that science was perfectly able to serve the soldier, if only the Board of Ordnance would let it. His own life at Waterloo he owed to the merest drop of fulminate of mercury, a percussion cap instead of a flintlock, which had allowed him to fire his soaking carbine when a flint, even if it had sparked, could not have ignited damp powder in the firing pan. Later he had petitioned the board on behalf of an American inventor who had shown him an astonishing revolving-chamber pistol. The authorities had not been impressed, however. Other than for a few riflemen to act as skirmishers, they required an army that could volley, on command, for it was volley fire that broke up massed ranks and columns. Would the enemy be always so obliging as to come on in such a manner?

The Sixth were handy with their carbines at least, observed Hervey as he took post on the right flank with the other officers, allowing the dragoons a clear line of fire, for unlike the gunners they would load live cartridge. 'By squadrons, carry on!'

The squadron officers now took over the practice. 'Load!'

Ramrods clattered as dragoons tamped the one-ounce balls.

'Front rank, even numbers, advance!'

14

One hundred dragoons pressed their troopers to the walk.

'Halt!'

They checked, inclining right in the prescribed manner so as to be able to fire to the flank rather than over the horses' heads.

'Present!'

Up came the carbines to the aim, though there were no targets.

'Fire!'

It was a good volley, but there were slow ignitions and misfires. Some of the horses shied; only one bolted. Hervey watched intently as next the odd numbers advanced half a dozen paces beyond the evens, presented and fired. And then the same again with the rear rank. Four volleys in all.

On the whole the horses stood them well, thought Hervey, but he could hardly be satisfied with the rate of misfires, and on a morning with not a touch of dampness in the air. 'Very well,' he said to the adjutant, as grey smoke drifted towards them. 'Have them re-form in double rank.'

'Sir.'

The adjutant moved to the front to give the executive commands, while the smoke rolled the length of the line, quite obscuring the front rank's line of sight. Hervey wondered if here, too, science might not serve them better. Was it contrary to the nature of the elements to require powder to burn without excessive smoke? Was there such a thing as fire without smoke? Smoke stood in the way of observation on the battlefield; he had only to recall the day at Waterloo, when it had been the very devil of a job to see what the French did. More than once had the duke's infantry fired on his own cavalry. But it was more than mere obscuration: every time a dragoon discharged his carbine he gave away his position. In line it mattered not at all, but on outpost duty it might make the difference between staying put or having to withdraw. Except that the weapon in these men's hands possessed neither the range nor the accuracy to exploit the advantage of smokeless powder. Hervey shook his head. Here they were on

Hounslow Heath going through the exact same evolutions of that day a dozen years ago, which was supposed to have been an end to the *Grande Armée* and the system that had need of it. There was no denying that there were armies still on the Continent, but he had seen enough in India these past six years to know there were other ways of war. If he, a mere acting-major of light dragoons, could see it, then there were sure to be those in the armies of France, and Russia and Austria – even Prussia – who could see it too. What if those armies were to embrace science (England had no monopoly in this field, even if she had the lead) and put to nought the superiority in drill and courage of His Majesty's men? He was sure the Royal Navy would be thinking 'scientifically', for in the navy there was no disdain of innovation. Quite the opposite, indeed: he could not easily forget the steamship in the Rangoon river in the late war with Ava.

But now they would end the field day with an advance in line, sabres drawn, exactly as they had done at the close of Waterloo. At that glorious moment, too, Hervey had been at the head of the Sixth, the senior officer remaining in the saddle, though still but a cornet. Well, he had them again now, and on the same terms (for as long as it took to replace him); he had better let them have their gallop after all! And he had better do it exactly as the drill book prescribed.

He turned to his trumpeter, whose mare stood composed at last. 'Draw swords!'

Corporal Parry, commanding officer's trumpeter since the Sixth had come back from India, put the bugle to his lips and attacked the *arpeggiando* quavers and semi-quavers as if the enemy were before them. It was not the hardest of calls, but neither was it one to falter over at the end of a field day.

Out came four hundred sabres, more or less as one.

'Forward!'

The simplest of the calls – just an E and a C, two semis and a quaver, repeated the once.

The line heaved forward, and the cursing began at once. Hervey fancied he recognized the NCOs' voices – 'Sit up, there!' 'Get back!' 'Close up, you idle man!'

'Trot!'

Short, bumping quavers on C, E and G.

Every horse recognized the call, but on different notes. The line billowed like sheets in the wind. 'Hold hard, damn you!' 'Get up, there! Get up!' 'Steady!'

Hervey glanced back. The sight was not propitious. But it was too late now. 'Gallop!'

Corporal Parry blew creditably – the same notes, but in different time.

Hervey glanced over his shoulder again. The line was about as straight as a gaggle of driven geese. He might as well prove to them just how much drill they still had need of: 'Charge!'

Corporal Parry managed the triplets admirably until the third repetition when he was bumped hard by a dragoon behind, and nearly lost a tooth.

Hervey heard him curse the man as foully as ever he'd heard from Armstrong. He glanced behind once more, saw the line of lofted sabres, and put his spurs into Gilbert's flanks for more speed: he was damned if he was going to be overtaken by what looked like a band of irregulars. Great God, what work there was to be done yet!

CHAPTER TWO

THE GRIM REAPER

Later

When they were come back to Hounslow barracks, Hervey handed over the parade to the senior captain and rode to the commanding officer's stables at the back of the officers' house. Here were four loose boxes, altogether quieter and more comfortable than the standing stalls of the troop-horse lines. Private Johnson was waiting.

These days, Hervey considered Johnson more soldier-servant than groom; except that the RSM would dispute that he answered any longer to the description 'soldier' (and even 'servant' would not have done in any proper establishment). The care of Hervey's two chargers, Gilbert, who had survived two crossings of the Equator and the siege of Bhurtpore, and Eliab, Jessye's foal, was largely given to Private Toyne, a good coper who prior to joining the Sixth three years past had learned his business around the horse fairs of Westmoreland.

18

Johnson was now about thirty-seven years old (the details of his birth were not recorded comprehensively), a year Hervey's senior, a single man still, with no home but that of the 6th Light Dragoons, which some were still pleased to call 'Princess Caroline's Own' although the title had long since been officially withdrawn out of deference to the Prince Regent, now King George IV. Johnson was a contented man, on the whole, given to speaking his mind, not always with optimism but unfailingly with honesty and absolute loyalty. He had joined the Sixth before the Peninsular campaign, a boy of fifteen-ish, lately of a Hallamshire orphanage and the Barmby Furscoe deep coal mine. Twice, when fire damp had ignited, and the explosion had brought down the roof, Johnson had been buried along with the pit pony he had been leading, and so after the second explosion, two months before Trafalgar, he had joined the army, certain that it must be an altogether healthier and safer occupation. His subterranean connection with equines had led him into the ranks of the Sixth rather than to the infantry's recruiting serjeant, though at that time there was more enlistment money to be had for a red coat than for a blue one.

Johnson had refused any promotion in the two decades since then, which seniority alone should have brought him (although he was not entirely without merit for corporal), convinced as he was that the extra duties and responsibilities were not worth the additional pay. In any case, he was content with his billet, so to speak, and the intimacy – the increasing intimacy – with the man to whom he had been groom for near a decade and a half. When Henrietta had died (he had been devoted to her in very high degree) he had left the colours in order to remain with 'his' officer; and when Hervey had rejoined the Sixth a year or so later, he had rejoined too without demur even though he was exchanging an agreeable life in a pleasant Wiltshire village for the uncertainty of one in the cantonments of East Bengal. As commanding officer's orderly now, although 'acting' because Hervey himself was acting

19

in that appointment, he enjoyed a position of some prestige, elevated above the ranks while still 'Private' Johnson, beyond the effective reach of any NCO since none would wish to incur the proxy wrath of the commanding officer, and yet with no responsibility beyond that which he had shouldered these past years attending to Cornet, now Acting-Major, Matthew Hervey.

Hervey handed Gilbert's reins to him, and Johnson in turn handed them to Private Toyne.

'There's an express for thee, sir.'

Hervey froze. 'From Wiltshire?'

'Ay, sir.' Johnson's tone was subdued. He knew that no one sent good news express; not that anyone had ever sent *him* an express.

Hervey knew it too: *For evil news rides post, while good news baits.* He breathed deeply. 'Who has it?'

'Adjutant, sir.'

It was a mark of the gravity of the news that Johnson was being punctilious in the formality of his address, and it did not escape its hearer. 'Do you know what it says?'

Johnson was surprised: Hervey must know that an express from Wiltshire, especially one held by the adjutant for his commanding officer, would not be revealed to a mere private man, for all the elevated position of his officer. Yet he continued evenly in his reply. 'No, sir, I don't.'

'Very well. You'd better come with me to orderly room. There might be need of . . . I might have need of you.'

Ordinarily Johnson would have protested at such an invitation. Regimental headquarters was no place to be when the commanding officer was dispensing summary justice to defaulters, which was what the day's Routine Orders said was to follow on the morning's drill. But he fell in behind Hervey without a word.

Hervey was not relishing this aspect of orderly room either. The Sixth, by long custom, did not 'touch over', as the rank and file, with delicacy, referred to flogging. Not, at least, flogging on the square, with triangle and cat and the whole regiment paraded to

20

witness punishment. A light-fingered dragoon, or a laggard, might find himself sentenced by a 'barrack-room court martial', presided over by the oldest soldier, to a good strapping, sometimes on the soles of his feet. But however humane the regiment's practice, the threat of flogging remained, for if the offence were grave a man might be remanded for a district, rather than a regimental, court martial; and since that court would invariably consist of officers from other regiments whose scruples might not be the same as the Sixth's in the matter of corporal punishment, the lash did indeed sometimes 'touch over' a dragoon. And it was not always within a commanding officer's discretion. The civil authorities had a right to jurisdiction for non-military offences, and where that was surrendered to the military, the courts would frequently insist on condign punishment.

'Atte-e-enshun!' bellowed the regimental serjeant-major as Hervey (and Johnson) entered the Sixth's smart, new, brick-built headquarters. The RSM's mirror-like leather and silver belied his morning's industry, for although he had not attended the field day, remaining in barracks instead to prepare for a proper orderly room, his feet had trodden every quarter of the lines, where his eye had alighted on legionary instances of dereliction of duty, and his bark had set reverberating the spines of the rear details.

Hervey passed him by with a courteous 'Good morning, Sarn't-major', but otherwise with a certain detachment, as befitted the commanding officer before orderly room. And in that form of address – 'Sarn't-major' – Hervey also displayed a proprietorial right, for by long custom the regimental serjeant-major was addressed as 'Mr' by all but the colonel and lieutenant-colonel. When the rank of quartermaster was replaced by that of troop serjeant-major halfway through the campaign in the Peninsula, 'Sarn't-major' was on the lips of every troop officer. There had never been cause for confusion or abashment, however, for although there were now eight 'sarn't-majors', there remained but one '*the* sarn't-major'.

Johnson, seeing no door through which to escape, stuck close to Hervey and hoped thereby to become invisible to the one man in whose sight he ventured only with trepidation. But vainly.

'Private Johnson!'

Johnson spun round and jerked to attention, back straight, head up, eyes front, hands pointing to the ground along the double stripe of his overalls, as perfect a figure of a dragoon as ever stood on defaulters' parade. But then, the summons had been unmistakable.

'When you have a minute,' said the RSM dryly.

'Sir!'

The RSM turned about and stalked to his office, leaving Johnson at attention in the corridor like a petrified tree. 'Carry on, Serjeant Plug!'

'Sah!'

The regimental orderly serjeant advanced on Johnson, licking his lips.

Johnson felt keenly the absence of his accustomed protection, but his only movement was an involuntary gulp as the ROS bore down on him.

Serjeant Plug halted half a sabre's length from the anxious Johnson and leaned forward so that the peaks of their shakos were almost touching. ''Ow'd yer like a little trip . . . dahn under, way of the 'ulks in the Thames!'

'Serjeant?'

'We's 'eard as there's some gen'l'men coming what wants a word with you . . . from Bow-street!'

What colour was left in Johnson's face drained away instantly.

'Nah, you little shirker, while we's waiting for 'em . . . 'op it!'

Johnson blinked, spun round like a top, scuttled down the corridor, and seeing the open door of the commanding officer's room, rushed in like a fugitive for sanctuary.

Hervey smiled wryly as he held out his shako for Johnson to

take. 'Was that Mr Hairsine's voice I heard? And then . . . Sarn't Plug's?'

Johnson shifted awkwardly. 'It were, sir.'

'I didn't catch what he was saying. Are you quite well?'

'Sir.'

'Don't "sir" me like that; I can see perfectly well that something's up.'

'Nothing, sir. Nothing.'

Hervey now knew otherwise; 'nothing' was most unusual idiom for Johnson.

'Sit down.'

'Ah'd rather not if yer don't mind, sir.'

Hervey sighed. This was rum indeed. Few men ever received an invitation to sit down in the commanding officer's office, and there were surely none who refused it.

'Sit down!'

Johnson looked for a chair, found the least comfortable-looking and did as he was told.

'How long have we been together?'

'Don't know, sir.'

Hervey sighed again. Heavy going indeed. 'Fourteen years, isn't it? Just before we crossed into France. Or perhaps a little before?'

Johnson made no reply.

'I could have you flogged,' he tried, thinking a little gallows humour might help.

'Ah'd better be getting thi stuff for tonight ready, sir,' was all that Johnson replied, making to rise.

Hervey shook his head, mystified. 'Well, I must say that I'm surprised. I do believe that if something had turned *me* the colour of the regimental facings I might confide in *you*.'

The adjutant interrupted Hervey's enquiries. He looked not entirely disapprovingly at the seated Johnson, but with something of a frown nevertheless. 'If I may, sir – the express.'

Hervey took it, saw the unmistakable, neat, round hand, and

forced himself to keep the mask at his face for a little longer. 'Thank you, Mr Vanneck,' he said, with a polite note of dismissal. 'And you, Johnson.'

The adjutant waited for Johnson to leave, however, and then approached Hervey's desk, confidentially. 'Just before you read the express, Hervey, I thought I should say that apparently there are two Bow-street men coming here to interview Johnson.' He had to clear his throat. 'I understand in connection with a serious crime against the Revenue.'

Hervey was astonished. 'Johnson? Revenue? He's . . .'

'As I said, it is only what I understand. Until they come I can have no perfect idea. In the meantime you might like to ask him . . . there again you might not.'

Hervey shook his head. 'I thought there was something, but hardly serious. The most I've ever known him do is take a case of brandy from a commissary waggon – and that was in snow up to your belt.'

'Let us hope that Bow-street and the Revenue have mistaken their man then.'

Hervey nodded, but none too assured. Vanneck took his leave.

When the door had closed, Hervey broke the seal on the express and opened the waxed envelope, steeling himself to the death, or expected demise, that it would reveal. Both his parents, though active still, were beyond their allotted span. It could not have been his sister, for hers was the hand. He trembled at the alternative; but Georgiana had been in good health for all of her ten years . . .

Horningsham
11th March 1827

My dear brother,

Do not be troubled for your kin by this letter, for we are all in the halest condition and most excellent spirits. I am sorry to have

24

to tell you, however, that Daniel Coates is grievous ill and Dr Birch does not consider he will survive the week. He was found by one of his men the day before yesterday on the plain near Wadman's Coppice, where he had fallen from his horse, Dr Birch believes of a stroke. He was brought back to Upton Scudamore but has scarce spoke a word nor eaten anything since, and Dr Birch is of the decided opinion that his condition cannot amend. I do not imagine that your duties will permit of any early visit, and I shall, dearest brother, endeavour to let you know by the speediest means if there is any change to Daniel Coates's condition.

Be assured of our love now and at all times,
Ever yr most affectionate sister,
Elizabeth.

Hervey sat down. *Dan Coates*: 'the shepherd of Salisbury Plain' as Archdeacon Hervey had dubbed him in the image of Hannah More's creation of pastoral wisdom and simple piety; first, foremost and forever to Hervey, though, riding-master, instructor in sabre and firelock, in fieldcraft, drill and in the lore of campaigning – a priceless understanding which Coates had gained in the ranks of the 16th Light Dragoons and as trumpeter to that able but much maligned general, Sir Banastre Tarleton. Could Daniel Coates be brought to this – a fall on Salisbury Plain – after the American War and the sick and muddle of the expedition to the Low Countries? Daniel Coates was not so very old; not an ancient, not so many years his father's senior; and he rode the plain every day tending his sheep. His flocks were not so extensive now, not since the end of the French war when demand for wool had fallen; but Daniel Coates had made his fortune during that 'never-ending war' and he had been astute enough too to sell half his sheep before Waterloo. He lived a godly and sober life, prudent – modest even. Poor Dan Coates: his fortune had in many ways made him unhappy, for he always felt keenly the loss of his wife, the more so because she had died so many years before he had been able to afford her more than a shawl and a mean grave.

'Mr Vanneck!'

The door to the adjutant's office opened. 'Hervey?'

'I shall go to Wiltshire this afternoon, after orderly room. Would you give my compliments to Captain Shute and inform him that the regiment will come under his orders?'

CHAPTER THREE

LAST POST

Horningsham, 13 March

The journey to Wiltshire, a hundred miles almost to the furlong, took nine and a half hours, the fastest time he had ever posted. The regimental chariot, lightly loaded, two excellent roadsters from Leicestershire for the first twenty miles, fair flew along the turnpikes, the estimable Corporal Denny astride the leader with scarcely a half-hour but in the saddle. Denny, a twenty-year dragoon who had been the chariot-man for the past five, knew the road as far as Andover well, so that Hervey had only to be alert for the last stretch across Salisbury Plain. Fortunately there was a good moon and the way was clear. They changed horses at Amesbury, the last posting house before the dozen miles of barren, hard chalk downland, a lonely tract of sheep and of isolated settlements where families kept themselves to themselves in a sturdy but sometimes unholy way.

They passed the Great Henge, an eerie, heathen place of, it was said, ancient sacrifice, though now but a silent, woolly fold. Then, slowing to a walk, they descended to misty Shrewton, still and dark but for the odd candle in a window, and the oil lamps of its empty inn. The loneliest stretch came next, five miles of high, windblown, rough grazing, the road rutted and potholed, only partially mended after the icy winter rains. They took it at a jogtrot, scarcely better than a good, stretching walk on metalled going, and in an hour slowed again for the steep descent into forlorn Chitterne, not a light to be seen, not a barking dog to proclaim any life at all, passing the dark shapes of dwelling houses every bit as ghostly in their stillness as the monoliths at Stonehenge. Then it was up to the high chalk again for the straight league and a half to graceful Heytesbury, off the plain at last and on to the rich plough of the Wylye valley, a village as different from its downland neighbours as a blood to a cob. In Heytesbury there were lights, in the street, in the upper windows, and in the lower ones too; and the sound of the fiddle from one of its inns, despite the steady approach of midnight; and one whole window of Heytesbury's abbey church was lit as if a dozen monks were yet saying compline within. The chariot picked up speed, on turnpike once more, rattling into Warminster as the clocks were beginning to strike the hour, and thence to skirt the great estate of Longleat, the seat of Henrietta's guardian, until at twenty minutes to one o'clock of the new day they were in Horningsham – poor, pretty, well-regulated Horningsham, the village of the Bath estate, the parish of the Reverend – indeed, the Venerable – Thomas Hervey M.A. (Oxon.).

They went first to the Bath Arms to arrange hay and a roof for the horses, and a bed for Corporal Denny, then Hervey walked with just his small-pack the half mile or so to his father's darkened vicarage, where he crept without a sound into the stable, lay down in the straw, as he had so many times as a boy, pulled his cloak about him and slept without stirring until dawn.

When he woke, the household was still abed (it was a little after six), so he shaved and bathed under the stable pump, and generally made himself presentable for the family's reveille before giving the stable's sole occupant – his father's driving pony – a peck of oats and an armful of hay. At seven o'clock, as had been the rule at the vicarage for as many years as he could remember, the door to the servants' hall was unbolted and thrown open, and the routine of the morning was begun.

The vicar of Horningsham did not keep a large establishment; he had not the means. There was a cook, Mrs Pomeroy, the same Hervey had known in his nursery, a housemaid, a manservant, a scullion and a gardener cum groom. Neither his mother nor his sister had a lady's maid, something Hervey had tried on several occasions to rectify, begging them to let him pay her wages in part compensation for the additional burden he imposed on them by Georgiana's 'wardship'. But they would not have it. Even when the Reverend Thomas Hervey had been made Archdeacon of Sarum, and the family had risen one whole floor in the society of Wiltshire, they were not inclined to relent, accustomed as they long were to the habitual economy of a poor country living.

Old Francis would have been the first to emerge, had he not occupied a corner of Horningsham churchyard these three years gone. Hervey considered that Francis had been as much a part of the household as his own parents. Francis had certainly known his father longer than had he, having been his scout at Oxford, accompanying him to his first parish as servant, and remaining with him thereafter. Now it was a new man, from the village. He had lost an arm tending the fire engine at Longleat, and Lord Bath had given him a good pension, which the Venerable Thomas Hervey now supplemented with the pay of an able-bodied indoor servant.

The heavy iron-studded door opened without its habitual creak, Hervey noted – testament, he imagined, to the single-arm industry of the new Francis. 'Good morning, Thomas Whitehead!' he called.

Thomas Whitehead, whom Hervey had known since they had both climbed the chestnut trees in Longleat-park, put down his bucket of ashes and knuckled his forehead in the naval manner. He

29

had never been to sea, but it was the Longleat way, for the marquess's younger son, Sir Henry Thynne – younger and *favoured* son ever since the elder and heir had eloped with Harriet Robbins, the turnpike keeper's daughter – held post rank in the Royal Navy.

'Good mornin', Major 'Ervey,' he answered, registering respect but no surprise. 'Reverend said as you'd be 'ere afore long.'

Hervey smiled back. It seemed strange not to be 'Master Matthew' any longer, as Francis had always had it. 'Is my father about?'

''E's at Upton Scud'more still, sir. Went yesterday to make arrangements, 'e said.'

Hervey started.

'Thou didn't know, Major 'Ervey?'

'I knew that he was gravely ill. Do you say . . .'

'I'm afeared so, sir,' replied Thomas Whitehead, suddenly awkward with the responsibility of informing of the death of one of the most prosperous farmers in West Wiltshire, churchwarden, guardian of the workhouse, justice of the peace. ''E died yes'day mornin', an' the Rev'rend went straightaway.'

The Venerable Thomas Hervey held the living of Upton Scudamore *in commendam*, as he had periodically for a quarter of a century, for it was not a rich living, and the three incumbents during that time had soon sought more lucrative preferment. Nevertheless, with his archdeacon's tithes, these days Mr Hervey was able to afford a curate, and so he no longer had to drive the dozen miles there and back each Sunday. But Archdeacon Hervey would not entrust the cure of Daniel Coates's soul to any but himself. That, Hervey knew full well. He felt a sudden emptiness. He was angry with himself for arriving too late to make proper farewells, but that was nothing compared with the change in the world now that Coates was no longer in it. Dan Coates had been forever there, a sure and certain guide, a man who had exercised wisdom and judgement, in uniform and out, a man whom Hervey had thought of variously as a father, brother and faithful NCO. Trumpeter-Corporal Coates, late of His Majesty's 16th Light

Dragoons, honourably discharged unfit for duty on account of the Flanders fever, had limped penniless into the Reverend Thomas Hervey's church two-score years ago, and from the depths of indigence had risen to yeoman respectability, to be on gentlemanly terms with the present Lord Bath where once he had watched the first marquess's sheep. No passing bell could sound loud or long enough for a man like Daniel Coates.

'Miss Georgiana's about, sir.'

Whether Whitehead disclosed this as an ameliorative or simply because he imagined it was what the father of a daughter would wish to hear, Hervey did not know, but he was grateful for it: there must be no unhappy introspection in the presence of his child, infrequent that the presence was. And if it were only Georgiana about then he could greet her without restraint (the company of her grandparents – not to mention her aunt and guardian, his sister – would somehow oblige him to maintain a greater reserve).

'Good! Then I shall go in at once and see her.'

He found Georgiana at the breakfast table, alone, spooning copious honey into a bowl of porridge. The hand stopped midway between pot and bowl as she saw him, her eyes and mouth wide.

'Beeswax is altogether better for a table than honey, I do believe,' he said, with teasing crustiness.

She looked at the spreading pool on the white cloth, frowned, placed the spoon down on her plate, and rose decorously to greet him.

He fell to one knee as she extended her arms.

It was never possible for him to see Georgiana without at once thinking of her mother. It was, indeed, like some perpetual penance for his cravenness in the events that had led to Henrietta's death. It was not merely the close similarity of features – the large, dark eyes, the high, prominent cheekbones, and increasingly the fullness of her raven hair – rather was it the mannerisms, the gestures. Georgiana's self-possession was uncannily familiar, and yet she had never known her mother.

The passage of time worked subtle changes, however. These days Hervey was able to acquit his penance speedily. No longer was he troubled for days, and nights. The pangs of guilt, though frequently sharp, were also short. But what had replaced the dull ache of his loss and of his own perceived fault in it was the conviction that he compounded his guilt by neglect of Henrietta's daughter. That was how he had thought of Georgiana, principally – as a relict of his late wife. *Had* thought, until quite recently. Since his return from Portugal he had begun to see Georgiana no longer as the mere image of her mother, like some miniature which had caught a good likeness, but as her own being, a child of ten with spirit, a quick mind, and decided opinions about things which he himself had not even thought about. In truth, he was beginning to find her engaging company. He wanted her to ride with him on the plain; he wanted even to hear her play the piano – and not just because he had bought a very fine one for her tenth birthday: he *wanted* to watch and listen. It was slowly occurring to him that Georgiana was not simply Henrietta's infant, and therefore his responsibility, but his own daughter – as much his flesh and blood as his late wife's. And the realization brought him feelings he could not yet fully understand but which he found wholly welcome.

Georgiana's arms met around his neck and she pressed her cheek firmly to his. 'I knew you would be come. I put a nightlight in my window for you.'

He had always been uncertain of the true warmth of her greeting, for he had, undeniably, neglected her. There could be no other word for it but 'neglect'. That he had cause to be absent, always, was without question: all his people knew of the calls of duty. Indeed, his father had forbidden him to send in his papers when he had once perceived it his duty to be at close hand to ageing parents. His sister had positively encouraged him to rejoin the colours when he had resigned in dismay after Henrietta's death; and even his mother had taken unconcealed pride in the common knowledge of West Wiltshire that her son braved so much in the service of the King. But in his heart he knew that he courted these absences, not for their own sake but for the chance of distinction. And, yes, for the money – prize money – that might accrue, for there could be no realistic prospect of promotion without purchase in these days of official peace.

He would not be apprehensive about his homecoming any longer, however. He had made his decision. Georgiana would have a mother, and he a wife. Then maybe Elizabeth, free at last of duty to all others, might find her own fulfilment (whatever that might be). It was, he confided, a noble course. And, too, it could only bring him tranquillity.

Daniel Coates's funeral took place two days later. There were no family considerations, he having died without issue, and never speaking of other kin, and early committal suited Lord Bath, who had parliamentary business to attend to in London. Nevertheless, the little church of St Mary the Virgin was full, its pews occupied in the main by the quality, with labourers and others whom 'the shepherd of Salisbury Plain' had variously helped standing by the walls inside and out. The three-bell tower had rung a muffled peal for a whole hour before the midday, when the coffin was to be brought from Drove Farm, and a dismounted party of the Wiltshire Yeomanry stood sharp by the lych gate to see in their late benefactor. Lord Bath and sundry JPs occupied the front pews, on the right, and on the Gospel side, in plain coat adorned with the star of the Knight Grand Cross of the Order of the Bath, sat old General Sir Banastre Tarleton, who had driven from Shropshire overnight on learning of the news of his former trumpeter's death. Hervey would have recognized him even without the coachman's prompting, for despite his seventy and five years the general was still the image of his Reynolds portrait, the dashing, conquering 'green dragoon'.

Punctually, a few minutes before the midday (for he would never have been late on parade), Daniel Coates's mortal remains were

33

borne to St Mary's on Drove Farm's best hay waggon. The men about the churchyard removed their hats, the women curtsied, and the Wiltshire Yeomanry stood to attention, resting on their swords, heads lowered. At the lych gate Coates's foreman, in black Melton coat, and his six longest-serving shepherds, in starched smocks, took charge of the fine oak coffin and began bearing their late, respected employer to his final entrance to the church in which for more than twenty years he had worshipped unfailingly. As they reached the porch at the west end, the Venerable Thomas Hervey, in surplice and stole – as Daniel Coates would have approved, if not so many of the archdeacon's clerical brethren in the diocese – took the head of the procession, and with open Prayer Book preceded his erstwhile parishioner and friend to the chancel steps.

' "'I am the resurrection and the life,' saith the Lord. 'He that believeth in me though he were dead, yet shall he live: and whosoever liveth and believeth in me shall never die.'" '

The congregation, standing, listened as the comforting yet chill words recalled them to their own mortality, and to the leveller that was the grave, each of them nodding some respect or other as the coffin passed.

' "I know that my Redeemer liveth, and that he shall stand at the latter day upon the earth. And though after my skin worms destroy this body, yet in my flesh shall I see God: whom I shall see for myself, and mine eyes shall behold, and not another. We brought nothing into this world, and it is certain we can carry nothing out. The Lord gave, and the Lord hath taken away; blessed be the name of the Lord." '

The foreman saw to the lowering of the coffin onto two trestles in front of the chancel steps, and then placed on top of it Daniel Coates's old sabre and trumpet, and the shepherd's crook and shears which had long since taken their place as the tools of his trade.

Archdeacon Hervey bowed to the congregation, and they sat. He began to read, as the Order for the Burial of the Dead required,

Psalm 39, *Dixi, Custodiam*. He had chosen this rather than the alternative since immediately before the doxology was a verse upon which he wished to reflect in his homily: 'O spare me a little, that I may recover my strength: before I go hence, and be no more seen.'

Hervey himself now rose and walked to the fine-carved lectern to read the Lesson, the words of which had become all too familiar during his two decades' sojourn in regimentals. ' "Now is Christ risen from the dead, and become the first-fruits of them that slept. For since by man came death, by man came also the resurrection of the dead. For as in Adam all die, even so in Christ shall all be made alive . . ." '

Yet even as he read he found himself doubting the promises. Daniel Coates would no more be seen; was that not the essence? He would never again be there to give counsel. He, Hervey, was quite alone in this world now that Daniel Coates had followed the only other person who had truly known his mind. Now he must fend entirely for himself. But not *selfishly*; that time was over.

It was a long lesson, and he read the words deliberately, with the emphases in the places he would once have judged imperative, and which now he did but from habit. ' "Therefore, my beloved brethren, be ye stedfast, unmoveable, always abounding in the work of the Lord, forasmuch as ye know that your labour is not in vain in the Lord." '

He glanced at Lord Bath as he left the lectern. The marquess seemed to nod his approval. The day before, Hervey had gone to Longleat to pay his customary respects to his late wife's guardian, and to Lady Bath, finding them both welcoming, though it was not long before the open wound of their son and heir's elopement was rubbed in some way, so that Lady Bath had to turn her face to dab at her eyes with a handkerchief. 'Of all the things I might have feared for Weymouth,' Lord Bath had said, 'an imprudent marriage never occurred to me. Mark you well, Hervey, the unhappiness when a son chooses such a way. I thank God there's no issue.'

35

Hervey had been of the opinion for some time that there must be a reconciliation, for the elopement was evidently no whim of the moment regretted almost as quick and to be 'dealt with' by money and the usual arrangements. No, Lord Weymouth and Harriet Robbins were evidently happy in their unusual match, and he saw no reason for Lord Bath to pursue his design to disinherit his son of title and land. He did not know Weymouth well – hardly at all (he knew his younger brother better) – but he ventured to believe that he was a rational man, of sound mind; should prudence in the marriage stakes be so narrowly defined as Lord Bath had it? But he had said nothing, for his own circumstances were far from exemplary. Except that he had resolved to put them into perfect order.

Archdeacon Hervey now climbed the steps of the pulpit. He did not intend detaining his congregation long: the office of the Burial of the Dead was an occasion to commend the soul of the departed to God, not his reputation to man. Yet there were things he would say.

' "*O spare me a little, that I may recover my strength: before I go hence, and be no more seen.*" ' He looked up from his pulpit prayer book. 'The Lord in his infinite wisdom did indeed spare Daniel Coates beyond his span of three-score and ten . . .'

Archdeacon Hervey went on to recount the story of Daniel Coates's rise from indigency to prosperity and respectability, and to praise the wisdom and generosity he displayed in both public office and private affairs. The silence in the church was remarkable, a reverencing not so much of Archdeacon Hervey's eloquence, adequate though that was, but of Daniel Coates's memory – before, as Mr Hervey at length recalled, drawing his homily to a close, ' "I go hence, and be no more seen." '

There was at this applause by nodding heads and, if not quite 'hear, hear', then from a sort of buzzing in the pews, which told Archdeacon Hervey that the unusual effort had been worthwhile. He glanced at the foreman and bowed his head – the signal – and then the foreman, with a simple beckoning nod, reassembled his bearers. They took up the coffin with all solemnity, the tools of Daniel Coates's two trades – and loves – still in place, turned slowly about and began the measured march from the chancel steps, their charge to be 'no more seen'.

The congregation rose and turned to follow as Archdeacon Hervey led the procession out of the church to the grave on the sunny south side, which Coates's own men had dug the day before.

Hervey accompanied his mother to the graveside, close behind Lord Bath, the principal mourner. And then came the words which he himself had had too frequent occasion to read when there had not been a chaplain to bury the dead. *Man that is born of a woman hath but a short time to live, and is full of misery. He cometh up, and is cut down, like a flower; he fleeth as it were a shadow, and never continueth in one stay. In the midst of life we are in death ...* More than ever they seemed to him a perfect if unhappy rendering of the condition of so many men who had worn the Sixth's badge. Indeed, they were apt, too, regarding his own condition, and for more time than he would have thought he could bear but for the company of regimental friends – and of two women who demanded nothing from him in return for that which they had so freely given.

Lord Bath declined the trowel, bending instead to take a hand-ful of earth from the fresh-dug mound. Old General Tarleton, cocked hat set firm as if he were in uniform, raised his hand in salute, making no attempt to hide the missing fingers (exactly as Daniel Coates had told Hervey of long years ago).

' "Forasmuch as it hath pleased Almighty God of his great mercy to take unto himself the soul of our dear brother here departed: we therefore commit his body to the ground; earth to earth, ashes to ashes, dust to dust; in sure and certain hope of the Resurrection to eternal life ... " '

When Lord Bath had sprinkled the earth on the coffin, Archdeacon Hervey began the closing prayers. It was a fine, sunny day. Somehow, Hervey thought, it assisted with the promise of eternal life. Many a time he had stood at the graveside when the rain had drummed on oak, or on simple shroud, and then the promises had seemed corrupt.

'"O Merciful God, the Father of our Lord Jesus Christ, who is the Resurrection and the life . . . who also hath taught us (by his holy apostle Saint Paul) not to be sorry, as men without hope . . ."'

He had never been a man without hope, had he? The trials of late years had brought him despair, but never quite that utter loss of hope of which St Paul warned. Or did he deceive himself in that? He picked up a handful of earth and cast it into the grave, then turned to walk after his mother.

'Major Hervey?' The voice was commanding.

He glanced to his right. The distinguished mourner was advancing on him. 'Yes, General?'

'I imagined it to be you,' said General Tarleton, jabbing his stick into the grass as he walked. 'Coates spoke much of you in his letters.'

'I'm very honoured, sir; I had no idea.'

General Sir Banastre Tarleton replaced his hat as they approached the lych gate. 'Read about the business in Portugal. Glad the Horse Guards have seen sense. Absurd notion, a court martial! When do you return to London?'

'Tomorrow or the day after, General.'

The grand old man nodded appreciatively. 'Good. I go to St James's this Thursday seven days. I would have you dine with me. Where do you stay?'

'We are quartered in Hounslow, General.'

He nodded again. 'Very well. I bid you good day then.'

Hervey bowed and let the general walk on to take leave of Lord Bath, before rejoining his mother, who had by now been joined by his sister.

'Matthew,' said Mrs Hervey uncomfortably. 'I would that we take your father home as soon as may be. The air is altogether too chill.'

'As you please, mother, but aren't we meant to attend first on the attorney in Warminster?'

Mrs Hervey had forgotten. She looked vexed, but then composed herself, for it was understood that Daniel Coates had left in his will some appreciation of her husband's early kindness towards him. Why otherwise should he have been summoned to attend its reading? Her son too: Coates had always spoken of his intention to bequeath him his horses; and, no doubt, there would be other tokens of their friendship ... 'Yes, of course, my dear; it is remiss of me.' She turned to Elizabeth. 'You are not summoned, are you?'

Elizabeth smiled patiently. 'No, Mama, not I.'

'You travel home in my carriage, mother,' said Hervey, replacing his hat. 'I will go with father in his.'

The reading of Daniel Coates's will was to be at two o'clock in the offices of Mr Simeon Tegg and Partners in the high-street, but when Hervey and his father arrived they were greeted by the clerk with instructions to repair across the road to the upper room of the Bell inn since a larger number than hitherto was now expected.

Archdeacon Hervey nodded benignly at the intelligence. 'He had favoured a great many during his life. I imagine that it will be so in death.'

His son thought him probably right, although he was of a mind that Daniel Coates's charity had never been of the sentimental kind. Coates had brought the Speenhamland system to this corner of West Wiltshire, but he had been a vigorous advocate of public works on which the destitute might labour in return for parish relief, and not everyone of the needy or the poor-ratepayers thought him laudable.

But when they entered the upper room they were taken aback by the number already gathered – four dozen by Hervey's rapid reckoning, and more still arriving.

'The entire board of guardians, I think,' said Archdeacon

Hervey, taking a glass of warm punch from another of Mr Tegg's clerks.

That much did not surprise his son; Elizabeth had told him often enough of Daniel Coates's generosity to the workhouse.

Before they were too much drawn into greetings and further speculation on the prospects of those assembled, the attorney called the proceedings to order.

'Gentlemen, I would beg your indulgence: there is a deal to attend to this afternoon. I propose to move at once to a formal reading of the will, thereafter to make some supplementary remarks arising from the late Mr Daniel Coates's instructions to me, whereupon I shall be at liberty to answer any questions. I should add that as soon as the will is read a copy shall be taken to the offices of the *Warminster Miscellany* for publication in tomorrow's edition.'

There were now, by Hervey's more considered reckoning, upwards of five dozen people in the room, of various degrees and of both sexes. He found himself wondering if Daniel Coates's estate could truly bear the evident expectations.

'Very well.' The attorney opened his portfolio and took out a single sheet of foolscap. '"I, Daniel Peter Coates of the Parish of Upton Scudamore, do by this my last Will and Testament give and bequeath to each man and woman in my employ the sum of twenty-five pounds, to my foreman William Costessey three hundred pounds and also to my housekeeper Anne Evans the same sum of three hundred pounds."'

There was a considerable buzz of surprise and appreciation. Hervey calculated that this munificence towards Daniel Coates's labourers, servants and two most trusted employees amounted to at least two thousand pounds.

'"The remainder of my estate, saving the items specified here-under, and subject to the payment of my funeral expenses, and to fees for the due management of said estate, I leave in trust to the principal benefit of the Warminster workhouse, with the urgent wish that a proper school and infirmary be established therein." '

The acclamation was loud and long.

At length Mr Simeon Tegg held up a hand. ' "And I do further leave under the terms of said trust an annuity of five hundred pounds to the Reverend Mr Thomas Hervey and Mrs Hervey of Horningsham, for as long as one or other of them shall live." '

The buzz of surprise returned, but respectful.

Mr Tegg paused only a moment. ' "And to Major Matthew Hervey of His Majesty's Sixth Light Dragoons I leave the sum of ten thousand pounds in trust for the purchase of a lieutenant-colonelcy in any of His Majesty's corps, and to him also my horses and all their appurtenances, and all military chattels of which I die possessed, this being my most certain act of service to His Majesty, so confident as I am in the loyalty and capability of this officer." '

The noise in the room was as great as for the bequest to the workhouse. Hervey, though both astonished and exhilarated by the scale of the generosity, was nevertheless equally discomfited by its proclamation.

His father laid a hand to his arm.

The attorney again had to hold up a hand to restore silence. ' "And I appoint the aforesaid Mr Thomas Hervey the executor of this my last Will and Testament, and to him the appointment of said trustees. Signed Daniel Coates, November 27, 1826." '

CHAPTER FOUR

IN THE MIDST OF LIFE

Later

The shivering began on their way back to Horningsham. Hervey pulled his coat tighter about him, turning up the collar.

'You are unwell, Matthew? It is not so cold.'

Hervey knew it was not cold. 'It will be nothing, father. The beginnings of a spring chill, perhaps.'

'I wonder you are scarce able to reason. I confess I am not. I had never imagined Daniel Coates planned such beneficence towards us. Indeed, I am wholly astonished that his fortune should permit of what we heard.'

Hervey hid his hands in his pockets to conceal the trembling. 'The attorney said there was twenty thousand in bonds alone.'

'He asked me, of course, if I would be his executor, but I had no idea it might require so much in judgement.'

'He evidently trusted you more than any man, father, and with reason, I might say.' He braced himself to master a vigorous spasm. 'But you had best appoint the trustees and let the board of guardians propose their plans for the workhouse. If I were you I'd make Elizabeth their chairman!'

Archdeacon Hervey looked at his son warily. 'That is by no means an idle suggestion.'

'I did not intend it to be so, father, I assure you.'

'But I may remind you, Matthew, that Elizabeth's duties in regard to Georgiana allow her little time already for her charity. You would not see her neglect the one for the other.'

Hervey, huddled in the corner of the hack barouche as if it were midwinter, though he could feel his temperature rising by the minute, was certain of his reply. 'I do not intend that Elizabeth has those duties for much longer, father.'

Archdeacon Hervey did not seem to hear; or if he did he did not question the intriguing notion that someone other than Elizabeth should have charge of Georgiana. 'Matthew, are you sure you are not sickening for something? Perhaps we should see Dr Birch?'

'No, father; it will not be necessary. A chill, that is all. I'll take a powder when we're home.'

By the time they reached Horningsham, however, the 'chill' had revealed itself unequivocally: fever, violent headache and muscular tiredness which, even transplanted from their tropical origins, were quite unmistakable. Hervey excused himself, explained that he would have to take his ease for several hours, and went to his room. There he scrambled in his small-pack, though he was sure there would be no quinine, for he had become careless of late since the remittent fever had not visited him these six months and more. There was not even any powder. He did not suffer from headaches as a rule, unless the wine had been bad, and he had become careless of this too. He took off his shoes, then his coat; he loosened his stock but took off no more, wrapped a travelling blanket around himself and got into his bed.

*

43

The old long-case clock in the hall was striking six as he came to. He heard each chime distinctly, and then counted them back to be sure of the hour. But was it morning or evening? There was no other noise. He felt better, much better. The headache was gone, he was no longer shivering, and the pain in his chest was no more. He felt the sheets either side of him and thought it odd, for he did not remember . . . They were damp, as they had been in India. He did not mind, beyond the inconvenience to the household, for he had evidently sweated out the fever and what caused it. And the recurrence was by no means as frequent as that first year, when the foul air of the Avan jungle had poisoned his blood, and the bouts themselves were not as long (though they were little less violent). Perhaps his restoration to full health would be faster than the doctors in Calcutta had told him? He had always believed it would be.

He sat up. His head swam a little. It was not surprising; it swam each time. But otherwise he felt in hale enough condition. He got up, swaying slightly, even having to steady himself on a bed post for an instant, then went to his window to see where the sun was. The day was overcast, however. He felt at his face: the stubble was thicker than an evening's. He decided to put on his dressing gown and go to bring hot water from the kitchen.

At the foot of the stairs he saw his sister.

'Matthew! You are better. I thought you would sleep for ever!'

He knew at once. It was as it had been in India in the early months: sleep, or delirium, a full cycle of day and night, without any sense of time's passing. 'I . . . I was thinking it only morning.'

Elizabeth's apparition was somehow troubling. The candles were not yet lit, but he could see well enough, and he saw a different Elizabeth. He had never thought of her in other than capable terms, his sister, always there, always knowing what to do, and never for herself. He had not observed the passing of the years, though he had been all too conscious of standing in the way of her prospects. But now he noticed how . . . grown to maturity she was. Gone were the ringlets; her face was that of a woman – not a

44

young woman, by which he meant girlish, but a woman of consequence, handsome, secure, as if possessed of title or family. He
wished for all his heart that it were so, for none was more deserving of it than she.

By the same light, too, Elizabeth could see her brother's pallor.
'I'm not sure you should be up even now,' she said, though without the tone that commanded him to return to bed. She knew her
brother well enough to judge these things prudentially. 'In any
case, we're not to dine until late; father is gone to Longleat. I'll
have Hannah draw your bath.'

Hervey did not object to that.

'And I shall fetch you tea. Go and sit by the fire.'

He had no objection to sitting by the fire either, but the prospect
of tea was somehow unappealing. 'I think I shall have a glass of
claret, Elizabeth. Is there any bread?'

She nodded. 'Go and sit down. I'll bring it.'

'Where is mother, and Georgiana?'

'They're both gone to Longleat too, though they went on foot.
Lady Bath generally sees them of a Thursday if she's at home. She
sends them back in a carriage towards now.'

Hervey inclined his head approvingly. It was good that Lady
Bath saw fit to receive Georgiana, for although Henrietta had lived
as one with the family, there were three Bath daughters, of whom
one still was at Longleat.

He sat by the fire. Whitehead had made it up well. It gave off a
good heat and he was grateful of it, for he ran a temperature yet,
and he knew that the shivers could come on again easily. In his
condition he reacted excessively to cold air which as a rule would
not trouble him.

Elizabeth returned with a decanter, a loaf of bread and a jar of
pork dripping. 'The wine is very possibly fine, for I hadn't the time
to search for the everyday.'

Hervey took a good taste, and smiled. 'Very possibly. You had
better not tell father!'

'He'll know right enough: Whitehead's entering it in the cellar book this moment.'

'Whitehead reads and writes, does he? I don't ever recall it.'

'Father had Mrs Strange instruct him. She said she never saw a man take to it so.'

He took another good taste, and helped himself to bread and dripping.

'He may not have Francis's ways,' explained Elizabeth, 'but he's a fine manservant. Papa is very fortunate.'

'Oh, I don't doubt it, and I never said ought about his ways. I've always found him obliging in the extreme.'

'And Georgiana likes him too. He's very good with her.'

'I am glad to hear it. But see, you'll have heard of the annuity that Daniel Coates bequeathed? Father ought now to be able to employ a lady's maid.'

Elizabeth looked uncertain. 'He is very exercised by the size of Daniel Coates's fortune. When he agreed to be executor he had no idea it would be to such an estate. The responsibility troubles him.'

'I told him he should appoint you to be chairman of the trustees.'

Elizabeth nodded. 'He told me. And I replied that I should have no objection. He also said that you had told him that you did not intend leaving Georgiana in our care for much longer.'

Hervey looked awkward. 'Ah. I had not meant it to sound so decided.'

'How had you meant it to sound, Matthew? Either Georgiana remains with me or she goes to Hounslow with you. It is not difficult, is it? You have a governess in mind, I suppose?'

He looked even more awkward. 'A governess, yes, well . . . no, not really, not yet; but a governess there may be. I am not certain of the arrangements.'

Elizabeth, who might have been put out, seemed instead vaguely amused by her brother's faltering thoughts of taking up the paternal reins. 'Perhaps you intend that Private Johnson does that duty, in between seeing to your uniforms and horses?'

Hervey raised an eyebrow, thinking to add 'And seeing to whatever it was that concerned the gentlemen from Bow Street!' He recalled that he might have to exercise himself in that regard when he returned. 'Georgiana would be happy enough with Johnson!'

Elizabeth ignored the tease. 'Well, I am ever at your disposal. And, as you say, Daniel Coates's bequest will enable Mama and Papa to employ a fuller establishment, so there would be no reason why I should not come to Hounslow with Georgiana. I imagine, too, that I might even be of help to you in respect of your duties in command?'

Hervey had not considered this, and he chided himself. Elizabeth was not a woman of fashion, but she was by no means incapable of taking her place in any drawing room. She would indeed be of help; with a certain outlay, she would even be an adornment. But, command was temporary; he had no expectations of remaining at the head of the regiment beyond the season. Except, of course, that he now possessed the means of purchasing the lieutenant-colonelcy for himself.

That reminded him. 'I really must write post-haste to Lord George Irvine.'

Elizabeth knew the business exactly. 'Shall your colonel approve?'

It was a good question. Hervey had every reason to believe he would. Lord George's solicitude on his returning from Portugal, his immediate entrusting of acting command to him, spoke volumes. And, indeed, there were very nearly two decades' association in peace and war. These were no mere things. But the lieutenant-colonelcy of a regiment of cavalry in peacetime was a much coveted prize. There would be no shortage of bidders.

'I believe he will.'

'And ten thousand shall be sufficient?'

Hervey was pulled up short again, as ever, by Elizabeth's percipience. There had been much speculation in the mess about the figure. Over time, officers had found more or less legal means to

47

circumvent the regulations, and the price had crept up, whatever the Horse Guards said. Ten thousand *ought* to be plenty but rumour was that the Ninth had just gone for *sixteen* thousand, and if that were so then the Sixth could not cost very much less, and perhaps even more, since they were just returned from India and therefore enjoyed the prospect of long and agreeable service at home.

'I think so, yes, with my own captaincy taken into account and a little extra.'

'You don't then have poor Benedict Strickland's majority?' Elizabeth knew the regulations only partially.

Hervey shook his head. 'If the enemy rather than the Oxford mail had killed him then I should have.'

'Well, I do not imagine that your amiable Colonel Joynson would wish to sell to anyone else once he knows that you are entering the lists.'

That was a highly questionable proposition. Hervey had not the slightest doubt that if command were in Eustace Joynson's gift he would have had it by now. But the lieutenant-colonelcy, although it had come to Joynson free on the death of Sir Ivo Lankester at Bhurtpore, was now the means of his subsistence in retirement. 'Frankly, Elizabeth, he'd be a fool to part with it for a penny less than the maximum bid.'

'Entering the lists' reminded him too: there was a procedure. He was meant to have submitted his name in the quarterly returns – 'suitable for promotion and willing to purchase'. It was for the general officer commanding the London District, now that Hervey was acting in command, to certify both, and the appropriate financial guarantees, but he himself had to instigate it. And he would have to make sure that the recommendation for promotion was to lieutenant-colonel, for he held the substantive rank of captain; his majority had come by brevet and by temporary assignment as second in command. There must be no bureaucratic slip: he held more than enough service to qualify for promotion to the lieutenant-colonelcy. Except that the deuced rules had changed, had they not? That is what Myles Vanneck had told him.

He made to get up.

'Sit still, Matthew! What is it you want?'

'The portfolio by my bed.'

Elizabeth went herself rather than ring for Hannah.

When she returned Hervey began searching the portfolio with a degree of anxiety. Then he found it, an extract from *The King's Regulations, 1824*. The adjutant had marked the apposite passage: 'The quarterly returns certified by Commanding Officers are to be the only communication made on the subject of promotion by purchase, and when a resignation is sent in, it will be considered unconditional and irrevocable and no successor is to be pointed out or recommended.'

He put down the file and cursed to himself. Did anyone take notice of this? In the past when an officer wanted to sell out it was all arranged decorously by the regimental agents: the one would name his price, another would offer to pay, and the colonel of the regiment would approve it. Now it seemed that *everything* was to be regulated by the Horse Guards. Just when the former system would have favoured him, for a change. It was so novel an idea – the Horse Guards' interference – he could hardly think how a regiment might properly regulate its officers if its colonel could not have his say in who was to be commissioned or advanced in his own fief.

He cursed beneath his breath. No, there was a way round every regulation: that much he had learned, and should have learned a dozen years before. He would write at once to his friend John Howard at the Horse Guards; and, of course, he would press his case in person.

'Elizabeth, I fear I shall have to return to Hounslow rather sooner than I had expected.'

His sister looked puzzled. 'But you said you would be able to spend a little time with us.'

Hervey looked preoccupied. 'Yes ... indeed. I'm sorry. But something has most unquestionably come up.'

CHAPTER FIVE

STABLEMATES

Hounslow, afternoon, 18 March

Hervey reached the cavalry barracks just as watch setting began. He had forgotten that today it would be at three o'clock since there was a levee at Windsor and every other dragoon was required for duty there. For all but the commanding officer the gates would remain shut until the inspections were complete and the guard posted, any who had business in or out of the barracks seeing to it that they were clear of the guardhouse by the orderly trumpeter's 'parade for picket', otherwise suffering the delay. It had been a long drive, but if he had remembered the advanced time of guard mounting he would have adjusted their speed over the last mile or so. He would exercise his privilege now of interrupting the sacred proceedings.

'Commanding officer!' shouted Corporal Denny from the leader of the regimental chariot, not allowing the horses to halt and thereby acknowledge that the commanding officer of the 6th Light

Dragoons, even an acting one, could be impeded at his own gates.

The sentry scuttled through the postern like a rat started by a terrier. Seconds later the big iron-clad doors swung open, dragoons heaving with all their strength.

'Details, atte-e-enshun!' bellowed the corporal for the inlying picket (the detailed men were not actually designated 'picket' until the picket officer had finished his inspection).

With scarcely checked speed, the chariot rolled through the gateway arch. Hervey acknowledged the salutes, the gate sentry with his carbine at the 'present', the picket officer, a mint-new cornet from his own squadron, and the orderly serjeant-major saluting with the hand, and the rest standing rigidly to attention.

Corporal Denny reined up outside regimental headquarters. The orderly dragoon, who had doubled from the guardhouse, pulled down the chariot's folding step, and opened the door. It had been six days since Hervey had left for Horningsham (the bout of remittent fever had detained him two days longer than he had intended) and he wanted to see District Orders and the adjutant's occurrence book before appearing at mess.

There was no one in the orderly room, but in his office were several letters. Three were in hands he recognized: Lord George Irvine's, Kat's, and that of his old friend Captain (sometime Commodore) Sir Laughton Peto. He hesitated before opening his colonel's, for likely it contained the reply to his express asking leave to purchase the lieutenant-colonelcy. Not that he entertained the slightest doubt as to Lord George's support. Nevertheless he laid it aside for the moment to deal instead with the four unrecognized hands. These, however, turned out to be matters of no great account, which could wait for the morning. Next he opened Kat's. Before he had left for Wiltshire he had sent her a brief note saying he would be gone some days, but expected to return within the week.

My dearest Matthew,

*I too am sorry at your news and trust that you will have a speedy
and a happy return. As I told you these two nights past, I go to
my sister's in Hertfordshire today until Sunday next, and beg
that you will join me there for as long as may be, for I believe I
shall soon thereafter go to Athleague and there stay a full month
until the work here at Holland-park is done. Pray let me know
immediately you return when it shall be.*

Your ever loving,
Kat.

Hervey felt a moment's unease at the intimacy of the endearment,
though he had seen it on the page often enough (and, heaven knew
right well, elsewhere too). Kat would expect him to drive this very
evening to Holland Park, but that was out of the question. He
must show himself at mess, and there was a field day tomorrow.
And besides, was he not resolved on . . . regularizing his life?

He laid the letter aside and opened that from Peto, which he saw
had been delivered in the day's London post.

The United Service Club
18th March

My Dear Hervey,

*I am attending at the Admiralty this week, and expect to travel
thence to Norfolk. Would you be so good as to dine with me
tomorrow evening?*

Ever Yr good friend,
Laughton Peto.

Hervey was much cheered by the revelation that his old friend was ashore and close at hand, and by the prospect of seeing him again so soon. He would reply first thing in the morning.

He picked up Lord George Irvine's letter again. It could not, of course, contain the positive information that the command was his, but he was confident that no matter what the Horse Guards' new regulations said, in practice all that was required was for the colonel of a regiment to make his wish known to the commander-in-chief, and the appointment was then but a formality. Yet he balked at breaking the seal nevertheless. There was duty to attend to first – District Orders and the occurrence book; he could not simply pick the cherry from the cake. In any case, and despite all reason, he still felt uncertain. He laid down the letter once more and turned open the file of orders.

In ten minutes he learned that nothing had materially altered in the London District during his absence, and that nothing was likely to do so – no notice of reviews, general officer's field days, levees nor the like. He looked at the copy of *The London Gazette* enclosed with the orders, noting its appointments – in particular that the King had been pleased to appoint his brother the Duke of Clarence to be High Admiral of the United Kingdom of Great Britain and Ireland, 'and of the Dominions, islands, Territories thereunto belonging' – and wondering what, if any, consequence there would be for his friend Peto. He turned the page and glanced through the honours: there were to be three new barons of the United Kingdom of Great Britain and Ireland: 'Sir John Singleton Copley, Knight, the name, stile and title of Baron Lyndhurst . . . the right Honourable Sir Charles Abbott, Knt, Chief Justice of the Court of King's Bench, the name, stile and title of Baron Tenterden . . . the Right Honourable William Conyngham Plunket, the name, stile and title of Baron Plunket, of Newtown, in the county of Cork'. There were several knights, and several more knights-commander of the various orders. *And* 'to be Knight of the Royal Guelphic Order, Eyre Somervile Esq., C.B.'!

Hervey smiled broadly. He knew Eyre Somervile to be worthy of any honour, but why so *singular* an order of knighthood puzzled him.

He read on: a report on the royal assent to several Acts of Parliament – 'An Act to amend and enlarge the powers and provisions of an Act, relating to the Heckbridge and Wentbridge Railway'; 'An Act for providing a further maintenance for the Rector of the parish of St John, Horslydown, within the town and borough of Southwark, in the county of Surrey'; 'An Act to enable the Birmingham Coal company to sue and be sued in the name of their Secretary, or one of the members of the said company', various Acts for more effectually repairing and maintaining roads in the Midland counties and Lancashire, various Acts relating to financial instruments (he shook his head: these were tedious details to detain him); and finally 'An Act for fixing, until the twenty-fifth day of March one thousand eight hundred and twenty-eight, the rates of subsistence to be paid to innkeepers and others on quartering soldiers'.

Hervey nodded at that. He considered himself more than a little fortunate to be in temporary command of a regiment quartered in barracks, for the vexations of billeting were many and unavoidable. Not least of these were the difficulties in maintaining a proper regime of feeding the troop horses, while in barracks the adjutant, the riding-master and the veterinary surgeon could cast their eyes over the entire regiment's stables in a quarter of an hour, and as a consequence every man was a better horsemaster.

But that was all behind them. He laid down the orders and took up the adjutant's occurrence book. He read it quickly, for it contained no more than the usual number of defaulters, routine comings and goings, receipts and issues, reports and returns. Then under the heading 'Veterinary' he saw 'three horses from A Trp confined in isolation, symptoms of the farcy'.

This was something he would rather not have read. There was always a certain number of the regiment's horses unfit for duty –

lameness, sores and abrasions, thrush, a cough – albeit a smaller number, the Sixth flattered themselves, than in other regiments. But the farcy was a different business altogether, an ulcerous death, and spread like the plague.

But he was jumping to conclusions. After all, the entry read *symptoms* of the farcy. The symptoms might as easily betoken something else: a cold, and sores from ill-fitting saddlery, or stall-chafing. Harmless enough. The trouble was, a regiment quartered in barracks rather than billeted on innkeepers and the like circulated its ailments all too easily. If it *were* farcy it might be round the entire lines in a week.

He cursed. He had seen the farcy only once before, in a livery stables in Sussex when first the Sixth had paraded for the Peninsula. He had taken Jessye there, and two of his fellow cornets had taken their chargers too, to rest before embarkation. The symptoms in one of the post horses had gone unnoticed, and the infection had spread, so that the lairage was put in quarantine and Jessye missed Hervey's first campaign – a thing he had always been grateful for since she would likely as not have perished with the others at Corunna. How she had not contracted the farcy there was beyond him – beyond any of the farriers even to explain. They had better pray hard that the symptoms here now were of something else. He would summon the veterinary surgeon at once. *No*, he would go to the infirmary lines and see for himself.

As a rule evening stables parade was finished by watch setting, and timings being advanced by three hours perforce made no difference to the routine. The mounting of the quarter-guard, which even in barracks the regiment knew as the inlying picket, signalled the change from the day's routine to the night's, just as in the field the evening stand-to-horses signalled that change. It was not customary for the commanding officer to visit in the barracks during the 'silent hours', the regiment at this time being in the care of the picket officer, but the commanding officer could go when and where he liked, and Hervey was of the mind that these were circumstances that permitted a variation in custom.

The infirmary lines were no different from the troop lines except that they were built with loose boxes rather than standing stalls in order to allow the patient to lie down at full stretch. They were high-ceilinged, allowing a good circulation of air, they were weatherproof, clean, well drained, and they smelled of new straw and tar. These lines were as good as they came, reckoned Hervey, and they were set well apart from the others. Not a bad beginning for quarantine.

He was surprised to find the veterinary surgeon still at duty, however, when there was scarce a dragoon to be seen anywhere else. 'Sam, I am sorry to see you here so late.'

The veterinarian was taking the temperature of one of the isolation mares. 'Good evening, sir,' he replied, without taking his eyes from the thermometer. 'Up five degrees,' he said matter-of-factly to the orderly, who duly recorded it in the book.

The Sixth's form of address among officers was a touch unusual. All except the commanding officer, who was called 'Colonel' by the newest dragoon, were on familiar terms, the rank-prefix used only very formally. Hervey, a brevet major in acting command, could hardly be addressed as 'Colonel', but neither did it seem correct for the officers – the more junior ones at least – to answer to him familiarly. Instead of 'Hervey' he was therefore 'sir', the form used by the dragoons for any officer, and for a serjeant-major too, as well as for any NCO when there was an officer on parade. As for the veterinarian, whose rank was always anomalous, the Sixth had for many years had their own custom: the officers called him by his Christian name.

Veterinary-Surgeon Samuel Kirwan was a 'respectable' practitioner. Indeed the Sixth had been lucky for twenty years in this regard, having been spared rough 'cattle doctors' little better educated than the farriers, getting instead men of learning from the new veterinary schools. Sam Kirwan had come to the regiment on its return from India, six months before. His father, a naval surgeon, had died after the Nile, his mother not long after that, and the orphan Kirwan had lived five years in the Yarmouth workhouse before a distant relative had claimed him. He had worked his way through the London Veterinary College and joined the artillery as assistant veterinary surgeon, until the vacancy with the Sixth gave him his own regimental practice. He was a little older than Hervey, but wholly inexperienced in campaigning, unlike the Sixth's past veterinarians. He appeared not to have the instinct of a Frederick Selden, who had seen them so sour-tongued through the latter part of the Peninsula and Waterloo, nor the hands of a David Sledge, who had lately endured with them in India; but there was something in him of the science of John Knight, the man who had elevated veterinary surgery in the regiment to a position of indispensability (though – a great mercy in Hervey's opinion – Sam Kirwan did *not* have John Knight's dyspeptic nature).

He gave the thermometer to the orderly, entered the mare's temperature in his own notebook, and turned to the acting commanding officer. 'Not at all encouraging.'

'How certain are you it's farcy, Sam?'

The veterinarian took off his spectacles as he turned. 'That would not be my diagnosis.'

'Indeed? It is entered in the adjutant's book.'

Sam Kirwan smiled thinly and shook his head. 'I reported only the symptoms. The farriers are quick to their conclusions.'

Hervey was encouraged. 'Then the symptoms . . . ?'

'The inflammation is as described in the farcy, but there is also, in two of the cases, inflammation of the pituitary membrane which lines the partition along the inside of the nose. It is discernible only by digital examination.'

Hervey approached the mare, took off a glove and, holding her muzzle down with his left hand, probed gently with his second finger. 'I don't know that I can discern anything, Sam.'

'Unless you are in the habit of such an examination, sir, it is unlikely to reveal itself. I would that you washed your hands now in that vinegar-water yonder; the disease – if it *is* farcy – is very contagious.'

Hervey did as he was told. 'Shall you put a name to it?'

Sam Kirwan sighed. 'I could, but it would be better instead to refer only to the symptoms, for this virus, if it is the type I have seen before, works in a mazey way. If I tell you it is glanders you will be alarmed.'

Hervey's jaw dropped. 'Good God. If we so much as suspect it then we ought to shoot every one of them!'

'I said you would be alarmed. No, I do not recommend that we shoot them, not now that they are in here. I've had sulphur pots placed between the lines. I've ordered them lit at dusk. They'll scrub the air well enough.'

Hervey shivered. An outbreak of glanders *or* farcy: besides the depredations on the order of battle (and the inconvenience and expense that would arise) there was the ignominy, the yellow flag flying at the barracks gate, the line in District Orders and all. It was not the thing of which a successful tenure of command was made.

'If there is the slightest risk of contagion then I am of a mind to shoot them forthwith.'

But Sam Kirwan shook his head. 'It would not be scientific to say that there is not the slightest risk, but I would not think it probable. I have observed that in such cases the virus takes a hold in the air even before the sick animal is removed, or even in the blood, yet does not show itself for several days. I very much fear that if it is glanders then A Troop's horses will be already infected. The important thing will be to keep them from the others. But I am unconvinced that it *is* glanders, only less so than that it is the farcy.'

'The two are horribly of a piece. Have you spoken to the adjutant so?'

'I have. He has given orders, I understand, for exercise at different times.'

They looked at the other occupants of the infirmary in turn, and then parted respectfully, though Hervey left the lines by no means certain they were following the right course. Destroying three troop horses which might perfectly well recover, which might indeed have nothing worse than a cold, was not something to be ordered lightly; but the well-being of four hundred more was his principal responsibility. What was certain was that his reputation would never recover if his troopers did not. He would consider it carefully and speak with the veterinarian again in the morning.

By the time he reached his quarters in the officers' house, the picket had alerted Private Johnson, and a good fire was taking hold in the hearth in his sitting room.

'Ah thought tha were comin back afore now, sir. Ah didn't know what to do.'

Perhaps it was the separation – Hervey was not usually without his groom for more than a day or so – but the vowels of Johnson's native county sounded particularly alien. It was curious: Johnson had left those parts twenty years ago and more, had never returned save once, and very briefly, and heard them only in the speech of Corporal Stray and a few others, yet they had not moderated in the slightest. Indeed, Hervey was quite convinced that they had become more pronounced of late, as if Johnson took some sort of perverse refuge in them.

'I was caught by the fever again, I'm afraid. Nor was I sure you would be still here.'

Johnson's brow furrowed. 'What's tha mean, sir?'

'The Bow-street men.'

Johnson muttered indistinctly and began poking the fire.

'Well?'

He stood up, though his shoulders remained hunched. 'T'serjeant-major says ah've got to go there in t'mornin, to Bow-street, ah mean.'

'What for?'

'Don't know, sir.'

'What do you mean you "don't know"? They must have given a reason.'

'Ah've got to see t'magistrate.'

'What for?'

'Don't know.'

Hervey sighed. Long experience told him that when Johnson was in such a mood it was better to drop the subject. He would speak with the sarn't-major in the morning. Even before the veterinarian.

'Will tha be eating in t'mess, sir?'

'I think, very probably, yes.' But he had not yet read Lord George's letter; and there was Peto's to reply to . . . and Kat's. 'There again . . . I've work to do, and it was a hard drive. Come back at five with tea, would you? I'll decide then.'

It was ten minutes before Johnson was satisfied that the fire had taken a good hold and the lamps were properly trimmed. He opened a bottle of claret, decanted it, poured a glass and set it down on the wine table beside the fire. He cleared a space on the writing table, muttered something about hot water, made to leave, and then remembered something. 'Oh, ah'm sorry, sir. This express came for thee about an 'our ago.'

Hervey stifled a curse. But he was easier when he saw the hand: Somervile's – most welcome. He nodded. 'You might fetch me cake, or some such?'

When Johnson was gone, Hervey sat in the leather armchair by the fire, took a long draught of the claret, and broke the express's seal.

Bedford-square
18th March

My dear Hervey,

Would you come and dine with us this evening, whatever the hour? I have a commission of which I would have you know at once, and a proposal.

Also, I go to Gloucestershire five days hence, and it would be advantageous, as well as agreeable to both Emma and me, were you to join us there too, for we are to make a party at the house of Sir Charles Cockerell whose name you will know from Calcutta. He keeps a fine establishment, in the Indian manner, and is sure to be appointed to the Board of Control erelong. I should say that accompanying us, at Emma's invitation, will be Lady Lankester.

Send word if you are unable to attend this evening and propose yourself for any other as soon as may be.

Ever yours &c,
Eyre Somervile.

That settled the business of the mess. He would go to Bedford Square; indeed he would spend the night there, or at the United Service, and call on Lord George or the Horse Guards in the morning – whichever seemed most expedient. His decision regarding the quarantine would be all the better for measured thought in the regimental chariot. And as to Gloucestershire and the presence of Kezia Lankester, he might have detected the hand of the Almighty Himself.

It remained only for him to open the letter from his colonel.

He noted the form of address again, as if it might reveal the letter's contents:

Major M. P. Hervey,
Officer Cmdg H. M. Sixth Light Dragoons,
The Cavalry-bks,
Hounslow.

It revealed nothing, however. It was the correct form; he would have expected no other. There was nothing for it but to break the seal and read.

He opened it hoping to see not too many words, for many words would assuredly be of explanation, and the only explanation needed would be of a negative. He was relieved: there were but a dozen lines.

Berkeley-square
17th March

My dear Hervey,

Nothing could have cheered me more than to receive yours of the 16th instant and its signifying your willingness to purchase. I have sent word to the Military Secretary and I hope profoundly that we may have it, though I wish I had had the letter but two days ago, for only yesterday I approved a list of bidders. I am travelling north this day for one week, but ere I go I shall write to Wellington, whom we may trust shall act favourably, and shall suffer you to call upon me the instant I return tomorrow seven days.

Believe me &tc,
Geo. Irvine.

Hervey folded the letter carefully. He was greatly encouraged, though annoyed that two days' fever could occasion such a turn. But it was not to be helped, and he was confident that Lord George would be able to see the business through. He had always been able to.

Johnson returned with two slices of seed cake. Hervey took one and offered him the other. 'Johnson, if you will, have Corporal Denny bring the chariot in an hour. And then present my compliments to the adjutant and ask him to arrange for the captain of the week to take tomorrow's field day.'

CHAPTER SIX

A DISTANT PROSPECT

Early evening

The chariot turned into Bedford Square a little fast, so that
Corporal Denny had to pull hard on the leader's reins to avoid
colliding with a removals van near half as big as the house it was
drawn up outside. In the gaslight, Hervey could see the bold red
lettering on the rear doors:

John Durham
Manufacturer
Successor to Morgan & Co
16 Catherine-st, Strand
London

Morgan and Sanders he had known: their ivory plates were on
the best camp furniture in India. He wondered who could be
taking delivery of so large a consignment. Then he saw Eyre

Somervile on the steps of number seven, tipping the van man a coin. What did Eyre Somervile want with camp furniture?

'Hervey!'

His old India friend, lately Third in Council of the Bengal Presidency, and before that Deputy Commissioner of Kistna, Collector of Taxes and Magistrate of Guntoor district and the Northern Circars, but now something suitably exalted in the Honourable East India Company's court of directors in London, looked exceptionally pleased with life. He had taken a house in this unfashionable part of the capital, albeit in a pleasant and modern square, to be close to the Company's headquarters in Leadenhall Street, in whose library and collection of Indian artefacts he could take daily delight (his official work did not detain him long). He stood on the steps of number seven in a fancy powder-blue coat made for him by his tailor in Calcutta, oblivious to the fashion of a dozen years and more for dark colours and plain cut. *Sir Eyre Somervile K.H.*: there was no one Hervey would rather see at this moment, save perhaps Peto.

He advanced on the steps of number seven and firmly shook Somervile's hand. 'I'm sorry I did not come before. I have been most particularly engaged.'

'Your old friend Coates, so I hear. Come inside.'

Hervey indicated Corporal Denny, who was standing holding the leader's bridle.

'Of course, of course. The chowkidar will show him the mews.'

When they were inside, Hervey grasped his old friend's arm. 'My dear fellow, forgive me: your knighthood – hearty congratulations!'

'Great gods what a frippery!' said Somervile, hardly raising an eyebrow, and making towards his sitting room. 'This king – "mud from a muddy spring", as your poet-friend had it. I am, anyway, more Ghibelline than Guelph.'

Hervey smiled. Eyre Somervile was never entirely predictable, but always diverting. 'Then why did you accept the honour?'

The khitmagar had already poured two manly glasses of sherry.

'Because, my dear Hervey, unlike you I do not scruple to use whatever means are put at my disposal.'

Somervile had once told him that he would be a disappointed man not to be made governor-general in Calcutta one day. And Hervey had been greatly impressed: not governor of Madras, or even of Bombay, but Calcutta – the *primus inter pares*, a position of (to all intents and purposes) vice-regal power. 'I rather think I meant why the singular order of Guelph.'

Somervile looked at him obliquely. 'You do know that it is the Guelph dynasty which rules in Hanover?'

Hervey made a pained expression. 'Shrewsbury was, of course, an elementary sort of school, whereas *Westminster* . . .'

Somervile raised a hand airily. 'Yes, Hervey, so you have sported with me before. And you gained a Greek prize, I seem to recall.'

'Homer, yes.' Then Hervey smiled again. 'But in translation.'

'*Really*, Hervey! You make yourself out to be a very simple soldier, and it will not serve. Sit yourself down, sir!'

Hervey did, and was grateful, for even though he had been seated for most of twenty-four hours, a chaise was not entirely easeful quarters. 'What I *truly* meant was why – if His Majesty's government wished to advance you in rank – did they see fit to do it in so outlandish an order. Why not simply *knight*?'

'How did your poet-friend put it? "A Senate – Time's worst statute unrepealed".'

Hervey shrugged. He knew the sonnet well; Shelley had written it not long after they had each left Rome. And he was as dismayed by its sentiment now as he had been then.

'I imagine,' continued Somervile, sounding magisterial, 'that it was to overcome some objection by others perceiving themselves more worthy than I. You know who are more usually made Royal Guelphs? Men of science and letters. I was honoured, so some gentleman-fartcatcher at the palace graciously informed me, for my translations of Bengali texts.'

Hervey raised his glass, determined to be cheerful. 'And most deservedly. But for what purpose, since you very evidently do not judge yourself to be meritorious, should His Majesty bestow that fetching blue-ribboned star on you?' He nodded to a table piled with books and everyday things, on which the order lay as if it had been discarded as casually as an empty claret bottle (unlike Somervile's Bath cross, of which he was enormously proud).

'Ah, didn't I say? I am to be lieutenant-governor of the Cape.'

It was so matter of fact that Hervey had to think twice what he had heard. 'Somervile, my dear fellow, my very sincere congratulations! This is most unexpected, is it not?'

Somervile leaned forward to refill Hervey's glass, though it was in less need of attention than his own which he then over-generously recharged and had to stand to find a cloth. 'While you were doing your best to carry war to Spain,' he began archly, dabbing irritatedly at the India cotton of his trousers and glancing uneasily at the door lest his wife should appear, 'you may have overlooked the little matter of Lord Charles Somerset's impeachment.'

'Who is Charles Somerset?'

'Who is Charles Somerset? Hervey, you astonish me.'

'Then let me guess. I fancy that he is Lord FitzRoy's . . . *elder* brother?'

'Quite.'

'And I fancy he is – or was – governor at the Cape.'

Somervile gave a look of 'I should think so, too'. He sat down again, laying aside the cloth. '*Is*, still, in name. Oh, he won't be impeached of course. The Whigs want to make mischief, but the Beauforts are too mighty. He was recalled last year, and there'll be no going back for him.'

'How has he offended the Whigs?'

'In a nutshell, by being altogether too autocratic.'

A smile creased Hervey's mouth the merest fraction. 'I imagine the elder brother, as the younger, was at Westminster. In your time, perhaps?'

Somervile sneezed and spilled snuff over the damp patch of his trousers. 'Great snakes, whatever next!' He stood up again to brush the offended patch, but there was now a smear of brown on the yellowed thigh, like the mark from a sweated saddle. He jerked the bell pull at the chimney-piece.

A khitmagar, turbaned, appeared almost at once. 'Sahib?'

Somervile rattled away in Urdu so fast that Hervey could not catch even the broadest gist of it. He thought his old friend might need to retire before Emma's appearance, and asked if they should adjourn.

'No, no,' replied Somervile, recovering his composure. 'Jaswant will be able to divert Emma. I shall go and dress, meanwhile. But to conclude – this part at least – do you know who is General Bourke? He has been sent to the Cape in Somerset's place, at least for the time being.'

Hervey looked thoughtful. 'There was a *Colonel* Bourke in the Peninsula, on Wellington's staff, as I recall. Might it be he?'

'It might. He is obviously not without influence, and I can imagine Wellington's interest in this.' He waved a hand airily. 'You understand that man will be prime minister one day!'

'*Bourke?*'

'No, Wellington!'

Hervey frowned. 'As well I should be Archbishop of Canterbury!'

Somervile shook his head. 'Mark my words, Hervey: Liverpool's a sick man. Who shall replace him? No one will serve with Canning! And Peel would have the Irish in arms in no time. No, it might be for a year or so only, and as – shall we say a *caretaker* – but I would lay good odds on it.'

Hervey rose, smiling at the notion. 'Well, be that as it may, what is General Bourke's situation to be on your arrival?'

Somervile shook his head. 'That will be nothing to trouble over.

He shall be commander of the garrison or some such. But he has sent in a scheme of military reorganization which I would question you about.' He looked at his trousers again, and then at the clock. 'See you, Emma will come down very presently, and your godson. I had better go. Pull for Jaswant if you want a bath, there's a good fellow. And he'll show you your room. I had better . . .' He put down his glass and quit the study with muffled apologies.

In the sudden peace of the little sitting room Hervey took a comfortable chair and began contemplating his old friend's news, but he rose again in a few minutes on the appearance of Emma.

'Lady Somervile!'

They embraced warmly.

'It sounds rather droll, don't you think?'

'Not at all,' replied Hervey, smiling warmly still. 'I am only diverted by the colourful order into which Eyre has been admitted.'

Emma raised her eyebrows. 'He has been declaiming on the subject of Guelphs and Papalists ever since he was first canvassed.'

'I can never remember: the Guelphs were the Papal party?'

'Just so. Not that he has the least objection to the Catholics.'

'Merely to medieval Italians?'

She smiled as she took the glass of sherry which Hervey had poured for her. 'You know very well how agitated he can become about these things. He somehow associates the Guelphs with the Tories.'

Hervey inclined his head. 'I had never thought of Eyre as a Whig, and still less a republican.'

Emma frowned. 'He is no more Whig than am I; or you. At present he is very contrary. He cannot make up his mind about this king. I think he would favour revolution if the Company could take over in government!'

Hervey was inclined to see more than irony. 'Things are awry, but not so great as to tempt such thoughts?'

'Oh, you know Eyre very well. He likes to imagine he could better arrange everything than people in Whitehall.'

'He is almost certainly in the right there!'

Emma held up a hand. 'Do not *you* begin! He needs no encouragement; rather the opposite indeed. By the way, shall you come with us to Gloucestershire? The house will appeal to you, I think. It is built in the Moghul fashion. Eyre is excessively keen to see it.'

Hervey looked thoughtful. 'I'm sorry, I had quite forgotten. And Lady Lankester is to accompany?'

'She is. We go on Friday, until seven days following. Eyre says we can post in just the one day.'

'I think it possible to post in a day, though I imagine your bones will be rearranged.'

'Shall you come?'

'I should like to very much, but there are one or two matters to attend. I didn't say, but there's a fearful bad eruption of something in our horse lines, quite possibly farcy.'

Emma was not dismayed. 'Can you be of particular service in that? I very much think that a week in the country would set you up capitally, Matthew. You have driven yourself excessively these past months, if I may say so. Eyre has told me of it.'

Hervey inclined his head. 'I think that it would not quite do for me to be absent with such a thing as farcy taken hold, though I won't deny a week in the country – or even a few days – would be agreeable. That was my intention in Wiltshire, though the wretched fever came again.'

Emma looked pained. 'You take the quinine still, I hope?'

'Not as a rule, no. Not since being in Lisbon.' He brightened. 'But hear: what Eyre does not yet know is that I may soon have the proper command of the regiment. You recall my speaking of Daniel Coates, who taught me to ride and shoot and all?'

Emma nodded.

'He died a week ago and left me a considerable sum to purchase a lieutenant-colonelcy. And I have applied, and Lord George Irvine, our colonel, is to support me.'

Emma sighed with true satisfaction. 'I am excessively pleased for you, Matthew. It is exactly as you deserve, and your regiment will be most fortunate to have you.'

Hervey basked for a moment in the warmth of her smile. 'Thank you. Though perhaps until the eggs are in the pudding . . .'

'Of course. But I should say, Eyre will not *entirely* share my joy.'

Hervey frowned. 'Oh? How so?'

'Has he spoken of the Cape Colony?'

'Yes. I'm sorry, I should have congratulated you before. It is splendid news. Except that I have no desire to lose your company. I imagine you shall go with him?'

It was not the answer to the question she had in mind, and Hervey's own question in turn surprised her. 'Of course!'

'And young Somervile?'

'Indeed! You would have me leave him here?'

Hervey thought of Georgiana and his own practice. 'No, Emma, I would not have you leave him for a moment.'

There was no awkward pause, as well there might have been had they not known each other for so long. But even so the appearance now of Jaswant was welcome.

'Memsahib, dinner is served,' he said, in rapid Urdu.

'Mehrbani, Jaswant. We shall dine as soon as Somervile Sahib is dressed.'

Again, the Urdu was so fast that Hervey was only just able to understand. He had neither spoken nor heard it in twelve months, and in truth he had never been nearly as fluent as Emma. 'You know, I have not sat down with you both since before . . .' He thought better of it, and returned instead to the unanswered invitation. 'You know, I might travel down to Gloucestershire on Saturday. Things should be in hand by then.'

Emma beamed. 'I am so pleased.'

'But what is it that prevents Somervile's unrestricted joy at my own news?'

Emma rose, holding the smile. 'I think I shall leave him to explain for himself.'

70

*

The Somerviles kept both an English and an Indian cook. This
evening it was the same Bengali whose sweet and spicy dishes had
delighted Hervey many an evening in Calcutta, when at times he
had been almost in residence with the Third in Council and his
lady at Fort William. In Bloomsbury, as there, the Somerviles
followed the Indian practice of beginning with the sweetest dishes,
so that they sat down to a table spread with pomegranates, grapes
and jujubes, oranges peeled and dusted with ginger, finger-lengths
of sugar cane, and slices of mango. When Hervey had attended
his first Indian feast, in the princely state of Chintal, he had sat
next to the rajah, who had half mocked the English way of pro-
ceeding through many dishes to a final sweet course, as though, he
had said, 'you must earn sweetness by progression through much
sourness – as in life itself.' The rajah had said that in India they
had no such coyness in their pleasures: 'We have earned title to
indulgence in this incarnation through preparation in earlier ones.'
That evening in Chintal, at his right hand, had sat the rajah's
daughter, the raj kumari, a beauty whose like he had never before
seen, or imagined; and later by some power that he thought a kind
of madness induced by the very air itself of those strange lands, he
had all but defiled his adoration of Henrietta in the raj kumari's
entitlement to indulgence. Only some years later, when he returned
to India, a widower, a bittering man, did he see the madness for
what it was – and embrace it warmly. But all that must end, he
had decided. Soon he would make regular the business of his
manly needs.

'Well, my dear,' said Emma to her husband, 'do you not think
it becoming that our guest may soon be lieutenant-colonel?' She
had told him the news at once.

'I do indeed,' replied Somervile, almost boisterous, as a
khitmagar began refilling glasses.

Hervey nodded in acknowledgement. 'But not forgetting there's
many a slip . . .'

'No, of course. But, you know, Hervey, I had thoroughly expected the promotion. Indeed, I had half arranged it.'

Hervey's face was screwed into a perfect picture of incomprehension. 'Somervile, I would not put anything beyond your reach, except that in the case of regimental command I rather thought the question lay between the buyer, the colonel and the Horse Guards.'

Somervile took care to check his enthusiasm just enough to swallow several jujubes, and then thought better of his game. He had a notion that at this moment the table, what with Hervey positively glowing at the prospect of command, was not the best place to reveal his hand. He had a better idea: he would tempt him with a display of the very artefacts of the life that Hervey knew best. But that, perforce, was a hand to play after dinner. Meanwhile conviviality would serve – as well as being the most natural of things in the company of his old, and supremely trusted, friend.

'How was your funeral? A fitting one for so eminently decent a fellow?'

Hervey found his glass being filled for a third time. He glanced at Emma, who gave no sign of noticing. 'Fitting . . . yes, very. The Wiltshire Yeomanry turned out smartly, Lord Bath was there of course, and General Tarleton came too.'

'Tarleton? 'Pon my word: a singular honour to an old trumpeter.'

'Just so. It was most affecting.'

'General Tarleton of the American war?' asked Emma.

'Yes. Do you know him?'

'No, except from his portrait. There is a print of it somewhere in the house. A very handsome one. You've seen it?'

'I have seen the image, yes,' said Hervey.

She smiled, indulgently. 'You yourself will be commissioning a portrait soon, no doubt. Somervile is.'

Hervey looked suitably impressed. 'Is this true, Somervile? Of course it must be if Emma says so.'

'Since I have a son and heir I feel it incumbent upon me.'

'*You* have good reason too, Matthew,' added Emma, detecting that her guest possibly considered the undertaking premature.

Hervey smiled but ignored the suggestion. 'Who shall paint you?' he asked, in a tone implying he was more sympathetic than Emma had supposed.

Somervile took a long, cogitative drink of his hock. 'Lawrence, I thought, though he's probably past his best; or Beechey, perhaps.'

Hervey's eyebrows revealed considerable surprise. 'I had not imagined ... Forgive me. I supposed the likes of Lawrence and Beechey would have years of commissions awaiting them.'

'Mm,' said Somervile, nodding, and draining his glass. 'That's what Emma says too. Well, there'll be a pupil, perhaps. There is not exactly an excess of time.'

'You mean before you leave for the Cape?'

'Quite.'

A khitmagar had begun clearing the sweet dishes, and another brought one of Hervey's favourites, which first he had tasted at the rajah's feast – *Mandaliya*, the entrails of young lambs, filled with marrow and spices known only to Emma's Bengali, and roasted over charcoal. The rajah, a man of startling sensibility and vocabulary, had spoken of *Mandaliya* as 'the very apotheosis of taste'. Hervey smiled at the recollection of it, such perfect erudition, such gentlemanlike manner. He had so much liked the rajah – his courage, humanity, integrity, each of a rare degree. He wished he had travelled to Chintal again during the long years of that second time in India ...

He braced himself. 'Lady Lankester – she will drive to Gloucestershire with you?'

It was quite a turn of conversation, but Emma was content enough to leave the question of portraits – for the time being, at least. 'She takes her own carriage, but yes, she will drive with us. Might you accompany us?'

73

Hervey did not know how to respond. Here was an unexpected, but not unlooked for, opportunity to present himself, and yet there was the business of the lieutenant-colonelcy to press, as well as the outbreak in the horse lines. 'I had thought Saturday ... but I rather think I might, if duties permit.'

Emma looked at him quizzically, though he did not see it, and then the conversation passed at Somervile's prompting to the week's obituaries, of which Hervey was still ignorant. And then, as it always did, to India.

Hervey began wondering if he would see India again, or yet if he even wanted to. They had been long years in Bengal, but wholly restorative. He regretted he had never gone back to Chintal to see the rajah, and indeed some of the other friends he had made there. But he had feared the raj kumari (if she were not to be quite the death of him) would somehow torment him to destruction. It had all been so long ago – ten years. And, of course, in Calcutta there had been Vaneeta. She had had but a small measure of the blood of Isabella Delgado's countrymen, but mixed with that of Bengal, Vaneeta's company had frequently been sublime . . .

He woke. *Sublime*: as indeed were the confections which now followed the *Mandaliya*, more sublime even than the *Madhuparka*, the honeyed milk which accompanied them. They drank the best hock and burgundy too, exactly as in Calcutta. Hervey sighed inwardly. Yes, he would like to see India again, where all tastes were intense and there was no 'coyness in pleasure'. Where, indeed, he might eat lotus and forget all 'obligation'.

When Jaswant appeared with coffee at the end of the feast, Somervile laid down his napkin and pushed back his chair. 'Come, Hervey, we shall take our coffee in my library. I would have you see the campaign furniture I have assembled!'

Hervey glanced at Emma.

'I will join you in a while, Matthew. From what I saw earlier it will take Eyre half an hour to assemble his bed.'

'Nonsense!' protested her husband. 'The catalogue says it may be assembled with one hand.'

Emma smiled challengingly.

In the library, a big room half filled with expedition baggage, Somervile was at once animated. He was a scholar of very considerable learning, and yet to Hervey he had often seemed never more content than when he was cocked atop a good horse, pistols at his belt and bandits in sight. Somervile handed him John Durham's catalogue, with its indications of what he had bought for the campaign in Cape Colony (not, to Hervey's knowledge, that there *was* any campaign in prospect).

He began reading the preamble. His own camp furniture in the Peninsula had been modest, for portage was ever a problem (he lost far more than eventually he returned to England with), and in India, where portage had been legion, his furniture had been substantial. Mr Durham's exhortation to potential customers was of another world, however:

> In encampments, persons of the highest distinction are obliged to accommodate themselves in such temporary circumstances, which encampments are ever subject to. Hence every article of an absolutely necessary kind must be made very portable, both for package and that such utensils should not retard rapid movement, either after or from the enemy. The articles of cabinet work used in such services are, therefore, each of them required to be folded in the most compact manner that can be devised; yet this is to be done in such a way as that when they are opened out they will answer their intended purpose. There are therefore camp or field bedsteads, camp chairs, desks, stools and tables ...

'My dear Somervile, don't you imagine that the position of lieutenant-governor shall require you to be resident in Cape-town, and that if you travel it shall be to where there are His Majesty's subjects, and therefore the usual comforts?'

Somervile looked dismayed. 'I do not so imagine! You don't suppose that Cape Colony is pegged out like a gymkhana. I shall need to beat its bounds! Indeed, I have every expectation of being instructed to *extend* those bounds!'

Hervey knew that at two bottles Somervile could become positively venturesome, though he had observed the same spirit at nothing more than a cup of arabica. The authorities would know his ardour well, as much as they did his scholarship in native affairs, and so he began wondering if his friend's appointment to an otherwise undistinguished station did indeed presage more active business.

'See first this bed, Hervey.'

Somervile had evidently been engaged in earlier practice, since he was able to unfasten and refasten the retaining hooks, pull the several levers and engage the various locking joints with facility, until there stood in the middle of the room a serviceable-looking single (occasional double) camp bed. When he threw the drapes over the canopy the effect was more of permanence than of the field. Hervey felt sure it would have been appropriate for the governor-general of Bengal, let alone beating about the dusty bounds of the Cape of Good Hope. 'You do expect to take the odd bearer with you?'

Somervile failed to recognize the tease. 'Yes, yes, of course. But I want to be certain of my equipage.'

Hervey nodded, smiling. 'That is very proper. What is in those large chests?'

'Ah, yes: my dining room.' Somervile lifted a lid to reveal four knocked-down, upholstered chairs. 'There are twelve in all. And a table in yonder flat box.'

There were also a brass-mounted secretaire, a travelling book-case with inset-brass grille doors, a caned mahogany sofa-bed, two folding armchairs, a mahogany washbasin, and a travelling bidet which Somervile unfolded from a leather carrying case no bigger than a lady's portmanteau. The whole effect was, indeed, of serviceability, of practicality and economy of labour (if not of materials), so that, as the blandishments of Mr Durham's trade card had it, when 'persons of the highest distinction are obliged to accommodate themselves in such temporary circumstances which encampments are ever subject to', they might do so in the greatest possible comfort. Hervey smiled even broader. He could picture Sir Eyre Somervile K.H. entertaining nobly both Dutch and English settlers in a style they almost certainly did not enjoy at their own farms – and perhaps even a native prince or two, who would surely be overawed by a demonstration of English cabinet-making skill. Or was the colony rather more civilized than he supposed? It had been Dutch-settled for two centuries and more. 'Somervile I am all admiration. This will have come at no small a price. Your devotion to duty is ever entire. I might wish, indeed, that I were coming with you!'

His old friend, who had been giving every impression of an eccentric among his collection of curiosities, spun round and fixed him with the same intense look that Hervey had seen in India when the wind of necessity changed suddenly. 'I wish you were. Indeed, I hope you will. I have need of you.'

Hervey quickened. 'My dear Somervile, I think you forget all that has recently passed. I have learned a little humility from the Portuguese affair – and a desire for a little ease!'

Somervile began fiddling with the handle to a secret compartment in a dispatch box. 'If by that you mean you are intent on toadying your way to advancement then I caution you against it very decidedly.'

Hervey frowned. 'It implies no toadying at all, merely the recognition that to move a mound of clay is better done with leverage rather than taking a kick at it.'

'And a good deal of money.'

Hervey did not hesitate. Indeed, he almost spat the words: 'I've nothing but contempt for it.' It was the first time he had admitted it since the prospect of the lieutenant-colonelcy had arisen – even to himself.

Somervile sprang the secret compartment, as in some show of revelation. 'There! I think you had better come with us to Gloucestershire, and we will discuss the terms of the undertaking.'

Hervey stood bewildered. '*What* undertaking? What on earth do you talk about?'

Somervile narrowed his eyes. 'The Cape Corps, the colony's militia and yeomanry. *More* than just militia and yeomanry indeed, for some are regulars. The Corps's to be reorganized, and radically. There's to be a new regiment raised, of mounted rifles. I want that you should have them. It would mean a lieutenant-colonel's brevet, substantive when parliament approves the plans. And then I should have a man whose judgement I could trust. There are native tribes on the eastern frontier threatening war again. Come and be enlivened by the touch of the spear!'

'The touch of the spear? Somervile, you're speaking riddles.'

'Oh, my dear fellow, I expected better of you. Do you not know the legends of your knightly caste? They were questing for more than the Grail, you recall.'

Hervey raised his hands, conceding. '"I was wounded by the spear and it alone can heal me"?'

Somervile thumped the despatch box. 'Just so! Hervey, it's a very fair prospect indeed in Africa! What paths of glory, what opportunity for distinction, shall there be in Hounslow?'

CHAPTER SEVEN

THE SECRET THINGS

Next day

Hervey had decided to return early to Hounslow instead of first
going to the Horse Guards. He felt certain that postponing his call
would not prejudice his purchase, as long as he did not leave it
more than a day or so more, and he was sure that the business of
the farcy, or whatever was to be Sam Kirwan's ultimate diagnosis,
required discretion. Soon after first parade was ended, he went to
his office resolved to give orders to have the three sick troop horses
destroyed. He was resolved, too, on getting to the bottom of what
it was that the thief-takers at Bow Street wanted of Johnson. But
waiting for him at regimental headquarters – and with every
expression of exigency – was a field officer in the uniform of the 3rd
Foot Guards, and a slightly older man in a plain coat, with the
appearance of a member of one of the professions, a lawyer perhaps.

The adjutant ushered them in to Hervey's office. 'Major
Dalrymple and Mr Nasmyth, sir.'

Major Dalrymple saluted; Nasmyth, carrying his hat, bowed.

Hervey, who had removed his forage cap, bowed by return. 'Gentlemen.'

Major Dalrymple advanced to Hervey's desk and held out a sealed folio. 'Will you be good enough to read this.'

He said it quietly, with due politeness, and in a manner that suggested it was by way of preliminaries. Hervey did not reply, instead taking the folio, noting the seal – the London District – then breaking it and reading the memorandum inside:

To the Offr Comdg
Sixth Lt Dgns.

The bearer of these presents acts on the authority of the General Officer Commanding the London District, and his instructions are to be followed accordingly.

Signed
The Honbl. Anstruther Home,
Lieut-col.
Brigade-major.
18th March 1827.

Hervey looked at the young major of Foot Guards who acted on this singular authority, and then at his plain-coated companion. 'Very well, won't you take a seat?'

They all sat.

'May I offer you some refreshment?'

'There is coffee being brought, sir,' said the adjutant.

Hervey nodded and gave him the letter of authority before turning back to his visitors. 'Capital. Now, Major Dalrymple, what will you have us do?'

'Major Hervey, you will know of the gunpowder mills at Waltham Abbey.'

It was not couched as a question, but the major paused as if for acknowledgement.

'Very slightly.'

'Information has been laid of an attempt this night by armed men to make off with a large quantity of powder. The mills and magazines shall be reinforced, three companies of the Sixtieth Rifles will be posted there after dark, and the conspirators are to be intercepted. You are required to furnish a troop for this purpose.'

Hervey nodded slowly. The experience of furnishing aid to the civil power was not unknown to him, and its attendant perils. 'Under whose orders shall the troop come?'

'Colonel Denroche, the district quartermaster-general, shall command all troops. He will follow the instructions of Mr Nasmyth, who acts on the authority of the Home Office.'

Hervey knew who was Colonel Denroche well enough. He looked at Nasmyth, wondering why a man with the authority to give orders to the district QMG should be at Hounslow now. 'May I ask who are these conspirators?'

Major Dalrymple turned.

Nasmyth replied, scarcely moving a muscle. 'I am not at liberty to divulge that information, except that I may say they are Irish.'

Hervey frowned. '*Irish?* Why should they want powder?'

'I cannot think the purpose too elusive, Major Hervey.'

'Well, it eludes me!'

'Major Hervey,' said Dalrymple, wanting to be emollient, 'I myself am not cognizant of the facts, simply that the orders are properly and legally given. An attempt to make off with powder from the royal mills would seem an unequivocal mischief. I do not think we need trouble ourselves further in these details.'

Nasmyth now leaned forward, better to lower his already *sotto* voice. 'I am by no means unsympathetic, Major Hervey. There has been enough these late years to make any officer wary in the circumstances.'

Never a truer word, thought Hervey. It was not the Sixth's doing, but 'Peterloo' and a dozen other affairs paltry by comparison had tarnished the happy Waterloo-hero image. He nodded appreciatively.

'I understand you to have been in India these five years and more, Major Hervey, but you will surely know that two years ago a bill for the so-called emancipation of Catholics was brought before parliament.'

Hervey knew of it full well. The bill was approved in the House of Commons but rejected by the Peers, and in the elections in Ireland a year ago the Catholic Association had campaigned hard on behalf of pro-emancipation candidates. 'But I understood that O'Connell was avowedly against violence?'

'Oh indeed, a most pacifical man is Mr O'Connell. He proclaims it often. But his cause is advanced by violence in the hedgerows, and he cannot be wholly averse to it therefore. Since the bill's defeat there has been steady word of Whiteboy insolence. You know of the Whiteboy terror, I suppose, Major Hervey?'

'I have served in Ireland.'

'Then I shall say no more, except that there are Irish navvies enough hereabouts to raise an army corps.'

Hervey said nothing for the moment. He told himself that he ought not to be surprised by this intelligence: the Whiteboy outrages, though long finished by the time he had gone to Ireland, had been savage. But all had been quiet these late years – especially since Peel had set up the Irish constabulary, the 'Peace Preservation Force'. There again, Catholic emancipation was a running sore: it had all but broken Pitt a quarter-century gone, and by all that he read and heard it would soon be doing the same to lesser men. 'One more thing, Mr Nasmyth: your . . . interest in this?'

Nasmyth did not reply.

Major Dalrymple spoke instead. 'Hervey, I hardly think it apt—'

But Nasmyth had second thoughts. 'No, Dalrymple, I can admit to that. I answer directly to Mr Peel, Major Hervey. That is all you need to know.'

Indeed it probably *was* all he needed to know. Robert Peel, Home Secretary, one-time Chief Secretary for Ireland, and as strong an opponent of emancipation as any man in the Cabinet – his intelligence would be assiduous. 'I'm obliged, sir.' He turned again to Major Dalrymple. 'You have details of the rendezvous?'

Dalrymple nodded. 'The mills are some twenty-five miles distant. Mr Nasmyth and I shall accompany the troop, and one of the Bow-street horse-patrolmen will take us by the most expeditious route. We are to make contact with Colonel Denroche by last light.'

Hervey considered the details. Twenty-five miles, by the regiment's standing orders for marching, would take them four and a half hours. His instructions from district headquarters specified a troop, but that would suppose a mounted strength of at least eighty, whereas at present no troop could mount more than fifty. He would have two troops do duty – a squadron; and *his* squadron, with him at its head (this was not an occasion for any mishap). He was glad, at least, that there would be a 'redbreast' as guide, for it was a road he did not know. Nevertheless he must allow a little extra time for the unforeseen.

The door opened, and Private Johnson edged in carefully with a silver service and the best of the china taken from Joseph Bonaparte's carriage after Vitoria.

'Coffee, gentlemen,' said Hervey, with a suppressed smile. He looked at his groom, solemnly. 'Johnson, you shall have to postpone your business in town. We march at one o'clock.'

When his visitors had retired to the officers' house, Hervey called for the regimental serjeant-major and told him of the night's assignment.

'Third Squadron shall do duty, Mr Hairsine, under my orders, but I should like you to accompany; I believe it may be a tricky affair.'

'Very good, sir.' Mr Hairsine was pleased. It saved him the trouble of insisting he should go, for although the squadron was Troop Serjeant-major Armstrong's business, Hervey was commanding officer as well as squadron leader, and the RSM's place was therefore with him.

'And this summons for Johnson to attend at Bow-street: I would that you send word to say that he's required for duty and cannot attend. I'd like him with me tonight. Are you any the wiser as to his offence?'

The RSM shook his head. 'Sir. The summons came last night, and said nothing other than that he was to present himself at Bow-street today. He won't say a word, sir, and neither would the Bow-street men when they came. They insisted on seeing him by themselves – a good two hours, they were. I confess I'm mystified. Generally you can have it out of the one or other.'

'By which we can assume this is no little affair.'

'Those was my thoughts, sir. But *Johnson*? Difficult to believe.'

'One of the Bow-street men hinted at worse to come,' said the adjutant, raising an eyebrow. 'He more or less accused us of having an outpost of the Seven Dials rookery here.'

'Did he, indeed?' Hervey could not credit it: the regiment had scarcely been returned from India six months. 'I don't want Johnson locked up for even a night.'

The RSM's brow furrowed deep. 'Sir, I can't see as how we can throw them off their line for ever.'

'They want names from him,' explained Vanneck.

Hervey now realized that the usual practice of not cooperating with the civil authorities when it looked as if the regimental strength might be diminished was not going to work in Johnson's case. He sat down, heavily. He could have no thoughts of Gloucestershire with his groom detained at Bow Street – nor, indeed, with the notion of a thieves' kitchen somewhere in his own barracks. 'Do we know what is the evidence against him? How was he collared?'

'I'm afraid we don't,' replied Vanneck. 'The Bow-street men would give away nothing.'

The RSM shook his head too.

'What do you make of the idea of the fencing?'

The RSM shook his head again. 'Sir, at any one time there's half a dozen little schemes going on.'

'True,' said Hervey. And providing they did not come very publicly to light or touch on the welfare or the pockets of other dragoons, no great efforts were made to extirpate them (the King's pay was mean enough). 'But I want to know what it is that Johnson's involved in. I can't believe his guilt in anything is bad enough to rouse the City magistrates.'

Vanneck raised his eyebrows, unseen.

The RSM frowned. 'He was the biggest progger in his squadron, sir!'

Hervey sighed. 'That I grant you, but only by the exigencies of field service. I don't recall we ever counted vigorous foraging to be theft.'

The RSM nodded. 'No, indeed not, sir. I meant merely that he is not without expertise when . . . exigencies are exigencies.'

'You will put the word out, then?'

'Ay, sir. There'll be canaries enough once they knows the *real* clink's beckoning.'

Hervey nodded appreciatively. 'I would sooner believe that . . .' Well, better not to say whom he thought more capable of miscreancy. 'I can't but think Johnson's unwitting of something. I confess it would go hard with me to learn otherwise. I'd go myself to Bow-street had not tonight's business come on.' He sighed, and made to change the subject. 'Have you seen Mr Kirwan?'

'Not since stables last night, sir.'

Hervey turned to the adjutant.

'I've not yet had the morning states.'

'Would you have him come at once. I believe we must destroy any horse showing the symptoms of the farcy . . . or of glanders.'

The RSM sounded a note of caution. 'Serjeant-majors report all's well, sir, barring those three in the infirmary.'

'I'm very glad to hear it, Mr Hairsine,' said Hervey, sitting down. 'But those three have something, and I'm damned if I'll have a yellow flag flying at the gates!'

The RSM put his hands to his side. 'With your leave, sir?'

Hervey nodded. 'Yes, Sarn't-major, thank you,' he said, then motioned the adjutant to stay.

'You will want me to accompany you this evening too, of course,' said Vanneck.

Hervey shook his head. 'No, I have something else I would have you do, which I confess is more in the way of personal duty for me than regimental.'

The Honourable Myles Vanneck, sometime lieutenant in Hervey's troop, but adjutant of three years now, had seen enough action in India not to crave a scrap with a rabble of Irish navvies. 'Very well, sir.'

Hervey's sabretache lay on his desk. He opened it and took out two letters. 'Would you deliver this personally into the hands of Colonel Howard at the Horse Guards. And this . . . would you have it sent at once to Lady Katherine Greville?'

The adjutant took the letters. He had not himself been to the Horse Guards before, but he needed no instructions in that direction. As for the letter for Lady Katherine Greville . . . the orderlies were practised enough to know where was Holland Park. 'Is there anything else, sir?'

'No, I think not; only the veterinarian.'

The adjutant bowed, sharp, in the regimental fashion, and made to leave, before turning with an afterthought. 'Once I have the orders out for tonight, I may as well drive for Whitehall . . . with your leave, sir?'

Hervey nodded, almost absently. 'Yes, thank you, Vanneck. I

don't mind telling you that Howard's letter is one of some moment.'

'It will be in his hand before noon, sir.'

Hervey smiled appreciatively again. 'And would you have Sarn't-major Armstrong come.'

He always had a care when he might appear to be favouring his troop serjeant-major, not least because he knew it would do Armstrong himself no good. Not that that would have been of the slightest concern to Armstrong; indeed, he might even have held the notion in contempt. But Hervey knew there were jealousies, and with precedence not in Armstrong's favour as far as promotion went (with a man his senior, his years left in service might not see him RSM) it was not wise to load things against his interests.

Armstrong came at once and was ushered into Hervey's office without ceremony. He saluted and bid his commanding officer, squadron- and troop-leader good morning. 'I was sorry to hear about Mr Coates, sir. A grand man.'

Hervey looked at his old NCO-friend. Armstrong was not a tall man, imposing by his frame alone; rather was there something in his air that commanded an immediate respect. He was compact yet powerful, and his face spoke of long experience and capability. He had a broken nose (not, as many supposed, the work of another's fist, but of the mêlée at Salamanca); there was a powder burn on his chin, from a desperate struggle outside Vitoria, and a short but vivid scar on his left cheek from the tunnel's collapse at Bhurtpore. In time the scar would grow fainter, to be just another mark on the tally stick of his service, but there were others, unseen, which might trouble him more than these mere blemishes. A little patch of grey hair on the back of his head marked the fracture, ten years old, memorial to the forlorn hope of saving Hervey's wife in the white wastes of North America. Hervey reckoned that Armstrong was the embodiment of the regiment: imperfect, as was any man, yet fighting-faithful.

'The funeral was a fine affair. General Tarleton showed.'

'Oh ay, sir?'

Hervey nodded. It was time to cut to the point. 'We're taking two troops to Waltham Abbey, the gunpowder mills.'

'I've just heard, sir.'

'I shall ride with them, and the RSM, but Captain Worsley shall have the squadron.'

'Ay, sir.'

'There'll be a deal of confusion tonight: there's a regiment of rifles as well. I don't want anybody dismounting unless it's an imperative necessity. I don't suppose there'll be mounted men against us, so the Rifles can know that anyone on foot is fair game. I shall rely on you to keep things from hotting.' It would be tricky, since Worsley was F Troop leader and Armstrong would not therefore be acting as squadron serjeant-major. That would be the privilege of Troop Serjeant-major Collins, not long promoted and for many years corporal in Armstrong's troop. However, Hervey was confident that Armstrong would find some way of asserting himself.

'Ay, sir. An' who are these men?'

'Irish.'

'*Irish?*'

'It seems they are not content with making trouble in the fair isle.'

'And they've come all the way over here to steal powder?'

Hervey knew he had opened a box, but with Armstrong he did not mind. 'Not especially for that purpose. They're working on the navigation nearby, apparently. Doubtless the poor dupes have been talked into it on the promise of drink and a few sovereigns.'

'Talked into it by who, sir?'

'O'Connell's party. It seems they're to force what they couldn't get from parliament.'

Armstrong grimaced. 'Well, sir, if you want my opinion, we'll be in for a long job of it if they start the trouble again. I don't see as why they can't give 'em what they want?' Armstrong considered himself by no means sentimentalized by his marriage to an Irish Catholic, but he fancied he took an interest in these things more as a consequence.

'You and I know that to be the sound course,' replied Hervey, shaking his head, 'but it's the dread of Home Rule again. There are times when I despair. But, that's not our concern tonight. We round up these gunpowder plotters as sharp as if they were Bonaparte's men come ashore!'

'Oh, we'll do that, sir; never you fear!'

'And you'll look sharp for Mr Fearnley.' Hervey had a special regard for his troop lieutenant: he was not long out of school, but he had the makings.

'I will that.'

'There's one last thing: *Johnson*. I think this business with the Bow-street men's no small matter. He won't say a word. The RSM's going to send someone there today, but would you see what you can do – here, I mean?'

'Ay, I will, sir. I heard he's been fencing.'

'Fencing?'

'That's what the wet canteen says.'

Hervey could scarcely speak, as if a horse had kicked him full with both feet. 'I can't believe it!'

'Neither would I, sir, but word is he's been doing a bit of running for a dealer in London.'

Hervey rose and went to a window. He looked out at the recruits drilling on the square, a timeless regimental scene. He had begun to think that after all these years he understood everything. But how could he? *The secret things belong unto the Lord*, said the Book of Moses; and something very like it obtained in the regiment. To each rank 'the secret things' were revealed differently.

He shook his head, resolved not to despair even if he did not comprehend. 'I can't even imagine he had the opportunity, let alone inclination. He was never averse to "progging", as he called it, but that was a sight different.'

'Ay, sir. Well, let's hope it comes to nought, but if you like I'll put out the word.'

Hervey nodded, slowly. 'Yes, if you would, Sarn't-major ... Why would he *want* to do it? If he were in need of money he knows that all he need do is ask me.'

It was half an hour before Sam Kirwan came to the orderly room, by which time Hervey had written another letter, to Peto postponing his calling on him. There were vexing things about tonight's commission – not least the probability that it would turn out to be another false alarm. Paying informers was a sure way of gaining intelligence, but it was also a sure way of gaining false information; and, from what he heard, the ratio of true to false was highly unfavourable. Nevertheless, if there were a plot to obtain gunpowder it could surely mean no other than an outrage was intended?

'I'm sorry, Hervey, I slept long. I didn't leave the sick lines until the early hours. There are another two.'

Hervey looked alarmed. 'Mr Hairsine said the sarn't-majors had reported all was well.'

'Two from the same troop, but they'd come in from the pay escort, late, which is why the serjeant-major wouldn't have known, likely as not.'

'Don't stand excuses, Sam: they should be able to account for every man and horse.' He stood up. 'The symptoms are the same, I suppose?'

'Not exactly, but the condition is the same, which is what is disposing me to think they have the virus from the others. I'll know better this evening.'

'I've decided we shall have to destroy them, Sam. There's no safe way otherwise.'

Sam Kirwan drew in his breath and inclined his head. 'I really don't counsel that, sir. Unless I'm able to observe the illness run its course there'll be no knowing for certain what it is. I'm by no means persuaded it's glanders, nor farcy.'

Hervey was ever open to persuasion in veterinary matters, and had Sam Kirwan been David Sledge then he would have taken the advice without question, but it seemed to him risky beyond reason. 'It will profit us nothing to know the cause if we lose a troop's worth of horses.'

'I am of the opinion that the virus will be already abroad in the troop. As long as any sick horse's confined to the infirmary then I'm sure there can be no serious chance of the contagion's spreading. If I can observe what is its true nature then I might treat any others that fall sick.'

The veterinarian's proposition was logical. The alternative, as he said, was to shoot every animal when it showed the first sign of sickness, no matter what; and if it were a virulent but curable malady then the cost could be great – as well as needless. It all depended on how strict might be the quarantine. But in any case, if the virus was abroad in one troop, could it be contained there as well as in the hospital lines? Hervey shook his head, though not in dissent as much as dismay at the unhappy alternatives before him.

'Very well. But we had better make a quarantine of A Troop's lines as well.' He looked his veterinary officer straight in the eye. 'I have to turn this over to you, Sam. I have other business, and I tell you frankly, I cannot afford to misjudge it.'

CHAPTER EIGHT

GUNPOWDER, TREASON
AND PLOT

Later

At one o'clock, Third Squadron paraded under the command of
Captain Christopher Worsley, F Troop leader. Hervey watched
from the edge of the square with the RSM, Major Dalrymple and
Nasmyth, the Home Secretary's man. Behind stood the commanding officer's trumpeter, Corporal Parry, the best of the
trumpet-major's men, with next to him Private Johnson and
the 'redbreast', a lantern-jawed man in the black top-hat, tail-coat
and breeches, and bright red waistcoat, of the Bow Street Horse
Patrol. Johnson was intent on keeping his distance, although the
patrolman, formerly serjeant in the 15th Hussars, was disposed to
be friendly.

Hervey decided not to address the parade. Although as aid to
the civil powers went this commission was a shade unusual, the
men were practised enough. He knew that the troop leaders had
spoken to them on the necessity of at first trying the flat of the

sword ('Peterloo' was ever in the forefront of an officer's mind when sent to do the magistrates' bidding), and the dragoons looked eager and capable. He saw no occasion for eloquence therefore. But the parade was his, and he rode forward to take the command.

'Third Squadron – five officers and eighty-eight other ranks – present in marching order, sir!'

Captain Christopher Worsley was a soft-spoken officer, not given to display, rather dull some said. He had joined the Sixth after Waterloo, gone with the regiment to India, but had come back after three years on account of a recurrent dysentery which defied every medical authority in Bengal. After extensive cures in Germany, he had returned to the Active List, bought F (Depot) Troop just before Bhurtpore, and brought them from Maidstone to Hounslow when the Sixth had returned in the autumn. Hervey had never got to know him well, for Worsley had been a bookish subaltern in D Troop, while he himself had spent a good deal of time on detached duty with E. But, dullness apart, Worsley was held in general respect among his fellows, and he possessed the very marked advantage of having a young and most active serjeant-major. Troop Serjeant-major Collins had been born the same year as Hervey, although there was a discrepancy of two years in the age on his attestation papers and that in the baptismal rolls of the parish in which his father, a miller, was churchwarden. Collins had, without his father's leave, enlisted in the Sixth the year before the French had invaded Portugal. He had given his age as eighteen rather than sixteen, and his first name as John rather than Angel, an early sign of his prudential judgement Hervey considered. Hervey was indeed the one man in the regiment who knew of these delinquencies, for he had once visited the Gloucestershire mill on his way to Ireland the year before Waterloo, where he had found a proud father and a good woman, his wife, long since reconciled to their only son's chosen way, happy that they received (as they always had) regular letters and assurances of his well-being. Hervey had told them – as far as he could without making

93

it appear that their son had been exposed to excessive danger – of young Corporal Collins's courage and skill, and that he was certain to come home one day with a serjeant-major's stripes. That had been all of thirteen years ago. It had perhaps taken longer to get the fourth stripe than Hervey had then imagined, for the reductions in the cavalry after Waterloo had been savage, but Alderman Collins had at last been able to see his son with four chevrons on his sleeve. In a week or so he would give a party in the great tithe barn at Ampney to celebrate the promotion, and the engagement to marry, both of which Alderman and Mrs Collins had long hoped for. Hervey fully intended being there.

He looked long at him, now. Serjeant-major Collins was every inch what a colonel in a fashionable regiment would want. He possessed that invaluable cavalry quality 'a good leg for a boot'. So did Mr Hairsine. Armstrong did not. Armstrong's leather and brass may have gleamed more, but Collins's was a frame made for a tailor. In fighting quality there was nothing to choose between them. In experience Armstrong had the better of his junior by a couple of years, in age by half a dozen. Hervey began to wonder if the old principle of promotion – seniority tempered by rejection – would indeed serve the battle-scarred Geordie Armstrong, or whether it would now favour instead the immaculate Angel Collins. He knew that with luck (and justice), the decision would be his, but it would not be easy, although seniority favoured Armstrong, and there could never be rejection of that record of service.

'Leave to carry on, sir?' Worsley sounded uncertain.

Hervey realized he had kept him long. 'Carry on.'

A march was a good time to think, to mull things over, especially if there was a reliable guide and no chance of ambush. Hervey was grateful of it. 'What path of glory's to be had in Hounslow?' Somervile had asked; yet here they were now, bent on saving parliament or the King himself from popish plotters and their

94

gunpowder. Hervey could not wholly rejoice in the mission, however, certain as he was that no *true* opportunity for distinction came in aiding the civil power. The best that any soldier could hope for was that his body came out of it whole and his reputation not too badly tarnished, for if every Tory reviled Shelley and his republican notions still, yet they half agreed his picture of 'An army, which liberticide and prey makes as a two-edged sword to all who wield'. Hervey shook his head. Thank God he had spent the past six years in India, where there were simple certainties – and no poets! Somervile was unquestionably right when he promised a surer path of glory in the Cape Colony. There he might wield his sabre freely and in no doubt as to who were the King's enemies. With Somervile his judge and patron, he would have his distinction, and his glory even; and with it no doubt further promotion. But it would not be with the Sixth. Would he think meanly of himself for ever thereafter?

They marched by way of Ealing, Brent and Enfield. As standing orders required, although the distance to Waltham Abbey was only half the daily march rate, they took the first ten miles slowly, with horses led in-hand the first half hour, and then, mounted, at a steady trot. Hervey had seen no reason to vary this, although the appearance of dismounted dragoons was of some curiosity to the population of Hounslow. After ten miles, nearing Brent, they halted on the common for the prescribed fifteen minutes, and gave each horse a handful of water to wash the mouth, and a wisp of hay. The dragoons themselves were allowed water but no pipe. The next six miles were done at a fast trot, and after forty-five minutes on short reins the regiment halted in the outskirts of Enfield. Here they rested for half an hour, the horses off-saddled and rubbed down, given a peck of corn and some water, and the dragoons allowed tobacco. It was nearing five o'clock as they set off for the final ten-mile stretch, the first fifteen minutes horses led in-hand again, and then a brisk trot as before. In an hour and a half, as the sun began closing to the horizon, they rode into a big field of spring pasture at the Four Swans in Waltham Cross, the furthest point of the Bow Street man's daily highway patrol, and there they dismounted.

While the RSM went with the 'redbreast' to negotiate with the landlord for the green fodder, and beer for the dragoons, Hervey took off his shako, put on a plain lowbrow hat and a plain green cloak, and unfastened the throat plume so as to make the bridle less military-looking. 'I want to spy out the road,' he said to Dalrymple and Nasmyth, looking at his watch, then springing back into the saddle. 'Is Colonel Denroche to meet us here?'

'He is,' said Nasmyth, looking at his own watch again. 'In an hour.' He gathered up his reins to accompany.

'No, if you please; I would rather scout on my own. It will arouse less suspicion, I think.'

Nasmyth looked irritated, but chose not to contest the matter.

'Do we meet the Sixtieth's colonel too? I must have words with him.'

'I do not know,' said Nasmyth curtly. 'That is a military matter.'

Hervey turned instead to Major Dalrymple.

'Neither do I,' said Dalrymple, apologetically. 'My orders are solely in connection with the cavalry.'

Hervey was angering. It did not seem too much to ask of the man acting on the direct authority of the General Officer Commanding the London District to know such a detail. It was, after all, not unimportant. 'Very well, I shall ride over to the mills while there's still daylight.'

Nasmyth shook his head. 'I wish you would not. The Sixtieth will have taken up their positions by now. It would be very perilous for all.'

'In God's name, man, I've got to speak with the Sixtieth else sure as fate we'll blunder into each other! Believe me, I've seen it more times than I care to remember, and in circumstances a deal more favourable than these!'

Nasmyth did not rise to the anger. 'I am sure we can arrange for the Sixtieth's colonel to come here, Hervey. I'm sure Colonel Denroche would wish it so.'

Hervey bit his lip. He was obliged, by the normal usages of aid to the civil power, to submit to any order from a magistrate, or in this case the representative of the Home Secretary himself, but that did not, in his view, mean submitting to orders as to *how* to exercise his military authority. Except, of course, where such action might be contrary to the law of the land. He chose to be emollient, however. 'I shall ride a mile or so yonder, to the crossroads – if this map's faithful. I want to see what is the going off the road.' He held his map out to Nasmyth, indicating his objective. 'This, I take it, is the road by which the intruders will come?'

'That is our intelligence. With one waggon, covered. And armed.'

Hervey nodded. 'And then I shall return by the old turnpike along the Lea. I shall be back in an hour,' he said, turning Gilbert about before there were any more protests and impediments.

There had been other occasions when he had felt acutely the want of time for reconnaissance. It made no difference whether the enemy was French or Hindoostani – or even Luddite or Irish: a thorough survey of the ground repaid any expense. He rejoiced that for once he had a good map, or rather plan – the Board of Ordnance's of 1801 – but he understood there had been extensive building during the late war, and it was as well to mark the changes while he could. Here after all was one of the biggest – perhaps *the* biggest – manufactories in England.

That, however, was not his immediate impression as he came into Waltham Abbey. The town was sleepier even than Enfield. As he turned north into Powdermill Lane and began trotting alongside the river he was at once struck, and to his immense surprise, by how pastoral, how green and pleasant, was the scene: no towering foundries, no 'dark Satanic mills', no winding gear to lower poor colliers to the infernal regions, no smoking chimneys to begrime the country thereabout. There were so many trees he might have been in Epping Forest still, or else nearby on good Queen Bess's old chase. There was no noise but for the creaking of waterwheels, no noxious vapours to sting the eyes and throat, no hurly-burly of any sort; only sailing barges which plied the sluggish Lea as peacefully as if they carried flour to City bakers rather than gunpowder to the Woolwich arsenal. But he knew full well how violence could suddenly intrude even on such a bucolic scene (he had drawn sabre and pistol in the English countryside before). And even here, in the quietness of birdsong and a light breeze in the oaks and elms, there was ever the threat of explosion as great as any he might hear on the battlefield. Greater, indeed: as loud as the magazines at Corunna and Ciudad Rodrigo when *their* powder had taken a spark; and as unpredictable as a volcano.

He rode north for almost a mile, and still the land was the Board of Ordnance's. In among the trees he could see the little curved-roof stone buildings, or else flimsy wooden ones which would blow apart readily rather than contain the blast and do fearful destruction to all inside. The more he saw the more astonished he was, for His Majesty's principal gunpowder mills would, he felt sure, have been at once familiar to great Henry himself when first the manufacture of powder began here three centuries ago. It was a most curious, almost primitive affair, the advances of science and engineering having passed by this very heart of the nation's machinery of war. There was not even a wall around the site to speak of, nothing to keep out malefactors, although he supposed the road might easily be closed at the southern and northern ends, and then the river on the one side would form a barrier, and the part-canalized Mill Head on the west another. Indeed there were so many cuts and sluices to channel the power-water or let small boats take powder from one process to the next that it appeared to him a veritable little Venice. He would have wished for a more thoroughgoing reconnaissance; all he could do now was gain an impression of the ground over which they might manoeuvre, if 'manoeuvre' was not too pretentious a description of a scramble at night after Irish hoddy-noddies.

He had yet to discover it for certain, but he felt sure the place must be stoutly patrolled by watchmen, to whom even a navvy fortified by spirits and armed with a pickaxe handle was not too formidable an opponent, for the watchmen would, of course, be firearmed, or have access to firearms. Doubtless the ringleaders would be carrying pistols; perhaps even muskets. They would think themselves well set up for the night's work, expecting nothing out of the ordinary of the watch, so that a sharp fusillade from the Sixtieth might confound them altogether. Not that it would be a fusillade: aimed shots was what the Sixtieth's riflemen would deliver, even in the dark, for there would be moon enough tonight to make out figures at fifty yards. And that was something that spoke of the intruders' inaptness too: a bit of a moon they no doubt considered to their advantage – enough to light their path but not enough to give them away. Hervey shook his head. Poor fools! It would be no hunter's moon tonight, but enough to give the pursuer his line; and with each dragoon carrying a torch those who escaped the Sixtieth's marksmanship would not evade the following sabre. Poor fools; poor, damned, gullible, Irish fools!

The ground to the left of the Powdermill Lane was firm enough. Hervey reckoned a man could run a good way before tiring. A pity it was not soft going, to let a horse overhaul a running man not too far from the road. He could see the odd fugitive getting into the woods on the common, where he would then have the advantage if he kept his head. If this were the only road approaching the mills (the parallel canal a couple of hundred yards across the common had a towpath, but according to his map little more), it would be well to put the better part of the squadron in the woods to begin with, leaving a strong party of carbines at the inlets where the Powdermill Lane and canal converged. The rest could picket the lane and the towpath and then drive the intruders north onto the carbines like beaters at a shoot. Unless they were given to panic (which of course, being Irish, was a very distinct possibility), or bent on murder, there was no reason why every one of them should not be taken prisoner. And that would be of the greatest advantage to the Home Office in their pursuit of intelligence. He needed to know for certain, however, where the Sixtieth were: close garrison of the corning mills and storage sheds was their task, but he must make sure there was no possibility of their mistaking his men for intruders.

'Halt!'

A rifleman, green-uniformed and grim-faced, stepped into the road from behind a rhododendron bush. Hervey pulled up at once. 'Good evening, Corporal. I am Major Hervey of the Sixth Light Dragoons.'

The Sixtieth corporal at once shouldered his rifle and saluted. 'Sir!'

'I was hoping to find your colonel.'

'Don't know where the colonel is, sir. The captain's just yonder a couple of hundred yards; at the flour mill beyond the big magazine, sir.'

Hervey was surprised by how far north the picket was posted, several hundred yards from any building; but that was a question for the captain. 'That will do, Corporal. Thank you.'

The corporal stood aside to let him pass. Hervey touched his hat in reply to the second salute, and put Gilbert back into a trot.

The metalled road now turned into soft track, which in turn all but disappeared at the Grand Magazine. Here was a safe enough place reckoned Hervey: it was entirely surrounded by water, though there was no sign of a guard. He picked his way carefully, wondering how they would fare if there were no moon, for the cloud was becoming heavy.

At the mill he met the officer commanding Number One Company, a young captain who quickly told him of the arrangements. The flour mill, he explained, was owned by the Ordnance; they had bought it to better regulate the flow of water from the

Lea to the powder-corning mills, and it was to be the forward company post. His orders were to picket the Powdermill Lane (which Hervey had just ridden) as far as the big bend in the Lea where the sentry had challenged, and, on the other side of the common, south along the canal as far as the old corning house.

Hervey noted the detail on his map, though not without some perplexity. 'I take it the second company will complete the circle, so to speak. But why are you posted so far from any of the buildings?'

The captain explained that such was the fear of causing explosion, no one with firearms was permitted within a hundred yards of any building.

Hervey knew well enough they sat atop a powder keg but he had rather supposed the intruders posed the greater risk of an errant spark. 'Very well,' he replied, a shade wearily. 'I've yet to receive my orders, but I fancy they'll be to patrol the road north of here, though I could do that well enough with a quarter of the men. Do you have a parole?'

'Shorncliffe.'

Hervey nodded. 'The same for both companies?'

'Ay. And yours?'

'We shall take "Shorncliffe" too. But I fancy, since we're hardly likely to meet Slattery's Dragoons, four legs should be a faithful enough sign. I shall now go to see your colonel. I'll see you again soon after dark, no doubt.'

The captain returned the wry smile. 'Join us for dinner if the colonel doesn't insist on your dining with him.'

Hervey touched his hat. He had always liked the way of the Rifles. 'With great pleasure.'

By the time Hervey got back to the Four Swans, the deputy quartermaster-general had arrived.

'Good evening, Colonel,' he said, dismounting and saluting. 'Major Hervey, commanding the Light Dragoons.'

101

Colonel Denroche remembered, and touched the tip of his bicorn.

'I have explored the mills and met Colonel Agar,' Hervey began, briskly. 'He's much agitated by the restrictions placed on his riflemen – not to approach within a hundred yards of any building. We've agreed that I should picket the road north of the Thorogood Sluice, the first inlet to the canal' (he pointed to the place on his map) 'and keep a reserve of dragoons to sweep the common land between the Lea and the canal in case anyone gets across the water.'

Colonel Denroche nodded.

Nasmyth stepped forward. 'Your exploration, Major Hervey: you did not go *north* of the Thorogood Sluice?'

Hervey was angering, but he spoke calmly. 'As it happens, I did not. Is there any reason I should not have done so?'

'Only that I have told my own men that no one would venture beyond there in daylight.'

'Your *own* men?'

Colonel Denroche held up a hand. 'I think we need not go into the details. Is your troop ready, Major Hervey?'

'It is, Colonel, but as yet they have no orders.'

Colonel Denroche narrowed his eyes. 'I know that, Hervey. Since I have not given *you* orders you cannot have given *them* any. Do not be truculent, sir.'

Hervey would not kick at pricks. He already sensed the night's work would be vexing enough. 'We stand ready, Colonel.'

'How many men can you dispose?'

'Just short of one hundred.'

'Very well. When it is quite dark you will take them into Waltham Abbey and await further orders. Muster in Bridge-street, which is perfectly suited. In the event of an attack, which the Rifles are well posted to repel, you will be called up the Powdermill-lane to pursue any who flee, and thereafter to patrol the environs to reassure the townsfolk and the mill workers.'

Hervey, incredulous, sought to clarify the otherwise

102

straightforward instruction. 'You do not want me to picket the sluice or place men on the common?' With so inactive a task, he wondered why he might not have had his orders from Major Dalrymple while it was full light.

'I do not believe that will be necessary. The Sixtieth have a close garrison.'

'The mills and the storage sheds, Colonel: who shall guard those in the event that anyone is able to slip by the Sixtieth?'

'I do not see how that could come about, unless by an amphibium.'

'A rowing boat is not beyond question, surely?'

Colonel Denroche was becoming irritated. 'Major Hervey, your thoroughness does you credit, but we are dealing with a band of Irish navigators, not His Majesty's forces. Besides, the mill watch will be attending to that.'

Hervey resolved to stand rebuked, seeing no prospect of persuading the deputy quartermaster-general to address the concern. 'One further question, Colonel. Mr Nasmyth's men – how shall they make themselves known if needs be?'

Nasmyth answered before the colonel was able to. 'You need have no worry on that account, Major Hervey.'

Hervey bridled. 'I am not mint-new, sir. I have seen affairs enough to know that what *may* go wrong usually does, and I neither want to shoot your men nor have them shoot mine!'

'Gentlemen!' snapped Colonel Denroche. 'There's no time for bickering. Major Hervey, just make sure your men stay south of the sluice; and Mr Nasmyth, keep your men well to the north of it!'

The first shot came just after midnight. Hervey, dozing on a straw bale in the Sixtieth's headquarters (the mill stables) woke at once and sprang up, fastening on his sword belt and reaching for his shako.

'Stand to horses!' he called to his trumpeter.

In an instant Corporal Parry was outside and blowing the triplets. They carried easily the hundred yards to Bridge Street where the dragoons waited. Keen anticipation of a chase thrilled through the ranks like a flame along a trail of powder.

Colonel Denroche had also posted himself at the stables. Hervey asked if he should bring up the squadron.

There had now been two dozen shots. Colonel Denroche checked his watch, and nodded.

' "Forward", please, C'Parry,' called Hervey as he went with the colonel into the yard.

Private Johnson was already standing with Gilbert's reins. Hervey mounted at once without checking the girth. Long years told him it was unnecessary – no matter what Johnson's misdemeanours.

Corporal Wainwright, his coverman, was already in the saddle; the RSM too. Hervey hoped Colonel Denroche was noting the address with which the Sixth stood to arms.

The firing was now brisk. Even the Sixtieth's commanding officer looked surprised. 'Not all Baker rifles, not by any means,' he muttered darkly.

Since there were no other firearms north of Bridge Street it could mean but one thing: the intruders were indeed well armed. Better armed than expected. 'Leave to take the squadron forward, Colonel?'

Colonel Denroche glanced at Nasmyth, who nodded. 'Very well.'

Hervey saluted and turned for the Powdermill Lane. 'Mr Hairsine, you and I shall ride for the Sixtieth's picket at the sluice. Corporal Parry, my compliments to Captain Worsley, and would he please bring up the squadron and wait by the old turnpike house. And no lights.'

'Sir.'

He put Gilbert into a trot.

The firing continued, sporadic now but still determined. He knew there must be riflemen in the shadows, but no challenge came until they got to the bend in the river where the corporal had checked him the evening before. A lantern swinging side to side brought them to a halt.

'Parole!'

'Shorncliffe,' replied Hervey, as quietly as he dare.

'Advance, friend!'

'Major Hervey, Sixth Light Dragoons.' He saw a serjeant's stripes. 'My squadron will be up in a few minutes. Have you seen anything?'

'Not a thing, sir.'

A scuffing on the road made the serjeant swing round. 'Halt! Who goes there?'

There were plaintive voices: 'Please, sir, just us.'

Two riflemen stepped from the bushes to take aim at the unknown shapes.

'Who's "us"?' demanded the serjeant gruffly.

'Sethy Wilks and Jack Cranch, sir. We was just doin a bit o' rabbitin' on the common . . . as we've rights to.'

'Raise your hands above your head, and step forward!'

The two shuffled into the pool of light. Hervey waited to hear them.

'Where're you from?' the serjeant barked, as if he were rousting recruits.

'The town, sir. We both of us work in the mills.'

'Have you seen anything?'

'No, sir. We just 'eard all the firin' and thought as how we'd better leave everythin'.'

Hervey saw they were of no help to him, except by way of negative intelligence – and the realization that commoners' rights might make the affair more hazardous than he had supposed. 'I think you might detain them, Serjeant, until it's all over.'

'Ay, sir.'

He kicked on.

The firing quickened again as they came up to the company

post. A sentry challenged them thirty yards short of the sluice.

Hervey gave the parole, dismounted and handed the reins to Johnson, then made his way to where he had last seen Number One Company commander.

The mill was still lit, and from the hatch-doorway at the top riflemen were firing – deliberate, careful aimed fire. He pushed open the door at the rear.

'Major Hervey!' The company commander was deftly reloading a pistol, but otherwise he looked as if he were at a drawing room.

'Captain Hallam. You are attacked?'

'If you could call it that. I was doing my rounds when half a dozen ruffians came along the road. The sentries told them to halt and the beggars opened fire at once. We've been returning fire since, but largely, I think, speculative. I estimate three dozen shots at us at least.'

'Are they still keeping up the fire? The intruders, I mean.'

'I've seen no muzzle flash for several minutes.'

Prudence suggested he wait a little longer, but Hervey was keen to follow up fast if the intruders had fled. 'You don't think it any sort of diversion – others slipping past while they fired on you?'

'I'm certain there's no one on the road or tow-path that came through us.'

'Very well. We'll go forward as soon as you order ceasefire.' He turned to the RSM. 'Mr Hairsine, bring them up, if you will.'

The RSM moved sharply.

'And F Troop to light torches,' Hervey called after him.

'Sir!'

Hervey took out his map. 'What do you make of it, Hallam? Why begin firing like that?'

Captain Hallam shook his head. 'I've been thinking the same myself. It's a deuced mazey thing. They even managed to shoot two of their own.'

Hervey's ears pricked. 'Indeed? Have you got them? Do they have any papers?'

'Just pay books. The beggars reek of beer and whisky, though.'

'No doubt. Dutch courage. Did they have firearms?'

'No. And I meant they're so soused I'm amazed they could stand.'

Hervey shook his head and began examining the map, intent on discovering what they might have overlooked.

But soon the squadron came jingling up, hooves thudding rather than clattering, the road no longer metalled, a green lane.

He folded his map quickly and made for the door. 'Cease firing?'

Number One Company Commander nodded.

Outside, he began blinking to recover his night eyes, trying his best to look away from the torches – one to every three dragoons.

'Here, sir!' called Johnson, standing fast where Hervey had dismounted.

He couldn't complain, but six months ago Johnson would have brought Gilbert up as soon as he heard the firing slacken. He wondered how long it would be before he recovered that assurance – if at all. 'Have you the torch?'

'Sir. Do you want me to light it, sir?'

Hervey blinked again, this time at the alien formality. 'No, not yet,' he said, taking the reins and remounting. 'Captain Worsley!'

'Here, Hervey.'

The voice was closer than he'd expected. He wished the lanterns in the mill had not been so bright; his night eyes were quite gone. 'There may be two dozen of them. They've firearms; how many, I don't know. They had a bit of a skirmish with the picket, but it looks as though they've fallen back. Send an officer and thirty along the sluice, the other side of it, for about three hundred yards until it bends like a hairpin, and then picket the hundred yards or so between there and the bridge on the canal to make sure they can't get any further south – or get back north, for that matter. See to it as well that the lock north of the hairpin's picketed. And keep torches well lit so we all know who's where.'

F Troop Leader turned in the saddle. 'Mr Thoyts!'

107

Hervey waited until Worsley had given his orders, then told him his own intention. 'You'll recall the map: from here on the Lea and the canal converge for about half a mile, and then there's a fifty-yard cut which practically joins them, albeit a narrow one. There's no bridge over the Lea, so if Thoyts stands on the canal they can't get across there either. We may just have them in the neck of a bottle. We'll ride straight for the cut now and then beat back towards Thoyts if there's no sign of them. Torches rear for the time being. Let's use the moon while we can.'

Captain Worsley touched his shako.

Although he had not seen the ground north of the sluice, Hervey said he would lead. He had had the most time to imprint the map on his mind, and although by simply following the river any dragoon could have found the cut, he judged that he could lead them there quicker by swinging north-west across the common.

Mr Hairsine had objections, however. 'Proper drill, sir, with respect! Best have scouts out.'

Hervey hesitated: the RSM was right, but every second counted.

'I'll scout with Lightowler, sir,' said Hairsine by way of deciding it.

'Very well, Sarn't-major. Head north-west for half a mile; if you run onto the canal then just follow it right.'

'Sir.' The RSM saluted, and nodded to his groom. 'Come on, Lightowler.'

They set off at a measured trot. It was moonlight to see well enough, and the treeless, marshy common ahead could hold few surprises. Hervey let them get a good fifty yards before signalling the rest of the troop to follow.

It took but five minutes to close to the cut, with not a sign of life other than protesting waterfowl. Hervey could see, too, that Cornet Thoyts's party had made equally rapid progress, the torches now halted in a line, and four more where he supposed the canal lock must be. If there were fugitives on the common they were as good as in the bag. 'Well done, Thoyts,' he muttered.

A sudden and violent fusillade brought him up short. He held up his hand and reined sharp to a halt. He couldn't work out from which side of the river, or even the canal, the firing came, for the two narrowed to a point at the cut. He took out his telescope. It revealed only that the RSM and Lightowler had dismounted. There were more shots – the muzzle flashes two hundred yards off at least. Not worth returning fire with carbines at that range. He had but one decision: dismount or not.

'Front form line!'

NCOs shouted the order the length of the column as Corporal Parry blew the repeated Gs.

Hervey supposed they had a frontage of two hundred yards at most, and narrowing. They would be tight packed, even with the torch men in the second line. But the NCOs would manage it somehow. 'Draw swords!'

Out rasped fifty blades.

'Forward!' He would keep them at the walk – all the better to hear the next words of command.

The moon disappeared behind a cloud as they swept the ground. Hervey cursed: the smiles of harlots! But the firing soon stopped.

They bumped, stumbled and barged on for a minute and more.

'Sir!' came a dragoon's voice, urgent.

Hervey looked right.

'Sir, it's Lightowler. I think 'e's dead, sir.'

He cursed again. F Troop could take care of Private Lightowler. Where was the RSM?

They found him twenty yards on, not a stone's throw from the cut. It was still near pitch dark, for the torches served more to light up the line than the way ahead. Hervey jumped from the saddle.

The RSM lay clutching his left shoulder. 'Other side of the cut they were, sir. Lightowler took a ball in the throat.' The voice was as determined as ever but a deal weaker.

'Johnson!' shouted Hervey. Johnson was no surgeon's mate, but he knew how to staunch and dress. 'Did you see how many, Sarn't-major?'

'Ay, sir, I did: quite a little knot of 'em – a dozen and more, and at least half a dozen shooters.'

Hervey angered. He clasped the RSM's right arm, then when Johnson came he sprang up and back into the saddle. 'Forward!'

The clouds parted suddenly and the moon lit their front like a stage at curtain-up. Another ragged fusillade crackled directly ahead.

Hervey saw his quarry. 'Charge!'

The canal cut was but a hunting challenge to any half-decent equestrian, especially now the blood was up. The squadron leapt, scrambled and tumbled across it. Sabres sliced left and right. There were screams, oaths and imprecations for a full five minutes until every dragoon had satisfied himself there was not a living thing on the marsh but in blue.

'Rally! Rally!' croaked Hervey.

Corporal Parry blew as well as he could, but he too had swung his sabre the while.

'Captain Worsley!'

'Think 'e's fallen, sir,' came a voice Hervey recognized.

'Sarn't-major Collins?'

'Ay, sir!'

'Hand over all your torches to E, then get your troop in hand fifty yards back and wait my orders!'

'Sir!'

'Sarn't-major Armstrong!'

'Sir!'

'I want every body and weapon recovered. Every last one. Get as many torches as you can forward.'

'Sir!'

'Hervey?' came his lieutenant's voice, breathless.

'Mr Fearnley, this is the rummest thing. Those wretches had no more idea of driving home an attack than a bunch of Methodists.

110

I can't think what in hell's name they were about. Take a dozen men and see what you find yonder.' He pointed in the direction the wretches must have come. 'Horses, boats, waggons – anything. Half a mile, no more.'

Lieutenant Fearnley touched his peak and called for his serjeant.

Hervey sat silently astride as the torches began revealing the butcher's bill, body after crumpled body in grey homespun, a dozen of them at least, more a scene from the plague than a battleground. These men, whoever they were, had not fallen like soldiers; he could not even see their weapons. They had certainly not *behaved* as soldiers. It had been more like that night at Elvas, when the rebels had opened fire in one of the squares to test the garrison. That was *exactly* what it was like. Except that the rebels had not been so inept as to get themselves shot. And where were Nasmyth's men in all this? Hervey cursed worse than before, and shook his head. There was a smell of rat. That, he was sure.

But why repine? To all other appearances, armed men had tried to storm the Royal Gunpowder Mills, and the 6th Light Dragoons, commanded by Acting-Major Matthew Hervey, had done their duty with economy and efficiency. And with thorough execution.

He swore again, stood in the stirrups and bellowed the one order he was pleased to give: 'Sarn't-major Armstrong, take Mr Hairsine's place!'

CHAPTER NINE

LIBERTICIDE

Hounslow, next day

The first streaks of a grey dawn followed the squadron into barracks, but it was another three hours before Hervey returned, insistent as he had been on seeing Captain Worsley, the RSM and two injured dragoons into the proper care of the surgeon at the mills, and the body of Private Lightowler into the hands of a decent undertaker.

He had not known Lightowler. Collins said that he was a waterman's boy, from Kent, but where exactly he didn't know. Hervey hoped the attestation papers would say something, though not every recruit would declare a next of kin, for his own good reasons. But however rootless a dragoon's life might appear in the official records, he had four hundred adoptive kin, the bearers of the numeral 'VI' on their regimental appointments. There would be a funeral with all due military honours, for Lightowler had died on the King's service, and no man in the Sixth would wish to see that go unremarked; for what would that say of the worth of his own life?

'The very devil of a business, sir,' said the adjutant, as he brought Hervey brandy in his office. 'I had it all from Fearnley.'

'Not all of it, I'll warrant,' came the rasping reply, the anger raw despite the four-hour ride and the lack of sleep. 'Those were no Whiteboys and Irish navvies. Not those who did the business at any rate.'

'Sir?'

Hervey unfastened the bib front of his tunic and loosened the necktie. 'We killed a dozen of them and rounded up half a dozen more, but they were so drunk they could scarcely walk. They could've done little harm firing.'

Vanneck was puzzled. 'Then who did?'

Hervey shook his head. 'I don't know. But they didn't shoot like bolting paddies; that's certain. The whole affair has a deuced rank smell to it.'

'Well, it has brought some distinction at least,' said the adjutant, handing him a sheet of paper.

Headquarters,
The London District,
20th March 1827.

The General Officer Commanding congratulates Major Hervey and detachment H. M. 6th Light Dragoons for their high efficiency and exemplary conduct in the incident at H. M. Gunpowder Mills last night. He much regrets the injury to life and limb among the detachment and assures the officer commanding that the facts of the incident, and the approbation of the General Officer Commanding of their part in the protection of a manufactory so vital to the Nation's defence, shall be placed this day before the Commander-in-Chief . . .

Hervey was impressed by the promptness with which it had been both written and delivered. Had it not been for the mention of casualties, he could have thought it composed in anticipation the night before. Why was the General Officer Commanding troubling to rise so early? Hervey had never known such despatch, not even in the Peninsula. But without doubt it brought distinction, and that was some consolation. An ill wind, such as could do no harm to his purchase of command . . .

'Gratifying,' he said simply, handing back the paper. 'You had better tell Sarn't-major Armstrong he will stand duty for Mr Hairsine until Tully is returned from leave.'

'He is already at orderly room, sir. Sarn't-major Tully is not due back for another month. Shall I recall him?'

Hervey did not hesitate. Tully may have been the senior, but he was not Armstrong. 'No. Would you have the sarn't-major come in. And I'll see him door-closed.'

The adjutant left him with his brandy. Moments later Hervey heard the words of command in the corridor: 'Staff parade, stand easy!' as the acting-RSM temporarily stood down his orderlies so he could attend on the acting commanding officer. To Hervey the voice sounded exactly as it ought: the ill wind had blown a little more good than he had first supposed.

'Sarn't-major Armstrong, sir.'

'Thank you, Mr Vanneck.'

The adjutant closed the door as Armstrong marched in, very formally, and saluted. 'Sir.'

Hervey, seated, put down the brandy glass. 'Stand easy, Sarn't-major.'

'How's Mr Hairsine and the others, sir?'

'His shoulder is broken, but it will mend well the surgeon says. Captain Worsley's leg is cut up, but he'll make good. The dragoons will be well, too, though Brunton's very poorly. We'll not see him at duty in months.'

Armstrong sighed. 'Bastards!'

Hervey stood up and walked to the window.

'What do you make of it all?'

'I can tell you what the men's saying, sir. They weren't no frightened paddies doing all the shooting last night.'

Hervey nodded. 'We walked into something, and I'm damned if I know what it was.'

'And I don't know why we couldn't have waited till morning and had a proper scout about.'

'We were ordered very emphatically to withdraw before daylight.'

'Bad business.'

Hervey turned. 'It is. But we'd better gather the reins up quickly. I want to put Wainwright in Brunton's place, make him lance-serjeant. What do you think?'

Armstrong tilted his head and raised an eyebrow.

Hervey knew from long years what this signalled. 'I know the objections, but the man is quite exceptional, and if we do not promote younger men then how shall we have sarn't-majors enough to find good RSMs?'

'An eight-year man for serjeant? They'll say he's your favourite, sir. That you're promoting him for what happened in Spain.'

'And Ava.'

'Ay, sir, and Ava.'

'And why not? If we promote alone by seniority then it's mere dead men's boots. Are we not to reward address and courage?'

'There's two men in E Troop alone his senior. There must be a dozen more in the regiment. What will that say to them as does their duty quietly every day?'

'It will say that exceptionally a corporal their junior merits superseding them. See, it wasn't so bad when there were eight troops, but the reductions—'

'He'll have the devil of a time from the serjeants, and some of the serjeant-majors won't be too pleased either.'

'He has the disposition to deal with the serjeants, and you have it to deal with the serjeant-majors. Do you oppose me in this then?'

Armstrong frowned. 'Not at all, sir. I'd make 'im serjeant tomorrow. You asked me what I thought, and I think there'll be trouble. But I wouldn't be frightened by it.'

Hervey nodded, slowly. 'Very well. I'll publish in today's orders.' He sat down. 'Now, if you can see to the day's routine, I shall go to see Mr Kirwan and A Troop's horses.'

Armstrong shook his head. 'There's a dozen of 'em down this morning, I heard.'

That was close to the last straw. Hervey felt as if one of them had kicked him in the groin.

'Mr Kirwan, a word, if you please.' It was entirely proper for Hervey to address the veterinary officer formally in front of dragoons, but it sounded so alien, even to Hervey's own ears, that he regretted saying anything at all. Yet say something he must, for the farcy had very evidently taken a hold of A Troop's horses, and the contagion might be abroad in others even as they spoke.

The veterinarian, coatless, was bathing the eyes of one of the older geldings. He peered over his spectacles. 'Why certainly, Major Hervey.' He gave the bowl to his assistant. 'Just a minute or so more sponging, Tress. Just see all the detritus is out.'

He took up his coat and walked towards the end of the stalls, where Hervey stood tapping the side of his overalls with his whip.

'Worm in the aqueous humour. You must have seen it often enough in India. Rare here, though. Can't think how it could have got there; certainly nothing to do with the other condition, though I wouldn't have seen it had I not been looking at them all so closely for the symptoms.'

But Hervey was unimpressed. 'I gave orders for the infected horses to be destroyed. Why did not you carry them out?'

Sam Kirwan looked surprised. 'Because you gave the orders when you believed the sickness to be farcy or glanders. But it is no such thing. I have observed it very closely, and I may with some certainty pronounce it to be influenza.'

Hervey in turn looked puzzled. 'Influenza? How can influenza be confused with farcy or glanders? And is influenza not bad horse-management? A Troop's men aren't greenheads!'

Sam Kirwan looked about. 'Hervey, may we go to my surgery? I should feel better able to explain myself.'

Hervey was not entirely placated by the news that it was neither farcy nor glanders, though in his own mind he was already conceding that the veterinarian was correct in staying the destruction of the horses. Except that influenza passed from horse to horse even more quickly than glanders, and the complications were sometimes lethal. It was not impossible, therefore, that the regiment's losses would be worse.

'Will you sit down?' asked Sam as they entered his surgery, a room lined with bottles, and enough bones for three skeletons. 'I can't offer hospitality, I'm afraid.'

Hervey was content to forgo coffee, smarting as he still was from the unnecessary order to have fifty troopers destroyed. 'Why the damned scare about glanders if all it is is a cold?'

'It's more than just a cold, Hervey,' said Sam, shaking his head. 'Any horse that gets it won't be fit for hard work this side of a month.'

'Very well, but how could influenza be mistaken for glanders – or farcy I think the first report had it.'

Sam shook his head again. 'It's not really that difficult, although you will recall I would not commit myself.'

Hervey shrugged. 'In truth, Sam, I do believe you said you didn't think it *was* glanders.'

'Well, to answer your question, the common symptom is catarrh; and fever. The trouble is, glanders takes several forms, as you're no doubt aware, but always with the glandular swelling – of the lymphatic specifically. In different years and places influenza, too, varies much in intensity and in some of its symptoms. Therefore it

117

is not unreasonable to be uncertain of which illness is present in the early stages.'

Hervey took off his forage cap and placed it on the table, a sure sign that cool reason was returning. 'How prudent you were. It would have cost you nothing to put them down.'

'Well,' said Sam, with a sigh, 'I confess it was not entirely without self-interest. I've been collecting blood and mucus from the infected animals – the ones recovering, that is – and I intend inoculating some of the others to see what is the effect. With your leave, of course.'

Hervey's brow furrowed. 'We're taking the most active steps to prevent the spread of the disease are we not, and you now want to spread it deliberately!'

'Both are true, but I should carry out the experiment in such a way that the animal I inoculated, if it developed the influenza, would not be able to infect others.'

Hervey looked gravely doubtful. 'Sam, we do not have the best of things at present – you won't yet have heard of last night's affair at the powder mills. This is not the best of times to be risking even one horse.' He took a deep breath. 'But I trust your science, God help me! How *many* horses?'

Sam smiled. 'Ten; perhaps not even that.'

Hervey nodded slowly. 'Very well. And all from A Troop?'

'No, I need some which have had no opportunity of infection.'

'Very well.'

Hervey leaned back in his chair, wishing now that there *was* coffee. 'What does your science say of these diseases, Sam? I know Clater, but he says little. I don't suppose you hold him in any regard.'

'On the contrary: some of his cures, his medicines – perhaps the majority even – are of no use whatsoever, but they are at least harmless!'

'He was no scientist.'

'He was writing thirty years ago and more. I think you should dispose of your Clater. I'll recommend a more scientific volume.'

'When you have written it?' He held up a hand to stay the protest. 'Tell me of *your* science, Sam. Why do we seem to do no different from when I was cornet?'

Sam shrugged. 'We have made *some* progress – much, I have to say, by observing what our cousins in human practice have learned. But as to the cause of illness, I confess it is true we have not made great steps. If you want my opinion it is simply put: that we may divide disease into two classes, the specific and the non-specific.' He took off his reading glasses and began polishing them. 'Each specific disease, into which class glanders and influenza fall, is marked by certain fixed and unchangeable features which distinguish it from any other disease, if not always perfectly to our observation, and it can only arise by propagation from the original source. The non-specific diseases are those of spontaneous growth, such as constitutional disturbance in the lungs, liver, stomach and so on.'

Hervey frowned. In one sense he himself might have observed as much. 'To what does this tend?'

Sam hesitated. 'Hervey, you look done in – if you'll permit me.' He stood and opened one of his medicine cabinets, taking out a bottle and two glasses. 'I would not as a rule prescribe this, but I myself have been about the whole night.'

Hervey smiled. 'I'm as happy to take my medicine from a horse doctor as from any.'

Sam poured two glasses of brandy. 'What do you know of germs?'

Hervey looked blank.

'You have not heard of germs?'

Hervey raised his eyebrows.

'Or animalculae?'

'No.'

Sam sipped a good measure of his brandy. 'What is the root cause of the influenza in A Troop?'

119

Hervey took his glass and began warming it between his hands. 'Since I do not know where precisely A Troop was when it acquired the disease, I cannot say.'

Sam nodded. 'That is reasonable enough. But you would ascribe the disease to place?'

Hervey looked wary. 'Ye-es.' He took a sip of his brandy.

'And what particular to the place would be the cause?'

Hervey frowned. 'The air, of course. What else? And wind-borne poisons. *Miasmas*, are they not called?'

'They are. And these are generated . . . ?'

'By stagnant water, rotting matter – by filth, commonly.'

The veterinarian shook his head. 'You would be entirely at ease in the Royal College of Physicians, Hervey. And indeed my own. But to my mind it is an insufficient hypothesis. You suffer from remittent fever, do you not, contracted in Ava?'

'Who has told you that?'

'Hervey, I am not so strange to the regiment!'

Hervey took another sip. 'Yes, I suffer from remittent fever. What is the connection?'

'Where do you suppose you contracted it?'

Hervey laughed. 'I know very well where I contracted it, I assure you! The stinking swamps of Rangoon!'

'*Mal aria.*'

'Just so.'

Sam took a longer sip of his brandy. 'The problem, you see, is that there are marshes without malaria, and malaria without marshes. And if this is so it surely cannot be that the circumstances alone – torpid water, decaying vegetable or animal matter, excreta – it cannot be that these of themselves generate the disease, else it would be invariable. And what might account for the different diseases? Do we suppose, say, that a rotting cat begets an influenza miasma, whereas glanders comes from a dead dog?'

Hervey looked thoughtful. 'I had not considered it in those terms, no. What do *you* say is the progenitor?'

120

Sam sighed again, but out of weariness with his own state of knowledge. 'There is no doubt, from extensive observation, that filthy conditions are associated with disease. But the connection is not for me sufficiently explained by the miasmatists. I am drawn instead to the notion of animalculae, germs – we may call them what we like: the most infinitesimally small creatures, which somehow invade the body. It is but speculation, and some hold it to be perilously wild, and yet I am convinced it is the future, at least so far as specific disease is concerned. For the non-specific I myself believe the cause remains an imbalance in the body's humours. Oh, not the bile and phlegm and such like; there is much more to it than that. But if we observe a spontaneous growth in the organs of an otherwise healthy horse we may conclude that the microscopical constituents of the animal's physiology are ... unbalanced. So far as I may see, the treatment of non-specific disease must tend to the restitution of that balance – by medication, by surgery perhaps, or by the proper regulation of the animal's regimen and environment. That is the business of farriery, Hervey – of horse-management as you progressives call it. And what every man in the Sixth should strive to excel in.'

Hervey drained his glass and held it out for more. 'That is understood. But are you implying that the other sort of disease, the "specific" kind, is beyond our management?'

'No,' said Sam, in a tone not altogether certain. 'Let me explain – so far as we may surmise, for positive knowledge has not yet been vouched-safe to us. What *is* a germ, animalcula, call it what you will? We do not rightly know. Imagine, however – for I believe the comparison apt, not least for its etymology – a germ is like a seed, wholly aboriginal. No wheat can grow but from a wheat seed, no oak tree but from an acorn. Likewise, no *specific* disease can be reproduced unless there is a germ of that disease present in the nidus.'

'Nidus?'

'Your Latin?'

'Ah, indeed.'

'Just so: the nest of the infection.'

'Which is situate where?'

Sam raised his hands. 'That is the question: in the air, or water, or feculence. That is what science must address itself to.'

For the moment, Hervey had quite forgotten the troubles of the night and his smarting over the vexed order. He wanted to know more, for it revealed as much about Sam Kirwan as it did of veterinary science. 'How do these "germs" get into the nest?'

Sam declared that that was yet another question. He explained that, taking the seed analogy further, in order for the acorn to grow into an oak the climatical conditions must be favourable, otherwise it would lie dormant. He believed it was possible for germs to be present in the horse *ab origine*, and that if the favourable conditions were understood, germination of the disease could be prevented. But the point was, what should be the treatment of the disease once it had developed? The symptoms must be treated, of course, for they were enervating, even fatal, but – and here he admitted that his analogy was uncertain – it was not known if the germ remained active within the body once the disease had developed. If it did, then only by destroying the germ could the disease be terminated, unless it somehow reverted to dormancy in the natural course of things. 'This,' he concluded, 'is another of the areas in which science must ask impertinent questions.'

Hervey, tired though he was, followed the reasoning well enough – testimony, he observed, to the veterinarian's powers of clear thinking. 'The farriers are well able to ameliorate the symptoms, under your direction, but how is the germ itself to be destroyed? To begin with, are you able to see it?'

Sam inclined his head. 'Were I to know where to look, perhaps, and had I a microscope with the power to see so small a thing. But how should I recognize it?'

'It would not be evident? I remember once being told that a bird was best recognized by observing what it did.'

'That is very true. And it would be well therefore to observe the blood of both the diseased animal and the healthy – and the excreta and mucus.'

Hervey now sat up, as if to say he had other things to be about. 'Eminently sensible. And that is presumably what you have been able to do in the case of A Troop's sick?'

'To a point, but, as I said, I do not have a microscope with one hundredth of the power I might need to see a germ at work.'

Hervey frowned, but with a wry smile. 'It seems to me therefore that you could never *disprove* your theory; only demonstrate the need of a more powerful microscope.'

Sam shrugged. 'Neither do I think this country is the best place to observe, for all the sick in A Troop's lines. Which is why, Hervey – and I would have wished to tell you in more agreeable circumstances – I have applied to the East India Company for employment. The tropics are the place to observe diseases. The virulence is much more marked.'

Hervey was on the edge of his chair, dismayed. 'There's no doubt the tropics are the place to *contract* the most wretched of diseases! Sam, I'm uncommonly sorry you want to leave us, and so soon. Your stock will be awful high in both mess and canteen, the way you've handled things. Is there nothing will induce you to change your mind?'

Sam smiled thankfully and shook his head. 'Believe me, Hervey, nothing would otherwise induce me to leave. The regiment is well-found, and, in truth, I find association with you wholly agreeable. But I have a most determined sense in this: I wish to make my science where it is hot, for heat is the nursemaid of contagion. You will be the first to read of my conclusions, I assure you!'

Hervey knew there were times when a prudent officer withdrew and let his subordinates carry on, whether they were other officers or NCOs. And now was such a time. Without him in barracks for the regimental staff to consult, or to make the troop officers look over their shoulders, what needed to be done would be done, and much the more expeditiously. Besides, he wanted time to think over a number of matters. As much as anything he wanted to dine with his old friend, Peto. He had no stauncher ally than Captain, lately Commodore, Sir Laughton Peto K.C.B. He enjoyed his company as much as he did Eyre Somervile's, and it was true beyond doubt that he owed his life – twice – to Peto's address, which made something particular of their friendship.

Hervey had but one duty to detain him in barracks, and that was to render a full account of the affair at Waltham Abbey, which both custom and discretion required to be submitted to the district headquarters within the day. Behind the closed doors of his office, therefore, he penned five close-written sides of foolscap, four of which comprised an entirely factual narrative of the night's events (with various commendations), and the last a submission that in his judgement the action of the malefactors was so strange as to make him conclude the enterprise was the work of *agents provocateurs.* He did not add, though he was sorely tempted, that such work was not unknown, and that perhaps the malpractices of the Home Office in Lord Sidmouth's time, not a decade before, had not been wholly extirpated.

When he was finished, he gave the despatch to the adjutant and asked that it be copied and taken by officer's hand to the Horse Guards. Then he went to his quarters, where Johnson had drawn his bath, and in an hour, refreshed and dressed, he set out for the United Service Club.

Corporal Denny and the regimental chariot had been engaged on business in connection with the night before, so Hervey had had to send Johnson to the posthouse in Hounslow to engage a hack chaise, with four horses at five shillings a mile to make the journey fast in one stage. He was able thereby to dismiss the coachman at the door of the United Service in Charles Street at precisely ten minutes to eight, a mere one hour and twenty minutes after leaving the barracks, although at uncommon cost to his pocket.

Peto was sitting in the coffee room reading the *Edinburgh Review* when Hervey entered.

'Would you not be better served by a Tory paper if you are calling on their lordships?'

Peto lowered his journal. 'Hah! You've heard then: Clarence to be Lord High Admiral! As well make my chaplain pope!'

Several members – some, officers of high rank – turned their heads, but Peto did not notice; or affected not to notice. He stood, and they shook hands.

'So you are come for admiralty orders?'

Peto grimaced again. 'Let us speak of it suitably victualled. Sherry?'

Hervey nodded, and Peto caught the waiter's eye.

'A dish apiece of the club Fino if you will.'

The waiter bowed and shuffled off, and both men sank into the tired-looking leather tubs that would soon be thrown out in the United Service's move to superior quarters.

'What *is* that stink?' growled Peto as he laid aside the *Review*. 'Worse than a whaler's bilge!'

'The gaslight, I imagine,' replied Hervey, with a shrug. He was quite used to it, for he was lately something of an habitué of the club, whereas Peto's time was divided between the quarterdeck and the wilds of Norfolk. 'You should have smelled the old oil-gas, before it was coal.'

Peto pulled a face. 'Rank stuff, sperm oil. Not cheap either: eight shillings a gallon at Lynn!' He huffed. 'Well, I think ours here are very moderate quarters, I must say. I had rather be at sea in a sixth-rate.'

Hervey knew full well he would rather be at sea. Peto had spent so little time ashore that even the gentlemanly estate he had taken nearby his childhood parsonage, provenance of two decades' prize money, could not divert him sufficiently. Not without a wife, at least; and that was an unlikely prospect by all the evidence of a dozen years' acquaintance. 'I imagine in Pall Mall we shall be altogether better provided for.'

'Nero's Palace?' sneered Peto (the new club was rising on the site of Carlton House, which had been the Prince of Wales's dissipated residence). 'Deuced lot of money just to be nearer the Admiralty and Horse Guards!'

'I don't think that touched on the decision. You've seen the rooms upstairs here.'

'I have. Tolerable, I'd say.'

Hervey pulled a face. He knew when his old friend was being perverse.

'Now, this business at Waltham Abbey: the coffee room was awash with the crack earlier. Talk of cavalry, and fire exchanged. Do you know of it?'

'I'm sorry to say I do. That is why I could not come before. We were most particularly engaged.'

'A pretty kettle of fish, by all accounts. Or rather, by those accounts to be had. And by God there were plenty to be had in the coffee room. None mentioned your gallants, though. I shall be all attention. You were not discomposed greatly, I trust?'

'Discomposed?' Hervey sighed. 'One of ours killed, and four more wounded.'

Peto looked suitably aghast. 'My dear fellow. Who was your man killed, any I should know?'

The waiter returned, and they took their glasses.

Hervey shook his head. 'A dragoon called Lightowler, not long with us, joined just before Bhurtpore. He had an uncle a serjeant. I always thought it a most pleasant name. A good sort too; never complained said the corporals. He had a blood-red right eye, most strange.'

Peto looked approving. 'I have always admired your knowing your dragoons as men.'

Hervey looked faintly puzzled. 'You, I recall, knew all your crew.'

'Hervey, do you suppose those fine fellows in red who drill each day over yonder' (he nodded in the direction of the Horse Guards) 'are known to anyone but as a number?'

Hervey's brow furrowed. 'That is rather different. To see a company of infantry load and volley is like seeing a machine working, a machine with a deuced lot of parts.'

'You have seen many machines working, have you?'

He reflected the smile. 'Now that you mention it . . .'

'Just so.' Peto looked solicitous again. 'Was anyone else hurt?'

'Worsley, one of the troop captains, and Mr Hairsine, the sarn't-major. You remember him?'

Peto nodded.

'And two others. They'll all be well in due course says the surgeon, but . . .'

'The *Evening Mail*'s saying it was a papist affair.'

Hervey inclined his head. 'And very convenient that is for the opposition to the Catholic Association. There'll be motions in parliament this very week to set the law on them, I shouldn't wonder.'

Peto took another sip of his sherry. 'Damned fine, this, Hervey,' he said, holding it up to the light to appreciate it fully. 'But I must say, I had not appreciated you were quite so strong for emancipation. You keep your opinion to yourself, I trust? Not exactly the way to honours with your new commander-in-chief.'

Hervey raised an eyebrow. The Duke of Wellington had always made plain his opinion, not that that would have made any difference to him. But above all the duke was pragmatic. 'I think now the Duke of York is dead you may find Wellington is of a different mind. That, at any rate, is what John Howard says. But see, I have no *very* strong opinion. I only object to being drawn into the game of it. And I very much suspect that last night was such a game.'

Rather to Hervey's surprise, for his old friend had never been what could be called circumspect, Peto glanced left and right and

127

lowered his voice. 'They buy at Berry Brothers, you know, as do I.'

Hervey was mystified.

'*Who?*'

'Our club!'

Hervey kicked himself. He was out of practice in his friend's methods of conversation. The signal to change subjects had not been *so* obscure. 'You will be laying in more for your next commission, then? Or shall you be able to buy directly whence it's shipped?'

But Peto looked suddenly pained. 'Hervey, my old friend, there will *be* no more commissions. I shan't get another ship. They're being laid up as we speak in every creek between Yarmouth and the Isle of Wight. I shan't even make the "yellow squadron". Certainly not now that Clarence is Lord High Admiral.'

Hervey was taken aback. His old friend was frequently acerbic, but never despondent. 'I cannot believe it. You were commodore twice. You were made K.C.B. but six months ago. I cannot believe the admiralty would dispense with such a record.'

'The record is by no means singular. And Clarence has no opinion of me.'

'After Ava?' Hervey was doubly incredulous. 'Wherefore does Clarence have no opinion of you?'

'Perhaps because I have none of him.'

'Ah.' Hervey recognized the condition. 'But Clarence will not be appointing captains, surely?'

'That is his prerogative, and I'm told he intends exercising it. I'd as soon throw in with Cochrane and his Greeks.'

Hervey nodded thoughtfully. He had read that Admiral Cochrane had taken command of the Greek navy. 'And do you see that Colonel Church is to be "generalissimo" of their army? I'd thought at one time to apply to him myself.'

'I don't know any Colonel Church,' replied Peto, absently.

'Nor do I, but I've read of him. He was with the Corsican Rangers, then raised a battalion of Greeks in our service.'

'What stands in your way, then? You'd have the sun on your back again.'

Hervey smiled, with a touch of modesty. 'I believe I shall soon have the regiment. I've been left a considerable legacy for the purpose – by Daniel Coates. You remember Dan Coates? He died not a fortnight ago.'

'I do remember. I'm sorry to hear it. Salt of the earth.'

Hervey nodded. 'Just so. And ever generous.'

Peto brightened. 'But this is good news: lieutenant-colonel! And not before time – long *after* time, indeed! We must have champagne. When is it accomplished?' He beckoned the waiter eagerly.

'Wait! It is *not* accomplished. There are formalities. I have applied to the colonel. I know he wishes me to have it, but there are other irons in that fire and it may be some time. Besides, Somervile's to be lieutenant-governor at the Cape Colony and has made me a most tempting offer.'

'And you're disposed to accept?'

'I'm certainly disposed to thinking of it, especially if the alternative is to be more as last night.'

Peto looked disappointed. 'I don't believe you would refuse your regiment even for a brigade of Marines! . . . We can at least have a good claret?'

Hervey smiled. 'I can see no reason why not; there is still your own honour to celebrate.'

Peto rose. 'It gets me a table next to the window here, but that, I think, is the extent of its usefulness. But let us go and dine. I hear they douse the galley fire at nine.'

The house dinner room was full, the window wall lined with KCBs and some more senior honours. They took the last table, in a dark corner but convenient for confidential talk, which Hervey at least was pleased with. A waiter brought the list.

'Great heavens,' growled Peto, holding it to the light. 'There's more crossed out than in! One soup, is there no fish?'

''Fraid not, sir,' said the waiter, matter of fact. 'We's been uncommon busy tonight, sir; on account of the—'

'Not even oysters?'

'I can ask M'seur Franswar, sir.'

'And who is he?' asked Peto, suspiciously.

'He is the new French cook, sir. Came on Monday.'

'I'd be obliged. Good and devilled, if he will.' He looked at his friend. 'Yours, Hervey?'

Hervey had been studying the list – not that the alternatives before him required great concentration, except that the excisions were of the French dishes that Monsieur François had evidently introduced that very week. 'Well, there is nothing for it but the vermicelly soup, and then the oysters, if there are any, and then the snipe pie, I think: it was good the last time I had it.'

Peto frowned. 'I think it must be extraordinarily old snipe. Oh, very well. I had hoped for something more choice, but . . .'

'You may have a beefsteak, of course, sir, or a chop.'

Peto shook his head. 'Have the wine steward come, if you will.'

'There's a very serviceable burgundy,' tried Hervey.

'I am pleased for it, but if your regimen tomorrow will permit, I should prefer we take something more robust.'

Hervey nodded. If his old friend wished to fortify himself in anticipation of their lordships' laying him up, then he had no objection to claret.

'Damnable business, beached like some dismasted man o' war, and at two-score years. Damnable. I applied to Hardy, you know, when I heard he was for Portugal.'

Lord Nelson's flag captain commanded the naval force which had accompanied the army to Lisbon. Hervey would rather not have been reminded, but he decided to make light of it. 'It was one of my several regrets that I never met him there. I think you would have been well to have been with him, for they're bound to see

130

action. The Miguelites are pushing hard again, I read. He had no opening for you?'

'No, though he said he'd remember me to Blackwood, who's to have the Nore.'

The butler came with his list. Peto assumed command, taking it and holding it to the light as if intent on studying every word.

'If you will permit me, sir . . .'

'I'm always glad of advice from someone who knows his cellar,' replied Peto, now turning through the hocks and the burgundies until he found what he was looking for. 'Is Ho Bryan ready?'

'Oh, yes indeed, sir, very fine. Lord Exmouth and Sir Philip Broke have just taken a second bottle over there.' He indicated a table at the further end of the room.

Peto looked with suitable reverence, and closed the list. 'I can't want for better recommendation.'

'Very good, sir.'

'Frigate men, Hervey,' he said as the butler withdrew. 'Swift and bold. None better!'

'Broke of the *Shannon*, is that?'

'Ay,' replied Peto, maintaining his watch and making no bones about it. 'I wonder what brings *them* up?'

'Do they serve still?'

Peto turned back to his friend. 'Yes,' he said thoughtfully. 'Though neither has an active command. Broke must be close to his flag: he's been post-captain a long time. He was damnably wounded taking the *Chesapeake*. I wonder if that's why he dines with Exmouth?'

Hervey knew how hard it must go with Peto, seeing a man promoted when he himself faced the Half-Pay List, albeit Broke was a captain older and much the senior.

The soup arrived, fortuitously, and a bottle, requiring Peto's close attention.

He tried it, sucking the wine noisily across his tongue. 'It is passable,' he said gravely. 'Though I would keep it another year. Open a second, if you will.'

131

When the waiter and the butler were gone, Peto gazed long again at Admiral the Viscount Exmouth and Captain Sir Philip Broke, as if they might reveal something of his own situation. Then frowning, intrigued, but with evident determination, he turned back to his old friend.

'Imagine they are come with the sole intention of enjoying a good dinner,' suggested Hervey, smiling.

Peto frowned even more. 'I shall try.' Then he resolved to hoist his spirits, and emptied his glass. 'But you must tell me more of your prospects. How are your people?'

Hervey picked up a spoon and began stirring his soup. 'They are very well, all.'

'Your sister?'

'Elizabeth especially.'

'And Georgiana?'

'Georgiana is very well. I intend she comes to live with me at Hounslow.'

Peto looked genuinely engaged by this news. 'Indeed? That is very agreeable. And as it should be.' He seemed then to hesitate. 'And your sister shall come to live with you too?'

'No,' said Hervey, drawing out the word as if thinking it over. 'Not for any length of time, to be exact. The truth is, Peto . . .'

'Yes?'

He hesitated again. 'The truth is . . . I intend marrying.'

His friend's mouth fell open. 'You have said nothing of this! Who?'

'You do not know her. Lady Lankester, my late commanding officer's widow.'

'Great heavens!' boomed Peto, turning a dozen heads in their direction. 'A widow!'

Hervey winced. 'My dear fellow, your discretion if you will! I have not yet proposed!'

'Bah! A widow? She'll not turn you down!'

'She is of independent means.'

'Of course she is. I'd never take you for a fool!'

Now Hervey frowned. 'She has a child too, not yet one year.'

'And evidently therefore of proper maternal sentiment.'

'Just so.'

Peto looked long at his old friend. 'Tell me, Hervey: you love this woman?'

'Peto!'

'Come, man: mayn't we speak of these things?'

'I . . . do not yet . . . that is to say I . . . have not yet had opportunity to form so deep an attachment.'

'You *have met* the woman?'

'Of course I've met her! We met in Calcutta after Sir Ivo Lankester was killed at Bhurtpore.'

'And how many times since?'

Hervey shifted awkwardly in his chair. 'Just the once. But—'

'Well, if it's a mother for Georgiana you're looking for . . .'

'Don't be absurd, Peto; it's not only that. She's a fine woman, a handsome woman – *very* handsome, indeed.'

'More handsome than Lady Katherine Greville?'

Hervey glanced anxiously at the ears still inclined in their direction. 'What is Katherine Greville to do with it?'

'You ask *me*?'

'You know very well the circumstances.'

'Indeed I do, as does, I suspect, half this dinner room, though they might not put face to the name.'

Hervey shifted even more awkwardly. 'I do wish you would lower your voice.'

'Well, I consider it a double occasion for celebration! You will be lieutenant-colonel, and with a rich and beautiful widow at your side. I envy you; I truly envy you.'

This latter was said in a tone of some fervour. And Hervey – for all that *both* occasions for congratulations were yet but aspiration – felt the true extent of his old friend's melancholy.

*

133

Hervey had instructed the coachman to return to the United Service Club at eleven o'clock so that he could be back in Hounslow by one. Several times during the evening he had wondered if instead he might go to Holland Park; his letter to Kat of the day before said he would call as soon as he was able, uncertain as he was when that might be on account of being summoned to the aid of the civil power. There were matters about which he must speak with her. *One* matter, rather. It was insupportable that he should press his suit with Kezia Lankester while continuing to call at Holland Park. He must make a clean breast of things, and at once; certainly before travelling to Gloucestershire. That was what he could do this evening at Holland Park.

Except that it was late. Kat kept late hours, it was true. The trouble was . . . the affair of Waltham Abbey, the uncertainty of getting the regiment, the offer of command at the Cape, the manly dinner: there would inevitably be but one purpose in calling at Holland Park . . .

He climbed into the chaise, not speaking.

'Hounslow, Major Hervey?' asked the coachman, holding open the door.

Hervey sighed. 'Hounslow, Peter; quick as you can.'

CHAPTER TEN

THE SERPENT'S COILS

Gloucestershire, three days later

Sezincote was the strangest house that Hervey had ever seen. It resembled the Pavilion at Brighton, with its Moghul turrets and tracery, its dome and peacock-tail arches, and yet it was very evidently a gentleman's house rather than a place of entertainment. The grounds called to mind the abundant gardens of the governor-general's residence in Calcutta, with all manner of plants patently not native to the country. On the balustrades of an ornamental bridge over a stream that watered the 'paradise garden' were little statues of Brahmin bulls – Nandi, 'the happy one' – and at a remove from the house itself stood Sir Charles Cockerell's bedroom, an octagon fashioned like a rajah's tent, tall poles supporting a canopy, and arch-windows, and a *chattri* – a minaret – in the centre. All was of local stone, but dyed yellow in the fashion of the native houses of Rajasthan. Yet within was as classical as any of the fashionable houses of not-so-distant Bath – 'Greek revival', as Somervile tersely dismissed it. Twenty years before Hervey had first set foot on the Madras beach (Somervile told him) Colonel John Cockerell, the present owner's brother, had returned from Bengal and bought the house from the Earl of Guildford to be near his friend Warren Hastings. On his death the house had passed to his youngest brother, who had been with him in Bengal, first as an official of the Company, later as a founder of the most successful of the Calcutta agency houses established to handle the affairs of Englishmen in India. Now Charles Cockerell was *Sir* Charles, denizen of Messrs Paxton, Cockerell and Trail of Austin Friars in the City – and member of parliament for Evesham.

'Wellington's brother got him the baronetcy,' explained Somervile, not entirely unkindly, as a footman unpacked Hervey's valises. 'I am very glad you could come. Cockerell's is not a bad ear to have.'

'Was it he who had the house Indianized, or his brother?'

'It was he. Another brother was the architect, with the Daniells. And Repton, I think, did the garden.'

'I liked it very much, after first overcoming my surprise.'

'The King visited, when he was Prince of Wales, which is why he decided on his pleasure dome in Brighton, apparently.'

'Indeed?' said Hervey, staring rather absently from a window towards the formal water gardens. 'I look forward to taking a good turn about the grounds tomorrow.' He turned sharply, as if steeling himself. 'What is the order for this evening?'

'A *small* party, I understand. Last night was rather a formal, parliamentary business, though not disagreeable. Your affair of the gunpowder was all the talk. I wish I had known it *was* your affair. You must tell me all of it later. I was vastly diverted by the notion of Westminster's being blown to the skies.'

Hervey looked at him, with a frowning challenge.

'Diverted by the thought that so many could imagine it possible. But we're in Tory country now, to be sure. As well not try saying "Catholic", Hervey. "Papist" is preferred among the gentry. They would have feted you last night, had they known.'

136

Hervey shrugged. 'That is as well. I should be loath to disabuse them and mistreat Sir Charles's hospitality.'

Somervile smiled conspiratorially. 'Oh, and I should say: there's music again, but Lady C has dismissed the band which entertained us so agreeably last night, and the party's to provide it instead. You'll not be expected to perform, though; not on your first night here. Emma and I have something, and your Lady Lankester.'

Hervey frowned again. 'Somervile, she is not *my* Lady Lankester.'

'Ah, then you have had second thoughts?'

'Not at all, only that it's a presumption to speak that way. I rather think I should not have said anything now. It was ungallant.'

Somervile threw an orange at him hard. 'Oh, perfect knight!'

Hervey fumbled the catch.

'Hands not what they were, Major Hervey?'

'They are quite safe, I assure you.'

Somervile rose. 'Come down at once when you're dressed to meet our host. It's a pity you did not arrive a little earlier: Emma and your lady were teaing together in the orangery – rather a useful *kala jugga*, I should have thought.'

Somervile was being frivolous, Hervey knew full well, but Somervile's frivolity was invariably laced with substantial intent. What the substance was this time, he could not be sure: but he would have need of a *kala jugga* – a secluded place – at some moment in the party. He most certainly *hoped* he would.

'And that dog of hers!'

'Dog?' said Hervey, as if this would mean some recalculation. 'I did not know there was a dog.'

'If you could call it that. An Italian greyhound.'

'I think them delightful!'

'Then you had better go to it, for it bit me.'

Hervey laughed. 'It sensed an unadoring presence perhaps?'

'Mm. Shall you wear regimentals this evening?'

137

'I had not thought to. Would it be remiss?'

'It is a private party. But our host might deem it a courtesy.'

No one seemed to be out much in regimentals in London, Hervey remarked, but the country was always a late follower of fashion. 'Very well.'

'No doubt it will serve your purpose, too. What female heart can withstand a red coat?'

'Somervile, you read too many novels! And my coat is blue, not red.'

'It is *metaphorically* red. And I was quoting from the *Edinburgh Review*, or are Whiggish journals beneath you?' He took his copy from the pocket of his coat. 'I at once resolved to save it for you when I saw it: "What female heart can withstand a red coat? I think this should be part of female education. As boys have the rocking horse to accustom them to ride, I would have military dolls in the nursery, to harden their hearts against officers and red coats."'

'Who writes such nonsense?'

'Hervey, my dear fellow, I could have written it myself! But we know that Lady Lankester must not have had military dolls in the nursery to harden *her* heart against red coats – though I should like to know what it would take to raise that heart's temperature above freezing!'

With some force Hervey threw back the orange (which his friend caught deftly with one hand). 'Somervile! I wonder that you asked her to accompany you at all with so low an opinion of her.'

'Not low, my dear Hervey, not low. Her temperature is of no concern to me.'

The acquaintance between the Somerviles and Kezia Lankester had begun firmly and happily in Calcutta, and after the death of Sir Ivo, Emma and her husband had stood not as mere friends but *in loco familiae*. Hervey understood this full well. What sense of obligation rather than true affection maintained their acquaintance now he did not know, but in truth it mattered not. That acquaintance had propelled the woman he was to ask to be his wife into circumstances that might otherwise have taken an age to contrive. The initiative was now his alone, however.

A hot bath had been drawn for him, which, after the early start and the clatter down from Hounslow, Hervey found welcome and restoring. He dressed in his levee coat, with white knee-breeches (trousers might be considered rather careless in such a place, even though Somervile had said they would be a *small* party), and descended to join his host and Lady Cockerell, and such of the small party that were assembled already.

'I read the Bhurtpore despatches,' said Sir Charles Cockerell, extending a hand. 'You captured that wretch Durjan Sal!'

'I did, Sir Charles. He was bolting the place like a manged fox.'

'And you saw off that desperate business the other night in Hertfordshire.'

'I would not have called it desperate, sir: I'm afraid it was a rather feeble affair.'

Sir Charles looked doubtful. But there were other introductions to make: Lady Cockerell, considerably younger than her husband's seventy-odd years, a woman of fashion, with an easy smile in contrast with her husband's cold aspect and manner; there was the vicar of the parish of Sezincote, an urbane man perhaps five years older than Hervey, and his wife, the Honourable Mrs Castle.

'Lady Lankester you know of course.'

Hervey turned. He had not seen her enter the room. She no longer wore demi-mourning, but instead a ball dress of embroidered net over cream satin, the décolleté distinct but modest. He was more taken by her appearance than he had somehow expected, and almost caught his breath. 'Of course,' he said, bowing.

Kezia Lankester curtsied, rather formally. 'Major Hervey, what a pleasure to see you again.' She smiled, but – he imagined it – perhaps rather distantly.

He sought too urgently to make reply. 'And a great pleasure for me, Lady Lankester—'

She had turned already to the Reverend and the Honourable Mrs Castle.

But Hervey's discomfort was soon relieved by the arrival of two local squires, one of them a baronet, both of them ten years at least his senior, together with their wives and the baronet's daughter and her betrothed. The squires were short and stocky, the untitled one perfectly round-faced and with a good many broken blood vessels. They were by no means mere floggers of the shire bench, however, and in the course of the evening would reveal a fair breadth of thinking, not viscerally against Reform, and sympathetic (if cautiously) to Catholic Emancipation. Both had served loyally in the militia during the French wars and were interested in Hervey's thoughts on military retrenchment. Their wives, however, would prove not so diverting, but since they seemed to prefer the company of the Reverend Mr Castle this would not trouble Hervey unduly. The betrothed daughter was, he estimated, not yet twenty. Besides a perfect complexion, some prettiness and good teeth, she had no conversation, nor little else to recommend her. What might pass momentarily as sparkle was, he discovered, mere silliness, although he would later chide himself for such a harsh judgement of one so young. Except that Henrietta had been her age when . . .

The fiancé was a tall, spare man – Hervey thought him his side of thirty – who bowed awkwardly and found it difficult to look him in the eye. He imagined him a poor catch for the young Miss —, although it was possible that he had considerably more money than breeding (Hervey noted that his coat was unquestionably well-cut).

Then came Sir Charles's country attorney, a gentleman, a little younger than his host and with the easy, unassuming manners of the earlier age, and an open face, an easy smile – a thoroughgoing picture of decency and common sense. And his wife was refined and equally at home. It was soon revealed that they had lost a son with the Twenty-eighth at Badajoz.

'Might you have known him, Major Hervey?'

'I may well have made his acquaintance, sir. Forgive me, but we were many in Spain. But Badajoz was a truly desperate affair. I do not think there were many officers in the infantry who were not wounded that night.'

The attorney maintained his enquiring smile throughout the exchange, his wife perhaps did less so, but there was no sadness, just a tender acceptance, as if it were the duty of a family such as theirs to officer the regiment which bore the county's name, and to accept the same fate as so many others who might not have their resource or advantage. Hervey wondered if the pain had eased in the dozen years since the siege. He had no experience of a grieving parent. When his own brother had died – in very different circumstances – he had been far away, and when he had returned there had only been happiness at his own safe homecoming.

When the attorney and his wife moved on to pay their respects to the representative of the cloth, Hervey was able to stand back from things a little and observe Kezia Lankester. She was, barring the betrothed daughter, the youngest in the party, and yet her self-possession was very marked. She took her leave of Lady — with cool assurance, spoke a few words to the happy couple, rather cut the fiancé when she considered their conversation was sufficient and then took up easily with her hostess. He could, perhaps, see what others meant when they spoke of a lack of warmth, but he knew at least as well as any man what the early and violent loss of a marriage partner might do; and he had no reason to presume that her love – indeed he might suppose *passion* – for the late Lieutenant-Colonel Sir Ivo Lankester had been one jot less than his own had been for Henrietta.

At dinner they sat beside each other. The fashion being to dine 'promiscuously' – male alternating with female – there was nothing suggestive in this. Indeed, had the two unattached guests not been

141

seated together it would have been something of a discourtesy. When Hervey had dined at Lord George Irvine's on returning from Lisbon, Lady Lankester had sat on his left. He had spent the first twenty minutes or so talking to the wife of a member of parliament, on his right, while trying to think what he might decently say to the widow of his late commanding officer when the time came. This evening Kezia Lankester sat on his left again, but although he was no longer quite the stranger, he had cause for even more unease. He had determined on marriage and yet he had not the faintest idea what were her thoughts on remarrying, nor the remotest notion of how eligible she would consider him. He chided himself. It was absurd that he should feel thus, a man who would face the King's enemies, yet who shrank from one of the King's subjects – *and* a subject ten years his junior at that!

Lady Cockerell had a French chef evidently keen to display his skill. Monsieur Anton's hors d'oeuvres – tunny and salmon canapés (cold), oysters with shrimp butter, oyster tarts, grilled oysters with herbs, cheese fritters and cheese puffs, all hot – engaged them a full half-hour, during which the untitled squire's wife was eager for Hervey's opinion on the prospects of her various nephews and more distant relatives who were in uniform, in which he endeavoured to oblige her while with increasing desperation trying to think how when the moment came he might open the conversation with Kezia Lankester.

The fish course came and went – a shrimp bisque, and salmon cooked in champagne – and still the untitled squire's wife had relatives and acquaintances in red to speak of. Only when a procession of footmen brought the entrées did Hervey find himself without conversation at last, his interlocutor having been taken up by the Reverend Mr Castle in the space of a footman's intervention between them.

Hervey was now left with nothing to distract him from the necessity of thinking of a favourable opening with the woman he intended marrying. His mind, however, was yet a bewildering blank. He watched as each magnificent entrée was brought to the table: boned quail filled with chicken mousse, ragout of pigeon with shallots and button mushrooms, braised sirloin of beef with stuffed tomatoes, stuffed mushrooms, potato croquettes, a vegetable mould and warm cucumbers in cream. Lady Cockerell's dazzling display of culinary hospitality served only to make his quest for an apt line more difficult.

Kezia Lankester turned to him and touched his sleeve. 'I am so glad to see you here, Major Hervey. We have had no opportunity to speak freely since India. My late husband thought very highly of you, you know.'

Hervey had to make a considerable effort to hide his relief. Her speaking thus was a gesture of much charm, without (it seemed to him) undue superiority, though perhaps with an underlying, rather distant formality. She was, he had to remind himself, ten years his junior, for all her apparent self-possession. 'You are kind to say so, madam.'

'No, Major Hervey,' she replied, with something of a smile. 'It was not meant as a kindness. Would you tell me . . . do you know how my late husband died?'

Hervey was not ready for this turn. He had supposed, somehow, that it had all been said in India – by the regimental major, perhaps. 'Well . . . that is . . . yes, I do. I . . . indeed I saw him fall.'

Kezia Lankester now looked down at her plate. 'I imagine he was to the fore?'

'Oh, he was. Indeed he was. He was at the head of one of the trenches closest the walls of Bhurtpore.' He was surprised she needed to ask.

'And was his death . . . was it done quickly?'

Hervey sighed. 'It was instant, madam.'

'You are certain of it, Major Hervey? You do not say it just for my sake?'

Hervey shook his head. 'I am certain of it.'

'So he was unable to say anything by way of . . . last words.'

'I am afraid not.'

He could not determine whether his reply was a comfort or the exact opposite. He wondered why she was so concerned with last words. They were rarely, in his experience, especially noble, and frequently they were entirely profane.

She seemed now to rally. 'And how do you like your command? Poor Major Strickland: I thought him a fine man.'

Hervey was momentarily thrown off what passed for his stride by the bitter-sweet in the connection of command and his old friend's death. 'Well, I . . . command of one's regiment, even temporarily, is the greatest satisfaction.'

'But Lady Somervile tells me you may have the lieutenant-colonelcy proper soon.'

Hervey wished Emma had not. 'I very much hope it may be so, Lady Lankester, but there are many formalities.'

'And your daughter, as I recall: she is well?'

Again, the sudden turn she took broke his stride. But he had surrendered the initiative . . . 'She is well, thank you.' He tried to form a question by return: her own daughter—

'And she is, as I remember, with your sister in Wiltshire?'

'Indeed.' He was now determined to wrest back the initiative, at least partially: 'And you will be staying in Gloucestershire long?'

But wresting was hardly necessary, for she seemed perfectly content to surrender the initiative. Glad, even. And so the initiative remained with him for the rest of their dinner, his fluency in finding question after question quite taking him by surprise, until, after a while, there *was* no initiative but free conversation – and on matters other than the here and now, the weather or family, the subjects by which a little prior study usually served in otherwise faltering table-talk. He was even composed enough to observe her closely as they spoke. He had admired her complexion when they had dined at Lord George Irvine's: it was fair, and she had applied a blushing stick, no doubt to relieve her mourning pallor, and he fancied she had again this evening. But soon he concluded that her face was more naturally suffused with colour, and altogether warmer than that evening in January. He found himself admiring the gentle swell of her breast, and although her lips were decidedly thinner than Kat's – or for that matter Vaneeta's – he began wondering, too . . .

'Whom do you think shall be prime minister?'

He woke sharply. He had heard the question plainly but evidently not what had preceded it. Desperately, he used one of the devices Kat had taught him. 'Whom do *you* think shall be prime minister?'

She smiled (did she recognize the trick?). 'I asked first, Major Hervey!'

Great heavens, he thought, and with admiration: this woman was assured! And her protest was not without a certain teasing – which these days he recognized as encouragement rather than the opposite. 'Sir Eyre Somervile believes it might be the Duke of Wellington.'

She frowned purposefully. 'Surely not, Major Hervey. Would the duke fit that office?'

'You mean, ma'am, may a soldier do ought but bark orders?'

She smiled again. 'Would you imagine the duke to be given to discussion?'

'I know him but a little, but I know him to take counsel, and even his time in the Peninsula required a good deal of diplomacy.' He tapped the table. 'Now, ma'am, perhaps *you* will tell *me* your opinion.'

She gave it freely and in such a manner as to command his considerable attention. He could not help but think that although Kat would have been able to say as much, it would have been hearsay and the whispered opinion of high-placed confidants. With Kezia Lankester it was very evidently her own thinking. And he liked what he saw of her serious mind.

At length came Monsieur Anton's *desserts* – baskets of glacé fruit and plates of *croquembouche*, charlotte *russe*, Nesselrode pudding, moulded jellies, coffee custard, praline and orange ices, chocolate *gâteaux*. Kezia Lankester was not greatly tempted, nor seemingly very impressed. Hervey had noticed how sparingly she ate throughout (neither had she drunk more than half a glass of hock), and wondered if it were yet a feature somehow of her mourning. But when their conversation resumed, he found himself more and more attracted by both her appearance and spirit, and encouraged by her complete ease of manner. He was disappointed when the conversation opened up to the table: it was, besides anything else, much the duller, despite the wit of a dozen more. And then once the table as a whole was engaged she made no attempt at further vocal contact with him, nor with her eyes – not even when they rose to let the ladies retire. He was suddenly anxious once more. Was it true indifference on her part? He was sure it could not have been shyness. Or perhaps she had thought that she – or he – had spoken *too* freely? As he sat down again he was wholly uncertain of whether she had in fact dismissed him.

When the gentlemen were all done with cigars and the price of corn – close on half an hour – they rejoined the ladies. Chairs had been arranged meanwhile so that the drawing room was now an auditorium, with a forte-piano and a harp at one end. Lady Cockerell at once began ushering her guests to their seats. After announcing that her house guests would provide a little diversion, she herself – very gamely, thought Hervey – began the entertainment, playing two rondos (which he had heard before but could not put a name to) and then a composition of her own incorporating several popular songs that he knew quite well. She played skilfully, earning vigorous applause, and hearty appreciation from the squires. Next came her husband in a worthy, if reedy, rendering of two Neapolitan songs sung in Italian to Lady Cockerell's accompaniment. There was again hearty applause, perhaps more in appreciation of hearing something so apparently out of character in their host as for any true appreciation of his voice;

but there was no encore. Then it was the turn of the Reverend and the Honourable Mrs Castle (the advowson being Sir Charles's, Mr Castle was deemed a permanent house guest). Mrs Castle played accompanying harp, and her husband sang something about virtue, and then about perseverance, and in a voice that Hervey recognized was capable though not to his mind attractive.

Next was Lady Lankester. An older man in a powdered wig and round spectacles came into the room, bowed and sat at the forte-piano.

'Must have stayed from last night,' said Somervile to Hervey, more or less *sotto voce*. 'There was a regular band.'

Lady Lankester bowed to her hostess and announced: '"*Se mai senti spirarti sul volto*", from *La Clemenza di Tito*, by Christoph Gluck.'

Hervey was at once all attention. He had heard of Gluck. He had no idea that Kezia Lankester possessed a voice that encompassed opera.

The forte-pianist began the introduction, a gentle melody in simple time, and Kezia Lankester entered confidently and with one of the clearest, sweetest voices Hervey thought he had ever heard. It was a slow aria, but with considerable range, and she sang it expressively. Hervey was charmed. He led the applause.

'She's been rehearsing all day,' said Somervile, as if he thought it mildly bad form.

Hervey frowned. 'I thought it enchanting.'

'My dear Lady Lankester, we must press you to an encore,' said their host.

Lady Lankester smiled indulgently. 'Very well, Sir Charles.' She turned to the forte-pianist.

He had already placed a new sheet of music on the rest.

She turned back to her audience. '"*Di questa cetra in seno*", from *Il Parnaso confuso*, again by Christoph Gluck.'

It was, once more, a slow melody, but in triple time and with a range perhaps even greater than the first. As before she sang with real expression, and Hervey wished very much that he had been able to understand the Italian.

The applause was even stronger. 'She can sing, I grant you that,' said Somervile.

Hervey was now inclined to ascribe her earlier sudden indifference to nerves, in anticipation of these choice pieces – except that she sang so effortlessly he could see no reason for them. Perhaps it was mere . . . preoccupation?

The forte-pianist took his bow, Kezia Lankester took another, and they left the 'stage' to the final diversion.

'Well, *a cavallo*,' said Somervile, in a resigned but by no means apprehensive way, taking his wife's hand and leading her forward.

Emma took her place at the forte-piano, while from behind a curtain her husband took a hunting whip and horn, sounding the latter to the immediate acclamation of the two squires.

'Ladies and gentlemen,' began Somervile, stentor-like. 'From the sublime heights of Italian opera I take you to the English countryside, and Mr Henry Fielding's "A Hunting We Will Go", with music by . . . I forget whom.'

There were appreciative *Yoicks!* from the squirearchy.

Emma began the jaunting little 6/8 introduction, Somervile sounded the off, slapped his thigh with the whip and took up the boisterous verse:

> *The dusky night rides do-own the sky,*
> *And ushers in the morn:*
> *The hounds all join in glorious cry,*
> *The hounds all join in glorious cry,*
> *The hu-untsman wi-inds his ho-o-o-orn,*
> *The huntsman winds his horn.*

Emma joined in the refrain:

> *And a-hunting we will go,*
> *A-hunting we will go,*
> *A-hu-u-u-u-u-u-u-u-unt,*
> *A-hu-unting we will go!*

Somervile sounded the off again, and Emma took up the second verse:

> *The wife around her hu-usband throws*
> *Her arms, to make him stay;*
> *My dear, it rains, it hai-ils, it blows;*
> *My dear, it rains, it hai-ils, it blows;*
> *You ca-a-a-a-a-a-a-a-not,*
> *You cannot hunt today.*

Somervile resumed the refrain:

> *Yet a-hunting we will go.*
> *A-hunting we will go,*
> *A-hu-u-u-u-u-u-u-u-unt,*
> *A-hu-unting we will go!*

And then the next verses:

> *The uncaverned fox like li-ightning flies,*
> *His cunning's all awake,*
> *To gain the race he e-eager tries,*
> *To gain the race he e-eager tries,*
> *His fo-orfeit li-ife the sta-a-a-ake,*
> *His fo-orfeit life the stake.*

> *Yet a-hunting we will go.*
> *A-hunting we will go,*
> *A-hu-u-u-u-u-u-u-u-unt,*
> *A-hu-unting we will go!*

> *At last his strength to faintness worn,*
> *Poor Reynard ceases flight;*

He stopped dramatically and sounded the kill – and then Emma joined for the finale:

> *Then hungry, homeward we-e return,*
> *Then hungry, homeward we-e return,*
> *To fe-east awa-ay the ni-i-i-ight,*
> *To feast away the night!*

> *And a-hunting we do go.*
> *A-hunting we do go,*
> *A-hu-u-u-u-u-u-u-u-unt,*
> *A-hu-unting we do go!*

The applause was long and vigorous. Hervey beamed with sheer pleasure at so uninhibited a performance. Here was a couple as perfectly matched as may be, full of refinement in the purlieus of the Court, dazzling in learning and conversation at Fort William, and yet as lusty as Fielding's best in the shires. At that moment he would have thrown in everything to go with them to the Cape.

Only Kezia Lankester seemed not to share the ebullience of the chase, though she applauded politely, smiling. No doubt it was a proper sensibility, thought Hervey, for the others were in familiar company, and of spouses, whereas she was not.

He went up to her as tea was brought in. 'Lady Lankester, your singing was delightful.'

She smiled a little, as if tired (Hervey realized that singing of such refinement as hers was not without prodigious effort, whatever the appearance to the contrary). 'Thank you, Major Hervey.' And then, seemingly as an afterthought, she asked, 'You are fond of music?'

Hervey cleared his throat. It was true to say that he liked the noise that music made, especially if it were played by a military band (the Sixth had always kept a good band), and he had liked what he had just heard of hers, but . . . 'Indeed yes, madam.'

' "The man that hath no music in himself, nor is not moved with concord of sweet sounds, is fit for treasons, stratagems, and spoils." '

It was familiar, but . . . 'Just so.'

She smiled a little broader, as if taking pity on him. 'Do you know the rest, Major Hervey?'

Hervey returned the smile, but he was suddenly determined that Kezia Lankester, at ten years his junior, should not get away entirely with her tease. 'It is some time, I confess, since I opened a book of Shakespeare, madam, but I hazard a recall of something about the man's dull nature?'

'You recall very commendably, Major Hervey. "The motions of his spirit are dull as night, and his affections dark as Erebus: let no such man be trusted." '

Hervey inclined his head. His guess had indeed been apt. 'Then I must take up the violin, ma'am, like the Duke of Wellington.'

She frowned. 'Then I would that you practised at a good distance from me, Major Hervey!'

It was strange, he thought: there were moments when Kezia Lankester seemed to be sporting with him, and with a distinct coyness – and then there would come a remark whose edge was decidedly cutting. But these were surroundings unfamiliar to her, and she had been widowed but a year . . .

Their hostess joined them, full of praise for Kezia's singing, and Hervey was able to content himself with the odd nod and word of agreement for a quarter of an hour. Then, as the first of the squires' ladies began gathering herself to depart, Kezia took a rather formal leave of her hostess, and withdrew.

The following day, Saturday, there was no hunting; or rather, the Fitzhardinge hounds were meeting with Lord Croome's, too far distant to drive. Instead the party spent the morning at archery. Hervey had not held a bow since his youth, and it took him a good deal of practice before attaining any consistent accuracy. Both Emma and her husband were capable – they had practised regularly in India – but the true proficient was Kezia Lankester, which was evident the instant she picked an arrow. Without the slightest ostentation she first examined the fletch, then held it to her right eye to look down the shaft. She took up one of the bows, flexed it and drew back the string twice, fitted the arrow, raised it to the aim at fifty yards (ignoring the nearer target positioned for the novices) and loosed it. The arrow flew straight, striking high on the straw roundel. She took another, corrected her point of aim and then loosed again. It struck in the centre of the bull's-eye, and with greater force than the first.

Hervey was at once impressed. Kezia Lankester had not merely corrected with a view to making a second and final correction, she had made the one adjustment and then loosed with certainty. Arrow after arrow of hers now struck firm, all within the six-inch white circle. Hervey was now captivated, for not only was the proficiency evidence of much application (as well as of a 'martial' side which stood in pleasing balance with the cultivated), the archer's posture and the drawing of the bow were admirably suited to displaying the female figure to advantage, its tautness of abdomen and prominence of breast. In Kezia Lankester's profile there was nothing of the mystery of the Bengal beauties (of Vaneeta, indeed), nor of the allure of Isabella Delgado, nor even of the statuary of Kat dressed for the Court, elegant but sensuous; yet he found the constrained grace powerfully attractive – reinforcing, *strongly* reinforcing, his resolve to make her an offer of marriage sooner rather than later.

Indeed, he was now resolved to do so before leaving Sezincote. He was certain he must, for he could have little opportunity to press his suit later; she would return to Hertfordshire and he to Hounslow, and thence . . . ? He could only hope that he had at least established his worth in her estimation, engaged her respect and interest. He would not, of course, expect an answer at once (let alone acceptance), but he would, in the parlance of the colony to which his great friends were bound, at least have staked a claim. She would have ample time to consider it, see its merits, come to believe that it was seemly (he was not without position and prospects, after all, even if he was perennially short of means). First, however, he would have to find the favourable moment to acquaint her with his proposal.

That afternoon the ladies of the party went visiting to the almshouses and with a new curate. Hervey and Somervile rode out together towards Evesham.

'I've been thinking over the Waltham Abbey business,' began Somervile as they started climbing the steep, wooded slopes beyond the house. 'I confess to being doubtful of your conclusions when first you told me last night, but I'm inclined now to think you may have something. There's a deal of resentment regarding the Catholic Association. I hear it frequently. Peel stays his hand as far as the suppression law's concerned, but he'd not be able to resist the clamour following an outrage on English soil.'

'That was the basis of my supposition,' replied Hervey, rather surprised that Somervile seemed not to have appreciated his own sensibility.

'But I hadn't myself come to any conclusions hitherto; it's one thing knowing the price of corn is high and quite another to judge the true political consequences. The point is, the business in Portugal may not be entirely unconnected.'

Hervey was intrigued. 'How so?'

'The government gives every impression of dither over the intervention, perhaps fearful of drawing the sword there with a discontented Ireland by our side.'

'I had not considered that.'

'You should dine more in St James's; or even Bloomsbury.'

'No doubt I should. So the import of what you are saying is that both Whig *and* Tory would have an interest in prosecutions against the Catholic Association? I am glad to avoid imputations of party in that case!' He smiled wryly.

'Do you have any Catholic friends?'

'Not since poor Strickland died.'

'That may be as well.'

'Great heavens! Don't say—'

'I say nothing at all, Hervey. And recollect that it is of complete indifference to me whether a man prays in English or Latin, so long as whoever hears him understands.'

Hervey was never fond of debating religion with Somervile at the best of times, and this morning was far from the best. He leaned forward along his mare's neck to avoid a low branch; it gave him the opportunity to return to the material subject. 'And so how do you suppose my submission to the Horse Guards will be received?'

'Pray you have a friend who keeps it in a drawer!'

Somervile gasped; his cob, chosen by the Cockerells' groom, supposing kindly but in error that this man of affairs had need of a schoolmaster, was taking a deal of urging up the slope, so that its rider was already short of breath a mile from the house. 'Great snakes, this screw!' he spluttered again, finally touching with his whip.

The horse picked up its feet a little, but still it plodded, so that Hervey had to keep checking his own hunter so as not to pull ahead. As for the friend and the drawer, he rather supposed he had no hope there – if holding back the submission *was* the right course. 'We may as well let them take it at a trot,' he sighed, conceding to poor practice rather than continuing the discomposure.

'If you haven't a friend at the Horse Guards, then you'd better come to the Cape with me! Have you given it any consideration?'

Hervey thought there was no need to reveal quite how much. 'I have,' he said, and with something of a rueful smile. 'But would I not need a friend at the Horse Guards in that case too? Or do you have plenipotentiary powers in that connection?'

Somervile did not see the tease. 'Oh, I think such things are easily arranged.'

Hervey was far from sure, but since he had reached no firm conclusion – or rather, he could not do so until he knew the Horse Guards' pleasure regarding the lieutenant-colonelcy – he was not inclined to argue. And so they continued their ride in a generality of conversation: the present state of legislative turmoil, the Corn Laws, the Greek war and the threats to the peace in His Majesty's possessions overseas. It was, as Somervile pointed out, and as Hervey sensed only too well, a difficult time for the War Office: it had been one thing calculating the number of men required to see off Bonaparte – every last one who could be found a red coat – and quite another to determine the size of that repugnant thing, a standing army.

'Soldiers in peace, Hervey,' Somervile reminded him. 'They are like chimneys in summer. You had better be done with it and come with me to the Cape!'

When they were back, and the ladies too, Hervey took a turn about the formal gardens with Emma. The talk was at first inconsequential, until at last Hervey stopped, and cleared his throat.

'Emma, I believe I should tell you that I intend making Kezia Lankester an offer of marriage.'

Emma looked astonished. She tried hard to recover her countenance nevertheless. 'Why Matthew, this is so very . . . sudden.' She rallied a little. 'If I say more by way of congratulations it would seem premature—'

'And tempt fate?'

'I do not believe in such a danger, as well you know. I meant . . . well, I had heard that there was an amour in Lisbon.'

Hervey became anxious at what exactly she had heard.

'A Portuguese lady of noble birth, whom you had first met there some years ago?'

'Ah.' His relief was palpable: she did not mean Kat. He lowered his eyes, and cleared his throat again. 'Isabella Delgado. She is engaged to another.'

Had he been on the point of making Isabella an offer of marriage? He had thought of it. He had certainly thought of the congress (rather too often). But there had been so many ... difficulties. The matter of her religion, for one thing: what would the parsonage at Horningsham have made of it? But he recalled that he had not much cared what they would think. Isabella had saved – if not his life – then certainly his military honour. And if Laming had not sent him the note declaring his intention to marry her, would he not have ridden that night to Belem and proposed? Why hadn't he anyway? Why had he not followed his true desire? Perhaps he had come to mistrust his own judgement (a cell in Badajoz was a powerful rebuke to self-esteem). And had he not thought that Laming was five times the better prospect for Isabella? But why had he *presumed*? Why had he not allowed Isabella the choice of which of them she would accept? Arrogant presumption indeed! But, in truth, had it not been because of obligation, obligation to the man who had just risked his own life and reputation to bring him out of Badajoz? Rather unhappiness than dishonour! But was that how a man of real flesh and blood acted? Was there not, truly, more honour in the breach than in the observance of such a desiccated code? He all but shrugged his shoulders: he, himself, could never judge it.

Emma looked excessively thoughtful. 'And there is issue of the marriage – of Kezia Lankester's, I mean. You have considered it?'

'I have. I think it entirely felicitous, indeed ... in the circumstances.'

Emma knew very well what he meant. And she admired him for his proper paternal instincts. She was not to be turned, however. 'Matthew, I will speak plainly. Kezia Lankester ... she is so very different from Henrietta.'

Hervey smiled in a mildly mocking way. 'Every woman is very different from Henrietta.'

'Do not be obtuse with me, Matthew; you know precisely what I mean.'

Hervey's brow furrowed. 'No, Emma, I do not believe that I do.'

Emma steeled herself. Their acquaintance went back a dozen years, to before Hervey and Henrietta Lindsay had wed. They had braved a good deal together in India. At one time she and Henrietta had been close, before Emma had given up society in London to join her brother in Madras. 'Matthew, as I remember her and as you have told me, albeit indirectly, Henrietta was . . . a passionate woman.' She reddened a little. 'Kezia Lankester is undoubtedly a very *fine* woman; she will make you a very proper wife, and no doubt be a very acceptable mother to Georgiana, but . . . I believe her to be—'

Hervey took pity on her, and himself. 'Emma, you are very good. I do not in the least degree mind what you have said, but Kezia Lankester is still, to all intents and purposes, in mourning. I do not suppose for one moment that we see her former self. Ivo Lankester was the very best of men.'

Emma sighed to herself. 'Matthew, I think you do not always allow for men being so very different from each other. Women too.'

Hervey was astonished. He knew men well enough, and he fancied he had not lived an entirely cloistered life. 'My dear Emma, I believe that these past twenty years have made me see entirely otherwise!'

Emma said nothing. She perceived that her difficulties lay not merely in having her fond friend see his intended for her true nature, but himself too. Instead she took his arm and deflected the conversation to the planting at the Moghul pools, thinking it altogether better to leave the matter until they were gone from Sezincote – for the long drive back to London, perhaps.

In the evening the party dined at Adlestrop. Hervey had opportunity again to speak with Kezia Lankester at dinner, but not so as to have any chance to advance his suit. Kezia herself was attentive, even at times almost talkative, but Hervey could gain no impression of what her answer might be were he at that moment able to propose. But, he reflected, the dinner table was hardly the place . . . though it had been at the table, those seven years ago, that Kat had first played him, quite without compunction.

The next day, Sunday, the party attended morning prayer at the Reverend Mr Castle's church. It was not an enlivening interlude, for Hervey at least, brought up as he had been in a less severe school of churchmanship, and it was at least half an hour too long (and that principally the sermon), but it did afford him a pleasant drive in the same carriage as Kezia, together with Somervile and Emma, who both talked prodigiously and warmly, thereby better disposing the atmosphere (he supposed) to his purposes.

In the afternoon, the four house guests were left to their own devices, and Somervile and Emma said they would take books to the orangery. Hervey asked Kezia if she would accompany him around the water garden (she had seen a part of it; he had not). She agreed at once, and evidently with some pleasure.

It was a warm, springlike day – abundant greenness, crocus and primrose everywhere, the birds full-throated. They strolled first through the 'Indian' garden and then on towards the thornery, with its thick planting of trees, many of which Hervey had not seen in England before. Kezia's Italian greyhound accompanied them. Hervey rather liked her – a pretty little dog, supple, alert, if somewhat aloof. She kept close to her mistress (Hervey was unsure whether by inclination or training) making not a sound. He thought to ask of her provenance, then thought it better to wait: he did not wish his interest to be misconstrued. Instead they walked for the most part in silence around the upper pool, with its temple to Surya (the sun god, he explained), then began following the stream, with Hervey selecting his line of advance as if they were in the forests of Chintal, for much of the daylight was shut out by a dense canopy of oriental maple, hornbeam and rowan, and Persian ironwoods already showing promise of vivid colour.

'I understand Mr Repton was responsible for the park,' said his companion at last as they came to one of the little pools halfway to the Indian bridge. 'But that one of the Daniells laid it out.'

Hervey knew of Repton well enough, but he was more familiar with the work of the Daniell brothers, for they had painted India from Rajasthan to Mysore, and when he saw one of their paintings he was at once transported. 'I understand that is so. The Daniells are fine painters. There's one of theirs in the house. I imagine when you were in India you were not able to see the Taj Mahal?'

Kezia showed no sign of painful memory. 'No, I was not. And I know that to be a particular deprivation. I should have liked to see it very much. You have, I take it?'

Hervey nodded. 'A little before we laid siege to Bhurtpore. It *is* a wondrous sight, and not merely the domes and towers: the gardens are a delight, and in truth, these here are not so very different. At least, they put one in mind of it by their singularity, by their not being so English, I mean.'

A rabbit, caught napping perhaps, darted from under a rose bush. Kezia's greyhound lurched.

'Perdi!' snapped her mistress, and the little dog froze.

Hervey marvelled at the command. Bringing a spaniel to a halt would have been impressive; stopping a greyhound, even the Italian sort, with a rabbit within reach was a remarkable achievement.

They continued, unspeaking, past hydrangeas and Plume Poppy, Honey Locust and bamboo. The place had grown quite silent but for their own footsteps. There was less birdsong now, the quiet time, nor sound of sheep or cattle in distant pasture. Hervey glanced at his companion – his intended. She looked content.

They rounded a big juniper bush to see the Indian bridge with its statuary of Brahmin bulls, the pride of the lower park.

'Nandi,' said Hervey, pointing to the balustrade above. 'The *happy one*, Shiva's favourite.'

Kezia smiled. 'They are very handsome. And they can certainly

159

transport one back to that dust and heat, even though I was there so short a time.'

They walked on, into the dark shade under the bridge, towards the pool beyond. Suddenly she stopped. 'Gracious! What a very . . . arresting thing!'

Hervey thought the same. Quite arresting enough to stop him too in his tracks.

'Do you suppose it a faithful image? Could there be a serpent so big, I mean – not its three heads,' she asked, sinking to the viewing bench as if quite overpowered by the monstrous bronze reptile.

Hervey sat down next to her (it seemed a perfectly natural thing to do), and began contemplating the question – as well as the figure itself. The gigantic snake coiled round the trunk of a tree in the middle of the pool, its mouths wide, fangs and forked tongues challenging any who would come from under the bridge. It stood full eight feet, perhaps more – eight feet of venomous danger, if venomous it was; otherwise its coils were perfectly able to crush the life out of any who defied its challenge.

'I cannot speak of sea serpents, madam,' he replied, shaking his head, 'but I never saw a python as big.'

Nor, certainly, a cobra. He had been surprised when first he had seen a cobra, ten years ago at the Rajah of Chintal's banquet, by how small it was in comparison with their reputation. But that had been the *cobra di capello*, the 'thing of the bazaars' the rajah had said, which rose from a basket to the charmer's pipe and swayed from side to side inches from his face as if determining the best moment to strike. But its mouth was invariably sewn up, the raj kumari had told him. If he wanted to see the real cobra – the hamadryad, the *king* cobra – they must go into the forest, for the jungle was the hamadryad's green fastness.

And he had seen the hamadryad there. He had watched as the male had approached the female, had edged the length of her, inch by careful inch, as cautiously as may be, for at any moment she might turn on him, sink her fangs into him, shoot her venom deep

160

in his vitals – and without warning. With the raj kumari he had watched their coiling, their writhing-mating. He had watched with a strange and increasing awareness of her at his side, and then there had been the beginnings of their own congress, the hamadryads potent and threatening only yards away, and the jungle all-concealing. There had been no consummation, however. The female hamadryad had taken sudden objection to the male's advance, and with a terrible hissing and thrashing she had put an end to him – and to herself, for the male had struck back, too late for self-defence but not for retribution. And Hervey and the raj kumari, the trance violently broken, had sped from the trysting place believing themselves in mortal danger – and Hervey certain that his soul had been.

'Major Hervey?'

He woke. 'I'm sorry, I . . .'

'I asked if the python were a water snake.'

'I . . . I think they may swim if needs be. I think all snakes may, though on this I am uncertain.'

He observed her closely. There was nothing of the forest in Kezia Lankester. She was of an altogether purer fire, as beautiful as the raj kumari but in so different a way. She was a civilized, thinking woman. When the raj kumari thought – that is when she had not been acting wholly on impulse – it had been to calculate, and her calculating had been her ruin (and his, almost).

'Lady Lankester, I . . . that is, would it be improper if I expressed to you my very great admiration, and . . .'

Her expression remained impassive but benign.

'And my wish that you would consider a proposal of marriage?'

Kezia Lankester entirely kept her countenance. She said nothing for the moment, seeming instead to be reflecting on what she had heard, utterly composed still, as if it had been an invitation to some diversion or other.

Hervey looked at her intently, trying not to reveal his mounting alarm. He had botched it; he felt sure.

She caught her breath a little before answering (alarming him the more). 'Major Hervey, I am most deeply obliged to you.' A faint smile came to her lips, as though she were dismissing a child, kindly, for some amusing excess. 'I can only suppose that you are moved by some sense of obligation, and it does not surprise me – and certainly does not dismay me – for in my short acquaintance with your regiment I have come to see its great virtue of constancy.'

He made to speak, intending to reassure her that his proposal was in no sense prompted by any sense of obligation (at least not to her), but he hesitated, and she stayed him with the merest gesture of a hand.

'Major Hervey, I assure you, I am by no means offended by these thoughts. On the contrary: they are very noble.'

Again he would have spoken to this point had not she anticipated him once more and bid him wait.

'I am flattered by your proposal. Such a one, to a widowed mother, might not be forthcoming again. *Your* prospects, on the other hand, are decidedly handsome.'

'Lady Lankester—'

'I have made myself plain, I trust.'

On the contrary, Hervey was wholly uncertain. And he would know with what finality he was being rejected. He frowned slightly, inclining his head a fraction, but enough to persuade her that she must repeat what she had presumed to be plain speaking.

'Major Hervey, I am honoured to accept your proposal.'

Hervey's mouth fell open. 'I . . . I had not imagined . . .' He took her hand. He bent forward to kiss her. Her lips were still parted slightly, and it was Hervey, not she, who ended the kiss.

He caught a glimpse of Perdita eyeing him – coldly, he sensed. She would get used to it; she would have to. If Kezia Lankester could accept him – 'the coldest woman', poor Strickland had thought her; but the widow of Sir Ivo, a man he admired in highest degree – then so could an undersize greyhound from that fickle, fiery country!

162

CHAPTER ELEVEN

RECKONINGS

Hounslow, 27 March

The last Tuesday of each month was the quartermaster's day for interior economy, as it was known in the Sixth, and so there was no general parade. Hervey had arrived back from Gloucestershire in the early hours; Emma had tried to persuade him to stay for another day and then drive back with them, but he had explained that there was Private Lightowler's funeral to attend to as well as business with the Horse Guards, and promised instead to call on them in Bedford Square at the first opportunity. At eight o'clock he breakfasted quietly in the officers' house, and at nine he stepped into regimental headquarters hoping not to hear too dispiriting a report of the weekend's 'crime'.

'Good morning, Hervey,' said Vanneck cheerily as the acting commanding officer passed through the adjutant's office and into his own. 'I trust that Gloucestershire was restorative?'

Hervey could not suppress a smile of satisfaction. 'Good

163

morning, Vanneck. Yes, it was.'

The adjutant followed him with a handful of letters.

'And I may tell you that I have certain news.'

Vanneck saw the distinctly pleased look, and was grateful for it. He had long been troubled by what he perceived as a lack of joy at the heart of his regimental hero.

'Lady Lankester and I are to be married.'

Vanneck smiled broadly, seeming not at all surprised, and held out his hand. 'My dear Hervey, my hearty congratulations!'

'I tell you of course, but I can tell no one else until her people know of it, which I shall have to address myself to soon.'

'I had no idea that you and Lady Lankester were ... on such terms. It seems rather remiss of me, your adjutant.'

Hervey smiled again and shook his head. 'Think nothing of it. Now, what deeds does the day quake to look upon?'

Vanneck shrugged. 'Nothing, really. Worsley and the sarn't-major are both recovering well. Mr Hairsine believes he will return to duty next week. Lightowler's funeral will be at eleven on Thursday; the coroner has issued the papers. Cornet Roffe delivered your letter to his father in Dartford – decent folk, said Roffe. He arranged for them to be present.'

Hervey nodded approvingly.

'There were the customary occurrences following pay parade on Saturday. There was no church on Sunday, as you know. The sick reports are usual enough – nothing of any moment in the horse lines. In all, a peaceful time.' Vanneck raised his eyebrows and lowered his voice. 'Save in one respect – Johnson.'

Hervey looked alarmed.

'No, in Johnson's own case I think all may be well. He's been a dupe, and an entirely innocent one as far as I can see. If he turns King's evidence then apparently there'll be no further action. But I'm afraid that it looks as if Snagge's the true criminal.'

'Snagge?'

Vanneck sighed. 'I know. I could scarcely credit it. But I would ask that you wait for Armstrong to return from quartermaster's, for he has the detail, and then you may best make whatever decision is necessary.'

'Very well.' Hervey thought for a moment. 'There is no word from the District? About Waltham, I mean.'

'Not other than a letter addressed personally to you.'

Hervey nodded to the bundle of letters in Vanneck's hand. 'Those are all mine?'

'They are. And two expresses. I would have sent them to Gloucestershire but they arrived only yesterday.'

Vanneck placed the little pile on Hervey's desk, and withdrew. 'I'll come as soon as Armstrong is returned. Shall I have someone bring coffee?'

Hervey shook his head. 'Just allow me half an hour with these.'

He sat at his desk and began examining each of the half dozen hands. The expresses were unmistakable – his sister's and his colonel's. Elizabeth's at once took priority.

Horningsham,
25th March

My dearest brother,

I scarce know how to begin. Captain Peto has made me an offer of marriage, and I am inclined by every instinct to accept! Papa believes it to be a very proper thing and I want therefore to have your blessing before I write back to Captain Peto to give my answer. Georgiana, who is very well, and our parents too, shall remain with me after I am married for as long as she is happy, which I am certain she must be, for although Norfolk is not Wiltshire it is agreeable country and she would be assured of proper company. As you must surely know, Captain Peto is given

command of a first-rate in the Mediterranean, and I should so
much like my letter to reach him before he leaves to join his ship.
And so, dearest brother, if you can revive yourself after the shock
of this joyous news, so wholly unexpected that it is, please hasten
your reply, for I shall not feel free to give my consent until I
receive it.

Your ever affectionate sister,
Elizabeth.

Hervey laid down the letter, shaking his head and smiling. 'And the old dog said not a word!' He pulled the bell cord by the fireplace. And he shook his head and smiled again: command of a first-rate! What double fortune this news was! He looked through the other letters to see if there was one from his old friend, but he perfectly understood why there was not.

A clerk appeared before Hervey could read over Elizabeth's letter a second time.

'Brayshaw, I shall want to send an express. In one hour.'

'Sir.' Brayshaw saluted, turned about smartly, and left to find an orderly to run to the post office.

Hervey picked up the second express, and with so light a heart that he broke the seal without hesitating.

My dear Hervey,

I very much regret having to tell you that the Commander-in-
Chief had already approved another for command – and had
informed him of it – by the time I was able to see him. Well do I
understand what a blow to you this will be, and for me it is only
ameliorated by knowing who shall be the officer, Lord
Holderness, whom I have known these many years past, as must

166

*you. It will be little consolation to you at this time to know you
will serve with such a man, but I beg you would commit yourself
to do so with all the zeal that has very properly brought you to
your position today, trusting that these long years waiting shall in
turn become past prelude.*

*I am leaving for the north this day, else I should have conveyed
this to you in person, and would beg that you call on me when I
return next Saturday seven days.*

You have my greatest respects in this, as at all times,

Believe me, &tc,
Geo. Irvine.

Hervey felt so acute a nausea that he thought he must get up at
once and leave the headquarters. Why did events take turns so
cruelly? His sister's happiness – his old friend's too – and then his
own expectations so peremptorily dashed. But instead he sat,
almost rooted, wanting something familiar to grasp at.

'Hervey?' Vanneck's voice betrayed concern.

Hervey looked at him blankly.

'Are you quite well?'

The acting commanding officer would have liked nothing more
at that moment than to confide his abject disappointment; but it
was unthinkable. 'I am perfectly well, thank you. Does Sarn't-
major Armstrong come?'

'He does.'

'Then call him, if you will.'

As Vanneck withdrew a second time, Hervey opened the letter
from his superior headquarters.

Head Quarters,
London District
26th March 1827

Major M. P. Hervey
Comndg 6th Lt Dgns,
Hounslow

Sir,

*I am directed to inform you that the General Officer
Commanding the London District has read your despatch
concerning the incident at Waltham Abbey mills of the 20th
instant with approbation. I am commanded to express once more
the General's approval of the conduct of the troops under your
orders, and to assure you that the despatch shall be forwarded to
the Commander-in-Chief of His Majesty's Land Forces forthwith.
I am further commanded to inform you that the General directs
that Regimental Serjeant-Major Hairsine's name be brought to
the immediate attention of the Commander-in-Chief for
consideration of a commission.*

I am, sir, your obedient servant,
James Fanshawe,
Lieut colonel.

As the adjutant, with the acting-RSM, came in, Hervey, blank-faced, handed the letter to him. 'An ill wind indeed. Hairsine earns a commission a dozen times in India, and it takes the smell of powder in Hertfordshire to have it!'

Vanneck raised his eyebrows as he read. 'The work of cavalry is rarely observed?'

It was the regiment's constant lament. 'Just so,' replied Hervey, the nausea now suppressed by the sudden requirement for action. 'I shall take the news to him myself. It may speed his recovery.'

He knew he ought also to be taking considerable satisfaction in his own commendation by the GOC, and the implicit promise that more might follow. Hairsine's reward was singular, but the praise heaped upon Hervey himself was, in truth, fulsome. To his certain experience, such praise was never so quick. He smelled fish.

Vanneck looked up. 'With your permission, I can publish this in tonight's orders. I think it would be well received.'

'I am sure of it,' said Hervey, nodding. 'Now, the Johnson business. Or should I be calling it the *Snagge* business?'

'With permission, Sarn't-major Armstrong might begin, sir?'

'Very well.' Hervey turned to the acting-RSM.

It was not possible to see Armstrong standing there without a moment's recollection of all that they had been through together, from the early days of subaltern officer and legionary corporal. It felt strange but also somehow fitting that at this time they held the regiment's good name and efficiency in their hands.

'I'm afraid you're not going to like it, sir.'

Hervey braced. 'Johnson?'

'Not Johnson, sir: he's right enough, though he needs the fear of God putting in 'im.'

Hervey, relieved to hear the exculpation, narrowed his eyes. 'Doubtless you will be able to do the Lord's work, Sarn't-major.'

'Depend on it, sir.'

'And the rest: do we have an outpost of the Seven Dials rookery here after all?'

Armstrong glanced at the adjutant.

'Go on, Sarn't-major,' said Vanneck.

'I'm afraid the bad apple's Captain Snagge, sir. It appears that he's been fencing coral and the like, all smuggled in. And half a dozen helpers about the barracks an' all.'

Hervey's brow furrowed as deep as Armstrong had ever seen it.

'I've been talking to the Bow-street men, sir, and pretty frank they've been. Seems there's some Italians in Stepney that deal in coral and olive oil and cheese and the like, and've been smuggling

169

the coral past the Revenue inside butter and parmijan cheese.'

Hervey looked askance. 'I should hardly think it worth the effort.'

'Not at all, sir: there's a shilling an ounce duty on coral.'

'And we are talking of a great deal of coral in a great deal of cheese?' He was still sceptical.

'The Revenue reckon they've lost three thousand pounds in duty.'

Hervey raised his eyebrows. 'And what exactly is the part played by Captain Snagge? And Johnson, for that matter.'

'Captain Snagge bought butter and oil and cheese from them for the messes' (Armstrong glanced at his notebook) 'from a Signor Guecco and another called Mazzuichi, and this were delivered from the bonded warehouse with the coral inside. Captain Snagge then removed the coral, here in barracks, and passed it on to . . .' (he consulted his notebook again) 'a fencer called Cetti in Holborn. Johnson used to bring the butter and stuff here, sometimes in the back of the regimental coach when you went to London. He thought it was provisions for the officers' mess, so was all right.'

Hervey was puzzled. 'But the regiment's only been under my orders for a few months. We returned from Lisbon only in January. How could Johnson be so materially involved?' (Snagge had exchanged from the previous regiment.)

'First it was Major Strickland's man who carried it, and then when you took command Captain Snagge told Johnson it was now part of his duty.'

Hervey sighed. 'And Johnson did not think to question it!'

'In fairness, sir, Captain Snagge said it were just a duty that went with the job, just bringing rations for the officers.'

Hervey began shaking his head. 'I don't understand why Johnson didn't say anything to me. After all this time.'

'I wouldn't fret if I was you, sir; he wouldn't say ought to me either.'

'Yes, but—' Hervey thought better of it. He knew it was a

conceit ever to suppose he might have gained so completely the trust of a private man, however much they had shared their lives in the twelve years past. But, no, Johnson was different. He was not merely a private man – not any more, not in essentials. 'Well,' he said, and heavily, 'we shall have to deal with Johnson's delinquency in due course. Where is Captain Snagge now?'

'He accompanied the detectors to Bow-street last night,' replied the adjutant.

Hervey nodded. There was some propriety in the sound of that at least; it would not have done for there to have been any sort of 'scene' in barracks. 'I despair that it is ever those officers from the ranks – Barrow in Calcutta, and now Snagge.'

Armstrong braced.

Hervey saw the look, and cursed himself for his crassness. 'I'm sorry, Sarn't-major; that was ill-judged.'

'And with respect, sir, incorrect.'

'Yes, incorrect.'

Had the adjutant not been present they might have had a robust exchange on this punctilio, for Hervey thought he could reasonably claim that while the 'gentlemen' officers were capable of dereliction of duty and all sorts of vice, pecuniary misdemeanour was not one of them – not in the Sixth at least.

'So it's Johnson in the clear, sir. He'll give King's evidence, and the Revenue will not prefer charges. We ourselves could, of course, charge him with disobeying a lawful command; he failed to divulge the facts of the affair when instructed to do so.'

Hervey permitted himself the wryest of smiles as he recalled the words of the Mutiny Act. ' "And every person so offending in any of the matters before-mentioned shall suffer death." That would certainly put the fear of God in him!'

' "Or such other punishment as by a Court-martial shall be inflicted," ' added Vanneck, intending to carry the exchange swiftly towards the material issue. 'I think the sarn't-major shall be able to inflict sufficient restrictions of privileges, sir. May I direct you

towards the question of Captain Snagge? He has admitted everything; that much is to his credit. And I took from him before he
left a letter of resignation. Unless you are strongly of a mind to
refuse the resignation on the grounds that it might be seen as
attempting to avoid court martial, I suggest the business can be
done with Greenwood and Cox quite expeditiously.'

Greenwood and Cox, the regimental agents, through whom all
things could be arranged – at a price. Hervey could see the
advantage of an expeditious selling-out, not least the (partial)
avoidance of scandal. But there was another advantage, and rather
more to his liking. Hervey had no intention of leaving any matter
for the new lieutenant-colonel that he could reasonably attend to
himself. For one thing it would be a discourtesy to delay decisions
unnecessarily; for another it would be equally discourteous to overwhelm a man with matters for resolution on his arrival. Above all,
if things were to be done the Sixth's way it was better that he,
Hervey, put things in hand at once. He had heard nothing but
good of Lord Holderness, but the unhappy memory – albeit a
decade ago – of a lieutenant-colonel intent on changing things was
never wholly out of mind.

'Well, there is a silver lining in this otherwise black cloud. There
will now be a vacancy in the rank of captain, which means in turn
there will be a vacancy for lieutenant and thence cornet – a
vacancy for Mr Hairsine.'

It meant also a vacancy for Vanneck, if Vanneck had the money,
which Hervey knew he certainly did have. *And* it might hasten the
promotion of Armstrong. But whereas Vanneck's captaincy was a
mere matter of financial procedure Armstrong's promotion to
regimental serjeant-major was a matter for executive decision.
Rightly the decision could not be Hervey's own, not now that he
had received word of a new lieutenant-colonel. But as acting
commanding officer, and soon to be Lord Holderness's second in
command, his opinion in the matter would undoubtedly be the
deciding one.

'Mr Vanneck, be so good, would you, as to allow me words with the sarn't-major' (Hervey was surprised to hear himself using the definite article, implying that already Armstrong *was* RSM). 'And then I would have words with you directly, before I leave for the Horse Guards.'

The adjutant withdrew, and Hervey sat down again. 'You are the senior serjeant-major, Geordie. As soon as Mr Hairsine is commissioned you shall take the crown. But I should add that it will be subject of course to a new commanding officer's approval, though I see no reason why that should be withheld.'

Armstrong was silent for a while. Though he was partly overcome by his own astonishing fortune, he recognized the implication in the words 'new commanding officer'. When he spoke it was in a lowered voice. 'Ay, sir, thank you. I never much thought it could come, what with America, and leaving an' all; but if it did, I always hoped it'd be you as colonel.'

Hervey cleared his throat. 'Well, I have not told even the adjutant yet, but I'm afraid it is not to be, at least not for the present.' And then he smiled. 'Just make sure you keep that crown on your arm until it is!'

'Oh ay, sir. Don't you worry on that account.'

'Very well. Give me your hand.'

When Armstrong was gone, Hervey took up his pen. He had two expresses to write. The first was to Eyre Somervile. He wrote quickly. He said, quite simply, that he wished to take up the commission at the Cape. The second express was his reply to Elizabeth's – a letter which on second reading he found more touching in its expression of their tie than ever he would have imagined.

My dearest Sister,

*I do not think that anything you might have written me could
have given such cause for pleasure. I am delighted for you to the
very depths of my being, for you know I owe you more than I
could ever repay, and can now at least rejoice that a man I so
fervently admire shall bring you happiness where I have for so
long stood in its way. And if I give a very imperfect account of
those feelings of joy here, it is solely on account of the expressman's attending and my knowing the urgency in which my reply
is held by you.*

*But Fortune favours us greatly, my dear Elizabeth, for not only
are you to be married, but I also. Lady Lankester – Kezia
Lankester – widow of Sir Ivo, has accepted my own offer. She
has a daughter, not yet one year old, and I believe Georgiana will
therefore be as completely happy in this as can I. I do not know
when the marriage shall take place, for much depends on a
commission abroad, which Eyre Somervile has asked me to
undertake with him . . .*

He wrote a few more lines, largely repeating his joy at
Elizabeth's news and assuring her that his own arrangements stood
in perfect accord with her own, then laid down his pen with considerable relief. It was a letter he had found strangely difficult to
compose, and not merely for knowing the expressman waited. At
a stroke Elizabeth's news removed a burden of guilt he had begun
to feel was intolerable. Besides her own happiness, therefore, he
had much to be thankful for, which in no small measure served as
balm to the wound of Lord George's letter. How often he and his
brother officers had spoken – and with black humour – of the
fortunes of war; yet here the fortunes of peace were no less

outrageous. In the space of but a few minutes his family circumstances were radically recast, and his military horizons transferred from Hounslow Heath to the wide Karoo. He would be lieutenant-colonel, at least, albeit in another uniform, and he had the satisfaction of seeing Hairsine on the brink of commissioning and Armstrong stepping into his shoes. These were mixed fortunes indeed. And, he had to remind himself, they were still to be safely decided. He must waste no time in thinking what might have been: he had to fashion the details of what now remained as his fortune.

CHAPTER TWELVE

AN UNDERSTANDING

_____

That evening

'Major Hervey, m'lady.'

Hervey entered the drawing room like a man arraigned before a court martial. He saw Kat rise, and the smile light her face as if she were a delighted child.

Lady Katherine Greville was but a month or so from her forty-third birthday. Hervey did not know her age precisely. Indeed there were very few clues to her seniority, and he would never have supposed it had not Sir Peregrine Greville himself been a man of – to his mind – advanced years, silvery and bald, paunchy and ponderous (though a kind man by all accounts); and had not Kat, too, from time to time hinted at worldly knowledge that came with a certain maturity. It did not trouble him in the least to know she was older than he. Most *assuredly* not when she appeared as she did now, for her looks and her figure would have made a woman half her age envious. But there lay something of a problem, for although Kezia Lankester was not exactly half Kat's age, she was undoubtedly close to it. He would not, of course, tell Kat this – why would there be need? – but she might suspect; she would certainly question him; she might even discover for herself.

'Matthew, at last you are come!' She embraced him unselfconsciously, even before the footman was able to close the doors of her sitting room. 'Have you dined? Shall you stay? Where have you *been*?'

Hervey found himself unable to answer any of her questions with candour. 'We have had much to do in Hounslow,' he tried.

'Indeed? You have always found the drive here and back an easy one,' she said, raising her eyebrows just enough to convey her meaning.

Hervey cleared his throat. 'I—'

'You have a chill or something, Matthew? Let me get you a little brandy.'

She pulled for the footman before Hervey could protest. He really had no intention of prolonging the call; to do so would be, to his mind, ungentlemanlike. 'Kat, I—'

The doors opened. 'M'lady?'

'I believe Major Hervey will have some brandy, Charles.'

Hervey bowed. He knew he should have refused – but how? Now he would have to wait until the footman returned before he could come to the point of his call; and it would be twice as difficult to get to that point with every minute that passed.

'Sit down, Matthew,' insisted Kat, indicating the place next to her rather than the settee opposite, to which he was mentally heading.

He did as she bid him. Kat placed a hand on his. He pulled away, glancing at the doors.

'My dear Matthew, are you quite well? Whatever is the matter?'

The footman brought him brandy, and a glass for Kat too.

Hervey took an unusually large sip of his. 'Kat, I ... I really don't know how ... that is ...'

177

She looked at him as if he had taken leave of his senses. She took his hand again, although he had tried to withdraw it to safety. 'Tell me.'

He sighed, heavily. 'Oh, Kat.'

She began stroking his hand. He did not pull away. It was the last thing he wanted to do. 'What is it, sweetest?'

He took a deep breath. 'Kat, I have asked Lady Lankester to marry me, and she has accepted.'

Kat stiffened as if by an electric shock. Her hand grasped his the harder, and the colour went from her face. 'Who is Lady Lankester?' she asked, in almost a whisper.

Hervey screwed up his courage once more. 'She is the widow of my former commanding officer in India.'

'How very convenient for all,' she said icily, letting loose his hand and folding hers in her lap.

He said nothing.

'And when did this . . . development occur?'

'Kat, I—'

'Oh, do not be squeamish, Matthew. I would know the worst.'

He placed a hand on hers. 'Kat, I . . . I have not been . . .'

'What are you trying to say, Matthew? That the business has entirely come about since last we met, all of a week ago?'

'Ahm, in a manner of speaking, yes.'

'Great heavens! Then what do you know of her? That she can take charge of the camp followers, and give orders to servants in Hindoostani!'

'Kat, I—'

'The widow of your erstwhile commanding officer, you say? How *old* is she, Matthew?'

'I don't rightly know.'

'Well, *imagine*. Is she older than I?'

'No-o.'

'Younger?'

'I . . . suppose.'

'*Very* much younger?'

'Kat, what has this—'

'Are you intending to *breed* from her? Is that your design, Matthew? Bear you a son and heir, will she?'

He cleared his throat again. 'She has a child, a daughter.'

Kat pulled her hand free. 'Ah, so now I understand. Do you love her, Matthew?'

'Kat, that is not—'

'I don't care one jot what it's not. If you loved her you would confess it at once, and with the greatest pleasure!'

He drained his glass. Kat immediately pulled the bell cord.

'Major Hervey has want of more brandy, Charles.'

Hervey did not gainsay her. Indeed, he said nothing.

Nor did Kat for some time, not until the footman had brought more brandy.

'Have you dined, or not?'

Hervey shook his head. 'In truth, Kat, I'm not hungry.'

She pulled the bell cord again. When the footman returned she said simply, 'Major Hervey and I will supper in half an hour, Charles.' She turned back to Hervey. 'Did you come by hack?'

'No, by the regiment's chariot. Corporal Denny is waiting.'

She turned again to the footman. 'Charles, please see to Major Hervey's driver and horses. They may all stay here the night. It's too drear out to be driving back to Hounslow.'

'But, Kat,' protested Hervey, glancing at the footman, 'I'm staying at my club. I go to the Horse Guards tomorrow.'

'Then that is all the more reason to stay here.' She nodded to her footman, who bowed and closed the doors behind him.

They rode out together the following morning. It was a frosted, quiet world, no one much about the market gardens or the green lanes of Chelsea, the carting traffic light, a mist on the Thames so that they could not see the south bank, and the cold air suppressing the worst stink of the laystalls. At the Royal Hospital, Hervey

179

raised his hat to two pensioners marching in perfect step together, though each man had a wooden leg. This was Kat's regular route of exercise; he knew it from many a morning. She took her exercise seriously, believing it to be in some measure a preserver of her youth. She knew women younger than she who were quite immobile. And they, poor souls, could not expect therefore to enjoy the company of any but men equally immobile.

Kat liked nothing better than the company of vigorous men, men in scarlet coats, men who would pay *her* attention rather than each other in their preoccupation with affairs of state, or of sport. Sir Peregrine was an undemanding, even accommodating, husband. She had once, in a heady, unguarded moment, thought she would leave him and live with her lover, but she had come to her senses in the double realization that she could no more forgo the luxury of Holland Park than could her lover throw up his regiment to live with her. And, lying awake in the early hours of this morning, her lover asleep beside her, content, she had concluded that there was no reason why the arrangement should not continue, with but the simple modification in her lover's marital status. Providing, of course, he would not be so insensitive as to fall in love with his bride (she knew perfectly well that that was not his present condition, and neither could it be his betrothed's). She must therefore find out what sort of woman was Lady Lankester. She could not expect to meet her very soon, but she had sufficient means of gathering intelligence on the gentry of Hertfordshire. She might even make a beginning this morning, and here, as they walked alongside the Physic Garden.

'Matthew, dearest, one thing intrigues me about Lady Lankester – by the way, what is her name? You have not said.' (As he had not said a lot of things, she felt like adding.)

Hervey changed hands with the whip as he came up on the off-side of Kat's mare, having at last got the young gelding round a hay-cart athwart the road. 'Kezia.'

'Heavens!' She kicked herself: it really wouldn't do to make any disparaging comment, no matter how provoked. 'What I wanted to ask, what intrigued me, is why did Lady Lankester – Kezia – why did she accept at once when the acquaintance was so slight? *Oh*, don't mistake me, Matthew: I can think of no reason why any woman should not at once accept an offer of marriage from you—'

'Kat, really, you—'

'No, Matthew, I do not jest. You are a most eligible man.' She would not add 'except in fortune', for she did not wish him bruised at this stage. 'But widowhood with a good name and adequate means would be a very respectable situation for her. Was she, do you know, predisposed to affection towards you; had she a *tendresse*?'

Hervey sighed, inwardly. It was a question he had asked himself; but that was very different from discussing the matter with Kat. 'In truth, I don't think I can say, except that perhaps Kezia Lankester is a woman of very decided . . . spirit. She went out to India with Sir Ivo, after all.'

'I would have travelled to India had you asked me, Matthew.'

'Kat!'

She loosed the reins a little, giving the mare a chance to stretch her neck after the collection of the previous half-hour. 'You do not suppose she wishes to become colonel's wife once more? I know what a powerful hold the prospect of command has for a man; does it, I wonder, extend to the female of the species?'

'Really, Kat, that is quite outrageous! I never thought it for a moment.'

'And she will not know, yet, of your disappointment in that regard.'

'Stop it!'

'Then we suppose that we do not in truth know why Lady Lankester accepted. *"Le Coeur a ses raisons que la raison ne connaît point."*'

Hervey smiled. '*Bonnes "Pensées".*'

181

Kat smiled too. 'You can be really quite clever, Major Hervey.'

He held the smile. He rather enjoyed being clever in Kat's company.

She had been turning something else over in her mind, however, and she now judged it the time. 'Your going to the Cape Colony, Matthew: a year, you say?'

'That is what Eyre Somervile proposes. But the Horse Guards will have to approve it first' (he smiled again) 'though Somervile thinks he can bend the commander-in-chief to his will.'

'I think it a capital idea. I think being second horse to Hol'ness – though he's a fine man, I know well enough – would be vexing for you in the extreme.'

Hervey was surprised. He had considered this news to be as objectionable to her as the first, and when he had told her, at supper, she had seemed to confirm his fears. 'You are very percipient, Kat. But I must say once more that this egg may miss the pudding just as did the first.'

Kat said nothing. But she had no intention of letting this egg break other than to her lover's advantage – and thereby to hers.

Hervey was determined that in the business of the Cape – unlike the business of command – he would not waste a moment in advancing his cause. And an ideal opportunity had arisen that morning, for he had received a letter from General Tarleton asking him to call at the United Service Club, where Hervey's newest supporter was staying for two nights on matters touching on his old regiment and the Horse Guards.

It was, too, a most promising meeting. The general's manner was cordial throughout, and when Hervey revealed his disappointment in failing to secure command, Tarleton commiserated with him in the strongest terms, saying that it was the fault of a dozen years' peace: he would have him command his *own* regiment had it not been so disgracefully disbanded! Indeed, he explained, it was in connection with this very matter that he intended calling this day on the 'new commander-in-chief', the Duke of Wellington (whom he referred to throughout as 'Wellesley' in much the way that a colonel might refer to a favourite cornet), for was it not time to re-raise every regiment of light cavalry that had so usefully extended the Line, now that Ireland looked set for trouble once more and so many regiments of Foot were being sent to the colonies?

Hervey had seen no immediate prospects for himself in such a petition – certainly not within a year at least – but he had recognized an opportunity to advance his 'Africa suit'. He did not know quite how these things were arranged between senior officers – he did not need to, only that they were – but he believed that General Tarleton might prevail on the Horse Guards to assign the duty to him. Indeed, it was in all probability but a mere detail, to be attended to in passing; perhaps a matter for the staff only and not the duke.

Tarleton had appeared delighted by the request. He thought it a capital idea that Hervey should have the Cape commission: he would be glad to recommend him to the duke, and gave his opinion in the most decided terms that the duke would at once concur. And Hervey had felt much relieved that his future lay in the hands of such an eminent soldier. He decided therefore not to call on Lord John Howard: that would be better left until the morning, after the general had visited. He returned instead to Hounslow, but with a vastly lighter heart than he had come up with the night before.

CHAPTER THIRTEEN

FRIENDS AT COURT

Next morning

Shortly after eleven o'clock Hervey was shown into a waiting room at the Horse Guards by a civilian clerk who eyed him as if he might be dangerous. He was puzzled: it was, after all, a perfectly routine visit – not even official, merely a call on the assistant quartermaster-general, Lieutenant-Colonel Lord John Howard. After not too long, however, his old friend appeared, with a man he did not recognize. Hervey, in a plain coat (he was visiting privately), rose.

'Lord Hol'ness, may I present Major Hervey.'

Hervey bowed.

'Major Hervey, I am excessively glad to meet you at last,' said Lord Holderness, with an easy smile and hand outstretched.

Hervey observed a man perhaps five years his senior, a little shorter than he, with fine, almost pretty, features, black hair cut quite short, an active sort of frame, and wearing the undress of the

4th Dragoon Guards, in which regiment he had been senior major, though for the last two years he had been on half pay, attending to his estates in Yorkshire. 'Good afternoon, Colonel.'

'I wish I had known you were to come. I have to be back in the House, presently. I am here simply to pay my respects.'

'And I to see my old friend, here. But this is very opportune nevertheless, Colonel. Might I take five minutes of your time? There are two things of some moment that would benefit from an early decision.'

Lord Holderness looked at his watch. 'If you press me, Major Hervey. They are not matters you are able to decide as acting in command?'

'One of them is not; the other is the regimental colonel's business, but he would expect your opinion.'

'Very well, of course.'

Hervey told him the circumstances of RSM Hairsine's 'field promotion' and the vacancy occasioned by Captain Snagge's sudden resignation, recommending that Lord George Irvine be advised to appoint Vanneck to the captaincy, and Hairsine to the consequent lieutenancy. Lord Holderness agreed that it seemed an admirable arrangement.

'And then there is the appointment of a new regimental serjeant-major—'

Lord Holderness held up a hand. 'Ah, on that I may spare you the burden of decision. I shall want to bring in my own man.'

Hervey was taken aback. The practice was not unknown, but there had never been an outsider, an 'extract', come to that appointment. 'Colonel, with great respect, I would counsel against it. The senior troop serjeant-major is a most experienced and esteemed man.'

Lord Holderness held his smile despite the unexpected and early questioning of his intentions. 'I'm sure he is, Hervey. And he will have his turn, but I wish to bring my late serjeant-major with me.'

Hervey saw there was nothing he might say now to have his new lieutenant-colonel change his mind. He did not know him:

persistence might even prejudice his opinion for good. 'Very well, Colonel.'

'And now, Hervey, I really must get back to the House: the Corn-bill, or the Catholics; I don't recall quite which.'

'Of course. And you are to come to Hounslow . . .'

Lord Holderness put on his forage cap. 'Next month, early, the second week, perhaps. I shall much look forward to renewing our acquaintance, Major Hervey. Good-bye, sir.' He held out a hand again.

'Good-bye, Colonel.'

'The devil of it!' said Hervey, when Lord Holderness had gone. 'Why must he bring his own man?'

'You would do the same, no doubt,' suggested Howard.

Hervey sighed. 'No doubt.'

After a moment or two, Howard pulled the bell cord at the side of the chimneypiece, and sat down. 'Your coming this day is most apt. Will you tea?'

Hervey nodded, as if resigned, and sat down. 'Thank you.'

A messenger came.

'Would you have tea brought us, please, Rayner,' asked Howard, with an agreeable nod.

Hervey sat forward as the messenger left. 'Howard, before anything, I would have you know my news, though it is as yet unannounced. I am to marry Lady Lankester.'

'Hervey, my *dear* fellow! Congratulations! This is most unexpected, is it not?'

'I did not expect a favourable reply from her so soon; that is sure. And when the arrangements are made, I would be very greatly obliged if you would be my supporter.'

His friend nodded. 'Of course, of course: a pleasure – an honour, indeed.'

Hervey leaned back in his chair. 'Now, why is my coming this morning so apt?'

Howard likewise leaned back, as if he too wanted to distance himself from the frivolity of nuptials. He smiled again, as a man about to impart welcome news. 'Two things. First, you shall have the Cape Colony commission.'

Hervey could not but reflect the smile, and he nodded his satisfaction. 'I imagine I am obliged to General Tarleton in this.'

Howard frowned. 'General Tarleton? No, I fear not; not at all. He called on the duke, but the duke would not see him. It was all a most disagreeable affair. The general insisted, but Wellington would not have it. There were pressing affairs to attend to yesterday, but not so pressing as to refuse old Tarleton. I confess I felt exceedingly sorry for him. There's clearly bad blood there.'

'Then how was the decision come to, and so quick?'

Howard raised an eyebrow. 'You have other friends do you not?'

'My *dear* fellow: forgive me; I hadn't realized—'

'Not *I*, you dolt! The duke wouldn't so much as allow *me* to move a sentry from here to Windsor!'

'I don't understand: Somervile? Irvine?'

Howard shook his head. 'Rather better looking than either of them – at least to the duke's eye.'

Hervey's mouth fell open. 'Good God! You don't mean . . . ?'

'They rode in the park together yesterday afternoon.'

Hervey shook his head despairingly.

'The Military Secretary will sign the authority tomorrow. And by the way – fortune favours you indeed – a troop of cavalry is to reinforce the garrison at the Cape. General Bourke has asked for it most urgently, though the duke is of the opinion that it should remain for but a year. You may imagine the arguments as to who shall pay for it!'

Hervey smiled ruefully. He imagined it all too well. Whitehall was a world he never wished to enter save occasionally to see his friend.

'The quartermaster-general will instruct the London District to furnish the troop, so it shall certainly be the Sixth.'

Hervey let his smile broaden. 'That is very gratifying, as well as sound sense.'

Howard nodded, but slowly, thoughtfully. 'The other matter is perhaps less welcome to your ears – your report on the affair at Waltham Abbey.'

Hervey sat up.

'Your *representation*, rather I should say.'

'Representation? Is it that? I was making no plea. Rather was I laying out the facts, as they appeared to me, of a decidedly strange run of events.'

'Is that your business as a soldier?'

Hervey's eyes widened. 'On becoming soldiers we have not ceased to be citizens.'

Lord John Howard held up a hand. 'Do not *Cromwell* me, Hervey! Or was that the wretched Lilburne? Be what may, I make no remark of my own.'

Hervey suddenly understood.

'If your report is to go to the Secretary at War then I am very much afraid you will be unable to take up the Cape commission.'

'Why?' asked Hervey, indignantly. 'I shall be punished for laying out the facts?'

Howard answered his old friend patiently. 'No, not punished. Lord Palmerston would want to consider it with close attention. He might wish to question witnesses, order an inquiry. At the very least you would be required to give evidence. You could not do so from the Cape.'

Hervey thought very carefully. 'Do you say that I should withdraw my report? That the commission at the Cape is . . . *contingent* on my so withdrawing?'

Lord John Howard looked grave. 'My dear fellow, I am very much of the opinion that it is indeed so.'

PART TWO
THE TOUCH OF THE SPEAR

Cape Colony

CHAPTER FOURTEEN

FIRST FOOTINGS

Cape Town, 9 August 1827

Teams of sweating Hottentots heaved on the ropes at the quayside, and one by one the horses of the 6th Light Dragoons were hoist from the *Leviathan*'s hold like so many jack-in-the-boxes. Out swung the booms, horse suspended mid-air in a canvas sling, yet calm as may be in its unaccustomed element, and then back edged the straining teams to lower the animal to the greeting hands of its dragoon and his corporal, and thence to join the growing circle of led horses stretching legs that for eight weeks and more had remained confined and idle. Besides the occasional whinny of delight from a trooper liberated from its Stygian stable, the only sounds were the barked commands of the NCOs and the unison grunting of the Hottentots. Hervey was pleased with what he saw. This was not a bustling harbour scene of the civilian kind, all last-minute coming and going, tearful embraces and lubberliness; here it was all good order and military discipline. Even the merchantman's crew cut about like hands aboard a man o' war, after two months at sea as fearful of Serjeant-major Armstrong's tongue as was any dragoon.

Hervey, impatient of the formality that acting command of the regiment had formerly imposed, made his excuses to Somervile standing beside him, got down from the saddle, gave the reins to Johnson and walked to the quayside. Dragoons braced or saluted as they saw him, the older ones hailing him by name, and he returned the greetings similarly, glad once again to be on the more familiar terms of troop rather than regiment, where he knew each man better than did his own mother, and in many cases loved them a good deal more.

'Not at all in bad condition, Sam!'

The veterinary surgeon turned, and smiled. 'Colonel Hervey, good morning!'

They shook hands. 'A few of them tucked up, but not nearly as bad as I've seen. How was the passage?'

Sam Kirwan gave him a favourable report. No voyage was ever without incident, however clement the weather, and the *Leviathan* had had its share of heavy seas. It was a springlike day at the Cape, bright sunshine and a gentle westerly, but Hervey had seen the South Atlantic five times in a dozen years, and perfectly understood the picture the veterinary surgeon painted.

One of the led horses, a bay gelding, stopped and began to stale. An orderly ran up and interrupted the flow with a big enamel bowl.

Hervey turned to Sam, quizzical.

'I've been taking samples since embarking. I want to observe what changes there are.'

Hervey nodded, pleased that the veterinarian was having his scientific satisfaction. 'What orders have you given for shoeing?'

'I understand it's but a mile or so to the barracks, so they can be led, and the farriers can make a beginning tomorrow on the fitter ones. You don't intend turning them away for a week or anything?'

'Not unless you advise it, Sam. I'd rather they began light work as soon as possible, while the weather's still mild.'

'Just so. Ah, here's Fearnley.'

'Good morning, Colonel,' said Hervey's lieutenant, saluting formally. 'And congratulations.'

Fearnley's boyish good looks and smile were a tonic, though tonic was scarcely needed; Hervey smiled by return and touched the peak of his forage cap. 'Thank you, Mr Fearnley. I perceive the exercise of command has been efficacious.'

'Yes, indeed, but never so easy.'

Hervey could imagine it. What with Sam Kirwan and Serjeant-major Armstrong there could hardly have been a decision to make, but Lieutenant Conyngham Fearnley, nephew of Lord George Irvine, the same age as Hervey had been at Talavera and eager for his first action, had clearly relished the independence, with its 'powers of detachment commander' giving him the disciplinary authority of the lieutenant-colonel himself. Hervey had known he could rely on Fearnley to exercise those powers prudently. In any case he had spoken on the matter very carefully beforehand with Armstrong.

Armstrong: there was rarely so ill a wind as did not blow some military good, Hervey had long concluded (exactly as his own disappointment in command gave way now to renewed appetite for sabre-work). If his troop serjeant-major was not to become *the* serjeant-major . . . well, there was the compensation now of having his old NCO-friend at his side once more. Rather, indeed, like the satisfaction of having Sam Kirwan with him. Sam's announcement that he wished to leave the Sixth in order to study his veterinary science in a tropical clime had come at exactly the right moment: the Cape Colony was no Indian furnace, but it had its attractions in this respect.

'Come and tell me of it,' said Hervey, nodding to the veterinarian as they left him to his samples.

Lieutenant Fearnley gave a full and enthusiastic account, as

favourable and encouraging a report as Sam Kirwan's had been –
yet with detail that Sam had modestly omitted.

'And Sarn't-major Armstrong?' asked Hervey, as a matter of
form rather than true enquiry.

Fearnley halted in his stride. 'You know, Hervey, in all truth I
would count myself worthy if I thought I were but half the man
that he is.'

Hervey turned to his lieutenant. Some things could still take him
by surprise, not least the humility of a subaltern officer who
otherwise and in the best sense had all the appearance of effortless
superiority. He put a hand to his shoulder. 'If you are capable of
thinking that, you are on the right road at least. Now, tell me
of Cornet Beauchamp. He looked likely, from the little I was able
to see of him . . .'

With both eyes fixed on the looming presence of Table Mountain
beyond the castle, Hervey swung his left leg forward so that the
knee was almost crooked over the saddle holster, and reached
down to loosen the girth strap. He reckoned he had done well to
bring Eli with him rather than leave her to come with the rest of
the troop on the *Leviathan*. Eli – Eliab – was Jessye's foal, now
rising nine years, fifteen hands three, a handy charger with all her
dam's sturdiness, and a fair bit of bone, her Welsh Mountain
blood evidently still strong although but a quarter. Eli was 'a good
doer' as the saying went – she did not lose condition too quickly
on changed or reduced rations. She had had a good passage, too.
The steamer *Enterprise* had brought them from the Thames to Cape
Town in fifty-four days, the fastest passage Hervey had ever made
over such a distance, whereas *Leviathan*, all sail, had set out a week
before her and had arrived this morning a fortnight after. Hervey
had therefore been able to ride Eli to the quayside with the
lieutenant-governor to watch them disembark, with his mare looking
every inch as if she had been at the Cape for a whole season.

'Yes, I thought them in very creditable condition,' said Sir Eyre

Somervile, having the greatest difficulty making his little kehilan walk rather than jogtrot. 'A week, perhaps, before they're ready for work?'

'A week, yes, to begin on lightish work. This is mild and bettering weather. In any event, they'll be fit enough by the time you're ready for us.'

'I shall still want you to go to the frontier meanwhile.'

'Of course. Fearnley knows what to do.'

The lieutenant-governor managed at last to get his mare to walk. Her flanks glistened, Somervile's face ran with sweat, and Hervey observed the spreading dampness under the arms of his long white coat and between his shoulder blades – and this despite the fact that they had done no more than trot for about ten minutes. Somervile was a good two stone plumper than when they had first met (and even then he had been carrying more weight than any handicapper would require). His opportunity for exercise these past months had not been what it had in Calcutta; but he had lost nothing of his gameness – nor his little arab mare her bottomless stamina. 'I'm determined to join you there just as soon as General Bourke is returned. I must meet him first.'

'I ought myself to be meeting him first, perhaps,' said Hervey, with more circumspection than usual. He had no wish to begin on the wrong foot with the general officer commanding.

Somervile waved a hand airily. 'Yes, yes, but I can attend to all that. The sooner I know your opinion of the frontier the sooner I can begin—'

The mare stumbled, throwing her rider painfully onto the saddle pommel. Somervile's face turned red as he struggled not to curse too foully. 'You are content with the barrack arrangements?' he tried, manfully, hoping the change of subject would prove a useful distraction.

Hervey looked almost as pained. 'For the horses, yes; for the men, no. One privy between twenty. We had better arrangements in India.'

'You have spoken to the town major, no doubt.'

'The garrison engineer's to do something.'

'The King of France's horses are better housed than a dragoon?' Hervey smiled ruefully.

'I was delighted to see your serjeant-major again. He is a most excellent fellow.'

'He is, and he ought by right to have been RSM now, but the new colonel wished to bring his own man, and I could not budge him on it.'

'You have a good opinion of him nevertheless, your new colonel?'

'Holderness? Oh indeed, he is very gentlemanlike.'

'And this sojourn of yours here, he will not resent it when you return?'

Hervey tilted his head. 'I do not believe so. Indeed he was most particular on that point. And I think, in a way, it is as well that I'm here, since a new man ought not to feel his predecessor – however temporary – looking over his shoulders.'

His old friend raised an eyebrow. 'Would that it were so with General Bourke. There's no doubt the colony is in want of true civil government, and yet it is in large part still an armed camp.'

Somervile had been in Cape Town barely a fortnight more than Hervey, but the best part of two decades in Madras and Bengal had given him a keen judgement in these matters (as well as a taste for powder and the edge of the sword). Hervey had long been certain that he would rather shoot tiger with Eyre Somervile than with any other man – save, perhaps, Peto. 'I would imagine that Bourke will be only too keen to address himself to the military side alone. Are you content with what he has proposed for the new regiments?'

Somervile answered very decidedly: 'I am, but I should wish for more of that article.' He indicated the platoon of the Fifty-fifth marching towards the castle.

Hervey nodded knowingly. It was good to see a regular regiment of Line here. Native troops – black, white, brown (or even, he supposed, yellow) – were all very well, but there was something about a red coat and the King's crown on the helmet plate. It was like seeing a brick-built wall, properly laid and pointed, when all else was undressed stone, or mud and daub. The Fifty-fifth he had never encountered before. They had not been in the Peninsula, nor at Waterloo, but they had sweated away in Jamaica and had been at the Cape for five years. He could not but suppose they were hardened to 'colonial' fighting. 'Indeed. It would be difficult to have excess of them. Except, you know, I've been reading that engineer officer's report of his exploration of Kaffraria, and I wonder whether such regulated drill as theirs is most apt.'

'They have a light company, do they not?'

Eli was now on her toes, sensing a return to quarters, so that Hervey had to sit deep again to try to collect her. 'Yes, and most usefully. It is merely that I imagine the country hasn't changed greatly since the exploration, and the sort of scrub he describes is the devil for manoeuvring in close order; you recall the like in Madras? I've been here but a week, but by all accounts the Xhosa fight from behind cover of the scrub, in which case I should sooner have a company of riflemen who snipe than three of muskets who volley.'

'Well, you may see the country for yourself right enough.'

'Just so. And I'm content to leave the Rifles recruits with Streatfield, their major, for the time being. They'll not be ready to begin mounted work for a month at least.'

As he settled Eli into a proper walk before starting on the long cobbled ramp to the gate, he glanced left and right about the curtain wall of the Castle of Good Hope. It would have been easy to imagine himself in Spain again, for the pentagonal fortress, with its bastions and ravelins, scarps and glacis, looked for all the world as if Marshal Vauban himself had been here. It looked, indeed, like the fortress at Badajoz. Hervey had a sudden moment's doubt, then told himself that Badajoz was all in the past, and kicked for Eli to walk on with more address.

It *was* a solid affair this place. It was not as big as Badajoz, but it was serviceable, although it had not saved the Dutch when the British had landed here to wrest the station from them in the early years of the French war. Already Hervey had spent hours in the castle library learning of it what he could. He knew each of the bastions by name, and why they were so called – Leerdam, the western bastion, followed clockwise by Buuren, Catzenellenbogen, Nassau and Orange. He knew that the bell above the gate was cast in Amsterdam in 1697 and weighed more than a quarter of a ton. The Dutch had used it to tell the hours and to warn of danger (it could be heard two and a half leagues away, said the librarian). Inside the walls were all the offices of an outpost of the Royal Dutch East Indian Company – church, bakery, storehouses, magazines, cells, workshops and living quarters, and all painted yellow to reflect the heat while minimizing the glare. It had been built with the utmost permanence in mind, the maritime replenishment station of the same undertaking as Britain's own John Company. Yet Hervey did not feel himself far-flung from the engine of affairs in London, nor excluded from the great enterprise in India; rather he felt – as he supposed must Somervile – that he was at a prime gearwheel in the vast machine that was the Honourable East India Company; a gearwheel that was set to expand somehow – and which at the same time was threatened with violent interruption. No, he did not feel himself to be without the opportunity for distinction; not here.

He woke. 'I beg your pardon—'

'I said that I feared Colonel Somerset was unfriendly. Scarcely a word to be had from him. He did not appear to share your pleasure in seeing a fine regiment landing its horses.'

'Ah, Colonel Somerset.' Hervey smiled, mock-pained. 'The army is divided into two classes of men: those who were at Waterloo, and those who were not.'

Somervile returned the smile, though wryer. 'I thought you were going to say those who are Somersets and those who are not!'

198

'That too! But the Waterloo Somersets were deuced fine. I met Lord FitzRoy a little before the battle, a most agreeable man; and Lord Edward had the Household brigade.'

'Well, FitzRoy is now Wellington's man at the Horse Guards. The Somersets' reach will be ever long, therefore.'

Hervey raised his eyebrows as he looked directly at his old friend. 'You could say, on the other hand, that since the duke is at the Horse Guards *my* reach is therefore long!'

Somervile was not sure what to make of the proposition. Was Hervey being entirely serious? 'At any rate, I should not wish anything untoward there. We must not forget that the reason I am here is that Lord Charles Somerset was recalled, and peremptorily. He will be brooding, still, in London, and there are plenty of ears there all too ready to be beguiled. He will be especially solicitous of his son, and, no doubt, the son will be assiduous in writing home his opinion of affairs here – Waterloo man or not. Caution, Hervey; that is my counsel.'

Hervey shook his head. 'Of course; caution. You may depend upon it.'

They rode on up the cobbled ramp without speaking, until Somervile gave voice to his other concern. 'It would have been well that General Bourke were here, and not just to welcome your troop. There are things I would know as to his thinking, although I must say that he has made admirable economies.'

'Better, I think, that we are able to lay on a proper parade for him in a month or so.'

'Just so,' agreed Somervile. 'But I do wish he'd not gone off to St Helena at the very time he knew I must arrive here. What in heaven's name possessed him to think there was any requirement for him there?' His mare began slipping and sliding on the cobbles, quite diverting him for the moment until she was back in hand, by which time he had resolved to change the subject. 'Quite a scientific sort of man, by the look of it, your veterinary surgeon. Quite particular he was about his urine samples.'

Now Eli stumbled. 'Damn!' Hervey was thrown off balance, and doubly to his chagrin since he had presumed her so capable. 'Not fit enough by miles. What? Sam Kirwan? Yes, exactly so. He'd applied to go to India, to study tropical infections, but I persuaded him here instead – for the time being at least.'

And already, he explained, thanks to his lieutenant's telling, he had cause to be grateful for those powers of persuasion, for Sam Kirwan had saved one trooper from choking when it swallowed its tongue in a gale off the Azores, and saved another's sight when it dislodged an eye from its socket. The War Office did not like sending horses to the Cape Colony. In the early years they had shipped them in their many hundreds, and a large number of those that survived the passage had broken down before they could be got fit for work (one in three did not see a second year in service). The alternative, which the War Office now preferred, was to buy the country-breds and native ponies, which, they believed, increasingly served. It had indeed been the War Office's intention in the Sixth's case to authorize local purchase rather than take on the expense of shipping, but Hervey had been able to persuade the Duke of Wellington's staff, and they in turn Lord Palmerston's, that the cost of shipping might easily be offset by the reduced time the reinforcement would need to remain in the colony training the country-breds to the trumpet.

'Much depends now, therefore, on Sam Kirwan's supervision of the regime of acclimation: three to four weeks, we reckon. Which is why I feel able to undertake your reconnaissance of the eastern frontier.'

'The Mounted Rifles will give your men a good run for their money in a couple of months, I imagine?'

Hervey nodded. He was not inclined to see any mischief in his old friend's suggestion. In any case it was undoubtedly true (neither was it a bad thing). The Rifles were already well found: there were eighty or so men enlisted, some from the former colonial corps, and a hundred-odd cob-ponies had been broken and backed thanks to the zeal and capability of the dozen rough-riders from the old Cape Regiment. Recruits had begun their drill with the double-barrelled rifles which Lord Charles Somerset had of his own initiative ordered from the Westley-Richards factory in Birmingham, and there were enough NCOs of sound experience to teach sharpshooting.

'When I have had a satisfactory parade state for the troop – in a day or so – I believe I should be ready to leave for the frontier. Shall you be able to give me more particular orders?'

'They are being copied as we speak.'

Through the arched gateway and into the bailey clattered the two mares. The quarter-guard presented arms, and Somervile acknowledged, raising his hat high.

'And there is another thing I would have you look to. Lord Charles Somerset says in his letter of relinquishment to me – which I must acknowledge is a handsome enough memorandum – that there is an officer in Cape Town who might render signal service. If he can be persuaded to bestir himself. I thought it appropriate that he accompany you to the frontier. His name is Edward Fairbrother, of the Royal African Corps.'

Hervey was puzzled. 'The corps was disbanded some years ago, was it not?'

They came to a halt outside the long, boxlike building that was headquarters of His Majesty's administration in the Cape Colony. Orderlies standing ready took hold of the bridles, and Sir Eyre Somervile, and Lieutenant-Colonel (Acting) Matthew Hervey, commandant of the new Corps of Cape Mounted Riflemen, dismounted with as little ceremony as possible.

'Five years ago, to be precise,' said Somervile, taking the steps to his quarters with impressive bounds, even though his breath was in short measure. 'The hard cases, I think you call them, were sent to Sierra Leone, and the officers who declined to accompany them were forced to transfer to half pay. One or two stayed here –

they were made land grants on the Fish River – but most returned to England.'

'And so Fairbrother knows the frontier?'

'Apparently very well, and speaks Xhosa – or Kaffir, as probably he calls it. Or yet Nguni, for that matter.'

Hervey smiled. His own facility with languages was entirely practical, whereas Somervile's delved deep into their history and character. 'How is *your* Xhosa, Lieutenant-Governor?'

Somervile did not immediately return the smile. 'I am not yet fluent, but I can converse perfectly reasonably with my *fundisa*. There was little else to detain me during the passage.'

Hervey nodded, chastened. 'Then I will speak with this Edward Fairbrother. There was a Fairbrother in the Eighteenth; I wonder if they are any sort of kin?'

CHAPTER FIFTEEN

ROYAL AFRICANS

Later that day

It began raining in the late morning, at first a mere mizzle, and then more decided, but it was no more to Hervey than the sort of late-winter downpour he had known on Salisbury Plain, though not nearly as cold. Johnson had complained about the weather since arriving. He had received the knowledge of the reversal of seasons in the southern hemisphere with considerable scepticism, believing his informants were intent on some joke at his expense (if anything, his brush with the Bow Street forces of the law had made him excessively wary). He had lit fires and worn woollens at every opportunity, and told Hervey severally that even when the weather took a turn for the worse in Sheffield in August they could at least go about in flimsy.

Hervey had quickly stayed his groom's grumbling protests this morning, however. He was determined on seeking out Lieutenant Fairbrother as soon as possible; and with the troop engaged on its march to quarters, and the Rifles in the capable hands of Major Streatfield, there was nothing that need detain him. He therefore called for his waterdeck cape and set off on foot for Fairbrother's lodgings, dismissing Johnson at the last minute, seeing how close were the lodgings and that he would not have need of the saddle.

He could reasonably have summoned Fairbrother to the castle, he told himself as he set off: the lieutenant was not on the Active List but he was still subject to military authority. And it might have served to do so, for it did no harm to remind a man of his duties. By convention, however, an officer on half pay was allowed the courtesies of formal retirement, and in any case, Hervey took the pragmatic view that persuading a man to do something he might find disagreeable was much the more likely if the persuader did not stand on his dignity.

The rain began to run down the back of his neck, and it troubled him that he was troubled by it. A soaking – like a baking, or a dusting or a freezing – was but a part of the soldier's life. Had he become soft of late in Hounslow? He wished he wore his shako instead of the forage cap, for it would have kept his neck dry. And he wished too that his new tunic were made, for he had a mind that Rifle green might make more of an impression on Fairbrother than would blue – unless Fairbrother was indeed related to the cornet of that name in the Eighteenth (whom Hervey had known in the Peninsula as a very dashing sabreur).

Lieutenant Fairbrother's lodgings were about half a mile from the castle next to an expanse of greenery known as the Company's Gardens, originally a market garden for the Dutch East India Company but now a handsome park filled more with exotic plants and the makings of some sturdy oaks. Hervey's instructions took him through the gardens to one of a dozen brightly painted timber houses on the western side. A Hottentot woman answered the bell. She was not a great age, but her hair was white; she wore a print dress of European fashion, but no cap. There was about her both dignity and authority. Hervey explained who he was, and

204

she admitted him and showed him to a flower-filled sitting room.

'I am Master Fairbrother's housekeeper, sir. I will see if he may receive you,' she said, with a certain formality. 'Please be seated.'

Hervey took a seat by a window with a prospect of Table Mountain. He sat for more than a quarter of an hour trying to remain composed, though inclining to exasperation at the delay in any sort of reply. There was a fire in the hearth, which at least began the process of drying out his trousers. He wondered what Sam Kirwan would be thinking of the prospects of studying his science in a tropical climate.

At length the housekeeper reappeared, and with a look that said she had had some difficulty. 'Master Fairbrother will come very presently, Colonel Hervey. May I offer yourself tea?'

Hervey was very content to take tea: the fire was drying him well enough, but he felt the need of something warming to the inner parts.

When the housekeeper returned, with a silver teapot, and blue china which looked as if it had come from the East, Hervey asked if she knew whether Master Fairbrother had any engagements in the coming weeks, to which she replied that as far as she knew there was nothing to detain him in Cape Town or elsewhere, explaining that he was engaged only infrequently in business, and that he spent his time with his books. Hervey was appreciative of her candour, and intrigued by the suggestion of a bookish disposition.

After five more minutes the half-pay lieutenant appeared, in a long silk dressing gown over day clothes, and perfectly shaved. Edward Fairbrother was a man of about Hervey's own height and not many years his junior. He had large brown eyes, thick black hair and noble cheekbones. Hervey rose, and in evident surprise.

'Mislike me not for my complexion, Colonel Hervey,' said Fairbrother, with a look almost haughty.

Hervey was no little discomfited. In India he had had so many native friends (and a lover) that a brown complexion had been nothing more to him than the clothes a man chose to wear. 'I beg your pardon, Mr Fairbrother,' he near stammered. 'I had not thought—'

'I take no offence, Colonel. It is of no consequence, and your surprise is hardly a thing of novelty.'

Hervey was uncertain on the first two assertions. Quite plainly it was something to which Fairbrother was sensible. Even in a corps so far removed from the regular order of battle as the Royal Africans a skin the colour of coffee, albeit with a good splashing of cream, would tell against a man. 'You speak Xhosa, Mr Fairbrother, as I'm given to understand,' he tried briskly. 'How did you acquire it?'

Fairbrother now looked positively disdainful. ' "I am as free as nature first made man, Ere the base laws of servitude began, When wild in woods the noble savage ran." '

Hervey sighed, and held out a hand, wondering if the bookish disposition was entirely favourable. 'Let us begin anew, if we may. Hervey, lieutenant-colonel-commandant of the Cape Mounted Rifles.'

Fairbrother took the hand, and smiled, conciliatory. 'Edward Fairbrother, late of His Majesty's Royal African Corps, and before that ensign, Jamaica Militia.'

Hervey now supposed he had a better understanding of Fairbrother's circumstances: a planter's family, English, with that admixture of the native blood which over long centuries shaded the complexions of many a good family there (or so Peto had once informed him, for he himself had never been to the West Indies).

'Well, Mr Fairbrother, I am much obliged to you. I have come to ask if you would be so good as to accompany me to the eastern frontier. I am to make a reconnaissance, and I should be grateful for the company of guide and interpreter.'

Fairbrother said nothing by reply, turning instead to his house-keeper. 'Mama Anky, would you bring me tea if you please.'

He sat down and crossed his legs, a gesture of independence that Hervey could not fail to observe.

'Colonel Hervey, I am a man of some affairs in Cape Town' (Hervey would learn that he imported rum from his father's estate) 'and I am not obliged to be at the governor's call.'

Hervey at once had to check himself. In law Lieutenant Edward Fairbrother was most certainly at the governor's call – the governor, the King's person. 'There is no question of *obliging* you, Mr Fairbrother. That is precisely why I came in person: to *ask* you. And as to any business interests, you may be assured that you would be properly compensated.'

Mama Anky brought tea. Fairbrother took his time pouring it, not appearing to be contemplating Hervey's proposition in the least. 'Colonel Hervey, when Lord Somerset – I should say Lord *Charles* Somerset – was governor, there were frequent opportunities for intercourse, but his lordship not once deigned to ask me to the castle, though he knew full well enough of my capabilities.'

Hervey sighed, though inwardly. He had no recommendation of Fairbrother other than that he spoke the language of the tribes on the Fish River frontier. This resentment of his would be altogether too tedious in but a few days' marching. 'I cannot imagine that Lord Charles Somerset would intend any slight on an officer who had served his king as you had.'

Fairbrother smiled pityingly and raised an eyebrow. 'Do you know the family?'

Hervey was beginning to object to the tone. He fancied he never stood on his rank, but lieutenant-colonel, even by brevet, required *some* respect; Fairbrother had an arrogant presumption . . . 'I had but a brief acquaintance with his younger brother, Lord FitzRoy – at Waterloo.'

Fairbrother at once sat up on the mention of Waterloo. He uncrossed his legs, turned his eyes to the teapot and occupied himself in replenishing his merely half-empty cup by way of allowing himself to begin anew. 'A very noble and gallant man, Lord FitzRoy, by all accounts. Were you there when he lost his arm?'

An understanding of the battle of Waterloo: Hervey was indeed obliged. He intended to press to advantage this unexpected turn. 'I rather think that at the moment Lord FitzRoy was hit there was so much smoke I could scarcely see the man next to me.'

The half-pay lieutenant's whole demeanour was now changed. He asked several more questions about the battle, most of which Hervey was able to answer, though not all by his own exact experience. As he explained, the battle was of a scale he could barely contemplate still; quite unlike any of those in the Peninsula – not Corunna, not Talavera, nor Salamanca nor even Vitoria.

At length Fairbrother smiled – a warm, conceding smile which Hervey found himself returning willingly, and thankfully.

'I believe I might arrange for you to be restored to the Active List, if that is what you wished. There are supernumerary posts in the Rifles.'

But Fairbrother shook his head, though still smiling. 'No, Colonel Hervey, I should not wish to be so restored. There is, I am afraid to tell you, an impediment – Lord Charles Somerset's son, whom his father promoted shamelessly during his time here. I do not care for his manners, nor much for his fashion of soldiery. I could not serve in a corps with such a man; and certainly not when he were my superior.'

Hervey now found himself saying what he would otherwise have regarded as improper. His instincts were ever for the correct practice of good order and military discipline (though he had rarely flinched, certainly of late, from respectfully speaking his mind), but he saw no reason to let that stand in the way of what seemed necessary for the execution of the King's business. 'Mr Fairbrother, between these four walls, I believe we may share the same opinion of Colonel Somerset. But it is I who have command of the Mounted Rifles, and I enjoy the confidence of the lieutenant-governor. You would need have no concerns on that account.'

Fairbrother said nothing, nodding slowly instead as if weighing Hervey's words. Then he rose and went to a writing desk and opened a drawer. 'See here,' he said, holding out in turn two miniatures. 'My father.'

Hervey saw a fine-looking man, as fine – and as white – as any he might see in the United Service Club.

'My mother.'

Hervey could not entirely hide his surprise. The likeness was of a black woman, unquestionably a pleasing-looking woman, though frankly no more than pleasing. 'I . . . I am not at all clear what is your purpose in this.'

'You might wish to ask yourself, Colonel Hervey, whether I am my father's son or my mother's.'

Hervey no longer concealed his surprise. 'You are both, I should imagine! Why should it be of any concern to me?'

Fairbrother took back the miniatures and replaced them in the writing desk, as if drawing a veil over his vexing provenance. 'You may not be certain of my ultimate loyalties. Colonel Somerset for one would doubt what would be my true feelings towards the Xhosa, cousins of my mother's people, albeit distant, that they are.'

'Great Gods! You took the oath to King George and all his heirs and successors did you not? And I imagine there was not a doubt when you were with the Royal Africans?'

'Hah! The Royal Africans – a greater gathering of rascals as ever you'd find. The scum of the earth – your Duke of Wellington's words – or rather, the scum of the scum of the earth, amenable to no discipline other than by the lash, and with no courage other than by drink. And yet, Colonel Hervey, *and yet*, every man of that infamous corps would have considered himself to be my superior on account of his fair, if pock-marked skin.' He shook his head. 'No, Colonel, the doubts about me in the Royal African Corps were not as elevated as to concerns about my loyalty. They were rather, I imagine, of my humanity.'

209

Hervey shifted awkwardly in his chair. These were depths with which he was unhappy, certainly on so recent an acquaintance. But his instinct was to sympathy nevertheless, even if sceptical. 'The officers – your fellow officers, I mean – they were not of an entirely prejudiced disposition?'

'My fellow officers, Colonel Hervey? Did you *meet* any officers of the Royal African Corps? Unread men. Not, I imagine, the sort that would grace the table of the Sixth Light Dragoons. That *is* your regiment, is it not?'

'It is. How did you know?'

Fairbrother tilted his head. 'I keep myself informed. I see the *London Gazette*.' He paused. 'I now know exactly who you are.'

Hervey decided it was time to bring affairs to a resolution, moving to the edge of his chair as if to rise. 'Then you are at an advantage, sir, for I know next to nothing of you. And I do not think I care to unless you are prepared to accompany me to the frontier. It would otherwise be mere idle gossip.'

For the first time Fairbrother looked discomfited, as if realizing he had momentarily lost the initiative. 'Very well, Colonel Hervey, if you would have it so immediately—'

Hervey drove home ruthlessly his sudden advantage. 'I would indeed. I have more than sufficient business to be about.'

Fairbrother quite flinched at the sudden display (and reminder) of martial briskness. 'Very well, Colonel Hervey, you shall have my answer at once. I will accompany you. But in the situation of gentleman, not of any military rank.'

Hervey sat back in his chair. He smiled, cautiously. 'Of course. And you may begin at once by omitting *my* rank too.'

'I'm obliged – very much obliged.'

Hervey, smiling more confidently, crossed his legs. 'Would you tell me of your people now?'

The lieutenant-governor's sitting room, as familiarly furnished as had been that same room in Bedford Square, was made all the more comfortable by a good fire and the warmth of Hervey's report. The lieutenant-governor drained his glass, rose from his writing table and nodded as if contemplating his assent.

'Truly, Somervile, he is a most intriguing man, and most engaging too – at least after the initial haughtiness is put aside. And, I believe, he may be a most discerning guide. He declined all rank.'

Somervile poured himself another glass of sherry, seeing Hervey's was full still. 'A mulatto having the King's commission – I never heard of it. The Duke of York was evidently of purer fire than I imagined.'

Hervey at last sipped a good measure of his sherry, content now that Somervile was of a mind with him. He would therefore tell him rather more of what he knew of Master Fairbrother. 'His story is really quite winning. His father – his *natural* father – owned extensive estates in Jamaica, and formed an attachment – I mean an attachment, not merely in the usual way – with one of his slaves, who does sound to me to have been a most agreeable woman. Be that as it may, the young Edward Fairbrother – a most unfortunate name, of course – played happily with the real Fairbrother heir, was raised with him indeed, schooled with him, and then the young master died of a fever when he was ten years old, the same age as our Fairbrother. At which the father formally adopted his natural son and sent him to school in Kingston – where I must say he appears to have had rather a fine schooling – and then bought him an ensigncy in the Jamaica Fencibles, and thence the Royal Africans.'

Somervile looked puzzled. 'I wonder, with his adopted father's money, why he was not able therefore to advance in rank.'

Hervey inclined his head and raised his eyebrows, as if to signal that it was 'the old story' again. 'He told me his father lost the greater part of his fortune in imprudent investments. He now lives on a modest annuity and his half pay – and such business as he can transact importing rum; though he says that now Cape brandy is improved, the commissaries are buying it for the ration rather than rum from the West Indies. He is of some independent means, however, and most certainly of independent mind; I believe we shall get on tolerably well.'

The lieutenant-governor nodded, this time unambiguously. 'I am glad to hear it. Just so long as he and Colonel Somerset do not ride together.' He finished his glass and reached once more for the decanter. 'I must say too that I am increasingly ill-disposed towards the colonel. His manner this morning at the quayside was really most improper, and I've heard murmuring from the colonial staff too. He is decidedly against the idea of the Mounted Rifles, apparently. He believes proper cavalry's what puts the fear of God into a black man. When General Bourke is returned I may ask him of Somerset's humour.'

Hervey accepted more sherry and unbuttoned his coat a little, warming to the atmosphere in every sense. 'May I ask of your own humour? Can you give me yet any enabling order for the frontier, and the limits if there be any?'

The lieutenant-governor sat back in his chair again, looking satisfied. 'I can. You may take them with you after dinner, together with, I am prodigiously pleased to say, some very serviceable maps. But let me tell you now of what I have in mind, in the broadest of terms.'

Hervey listened keenly as Somervile began. They had known each other, and indeed had worked together, long enough for the one to inform the other of his intent without recourse to many words, and for the one to know precisely what the other had need of hearing. Somervile did not therefore itemize his requirements, as if a list for attention by a quartermaster (though he made sure that such detail was recorded in his written orders for the benefit of his staff and the record); instead he told Hervey what was his mind regarding the Xhosa. He wished to know, if it came to a fight – and he earnestly hoped that it would not – what was the best course of victory. He wished to know if in that regard the Cape

212

Colony was in essence like India. If it were, then he, the lieutenant-governor, would have no concerns: if his pacific policies failed then he would rely on the correct application of his military resources. If it were not like India, then he would first have to recast that military strategy before gambling with his 'diplomatic' means. And this, he confided very readily, he would do on and with the advice of his old friend rather than by that of any general.

CHAPTER SIXTEEN

THE SETTLEMENTS

Algoa Bay, 23 August

With the fairest of winds, the passage from Cape Town to Port Elizabeth was ten days. Assisted by steam, as Hervey and his party were in the *Fortune*, a brig with just enough room to ship five horses as well as half a dozen passengers comfortably, the passage was made in six even though the winds were at times light.

They messed together during that time: Hervey, Fairbrother, Corporal Wainwright (whose lance rank had been another casualty of the change of command), Private Johnson and two Cape Dutch merchants returning to Port Elizabeth, whose English was limited to the needs of their trade and who therefore kept themselves much to their own society. Fairbrother himself, perceiving some antipathy towards him initially on the merchants' part, was quick to pick a fight with them in their own language – some trivial thing, a little matter of history concerning the settlement of the Cape, but enough to promote an atmosphere of unease – although after two days they managed to bring themselves to some repairing civility, which made Fairbrother content. Hervey observed in this both a combative streak, which was admirable in a soldier if kept under strict regulation, and a propensity to see insult at every turn, which in combination was tiresome and altogether too volatile. What he also observed, however, was the effect of Fairbrother's sharing a table with Wainwright and Johnson. At first it was all polite formality, but after a while Fairbrother noticed the happy familiarity between the two dragoons and Hervey, the warmth, the confidence, the mutual trust and respect – all the things that at one time he had thought the mark of an Englishman in his dealings with another. For as Hervey had already concluded, Fairbrother thought himself first an Englishman. That, indeed, had been his education, his upbringing – to begin with as the half kin and inseparable companion of a fair-faced Fairbrother, and then as the adopted heir of one who seemed to him the personification of all that Shakespeare and the misty-eyed poetry to which he was drawn spoke of distant England.

Fairbrother in turn spoke of it to Hervey as they neared their harbour.

'You know, Hervey, I have observed much in the past few days that restores my spirits. These men of yours are vastly different from those of the Royal African Corps. You may not believe how so.'

Hervey could believe it only too well: he doubted that Edward Fairbrother had ever had to put a ball into the chest of a man in a red jacket, as *he* had at Badajoz. 'I do not know what conclusion you draw from that observation, but it would be perilous to be sentimental.'

Fairbrother smiled. 'Oh, you must permit me a little sentiment, if it is of the good sort. It is merely that I marvel at your way with these men, almost as if they were fellow officers indeed.'

Hervey knew what Fairbrother meant. He had himself observed the stiffness, the necessary distance between officers and men in the

215

ranks of red, but he was intrigued to know more of this impartial observer's opinion, for such things were ever flattering. 'The regiment has always been under very strict regulation, but never by the lash.'

'Of course, in my former corps the men were enlisted for ignoble reasons – to escape the hulks, or the gallows even. We were little more than a penal battalion. They were men from, as I believe, the more disagreeable parts of England.'

Hervey now smiled, and clapped a hand to Fairbrother's shoulder. 'Do not imagine that because mine is a regiment of cavalry we invariably recruit a nobler sort! Johnson is from one of the meanest cities, a workhouse pauper, a refugee from the coal pits; and Wainwright I myself found in the filthiest of hovels that would disgrace, I imagine, a plantation in Jamaica.'

'Then your regiment has made of them a very great deal, Colonel Hervey. That, or Nature would claim them as her gentlemen.'

Hervey smiled the more. 'Come now, that is a little high-blown; though I concede they are men of special worth. Wainwright has enough courage for a whole troop.'

Fairbrother shook his head to re-emphasize the point: 'I do not think I have admired anything so much as what passes between you and them. It is as if rank has become of no need. I once heard it said that in an English regiment, the superior officer, if he is a gentleman, will never think of it, and the subordinate, if he is a gentleman, will never forget it. I am sorry to say that I did not observe as much in my former corps. And now it seems to me that it is possible to omit the word "officer" from that dictum.'

Hervey squeezed Fairbrother's shoulder again. 'You are a very delightful observer, if perhaps susceptible to sentiment. But I cannot laugh at that. I am glad you think the Sixth thus; I am proud, indeed. And I must say that I have greatly enjoyed these past days. You are – I *will* say it – exceedingly agreeable company.

I would not have better conversation in my mess than I have shared with you at table.'

'You mean you have been agreeably surprised by the conversation of one who wears the shadowed livery?'

Hervey withdrew his hand, and frowned very pointedly. 'Fairbrother, I will speak plainly, for I have known you now long enough. If you persist in this resentfulness you will drive away any friendship and embitter yourself terribly. Give it up!'

Fairbrother turned his head from him for a moment, and then back, as if to make a firm break with what had gone before. 'Hervey, I do most sincerely beg pardon.'

Hervey thought Algoa Bay one of the most beautiful sights he had beheld. On his passages to and from India he had not seen the bay before, his ship standing well out to catch the south-west monsoon, east of Madagascar, or the reverse on the passage home. The shore was white, whiter than anything he recalled of Madras – which in other respects he was minded of – and beyond it was a green that invited rather than threatened (the forests of the Coromandel coast had threatened): a green that promised life, and good life, shared, rather than the fortress-forest whose repellent and repelling occupants persuaded all but the most inquisitive to keep well clear. Hervey felt a powerful desire to be in that inviting green, as others had before him: first the Dutch, and then more and more English, by which of course he must include Irish, for here was land whose title an Irish peasant might own instead of paying the rack-rents to the absent landlord. And surely, in all this country (they had sailed eight hundred miles from Cape Colony), there was enough green for everyone?

But Hervey had read the colony's historical record, Somervile had revealed to him the contents of the most confidential of papers, and Fairbrother had told him what so many outside the castle believed: the white man lived precariously at the Cape. He knew that what he observed inland of Algoa Bay was not a

217

wilderness, and that out of the abundant green might come at any time native hordes to reclaim all that was settled. And even if those native hordes could be checked, there would surely be more. Could these Cape settlers, a few thousand adventurers, ever know what was to come out of that green heart of Africa – or when? *Ex Africa aliquid novi semper*: Atilius Regulus had killed the huge African snake, and the spoils of the creature were shipped to Rome for public display. The snake had been real enough, and yet the poets had seen it as boding evil for Rome, so that Africa to their minds became Rome-hating. The Carthaginians – black Hannibal – had almost destroyed the city: the Romans in their revenge had destroyed Carthage, poisoned the wells, ploughed salt into her fertile soil. Would that be what they would have to do here, at the very extremity of the continent, just as Rome had had to do?

Hervey knew that Somervile was right. There was no prospect of a diplomatic peace without the military resources to crush the Xhosa if they refused diplomacy: *si vis pacem, preparate bellum*. But if the Xhosa were only a fraction of the native hordes that might pour into the colony, how might there ever be a settled peace? As Somervile pointed out, the Secretary of State for War and the Colonies was not of a philosophical mind. From the perspective of Downing Street, the shores of southern Africa could be colonized in the usual way: cleared, fortified, settled, regulated – and with trade, the benign influence, conducted beyond the pale. Moreover, to Hervey there was no ill in such a vision. Why could not the Xhosa stay east of the Fish River, where by 'treaty' they had settled after the terrible fighting seven years ago? What accounted for their recent depredations across the Fish into the Crown Colony? They must know that it brought nothing but retribution. These Cape-Dutch farmers, these *burghers* (and for that matter the newer British settlers), were not men who would be satisfied with merely recovering their stolen cattle: they would want a reckoning – compensation, reparation, condign punishment.

And so the trouble would inevitably increase. Did the colony possess enough troops to fight a full-scale war with the Xhosa? That indeed was the question to which this preliminary reconnaissance was directed. History was no good presage: the fighting seven years ago had been savage, unpredictable, unconfined, the Xhosa attacking not just isolated farms but forts and the bigger settlements. Even Graham's Town had been all but overrun. The equal savagery with which the insurrection had been put down – necessary savagery, said everyone, for there had been no alternative – had then sown the seeds of the present state of frontier insolence. In the aftermath of the French war, and with Bonaparte on St Helena, there had been plenty of troops at the Cape, but since Bonaparte's death and the Xhosa rebellion there had been severe retrenchment; how much more savage now would they need to be if the Xhosa made war again? Must they destroy every kraal, poison the wells and plough salt into the soil beyond the Fish River?

If this magnificent landing – the sea, the beaches and the green beyond – minded Hervey of his first footing in Madras, he was soon persuaded of the difference. Madras had been all white villas the length of the shoreline (and a bustling shore at that), and a massive stone fortress, with the roofs of fine-looking buildings and the spire of St Mary's church topping the walls, like a Hanse port. Here in Port Elizabeth there were few signs of comparable civilization. The place had been scarcely more than an empty beach not seven years before. On the heights above the Baakens River was not so much a fortress as a redoubt, wood- and earth-built in 1799 when the British had first taken the country from the Dutch. It was named Fort Frederick in honour of the then commander-in-chief, the late Duke of York, and close by were the Batavian barracks, to Hervey's eye in no greater state of comfort than the day they had been rudely put up. He understood them to house two companies of the 55th (Westmoreland) Regiment – fretting to be on to India, their original destination, Fairbrother had told him.

He could not blame them: in India there would be legions of little brown men who for a few annas would shave a private soldier of a morning, dhobi his linen, attend his uniform, black his boots and pipeclay his equipment. Here there were a few Hottentots who couldn't be trusted with a sweeping brush. As for women, Hervey saw none to compare with that day when he came ashore in Madras.

On a promontory above the beach there was a stone pyramid. Hervey pointed as he and Fairbrother walked along the landing stage. 'To a colonial pharo, no doubt!'

Fairbrother looked pained. 'Do you not know?'

Hervey looked askance. 'It is of some greater significance, evidently.'

'Hervey, it is all you need to know of a man.' Fairbrother said it almost wistfully.

Hervey had unconsciously reassumed his military mask on touching dry land, and bridled somewhat at his companion's obliqueness. 'Do stop riddling.'

Fairbrother was not in the least perturbed. He was not under military orders in any significant sense (he could walk away at will), and by now the two had struck up more than a professional friendship; indeed, they had forgone all rank. 'Hervey, do you know what it *is* to grieve for a woman?'

Hervey spun round. At that moment he felt the most powerful urge to strike Edward Fairbrother, an urge he had rarely felt other than in close action. The impudent assumption! Henrietta was in truth a saddening memory now, not the agonizing daily presence of the first years, nor even the dull remittent ache of the India sojourn. Yet his grief had driven him from the army, had made him for many months a melancholy companion, had sapped at his confidence and his will, distorted his view of humanity and duty, and ultimately led him to question – in many cases without an answer – so much of what he had once held dear. He knew what it was to grieve for a woman.

'I believe you have lived too long outside decent society else you would never have presumed.' He spat the words icily, intending to wound as deep by return.

Fairbrother froze. Then he put both hands to Hervey's shoulders.

Hervey did not recoil, although it was so alien a gesture.

'My dear fellow.' The voice was as warm with sympathy as Hervey's had been cold with anger. 'I believe I may indeed have lived for too long outside decent society. And in that case, for it was not principally of my own choosing, I beg you would forgive me. It was a most arrogant presumption, and I am sorry for it. I confess that I am altogether too disposed to it.'

Hervey's face softened. 'Then we have more in common than you suppose.' He turned and continued along the broad wooden walk to the quayside. 'Hadn't you better tell me what *is* the pyramid?'

'Have you heard of General Donkin?'

'I saw much of his brigade at Talavera.'

'He was briefly governor here at the Cape. He had been in India, and his wife – of but a very few years – died there, and he was returning with his young son when he received orders to assume the governorship to allow Lord Charles Somerset to return to England. It was he – not Somerset – who put the frontier onto a proper footing. There were settlers arriving from England, and there were many from my old corps too who were being promised grants of land. He surveyed the whole area. And that pyramid is a memorial to his wife.'

Hervey stopped again. He looked at the monument, then back at the brig, from which flat-bottomed boats were already warping her cargo to the landing stages, and then at his new friend. 'Her name, I imagine, was Elizabeth?'

Fairbrother nodded.

Hervey found himself vowing he would one day do the same, before recalling himself to his senses. 'I think we may delay our

221

necessary calls and business here. It is a warm day, and I think I would have you know something. Let us find a quiet spot, and I will tell you of why I spoke so sharp.'

Thanks to the fleetness of the lighters, and the address of the postal official and his steam barge, it took but a couple of hours to arrange for the officer commanding the frontier, and the district magistrate – the *landdrost* – of Port Elizabeth, to receive them. They met at the garrison headquarters, a thatched, stone-walled, single-storey affair the size and shape of the nave of a small English parish church. The officer commanding, Major Hearne of the 49th (Hertfordshire) Foot, greeted them cordially. Hervey had taken the precaution, though his friend wore only semi-military dress, of introducing Fairbrother as 'Captain' and aidant. The landdrost, a former officer in the Cape Regiment but now with a prospering farm and waistline, was equally welcoming. They explained that they were of course aware of the arrival of the new lieutenant-governor, and hoped that this presaged greater attention to the frontier, declaring very candidly that General Bourke appeared too encumbered with matters of economy to cast his customary soldier's eye on the situation.

The four of them sat down to coffee – a fiercely strong liquid made from beans brought from the East Indies – and Cape brandy, much rougher than its French begetter, if not as strong.

'How much am I to assume you know of the frontier, Colonel Hervey?' asked Major Hearne.

The officer commanding the frontier was a little older than Hervey, with a broken nose and powder-burn scar on his cheek bone. It was the first time that Hervey could remember an officer of evident seniority – and experience – who was now his subordinate. 'I have read what there is to read, Major Hearne, but I believe it would be better to assume no knowledge. I have scarce been at the Cape a month, after all.'

'Very well, Colonel. Perhaps we need go back no further than to

222

1819. The Xhosa all but overwhelmed the settled frontier, even Graham's-town. You may imagine they dealt most savagely with either sex. And they in turn were dealt with very severely, at Lord Charles Somerset's perfectly reasonable bidding. But then, with a most contrary magnanimity, he proceeded to treat with them as if he were at the Congress of Vienna.'

Hervey sipped at his brandy. This much he knew, but he would not interrupt since it was as well to know what those at the frontier believed.

Major Hearne unrolled a map on the table. 'The principal Xhosa chief was – *is* – a wily old bird named Gaika. Somerset had him sign a treaty which pushed the frontier east to the Keiskama River' (he pointed to the map) 'with the idea that the country between there and the Fish should not be settled, but patrolled to make sure the Xhosa weren't encroaching – patrolled principally from here, Fort Willshire.' He indicated the point on the Keiskama nearest the Fish, not five miles north-east, and ten miles due north of the ford and military post at Trompetter's Drift.

Again Hervey knew this, but he studied the map closely nevertheless; there was nothing like the proximity of the country to give a map life. He saw that the furthest distance between the two rivers was perhaps twenty-five miles, about the same as from Fort Willshire to the sea, and if the same distance was patrolled north-west of the fort it meant a troop mounted on good horses might make a detailed reconnaissance of the unsettled territory in two days. If they were to make but a cursory search – if the Xhosa left spoor – they might do it in only one. He thought the territory a prudent 'glacis' if the Fish River was to be the true limit of the settler parties. But so rangy a border was bound to be a temptation to both sides. 'And has the scheme been successful?' he asked, not entirely expecting the answer to be 'yes'.

'To begin with, it was. The settlements were well regulated, all of them between the Bushman's River and the Fish.' The major glanced at the landdrost.

The landdrost, sweating remarkably heavily thought Hervey for one accustomed to the country (in truth it seemed not greatly warmer than a spring day in Wiltshire), took up the invitation. 'There are two townships east of here, Colonel: Bathurst, about five miles inland from the estuary of the Kowie, which is the next river west from the Fish, and Graham's-town, fifteen or so miles further up the Kowie. There is a landdrost at each, who answers to me. They have had a difficult job. Most of the settlers were unsuited to the requirements of agriculture here: they simply did not know how to work the land. General Donkin originally stipulated that only vines and wheat were to be cultivated, since cattle were bound to attract the Xhosa. All other supplies were to come from here, or from Cape Town. But there was persistent corn blight, and many of the settlers began drifting to the townships where the Cape commissariat had set up ration depots. Not surprisingly, the landdrosts began turning a blind eye to the grow- ing practice of keeping cattle – I confess that I myself did so – for without them the settlements here would have failed half a dozen years ago.'

Hervey nodded. 'And between the Fish and the Keiskama?'

The landdrost tilted his head.

Hervey wanted to be sure. 'The cattle have been ranging into the unsettled territory?'

'Some of the Dutch burghers, especially, found the temptation too great. They even began supplying the company at Fort Willshire.'

Major Hearne took back the reins. 'In the early days the patrols from Willshire were effective in keeping the Xhosa out. And the burghers themselves are sturdy souls: they were more than capable of driving off a reiving party. But of late the incursions have been more determined.'

The landdrost, wiping his brow with a towelling swatch, reasserted his primacy. 'There has been of late a troubling affair east of Graham's-town; and Colonel, if you wish to be of assistance to the new lieutenant-governor, I believe you would do no better than take yourself there.'

Hervey looked at Major Hearne.

'I concur,' said the officer commanding the frontier.

Hervey glanced at Fairbrother, who shook his head just perceptibly, indicating he had nothing to ask.

'Very well. You had better tell me of it. And I shall want to see beyond the Fish – see Fort Willshire and the country there. Perhaps we might set out tomorrow morning, to make Graham's-town in the day.'

'I will accompany you, of course, Colonel.'

'That won't be necessary, Major Hearne. Captain Fairbrother knows the country, and your detachments at Graham's-town can give us what else we may need. You will have duties here, I know.'

The major looked relieved. 'Thank you, Colonel. In truth, my wife is close to her time and—'

Hervey held up a hand. 'Then I should positively refuse you permission to accompany me.'

'Perhaps you will dine with us, Colonel? And the landdrost too.'

Hervey smiled politely. 'That would be most welcome.'

'And Captain Fairbrother, of course.'

Fairbrother looked faintly surprised. 'Thank you . . . sir.'

CHAPTER SEVENTEEN

BUSH CRAFT

Next day

The officer commanding the frontier provided the party with a
dozen good country-breds, some with a fair bit of blood, all with
a good measure of bone, and none with feathers. The biggest, by
Hervey's reckoning, stood fifteen hands two, the smallest a full
hand less. They would not have done for a regiment at Brighton,
but he knew at once they would serve here. They would have
served in India, too, he felt certain, though requiring a little more
corn perhaps than the Marwari with which the regiment had lately
become so attached. These, he imagined, would be the look of the
remounts for the Rifles once the rough-riders had finished with
them – the quarters muscled through collected work rather
than, as now, merely on the shoulders through galloping freely,
and the coat flat and glossy rather than staring. Any of these
Algoa troopers would carry him well, for they looked handy and
no doubt possessed a good turn of speed over a quarter of a mile.

Just the sort of horse to have under him in a sudden brush with Xhosa.

Twelve horses: a second saddle horse for each of them, and a bat-horse apiece too. Corporal Wainwright had at once begun making the arrangements.

An hour or so into the march, the morning fresh and the sun climbing, Private Johnson edged his mare up alongside Hervey's.

'Does this remind thee o'anywhere, Colonel 'Ervey?'

Johnson had not spoken much to begin with on the march. Hervey suspected he had a sore head, for the Fifty-fifth's canteen had been a hospitable place, and the bingo – 'Cape Smoke' – improbably cheap. But in truth Johnson had drunk no more brandy than he was capable of, which was not a great deal: he was, anyway, long past the soldier's practice of drinking, camel-like, all that was available in order to sustain him through weeks of drought. Johnson, for all the appearance at times to the contrary, had a sense of occasion. And on those *contrary* occasions, Hervey had come to recognize that Johnson had invariably discerned something of the circumstances that he himself had not. What Johnson in his silence had been doing was allowing – consenting to – the growing attachment between Hervey and Fairbrother, for Johnson misliked (or liked) no man for his complexion. True, he thought Indians were detestable (except the ones he knew), Spaniards despicable (except all those brave *guerrilleros*), Portuguese shameless (except General de Braganza, the army and most of all Dona Isabella Delgado), and the Hottentots and Kaffirs – if that was what they were here at the Cape – beneath contempt (except that he had enjoyed the crack with several black faces in the canteen last night). But this Mr Fairbrother – *Captain* Fairbrother – as Hervey insisted on calling him, was not Indian, or Spanish or Portuguese or African: he was a gentleman; and that was all there was to be said of the matter.

Perhaps not all. The other officers whom Johnson had known

227

did not talk much about books and such like. And it seemed to him that Hervey was enjoying it a very great deal. If Captain Hervey – or Major, or Colonel, or whatever it was today (he truly thought brevets more complicated than . . .) – if Captain Hervey needed one thing it was a good friend. And not a woman-friend (Johnson had his decided opinions on these) but another officer. There was Captain Peto, but he was always at sea, and there was Colonel Howard, but he was always in London; and since poor Major Strickland was killed there was no one in the Sixth with whom Hervey could talk on what it was that officers talked about – officers and *gentlemen* talked about.

Colonel Hervey sometimes talked to him, but he knew it could not be the same. And in Hounslow it had all so nearly come to an end. He did not think of the prospect of a prison hulk so much as the deprivation of that life that had come to mean everything to him: the Sixth and 'his' officer. People had always been good to him – or at least *fair*. And over the business of the coral . . . well, he had not expected to remain the commanding officer's groom after that. Yet here he was, taken back like the son in the Bible who went off and ate with the pigs. What had he to complain about ever when such a man as Colonel Hervey was his officer? He had never known anything of the coral; he was only doing as he was told. But he supposed that wouldn't have made any difference if Colonel Hervey – and Serjeant-major Armstrong and the others – hadn't been there to help him.

Yes, he certainly approved of 'Captain' Fairbrother. He was the sort of friend that Colonel Hervey needed. Perhaps if he had had a friend in Hounslow . . . No, he must not think like that. But why else would his officer want to marry this Lady Lankester, someone he'd hardly ever met? It was none of his business, of course: what an officer chose to do was his own affair, and quite beyond the understanding of the rank and file. But he did not relish the idea of serving a new mistress. There would never be anybody like Mrs Hervey – not even Mrs Delgado (although she was the one he wanted most to see filling her shoes) . . .

Hervey concluded where Johnson was thinking of. 'It puts me in mind of Salisbury Plain. On a fair day, that is.'

'That's what I reckoned, sir. Is it all like this? Ah thought there were jungle, an' lions an' things.'

Hervey turned to Fairbrother, with a rueful smile that invited a response to Johnson's boundless question on the natural history of the Continent.

'Well now, Private Johnson,' began Fairbrother, endearing himself at once by the appellation of rank, however lowly. 'Do you recall how many days you were sailing to the Cape?'

Johnson frowned. 'Abaht fifty, I think it were, sir.'

'About fifty; and perhaps some forty-five of those were spent traversing the coast of Africa, one way or another; perhaps a hundred and fifty miles in the day. You may therefore calculate the very great distance that is this continent from north to south. And in the space of those several thousands of miles, there is all manner of country – desert where a man would bake like bread in an oven, and be dried like a piece of leather for want of water. Then there is grassland, as here, where there are great herds of all manner of beasts – lion, elephant, antelope, camelopard, though here there are not so many, for the Xhosa and the Dutch have driven them out of the grazing lands to make room for their cattle. And in the middle of the continent, where the rain falls very heavy, and the growth is prodigious, there is jungle – the deepest forest you might ever see, with apes of every description living in the trees without ever placing a foot upon the ground.'

Johnson's brow was screwed up very tight. 'Don't think ah'd like that, sir. Ah wouldn't like being somewhere there were things over thi 'ead.'

Fairbrother's expression almost matched Johnson's as he struggled to make sense of the pronunciation and vocabulary. 'And things underfoot.'

'Ooh ay, sir. When we were in India, or wherever it were – in

229

t'jungle there – there were all sorts o' things, an' snakes as thick as thi leg.'

Hervey smiled to himself. Johnson was allowed his exaggeration – except that in Johnson's imagination it was no exaggeration at all.

''As tha been in t'jungle then, sir?'

Fairbrother was increasingly charmed by Johnson's candour (there had been occasions, when first he had joined the Royal African Corps, when he had been derided for his presumed jungle origins). 'I have. But not, I imagine, as much as Colonel Hervey. And, of course, I have no knowledge of how similar are the forests of India to those of Africa.'

Johnson was not inclined to think the differences very great; he had disliked the forests of India, and he had no doubt that he would dislike those of Africa just as much. 'So there isn't any jungles 'ere, then, sir – in t'Cape, I mean?'

'No, there is no jungle. There is forest, quite dense, but we are not near enough to the Equator to make it so . . . fearsome. We may see elephant – I think we *shall* see elephant – and leopard; or rather we shall *hear* leopard, in the night. And the going will become thick with scrub near the rivers . . .'

Although he gave the impression otherwise, Johnson was not greatly exercised by the topography, or fauna, of the Eastern Cape. It was merely that the place did in truth resemble Salisbury Plain so much, which he had grown almost as fond of as Hervey had been during their sojourns in Wiltshire. He was intrigued by how quickly the country here might change, and into what. At the edge of the Wiltshire plain there were fields of corn or cattle; what was at the edge of this plain?

Fairbrother truly did like Johnson. Hervey could see it. And yet Hervey could only wonder what would have been his new friend's reaction had he seen the *real* Johnson, the man undiminished by the business of the coral smuggling. Johnson had lost a measure of his cheeriness, his unbounded – at times almost senseless –

optimism. At first Hervey had enjoyed the respite, for Johnson's chirpy certainty he at times found decidedly wearing; but after a while he had come to feel it like the loss of an old, if irascible, relative, the loss infinitely greater than the respite. This presage, first-swallow-like, of Johnson's return to a state of (respectful) familiarity was therefore much to be welcomed. The leaving of Hounslow – of England – had in the end been so precipitate, what with endless duty calls as well as family, and then the requirements of his betrothal, that he had not been able to give his groom-orderly more than passing attention. He had been rather thankful of it in fact, for anger, exasperation and disappointment had been mixed in powerful measure, and it was as well there had been no opportunity to delve into it. Now it was meet to restore their former relations.

At Graham's Town, a settlement of few stone buildings but to Hervey's mind a busy, optimistic sort of place nevertheless, they found the detachment commander was laid low by an attack of dysentery. His lieutenant was new, so it was the landdrost who received them and told them of the 'Clay Pits Trouble', as already it was becoming known on the frontier. Hervey listened to the landdrost carefully, glancing periodically at Fairbrother for any sign of dispute, but seeing none. The landdrost was an old Cape hand, who had seen service with both the Cape Regiment and then the Albany Levy. He took the view that General Donkin – and Lord Charles Somerset – had made admirable plans, but that in reality the life of the frontier was not to be regulated as if it were a place subject to the usual laws of property and the border itself a mere party wall. The affair of the clay pits, he observed, was but one example of the 'untidiness' of the frontier and the difficulties in applying the 'Donkin doctrine' to the letter.

The clay pits, explained the landdrost, were about five leagues due east, an easy enough three-hour ride – two with fresh horses at a gallop. And the Fish River was two and a half leagues beyond.

231

The pits were firmly within the colony itself therefore, not the unsettled, patrolled tract. The clay had been used for generations by the Xhosa for dyeing blankets and to paint themselves. The trouble was, he told them, the clay pits were on the farm of one John Brown, who had come east with the first 1820 settler parties. Brown complained that of late he had lost a hundred and sixty cattle and a dozen horses, and that the occasional patrols from Graham's Town, or Fort Willshire in the unsettled tract, were no protection. The soldiers, he claimed – Hottentot troops – merely hid in ambush, shot at the Xhosa as they approached the pits and then cut off the ears of those they had killed as proof of their zeal and prowess. This, suggested the landdrost, accounted for growing Xhosa enmity. The trouble was, other settlers in the area were trading with the clay-seekers: cattle, ivory, hides and gum in exchange for beads, buttons, wire and trinkets. And since the settlers' cattle was for the most part unbranded, it was not difficult to imagine the temptation for the Xhosa. One of the settlers had been killed not many months ago when a patrol had appeared unexpectedly and the Xhosa thought they had been betrayed. It was therefore no longer merely a matter of petty lawbreaking but of murder, and – though he was guarded in his expression of it – the landdrost evidently felt that the military were not cooperating as fully as they might in his investigations.

'What's to be done?' asked Hervey.

The landdrost's jaw jutted. 'I would wish to have one of Brown's neighbours by the name of Mahoney arrested for illegal trading, and his land confiscated. That ought to still the activity. I have asked the military to station two men on Brown's property until such time that I can determine on a conciliatory course with the Xhosa. Brown's claims of losses I find loose and exaggerated. They'd be wholly impossible to verify without actually tracing the cattle to the Xhosa kraals. Might I accompany you? At least as far as to Brown's farm and the clay pits.'

Hervey had no objection. He trusted his own powers of

232

observation and discernment in strictly military affairs (if there could *be* such a thing as strictly military), but in judging the civil conditions at the frontier he knew he would be wise to have counsel of the civil authority.

The following morning, Hervey and his party, accompanied by the landdrost and three pandours who would act as scouts – Hottentots from the Cape Corps detachment – left Graham's Town for Brown's farm and the clay pits. It was another fine day, with a few high, barred clouds to remind them that the sea was not so very distant, but otherwise in the vast carpet of green and yellow – rich grass that sorely tempted the horses, and a flower he did not quite recognize – Hervey could have believed himself in the middle of a continent rather than at its furthest edge. Johnson, however, was soon voicing his disappointment by the lack of game, big or otherwise. They saw the odd bushbuck, and plenty of birds, but nothing, he reckoned, they would not have seen in India. The landdrost, drawn in by Johnson's simple curiosity, as Fairbrother had been the day before, explained that when they reached the Fish River they would see more; and if then they were to ride south towards its estuary, they would see hippopotamus, buffalo, antelope in many guises, and perhaps even the black rhinoceros.

The names meant less to him than the landdrost supposed, especially since Johnson did not reveal his ignorance. He knew what a buffalo was, and for that matter antelope (he understood, too, that there were different types), but hippopotamus and rhinoceros were wholly novel. In any case, what he wanted more than anything to see was elephant. In India he had become quite used to them: they were but a part of the scene of daily life, domestic even. In Africa, however, he had heard that elephants were twice the size of their Indian cousins, with tusks that might gore a horse in an instant, toss it aloft indeed; and that these beasts ranged in herds ten times more destructive than a whole brigade of charging cavalry. This he wanted to see at a safe distance yet close enough to judge for himself the power of those massive tusks – any one of which, besides spelling death, might also bring him considerable fortune.

The road to Brown's farm was a good one. It was not so much made as well travelled, though not by waggon, so that it was evenly worn rather than rutted, allowing a comfortable pace at both walk and trot. In two and a half hours, as the sun was nearing its highest, though its heat was no more than a June day on Salisbury Plain (and certainly nothing to what they had been used to in Bengal at this season), the party arrived at the farm. There was no marking its boundary save for a stone at the roadside, no fence or cleared perimeter, but half a mile distant they could see a cluster of white-washed buildings, and wispy smoke rising from a single chimney.

'Do you know where his cattle graze?' asked Hervey, puzzled that there was no sign of them.

'Beyond the buildings yonder,' replied the landdrost, looking about him at the good spring grass. 'He ought by rights to have driven them up here by now, but the water's all on the other side of the farm, and it's easier. Brown's not the most industrious of men. This is good soil here, and he ought to be growing maize, wheat even; but ploughing's hard work, especially when cattle take no looking to at all.'

'Except when the Xhosa take a fancy to them.'

'Exactly so.'

When they came to the farmhouse, a plain, single-storey, stone-built affair with an iron roof, they found the two men of the Cape Corps saddling their horses in the lean-to stabling.

'Is John Brown hereabout?' called the landdrost.

The men, both Irish, red-coated but hatless, looked tired and dirty. It appeared to dawn on them slowly that here were reinforcements. 'Ay, sor,' said one of them, belatedly knuckling his forehead and standing to attention. 'T'other side of the farm.

Xhosa were thieving again last night, sor. Drove off a hundred head and more.'

Hervey decided that this was now as much military business as civil. 'Stand easy, Corporal. What is Brown doing about it?'

The man turned to him, looking relieved to be in receipt of orders again. 'Sor! Him and his men are trying to catch loose horses, and then he says he's going to ride to Blaufontein to get up a posse of burghers, sor – Dutchmen.'

Hervey looked at the landdrost.

'He's within his rights, though I would wish he didn't take the Dutch. They're a good deal more savage, and that's the last thing we need.'

'I think the Xhosa've taken one of the boys with them as well, sor,' said the corporal, looking now to the landdrost. 'At least I hope they've taken him, and not just stuck a spear in him.'

'One of the Hottentots?'

'No, sor, one of the white boys.'

'Oh God,' groaned the landdrost. 'That gives us little option but to chase them hard. What do you think, Captain Fairbrother?'

Fairbrother and the landdrost had got on well together the previous night. They had met before, when Fairbrother had come with his company of Royal Africans in the late troubles. The landdrost was evidently more disposed to take his advice than he would have been the Graham's Town lieutenant's. 'I am of the opinion that if the Xhosa are chased by Dutch burghers they'll fight as if it's one band of brigands against another. If they're pursued by red coats – they're not stupid – they'll know it's a matter of government.'

'And?' asked Hervey.

'I doubt the boy would survive a fight between brigands. If they see that government is after them then they'll be forced to think. As I said, they're not stupid. And in Xhosa law, the tribe as a whole is responsible for any felony.'

'Sor?'

'Carry on, Corporal,' said Hervey.

'Sor! We heard yesterday the Xhosa've been raiding north of here as well, in the Dutch lands. I think the burghers'll be turning out anyway, if they haven't already.'

The landdrost's brow furrowed. 'That changes things. If there's a general irruption of Xhosa, as it seems there may be, then I think, Colonel Hervey, we must send word back to Graham's-town for troops to come forward. And to Port Elizabeth too.'

Hervey nodded. 'By what means does Fort Willshire communicate with Graham's-town? Will they not have detected the trouble? I should very much hope so.'

'And should I. They communicate by messenger via Trompetter's Drift. We'll know if they've detected anything when we get there.'

Hervey looked thoughtful. 'I think, Landdrost, you had better go yourself, had you not?'

The landdrost was uncertain. 'I can scarcely leave you to wander the frontier, Colonel Hervey. I thought I would accompany you to Fort Willshire.'

'Indeed, of course,' conceded Hervey at once, 'but the situation has changed markedly, as you yourself have said. Your influence at Graham's-town will be – if I may say it – of considerably more profit than chaperoning me here. It's not as I would have wished, but there's opportunity now for a meeting with the Xhosa, and I would observe them closely. Indeed, it is a quite exceptional opportunity.'

The landdrost looked troubled. 'Colonel, with respect, you cannot treat with the Xhosa as did Lord Charles Somerset, believing them to be honourable men.'

Hervey smiled a little. 'I have no intention of doing so, not until they are capable of proving it beyond question – which I don't imagine for one minute they will be able to do. No, I think we may bring them to a fight of sorts, and then see how they acquit themselves.'

'You will deliberately bring on a fight, Colonel Hervey?'

Hervey smiled again, but wryly. 'I should rather they gave back the boy and the cattle *without* a fight, but in the circumstances I hardly expect they will. I shall be most careful in it, I assure you!'

The spoor of a hundred or more head of cattle was not difficult to follow. In any case, Fairbrother was certain the Xhosa must drive them due east to begin with, for they could not afford to go near the post at Trompetter's Drift. At this time of year, he explained, the river would be full but not swollen, and there were several deep fords downstream of the drift. There were two other rivers the Xhosa must cross before getting to relative haven the other side of the Keiskama, he said, pointing them out on his own much-embellished map. The Baka River was the greater obstacle – greater even than the Keiskama, though not as extensive – and he reckoned the Xhosa would want to make its banks by nightfall to be able to ford it at dawn; or perhaps even to attempt a crossing after dark since the moon was so full. It was about twenty miles, easily within a day's march for the Xhosa, even driving a hundred head of cattle. However, although the first river after the Fish, the Gwalana, was not much of an obstacle, it might slow them down more than they were prepared to accept: tired, thirsty cattle could become unmanageable when suddenly presented with water. In which case, Fairbrother argued, the Xhosa would be more likely to head *north*-east after crossing the Fish, skirting the muddy source of the Gwalana, and then continuing north-east to the Keiskama. So, if instead of tracking them across the Fish they rode fast for Trompetter's Drift, changed horses, and then made for the head of the Gwalana, they would *intercept* the Xhosa rather than merely trying to catch them up.

They rode hard on this prediction, reaching Trompetter's Drift in the middle of the afternoon. Here they changed horses, and Hervey, concerned lest the Xhosa were taking the different course,

237

ordered the post serjeant to send men to patrol the far bank of the Gwalana. They then rode on without rest, reaching the muddy head of the Gwalana an hour and a half later.

'I think we must remain mounted at all times,' said Fairbrother as they approached the darker scrub about the headwater. 'The Xhosa would fancy themselves superior in any fight, but they know they can't out-run a horse.'

Hervey saw no reason to dispute it. He was, in fact, surprised by the thickness of the *bushveld* here, and the thorns and tangled grass. The country had been getting trappier by the mile since they crossed the Fish, but here it was *so* trappy they were obliged to follow animal trails – and much to Hervey's unease, for he imagined a charging elephant or rhinoceros would deal horribly with half a dozen men and horses in single file. Moreover, the country was ideal for ambush; he was grateful for the saddle's extra height.

'I'm beginning to wonder if the notion of mounted rifles is a sound one,' he said, as if turning the idea over in his mind as he spoke.

'As long as they're trained to fire from the saddle as well as on foot, they should serve,' replied Fairbrother measuredly. 'The country's not universally close, as we saw. And the Xhosa *throw* their spears, they don't thrust them home – not unless their situation's desperate. I should say that the rifle is the very best way to hold them off.'

Hervey searched the cover intently, though since it was too dense to reveal even the crouching leopard, he felt his chances of detecting a black spearman were next to nothing. By what sign did the Xhosa reveal themselves? Was it by the spear itself, the sickening thud of its point in flesh? If they were to confront the reiving party it would be well that *they* ambushed *them*, for the Xhosa's scouting skills would surely be at least the equal of their own.

'Well, we have half a dozen carbines. It will have to do. Assuming they drive the cattle through that open stretch yonder' (he nodded to the scattered scrub they had just ridden through) 'if we show a surprise front I don't imagine there'll be much throwing or stabbing. And they can hardly run back since they must think they're pursued as well. We shall call on them to lay down their spears and then interrogate them about the boy. One of them – the leader, if we can find him – we'll take to Graham's-town to be dealt with judicially. I would think he'd be willing to talk to us about what the Xhosa are up to in exchange for his neck, would you not? The rest can leave without their weapons once we get a patrol from Fort Willshire to escort them across the Keiskama.'

Fairbrother nodded. 'You know, Hervey, what I should really like is to meet Gaika. He *is* the Xhosa's paramount chief, after all. He has questions to answer – why he breaks the 1820 treaty, for instance. Oh, I know at Graham's-town they said Gaika has no more idea of a treaty than a monkey, but Gaika's no fool, and he must know the consequences of what his people are doing. So why does he permit it? This is what your Somervile ought most usefully to know.'

Hervey pondered the proposition. 'I think you are in the right. But are there not officials who speak regularly with him?'

Fairbrother smiled. 'I very much doubt it, Hervey. This is Africa; it is not India – or even America. There has not evolved that notion of subtle dealing with the native tribes. I have read much on this, and I confess – against my better instinct – that I am sorely impressed with the method. In Canada, for instance, you have a most estimable corps of men well versed in native affairs, and there is in consequence little trouble with the Indian tribes. And in India you send fine men from Oxford. Here, those who do the King's bidding are not in the main men you would share a gentlemanly bottle of claret with, and—'

A shot. So loud as to make every horse start. One of the pandours rolled backwards from the saddle, hitting the ground hard and with a scream like a woman. Corporal Wainwright barged past and fired into a thorn bush (he alone had seen the flash). He fired his second pistol. There was a shriek. He sprang from the saddle and began cutting at the thorn with his sabre as Hervey jumped down to tend the motionless redcoat. Without a word Johnson made to gather up the loose reins, even as the other two pandours were high-tailing back towards Trompetter's Drift.

'Stop! Damn you!' shouted Fairbrother, drawing his pistol.

They neither heard nor cared.

Fairbrother sent a ball after them, but it only hastened the flight. 'Bastard coward-Kaffirs!' he spat.

Two spears struck the held horses. They squealed and reared. Two Xhosa, hair reddened, wide-eyed and naked but for civet aprons, rushed at them whooping wildly, clutching broken-shaft spears like short swords. Hervey sprang up and drew his sabre; Wainwright stood square to parry. But Fairbrother spurred forward, just getting in front of the dismounted pair as the Xhosa closed. He swung his mare's quarters left into them, drawing his sabre as he did so, gaining the crucial moment's surprise and getting in a nearside cut, almost severing an arm at the elbow before either of them could strike.

The second Xhosa thrust the spear-sword at Fairbrother's thigh. It hit the cheroot case in his pocket and glanced off into the thick leather of the saddle arch. The Xhosa's eyes rolled with sudden horror as Fairbrother brought the handguard of his sabre down hard into the man's face, splitting open his nose like a ripe fruit. As the Xhosa crumpled clutching his bloody flesh, Fairbrother drove the point of his sabre deep behind the clavicle, then drew his second pistol and fired a following shot at the other man. The ball struck between the shoulders, and he fell writhing – then twitching; then still.

Fairbrother sheathed his sabre and took out his little Collier revolver. But he had no target. The Xhosa were gone as fast as they'd come.

Corporal Wainwright, hacking furiously at the thorn, shouted suddenly. 'Here! And alive, sir!' He pulled the terrified man from cover, and saw the hole in his shoulder.

Johnson had had to dismount to get the led horses in hand. He was struggling still, though one of them, the spearhead deep in its belly, was weakening.

Hervey saw that the pandour lay lifeless, so he closed to the wounded Xhosa instead. The ball had struck in the same place as the Burman ball had struck *him*, three years before. But there would be no surgeon of Mr Ritchie's vulnerary skill to save this man's arm; not unless they could get him to Graham's Town, which they could not do inside of twenty-four hours – even by way of Trompetter's Drift and with no Xhosa to trouble them. Not unless they rode through the night; even supposing they could find their way by moonlight.

Fairbrother had already calculated the odds, and the time and the distance. 'We must back-track for Trompetter's Drift at once,' he began, calmly but insistently. 'We might make a couple of leagues before nightfall, and every mile we get nearer the post is another mile further from the Xhosa, except we can't be certain they won't follow. We might run into the patrol, too.' He looked hard at their captive as Wainwright dressed the wound.

'We can't leave him, I think,' said Hervey.

'Would you leave the pandour if he weren't dead?'

'No, indeed: not in a red coat!'

'And an enemy of that red coat?'

'A *wounded* enemy, Fairbrother. I would not chance him to the wild things here. Are you trying me?'

Fairbrother smiled grimly. 'I am.'

And Hervey thought he knew why. Did Fairbrother imagine he might somehow think the worth of a man's life, the effort to be expended in its preservation, was in some measure dependent on the shade of his skin? That the white – the grubby white – of a British soldier entitled him to the greater effort, more than any half-caste, and infinitely more than an ebony-coloured savage, who was so far removed from the decencies of good society as to be little more than an animal, to be killed to prevent its predation? 'I believe you are more a soldier than you will admit. You are content to shoot a pandour in a red coat – in the back – and yet I surmise that a stricken enemy engages every last sentiment.'

'It is not possible to shoot a fleeing man anywhere but in the back, Hervey.'

'I know that!'

'And by what right do we expect quarter, and aid, when we are fallen if we do not treat with an enemy, however base, in the same way?'

'You push at an open door.'

Fairbrother sighed. 'I wanted only to be sure. It has not always been the way on the frontier.'

Hervey could believe it. It had not always been the way any-where. He looked about him: a dead redcoat, two dying horses, two pandours fled: not circumstances to be proud of. An ambush, not much less; an affair of bad scouting (or at least *superior* scout-ing on the part of the Xhosa). This was no adornment to his reputation. But much more than that, it was notice that they them-selves might yet end as vulture-meat in a tract of country that could no longer boast the King's peace. He was not afraid, how-ever. That sort of fear did not trouble him (he would stand his ground abler than any man who might challenge him hereabouts). Rather was he suddenly aware of how much he had taken for granted – that the Xhosa, whose reputation was hardly fearsome after all, were not as the Burmans or Maharatas, the Pindarees or the Jhauts. Neither was this country desert or tropical forest, nor like anything he had seen in the Peninsula or in France, or Canada. He knew he had been worsted. Courage and address on Wainwright's and Fairbrother's part had saved the day. And he was already drawing his conclusions. He had proceeded to the frontier in pursuit of the reiving party as if he had been commanding a troop of His Majesty's Cavalry of the Line. It would not serve.

CHAPTER EIGHTEEN

THE SUN NEVER SETS WITHOUT FRESH NEWS

Later

An hour of straining every muscle and of bending every sense to the detecting of concealed Xhosa induced a feeling of exhaustion quite unlike any Hervey could remember. Although reason told him that every mile meant greater safety, in his water he could not quite feel it. Only when the scrub began to thin – both in thickness of the thorn and its occurrence – did he begin to feel the advantage shifting back in his direction. He had been in closer country – the Burman jungle, the Canadian forest – but he had never before supposed that the country gave the natural advantage to his opponent. The Burmans had known their jungle, and the Iroquois their forest, but Hervey had been certain it was possible to match them; here, in this strange mix of country, he half believed the Xhosa had some magic by which they transported themselves. How else had they covered the ground so quickly, and taken them unawares at the Gwalana's head?

The wounded Xhosa had soon lost consciousness, and a fever now burned. Fairbrother had tried at first to question him, and to dull his pain and loosen his tongue with brandy; but he had learned nothing. Neither had they met the patrol from Trompetter's Drift (it was not surprising: their charge, as Hervey himself had given it, was to scout the *east* bank of the river), nor even one of the routine patrols from Fort Willshire. Were the patrols diverted north, dealing with an irruption into the old Dutch areas?

The party's one piece of fortune was that the pandours had returned to duty. Fairbrother had found them crouching in the scrub a mile or so from the Gwalana's head, frightened, confused, only too pleased to see authority again and willing to submit to any punishment. Hervey had berated them in English – which they partially understood (and his manner had left no doubt) – and then Fairbrother had berated them in their own language, calling down every ancestral curse he could recall, shaming them to the point that they looked broken men.

'Don't let them fool you,' he said, when at length Hervey dismissed them with but a day's stoppage of pay. 'They're contrite now, but they'd run again as soon as look at you. We neither pay 'em enough nor treat them as men, half the time. That and the Hottentot's natural disinclination to soldiery. You have your martial races in India, do you not? Well, Hervey, these Hottentots ain't no martial race.'

For the time being, however, the pandours worked willingly cutting thorn bushes, gathering wood, chivvied by Johnson, encouraged by Wainwright. There was perhaps an hour's daylight left when they halted for the night – another league between them and the Xhosa, another league nearer the post at Trompetter's Drift. *If* they had been capable of it. The horses were done, needing water and rest; they had led them for at least half the way. They themselves were footsore and just as weary. Half their kit and provisions they had abandoned (two horses destroyed and the priority to powder and cartridges). But they could not be certain that they *were* putting any distance between them and the Xhosa. Fairbrother had said he could not imagine why they would follow, but then, he had been first to admit his surprise that a Xhosa should carry a musket. Hervey had been sure they needed time to prepare for the night, to meet the Xhosa on ground of his choosing, properly disposed, ready. It was what he would have done with the Sixth in any rearguard, and he would do the same with a troop of mounted riflemen too. Thus far the prudence of the Peninsula applied as well in Africa.

When he had done all that he could for the security of the party – thorn bushes across the approaches to the bivouac, just out of spear-throwing distance, fires laid at the four points of the compass, with powder trails to each, and every man told off to an alarm post – Hervey spoke quietly to his coverman. 'Rather a scrape, I'm afraid, Corporal Wainwright.'

'Ay, sir.'

'One of us must be awake at all times – you or I.'

'Ay, sir.'

'The pandours will stand sentry at the thorn in turn, but one or other of us will have to see they keep post.'

Corporal Wainwright nodded. He understood perfectly well. Johnson was probably as capable, but he did not have the rank, and it would be unfair. And Captain Fairbrother, for all that he had fought with as much nerve as he had ever seen, was not *regiment*. 'Sir.'

'It will be dark in half an hour. Captain Fairbrother says the Xhosa don't as a rule attack during the night unless they're sure of their advantage, but I wouldn't rule out an attack at last light, perhaps to rattle us, and then a full-blown affair at dawn. So we may hear them all night, keeping us from sleep, or else they'll use the dark to creep into position for the dawn. Either way, not a happy prospect.'

'We'll be right, sir.'

Hervey smiled to himself. This was not bravado, just the proper confidence of a non-commissioned officer who had learned his trade in a dozen different scrapes. 'I would have wished those pandours had a faithful taste for scouting, that's all. We should have a better notion of whether we'd been followed.'

'Maybe, sir; but not certain. We're doing only what we'd be doing anyway.'

Hervey nodded. Wainwright spoke the truth. There could never be a time to take the night's ease for granted.

'Do we break camp *before* first light if we hear nothing in the night, sir?'

It was the usual practice, so long as the enemy could not get wind of the move: not an easy thing to manage even with some distance between the lines, so to speak. Here, where the Xhosa might rush in from no further than the spear's flight, and with the moon set, it would be the very devil of a fight. No, Hervey's instinct was to let the dawn come, when they would then have the advantage of their firearms. He shook his head. 'We'll stand to as if defending our position, Corporal Wainwright.' And then, fearing he had exposed his own doubts too much, he half smiled. 'It's of no matter. I do not count the Xhosa especially brave. Had they pressed a little more determinedly we should have been caught, I think. There cannot have been but the three of them.'

'I reckoned so too, sir. But I think as I should do the scouting in the morning. If they gets behind us tonight then I don't think the pandours'll be right. I mightn't know the country as well as them, but I'd do a better job if it comes to another fight.'

Hervey put a hand to Wainwright's shoulder. 'I don't doubt it – than both of them combined. Very well. And you'll take the first watch, until midnight?'

'Sir.'

'Good man.' Hervey turned; but then he had second thoughts.

'We've come a long way since that morning on Warminster Common, have we not, Corporal Wainwright?'

'Sir.' Wainwright smiled ruefully. 'And not yet five and twenty.'

Hervey had not considered it. 'Indeed?'

'Tomorrow, sir.'

'The strangest thing!'

'There's not been too many birthdays since the Common when I haven't heard a shot, sir.'

'The devil!'

'But I reckon it must be the same with you, sir.'

Hervey knew it, but he doubted he had ever been in such position: no notion of where or how many the enemy, and so little with which to defend himself – and his reputation. He smiled back, dutifully. 'What should we do with peace, eh, Corporal Wainwright?'

'Ay, sir,' replied his coverman, just as dutifully.

Hervey nodded, fixing him with a look that said everything that would not be permitted in words, and then turned and stepped sharply to where Johnson was crouching by the pack saddles.

Johnson stood and held out a mess of tea. 'Just mashed.'

Hervey took it, again with but a nod. It had been more times than either of them could count: Johnson's ability to make tea in the most unpromising conditions seemed rarely short of miraculous. There had been tea before dawn on the morning of Waterloo, when the rain had lashed down all night (Hervey reckoned there could have been few general officers so favoured), and Johnson had since perfected what he called his 'patent storm kettle', first fashioned ten years ago in an Indian bazaar. It was rather easier now to get a flame, though: no need of flint and tinder-box with Mr Walker's new sulphur friction matches.

'Thank you, Johnson. You must remind me, when we get back to England, to see if Welch and Stalker will give you a pension for your storm kettle.'

'Ay, right, sir. So tha does think we'll get back then? Ah sort o' thought we'd end up 'ere wi' an ass's thing up us arse.'

247

Hervey could not have suppressed the smile if he had tried. '*Assegai.*'

'Summat sharp, any road.'

Hervey shook his head. 'Johnson, after all we've seen, I don't think we shall meet our end by a gang of cattle reivers carrying spears.'

'Well, ah'm right glad tha's sure on it, sir. Them spears looked the job to me. Wouldn't 'ave managed if Cap'n Fairbrother 'adn't got in first. Ah reckoned ah weren't long for this world.'

Hervey was determined to be bright. 'Oh, I think "Guard" and then "Cut One" would have done the business.'

Johnson frowned. 'Well, ah'm right glad tha's sure on 't, sir. Does tha want any snap?'

Hervey nodded. 'I think I'll have one of those corn cakes. Has Captain Fairbrother had anything?'

'Ah took 'im some tea, but 'e said 'e didn't want owt else. 'E's been cleanin them guns o' 'is since we stopped.' He shook his head. 'That blackie's poorly, sir. Ah tried to give 'im tea an' all, but 'e weren't wi' it.'

'That was good of you. I doubt he'll see the morning, I'm afraid.' Hervey took a second corn cake, for Fairbrother, and a bottle of brandy. 'We'll stand to in about half an hour.'

Johnson nodded, the sideways nod that said he understood and would get on with it, come what may.

Hervey took the bottle and the corn cakes to where Fairbrother sat under a milkwood tree reloading his pistols after their vigorous cleaning. 'I can't say I like these, but we must eat something.'

Fairbrother took the corn cake with little pleasure. 'You are content with things for the night, now?'

Hervey sat down next to him, uncorked the bottle and poured brandy into Fairbrother's mess tin, and then his own. 'As content as may be. I only wish those pandours had been able to show more address. It's the strangest thing to have no idea what your enemy intends or where he is.'

At that moment one of the pandours started suddenly, scuttling back a good ten feet from the bush he was posted next to. Hervey reached for his pistol, but it was soon evident the man had given himself a fright.

Fairbrother continued calmly sipping his brandy. 'To the man who is afraid, everything rustles.'

Hervey laid down his pistol, and looked at him ruefully. 'Colony lore, or your own observation?'

'Sophocles.'

'Oh.' Hervey half smiled. 'You would get on famously in the Sixth.'

'I think not.'

Hervey tutted. 'I shan't indulge you in your self-disregard. You would be received handsomely for what you did at the river.'

Fairbrother finished his brandy, and Hervey poured him more. 'You are not a poet, Colonel?'

Hervey braced himself: Fairbrother was the most intriguing mix of superiority and resentment he had known, a man who had sat with his books in Cape Town for ... how many years he didn't rightly know, and yet able to comport himself in the field as if he had been continually on campaign. Neither did it seem to him a contemptuous sort of courage, a display of scorn for the fears of the common herd, despite the Sophocles. When this sojourn at the frontier was over, Hervey was determined that Edward Fairbrother should have some proper place in the military society of the Cape. It was not merely a matter of desert, but of resource.

'I am not a poet. Though I am fond of Milton.'

Fairbrother nodded gravely. 'I was rather minded of Wordsworth.'

'I confess I've never read him.'

'Really? You astonish me, Colonel Hervey. So martial a man, Wordsworth.'

Hervey frowned incredulously. 'Martial? I thought him pastoral.'

'In part, of course. But he was an enthusiastic militiaman, as I have read.'

'I did not know it. Good.'

'So you will not know "The Happy Warrior"?'

'No.'

'"Who is the Happy Warrior? Who is he that every man in arms should wish to be?"'

'And the answer?'

'The answer is contained in but a single sentence.'

'Then it must be trite.'

'Ah, indeed you are the man I thought! A single sentence, but of many dozen lines!'

'Then I would have no more of it now, unless it contains anything of defence against the Xhosa. I shall read it when we return to the Cape.'

Fairbrother smiled. 'I leave the comfort of my hearth and the solace of my books, come within a trice of death, and shall pass the night in anticipation of a murderous onslaught, and yet I am content to do so in the company of a happy warrior.'

'And a Collier revolver.'

Fairbrother smiled even broader. 'Yes, I confess I am excessively content to be in the company of Mr Collier.'

'Then tell me, what do you believe the Xhosa will do?'

Fairbrother sighed as he took another sip of his brandy. 'The Xhosa are a simple people, Hervey. They are superstitious, as are all the native tribes, but they aren't troubled greatly by the spirits of their ancestors, as the Bushmen are. They will not have a fear of the night, only inasmuch as they might meet a leopard. And *unlike* their cousins the Zulu, of whom you will have heard, they fear death' (he smiled wryly) 'which is to our advantage, of course.'

'But they do not fear it any more at night than day.'

'No. Indeed, if anything, they are quite animated by the coming of the night. They have a saying: *alitshonanga lingenandaba* – the sun never sets without fresh news.'

It was not what Hervey wanted to hear. 'I don't think *our* Xhosa will see the morning.'

Fairbrother thought for some time before speaking. 'We should try to take out the ball from his shoulder.'

Hervey looked bemused. 'I once had a ball taken from mine, but I knew very little of it. Do *you* know how it is done?'

'I have seen a ball removed, yes. Several, indeed.'

It was not the same as knowing what to do, but he was in part encouraged. 'Shall you try?'

Fairbrother rose. 'Bring the bottle.'

They removed the bloody dressing from the unconscious Xhosa. He did not stir. Fairbrother decided not to force brandy into him, giving the bottle back to Hervey instead.

'If he wakes, pour this down his throat in as big a measure as you can.'

The light was beginning to fail, but it made no difference, for Fairbrother had no surgeon's instruments and therefore no need of light. His would be all probing with the finger, hoping he could identify iron from bone. How he would extract the ball he had no idea: only when he saw how deep it lay might he begin thinking.

'At least the wound's clean,' he said, rolling up his sleeves. 'There's no cloth and such taken in by the ball, as far as I can see. It's that which makes a wound putrid.'

He found the ball easily enough, and not deep. At least, he was fairly sure it was the ball; he would need more light to be certain.

'His pulse is very weak,' said Hervey, thinking that so deep a sleep must be close to death.

'I can't help it,' said Fairbrother, dabbing away some of the dried blood about the wound, though fresh soon followed. 'And it's as well, since he'd now be screaming like a hyena.' He turned. 'Johnson, would you fetch me a small spoon, please.'

Johnson brought a silver teaspoon, which he had had since progging in Vitoria a dozen years before.

251

Hervey watched as Fairbrother began easing it into the wound, as carefully as he might spoon for the stone in a ripe plum.

'I think I have it.'

Indeed, out came the one-ounce ball with not a great deal more trouble than the stone from the fruit, and clean with it.

'I am all astonishment, Fairbrother. I never saw anything as neat!'

Fairbrother sighed. 'I confess it has been some time, but it was a sight easier than anything I had to do with the Royal Africans.'

'You were not their surgeon?'

'I assisted the surgeon on many an occasion. He was in want of it, poor man. Johnson, do you have needle and thread?'

When, an hour later, they were stood down and attuning to the sounds of the night, just as their eyes had by degrees become accustomed to the black dark, Hervey and Fairbrother sat under the milkwood once more.

'You did not say before, directly, if you thought the Xhosa would attack, only that they did not fear the night.'

Fairbrother replied extra softly, just as Hervey had spoken. 'Be thankful they are not Zulu. They would now be bringing on re-inforcements, scenting blood. The Xhosa are more likely to lie up, taking their ease. They chanced with us back at the Gwalana, and we beat them off. They still have their cattle, though; and we should not forget that it was cattle they came for. Neither do they guard their honour as jealously as the Zulu: they will not feel bound to avenge their defeat. In that they are most pragmatical.'

'They'll not feel bound to recover a fellow tribesman?'

'Not obliged, no. Not unless he's of some consequence; and I saw nothing about ours that marked him thus.'

The brandy was now filling their mess tins again, serving a therapeutic purpose as welcome as it would have been to the Xhosa had he woken. Hervey settled back against the gnarled trunk of the milkwood and pushed his legs out straight. 'It occurs to me the Xhosa's chief – Gaika – might ponder with advantage on the return of one of his tribesmen who has been tended well, especially one who has sought to steal cattle and shoot one of the King's men. If he lives, it will only be because of your address.'

'And your decision that he should not be abandoned, or summarily executed. You do intend that he stands trial for shooting a redcoat? That, surely, is the landdrost's business.'

Hervey crossed his legs. 'He must stand trial, well enough. But it were better that it were Gaika's punishment and not ours. It would at least be the better seen to be done.'

'You may be right, Hervey. But you know, the Xhosa call us *omasiza mbulala*: "the people who rescue, then kill". It began when Somerset made demands on the Xhosa in return for our protection.'

Hervey had well understood the difference between Britain in India and Britain in the Cape Colony before leaving England; but perforce in the abstract. The purpose of the British in India, to be precise the 'Honourable Company of Merchants of England trading to the East Indies', was just that – trade. Its crab-like expansion from the coastal factories of Malabar, Coromandel and the mouth of the Ganges was not so much intentional as consequential. The directors of the company had no wish for the expense of campaigning and conquest, even where the territory acquired yielded riches more than enough to compensate: they had wanted the prosperity of what they understood best – commerce. They did not wish for war, but if native adventurists would challenge their right to their perfectly legal business, then the Court of Directors would not flinch from opposing them. They had not tried to *settle* India, however. On the contrary, outside the cantonments the Company had been strict in discouraging the activity of missionaries and others who would try to turn the native population from its own ways. Land was not given to white-faced immigrants; and those who had title to it, or even nomadic rights to range, were not displaced and forbidden to set foot on the land again. Not that Hervey had observed perfect peace in the one and nothing but war in the other; both places seemed to him just as hostile.

He would have to admit, however, just a certain unease here in Cape Colony. If the British – and before them the Dutch – had taken land from the native tribes in the belief that there was plenty of land for them to have instead, then where was the evil in that? If, however, they had taken the *best* land, and the tribes now suffered because of it, then that was an offence against the most fundamental instinct of right and wrong. In which case there would be no end of trouble on the frontier until the Xhosa, and any other of the aggrieved tribes, were comprehensively beaten into submission. That meant, quite simply, the slaughter of so many of them that those remaining feared extinction if they continued to resist. It was not a prospect that appealed to any part of him. But he had read, as was only expedient to a soldier of tender conscience, the doctors of the Church, Augustine and Aquinas. He could take some comfort from the knowledge that as a soldier he was not obliged to consider *jus ad bellum*. That was a matter for the lawful authorities of the nation. His concern must be *jus in bello*. And yet had he himself not said to Lord John Howard, 'On becoming a soldier I have not ceased to be a citizen'? He smiled to himself. 'Do not Cromwell me, Hervey!', Lord John had replied, ever practical. The trouble was, Lord John Howard, far from the field, was so busy about the commander-in-chief's business that thinking was an indulgence. He, Hervey, on the other hand, between bouts of intense action frequently had a great deal of time to think. It was a cruel sort of irony.

'Do you consider the Xhosa might be pacified other than by military means?' he asked, in an absent sort of way.

Fairbrother detected the change of tone. 'Not as long as there are men in Cape-town like the Somersets.'

Hervey understood the response, but it was not enough. 'I mean, are they susceptible to making peace at all?'

'Ah, Colonel Hervey, you declare yourself not a poet, but you are evidently something of a philosopher! You really must read the Wordsworth.'

Hervey scowled. 'Fairbrother, do not try me. There was never yet philosopher that could endure the toothache patiently.'

Fairbrother thought a while before answering. 'The Xhosa are not a warlike people, for all that they may fight savagely. But they have begun to speak of a deliverer; they say *kukuza kuka Nxele* – the coming of Nxele. Makana Nxele was a warrior, and a fine one. Before Nxele, the Xhosa had been mere herdsmen, and Gaika a grey-haired old chief whom both tribesmen and Somerset treated kindly but otherwise ignored. Nxele was their leader in the frontier war. He led the attack on Graham's-town, and believe me, Hervey – I saw it with my own eyes – it was not for want of courage that they failed. Afterwards, Colonel Willshire's punitive raids on the kraals were – I speak my mind in this – brutal. Your Duke of Cumberland could have done no worse.'

'Why do you say *my* Duke of Cumberland?' demanded Hervey, a shade impatiently. 'He was no more mine than yours.'

Fairbrother thought to leave explanation to another day. 'A mere lapse of speech. But hear me continue. Nxele gave himself up to Willshire rather than have his people subjected to greater hardship, and Somerset dealt with him very ill. He put him on Robben Island, a damnable place, and he died the following year trying to escape. The Xhosa have begun speaking as if he's immortal, which is a sign to beware. They are as a rule a level-headed people, for all their superstition.'

Hervey thought for a while. 'I did not ask before: how did you come to speak their language?'

'I took a fundisa, a munshi as you say in India, when the Corps first came here. It seemed a perfectly natural thing to do.'

'Though not, I imagine, to everyone.'

'Decidedly not. But you know, Hervey, it was far from an unpleasant labour. The Xhosa are not without their charms.'

Hervey frowned, unseen, though the tone of his voice betrayed it. 'I confess I saw no charm today. That was a deuced near-run thing at the river. I shall ever be grateful to you.'

Hervey heard the smile in the reply: 'My dear Hervey, think nothing of it.'

And there was just something, too, that convinced him of Fairbrother's utter sincerity in the dismissal. His courage had been so matter of fact, his manner afterwards unassuming, retiring even. 'Nevertheless, I would commend your valuable service when we return. I would have you meet Eyre Somervile; you and he will get on famously. And you should know that it was in Somerset's papers that he found you recommended. Somerset may have had his faults in your regard, but on this occasion he had been keen to set the record straight.'

Fairbrother smiled again, part unbelieving. 'As you wish.' He finished the brandy.

They sat listening to the sounds of the night. The dusk's chorus of cicadas had finished before they stood down (it would have been imprudent to rest arms with such a noise masking the tell-tale signals of approaching attack). An African night was eerily different from an Indian. No monkey could keep quiet in India, however black the darkness. And in forest or desert the jinnees in their temporary corporeal form – human or animal – rustled about their supernatural business. But here it was the deepest silence, and what occasional sounds there were came from a distance: yet a hunting leopard, half a mile off, might snarl at another and sound as if it were but an arm's length away. This was the sound of emptiness, an empty land, empty even of spirits. Hervey did not believe in the jinnees, but he believed in the sounds they made, and that an Indian night was not empty but peopled by a something that could not quite be touched, yet was not so far removed from the spirit of the day. This African night was somehow barren, a desolate time when the sun had forsaken the land – just as Fairbrother had told him the

Xhosa said of the beginning of war, that 'the land is dead'.

'Did you ever think of being anything but a soldier, Hervey?'

It was a very *sudden* change in the degree of their intimacy. Hervey was quite taken aback. And yet, sitting here in the alien darkness, owing his life – almost certainly – to this man (and in all likelihood, too, dependent on his judgement to see them safely away), it could not be other than natural. And, indeed, welcome. 'I don't believe I did.'

'Nor any second thoughts since, I imagine.'

Hervey thought for a moment, and decided on candour. 'Once, yes: ten years ago after the death of my wife. I resigned and was an ordinary subject of His Majesty – for a year and more.'

'My dear Hervey,' began Fairbrother, the tautness in his voice at once apparent, 'I owe you the greatest of apologies for what I asked about grieving for a woman.'

Hervey shook his head gently, as if Fairbrother might see. 'And yet, time does bring its balm. I am able for the most part to think of her now with a happy composure. Even three years ago I could not have done so.'

'And – I press you impertinently, no doubt – there has been no other claim on your affection?'

The intimacy had progressed to a degree Hervey had not imagined possible. He found it warming. 'I am to be married.'

'Indeed! Then I am most happy for you. May I ask who is the lady?'

'Of course you may ask. She is my former commanding officer's widow. He was killed in India.'

'Fighting alongside you at Bhurtpore?'

'Yes.'

Fairbrother nodded. 'I had heard of the custom,' he said, respectfully. 'The widow of a fellow officer: it is most noble.'

Hervey balked at the assumption of nobility. 'Truly, Fairbrother, you presume too much again! I do not marry out of

257

duty.' He found himself hesitating. 'That is, I do not marry out of duty to my commanding officer's widow.'

Fairbrother was pained. 'I do not presume, my friend. I do not presume by speaking of noble motives that there is any absence of love. A man's motives may be mixed, but it is not to say they are consequentially ignoble.'

'I take no offence.'

Indeed he did not. He wished only for no questioning of his feelings towards Kezia Lankester. In truth, he was only yet discovering them for himself.

Hervey woke with a start. He seized his pistols and began making for Corporal Wainwright.

'Hold fire! It is I, Fairbrother!'

Hervey, numb with the peculiar sensation that sudden wakefulness brought, could not make out where the shouts came from, or why. 'Wainwright?'

'Here, sir!'

He groped his way in the pitch darkness to where Corporal Wainwright crouched, carbine levelled. 'What is it?'

'It is I, Fairbrother; give me a voice!'

Hervey hesitated. It made no sense; and yet this was the man who had saved his life. 'Here, Fairbrother, here!'

He repeated the call, twice, until after what seemed an age, Fairbrother reached him. Hervey could just make out a second figure. 'What—'

'Xhosa. There are two more, dead, yonder in the scrub.' He pushed the man down, commanding him to sit: '*Hlala phantsi!*'

'How in God's name—'

'Your Corporal Wainwright reported a noise,' he said, breathless.

'And you walked out and found them?'

'I crawled out; circled across their line. They weren't difficult to find. I could smell them. And they *will* stand erect.' He held a long knife in his hand. He dropped to one knee and put it to the Xhosa's neck. 'Tell me, who are you? How many?'

'*Izinto azimntaka Ngqika zonke.*'

Fairbrother jabbed in the point further, almost breaking the skin. 'Do not sport with me!'

'What does he say?' whispered Hervey.

'He says it is not everyone who is a son of Gaika. It's a saying they have: he means not everyone is fortunate.'

Fairbrother began fingering the Xhosa's necklace.

'Lion claws. Well, well. Methinks he protests too much.' He jabbed the Xhosa's neck again. 'Not everyone is a son of Gaika, but *you* are!'

The man made no sound. He dare not deny his affinity with so great a chief.

'Bull's-eye, Hervey! God only knows how many Xhosa there are in that scrub, but they'll be powerfully determined to be in on us now. Our best chance is to set light to one of the fires so they'll know he'll be a dead Gaika's son if they attack.'

It went against Hervey's every instinct to light up the camp when they were not being attacked: the Xhosa could stand off and observe them all night, counting the odds, reckoning an assault would be an easy affair. Yet what option did they have, for the attack must now surely come? 'Light the fire,' he said.

'Pandours've 'oofed it, sir!' came Johnson's cheery report.

Corporal Wainwright fired his carbine and then reached for the pistols at his belt.

In the flash from the second shot Hervey saw a Xhosa fall. 'Good shooting,' he said, quietly. 'Now the fire.'

Wainwright struck a match, searched a few seconds for the powder trail and then lit it. The flame ran fast and strong, and the dry brushwood, sprinkled liberally with more powder, exploded in a fiery crackle.

Fairbrother immediately began dragging his captive towards the blaze, knife still at his throat. 'Let them have a good look first,' he growled.

259

Hervey had already decided they couldn't sit it out, not with the two pandours gone. 'Johnson, get the torches and bring five horses.'

'Ay, sir.'

It took him a quarter of an hour – which seemed an age. Meanwhile the fire gave a strong and steady light, so there were no false alarms. Wainwright, his carbine reloaded, turned about continuously, slowly, to cover any approach. Hervey explained his intention meanwhile: they would walk towards Trompetter's Drift until it was safe, and then they would outdistance the Xhosa in a mounted dash. They had six torches – if Johnson could find them: one and a spare he would take himself to lead; two torches Johnson would have for Fairbrother, and the other two Wainwright would carry at the rear. The Xhosa from whose shoulder they had removed the ball would be left by the fire: there his fellow tribesmen would see him, and Hervey's obligation to a prisoner would be discharged.

''Ere, sir!'

Hervey could not see a thing except what the fire illuminated, his night eyes quite gone.

'Can you come closer?'

'I'll try, but one of 'em's being a dog!'

Hervey edged towards the voice, sabre drawn (a pistol would need reloading). He smelled the horse sweat before he could make out the shapes. 'Well done, Johnson. Five in hand: the sarn't-major shall hear of it!'

'That's all right then.'

Hervey could picture the expression on Johnson's face. Things were becoming desperate, yet there was no cause for despair for as long as the Sixth remained the Sixth, however small a detachment or far-flung. 'Where are the torches?'

'Under t'stirrup leathers, sir – fust three on mi left.'

Hervey felt his way until he found the end horse's saddle, uncrossed the stirrup leathers and took one of the torches. He found his matches, struck one and held it to the tar-cloth. In a minute or so the flame had taken a good hold. 'Follow me.'

The horses were untroubled by the torch, which was as well since every one of the party would have his hands full. By the light of the fire, Hervey distributed the reins and the other two torches, told Johnson the plan, found his bearings and with no more than a 'good luck!' made ready to strike out for the trail they had come by from Trompetter's Drift.

The captive Xhosa, his hands now bound, and prompted by the point of the knife, shouted something half-defiant, half-pleading. '*Abantu* . . .'

Hervey started.

'He says what I told him to say,' rasped Fairbrother. 'That I'd cut his throat if any of them tried to stop us.'

'Has he said how many of them there are?'

'A dozen or so. But how can you believe a man with a knife at his throat?'

Hervey smiled to himself. What fortune had brought them together, this man so skilled in the ways of ruthlessness, and of fieldcraft, and yet of such sensibility? And how had these qualities been dismissed to the Half-Pay List?

For three wearying hours they tramped – edged – along the Trompetter's Drift trail, seeing, hearing, smelling the sudden death that lurked in the dark beyond the range of the torches, as deadly as the night cobra. The captive Xhosa kept up his distancing calls, the point of Fairbrother's urging knife twice drawing blood, and a dozen nerve-tearing times Wainwright fired at shadowy shapes, dextrously reloading his carbine with one hand.

The close scrub at last gave way to open grass. Here, Hervey reckoned, was their best chance of remounting without the Xhosa overwhelming them in a sudden rush; and from here they could kick hard and put a safe distance behind them.

He stopped, and turned. 'Johnson and Wainwright mount! Close up and put your pistols to the Xhosa's head.'

It took but a few seconds.

'Now you, Fairbrother.'

Fairbrother took the reins from Johnson and swung into the saddle, leaving Hervey with the point of his sabre at the Xhosa's throat.

'Pull him up!'

The three of them hauled the Xhosa astride the fifth horse.

'Go!'

Fairbrother, with the fifth horse's reins looped over his left arm, and his right holding the Xhosa in the saddle, kicked hard, with Johnson on the other side gripping the man as firmly.

Hervey's horse swung round in the excitement, Hervey's left foot dragging in the stirrup.

It was all the lurking Xhosa needed.

An ear-splitting shriek and then a shot, and then the weight of a dead man knocking him to the ground: Hervey lost grip of the reins. The horse took off with his foot still caught in the stirrup. Wainwright fired again – a Xhosa at his bridle – and then spurred after the runaway, barely able to see ahead.

Fifty yards it was before he caught the horse – close enough for the Xhosa to be at them yet. He jumped from the saddle, drew his sabre and cut the stirrup leather. Hervey, so racked as to be semi-senseless, groped for the reins and the saddle. Wainwright shouldered him astride and then made to remount.

A Xhosa ran in at him. Wainwright neither saw nor heard. Some other sense told him to parry then cut, the blade slicing deep and audibly. He vaulted into the saddle. 'Go on, sir! Go on!' he shouted, grabbing Hervey's reins.

Hervey in his half-daze knew he had heard those words before.

CHAPTER NINETEEN

RIFLES

Cape Town, three weeks later, 14 September

Colonel Hervey stood at the end of the line of riflemen on the firing range. The practice was conducted by a former serjeant of the Ninety-fifth commissioned in the field after Waterloo and now adjutant of the Cape Mounted Rifles.

It was the first opportunity Hervey had had to observe the Rifles at drill. In his month and more's absence, his major had seen to completing the dismounted training, and soon the recruits would begin riding school. It would be six weeks, at least, before he could take field drill, though he could make a beginning in the sand tray with his company officers.

The fortnight at the frontier had formed his thoughts very particularly. It was not merely the ambush that had shaped his thinking, but the notion of men – the Xhosa principally, but he imagined the other native tribes to be the same – the notion of their acting as individual warriors, intent on pressing home the

263

attack in ones and twos as the country permitted. It was not unlike what he knew to be the practice in North America, but here in Africa, by all accounts, the warriors also adopted regular formations when the country was otherwise too open. After reaching Trompetter's Drift, exhausted, the party had rested for twenty-four hours before continuing on the trail of the reiving Xhosa. Hervey had marvelled at the changing country – from close thorn to scrubby bushveld, and then to rolling grassland. He knew that if the Xhosa could be made to fight in open country then musketry and cavalry ought to defeat them roundly. If they could not be brought to battle in the open, then his volleying infantry and his well-drilled light dragoons might as well hold parades as go into close country after them.

This much might have been in the mind of Lord Charles Somerset when he set in hand the reorganization; except that Hervey had seen no reference to any cause but economy. And whatever the intention of the former governor, the fact was that the officers of the Mounted Rifles were already thinking like skirmishers – as if they were preparing for the sort of general action in which riflemen took post ahead of the red lines of muskets. Hervey was certain there was a place for that, but it was not in two-thirds of the country he had ridden over. There, it was the Rifles themselves who would have to close with the enemy, for there was no more chance of Line infantry advancing shoulder-to-shoulder than there was of discharging a single volley to effect. In truth, he had concluded, if there was to be another war on the frontier the proportion of such troops as the Rifles to those that fought in close order must be at the least three to one.

'At two hundred yards . . . targets, five rounds, *shoot!*'

The fire was ragged compared with that of volleying redcoats, but it was through no idleness or slow burn: riflemen fired as individuals, taking individual aim, firing only when their sights were properly laid, and stopping their breath to keep the aim true. Two hundred yards! Redcoats might volley at a hundred, but more likely fifty.

When the firing ended, the adjutant shouted 'Stop', and each man sprang to his feet.

'In double time, *march!*'

Fifty green-coated recruits, rifles at the trail, began doubling the two hundred yards to the targets. Hervey doubled too. He could not recall the last time he ran as far. In a couple of months these men would be able to fire five rounds, spring into the saddle, gallop two hundred yards and then dismount to fire another five. Such speed and accurate fire could confound an enemy ten times their number. He was convinced they were the answer – not the complete answer, but one that might shock the Xhosa out of the fastness of the bush and into the very country in which red- and bluecoats had the advantage.

He walked from target to target. There was none without five neat holes, and many where the holes were drilled in a cluster the size of a soup bowl. Here was impressive shooting, by any measure. But then many a recruit had been a cradle rifleman, schooled in marksmanship for the pot; though many more had been well-chosen volunteers whom the corporals and the adjutant had coaxed in their shooting rather than drilled by sharp words and the jab of the pike staff as if they were musketeers.

'Stand to your front!'

Fifty riflemen braced up. The corporals walked along the line giving each man a new white target, a piece of white canvas in a wooden frame eighteen inches square.

'Even numbers, double *march!*'

Hervey watched, deciding not to distract the adjutant by asking the purpose.

When the even numbers had doubled a hundred yards, the adjutant blew his whistle, the riflemen halted, faced about, grounded arms and held the targets aloft.

Hervey's mouth near fell open.

'Every man a volunteer, Colonel,' said the adjutant. 'They do things different at the Cape.'

Hervey shook his head: they were indeed a long way from Hounslow.

'Odd numbers, prone position, two rounds in your own time, *go on!*'

The adjutant explained that the riflemen had been numbered off a fortnight ago in permanent pairings, and that this was to be the final test of mutual confidence.

Single shots rang out the length of the line, impressively deliberate. There was a pause of several seconds to let the smoke clear, while each man took aim with the second barrel, and then it was the same again: the most purposeful shooting Hervey had ever seen. He could not tell yet, of course, how wide or high the riflemen had aimed, but he greatly admired the steadiness of the target-holders nonetheless. He would not have wished to stand at a hundred yards and have a line of redcoats fire even wide and high of him, so inaccurate was the musket!

The adjutant blew his whistle, and the even numbers doubled back to the firing point. Hervey began examining the targets eagerly. Every one of them had two holes.

Now the practice was repeated, odd numbers doubling out with the targets for the evens. The shooting was the same, deliberate business; and when the targets came back, the results were as before.

Hervey was minded to address the rifle-recruits, and then thought better of it: let them think this was nothing remarkable and they might achieve even more. There would certainly be need, and much of it at close-quarters. He knew he might see shooting as intelligent as this at Shorncliffe, but there was a distinct edge to what he had just witnessed. He was thoroughly heartened. He could tell Somervile that already there were the makings of a force to tackle the frontier on its own terms – could tell Somervile *and* General Bourke (he must make no mistake on that account).

'And the other recruit platoons are as good,' said the adjutant as Hervey began walking from the firing point towards where Johnson stood with the horses.

Hervey nodded. 'I congratulate you most heartily, Captain Brigg. And I'm grateful to you for sending me word of this. I landed only a little before midnight, but the effort has been repaid handsomely, I assure you. And now I shall go and see how my dragoons are' (he smiled wryly); 'carbines and all!'

Hervey gazed at the corral in horrified disbelief. Never in all his service had he seen its like. 'How many?'

'Fifty-seven,' said the veterinary surgeon.

Not a horse moved: two-thirds of the squadron's sabre strength stood head down, as if bawled out by the harshest-mouthed serjeant-major, their coats looking like nothing so much as old blankets with half the nap plucked away.

'And the others?'

'Not one of the chargers, thank God. They were stabled well apart. For the rest, I can discern no pattern. The better quality have fared as bad as the rest. It's difficult to say what's the nature of the illness, let alone the cause or cure. The depression you see in their condition is undoubtedly respiratory, but there's some poison in the blood too. There's a good deal of inflammation about the eyes, and the fossa's much swollen. That will account for some of the immobility. And the fever too.'

'What do the authorities say?'

'Nothing of real help. The Dutch call it *perdesiekt*. It strikes from time to time, though without obvious cause, the only common factor being that it tends to come at the onset of summer. It's highly contagious and they've no treatment for it. The chances of recovery appear to be about one in five.'

'Could it be something else, contracted in England?'

'I could not dismiss the possibility, but I know of no disease which takes longer than twenty-eight days to manifest itself, which is why we fix the period of quarantine at twice that time. If it is

267

this *perdesiekt* then there's consolation that those that recover will be salted.'

Hervey sighed. 'That is cold comfort, I think.'

'At this time, perhaps. The Dutch have been clever about it, though. They've built their studs with salted stock. Any Caper we buy – and we'll have to buy – will be warranted resistant to it.'

Hervey thought for a while. 'There's nothing you can do?'

'On the contrary: I'm doing a great deal, but it can be of little prospect, for I can only treat speculatively – and variously, so that if there is any amendment it will likely as not be confined to a quarter of them.'

Hervey felt himself tired, but even so he thought Sam Kirwan a shade difficult to follow this morning. 'Would you explain?'

'One quarter of them I'm not treating at all. One quarter I'm dosing strongly with acetic acid, another I'm purging with calomel, and the rest I'm bleeding.'

'Bleeding? But you always said—'

'Unless I can show that I've bled, the College will dismiss any findings.'

Hervey's brow furrowed. 'Sam, if you believe that bleeding does nothing but weaken a sick animal, then a quarter of these are condemned for the sake of science.'

'Not a quarter, Hervey, but one in five of a quarter; unless – and it would be perverse in the extreme – all the animals in that quarter were the ones that would recover naturally.'

Hervey had questioned Sam Kirwan's judgement once before; tired though he was, he would not do so a second time. 'Very well. You did not say: have any died yet?'

'No. Death generally occurs in about a week, say the Dutch. The disease only manifested itself four days ago.'

'And a very strict quarantine of the chargers is being enforced?'

Sam glanced at Hervey from under raised eyebrows.

'Very well. But you know, come to think of it, we may have a dozen of these saved, but meanwhile we run a terrible risk of contagion. I've half a mind it would be better to destroy the lot.'

Sam nodded. 'I understand your concern perfectly. And I acknowledge I am keenly studying the science in all this, but the chargers are separated by a mile and more; and only I and my assistants travel between them. I do not see how there could be any contagion.'

Hervey was in truth only too pleased to be persuaded that there was no need for destroying the best part of a troop's worth of horses. 'Has Fearnley done anything about remounts, do you know?'

Remounts were the regimental officers' business, not the veterinary surgeon's, though a prudent buyer would take his opinion. Sam Kirwan had not waited to be asked, however. 'I've made arrangements to go with him to a farm at Eerste River, about fifteen miles east. The Dutch say there's a good breeder there. He sells to the Company in Madras.'

'They'll be tits, no doubt.'

'But hardy, and good doers, and salted, so you might care to sit a little shorter in the saddle.'

Hervey shrugged. 'If they're up to weight then I've no very great concern for appearance. When do you go?'

'Tomorrow.'

'I may go myself, depending on duties at the castle. But Fearnley's perfectly capable of choosing remounts – once he's got over his dismay at not seeing blood. I would have Armstrong go with him too.'

They watched in silence for a while as one of the assistants went to work with a bleeding stick.

'Two quarts only: enough to keep the antediluvians at the College content. And from the toe: least damage.'

Hervey looked sadly on the scene. He knew Sam Kirwan to be a man of genuine love for the horses in his care: Sam would never have wished such an event. But at least he had his science to compensate him. For the rest – even the roughest dragoon – it was a melancholy affair. No one of his troop had paraded with his own

269

horse longer than a year, for they had brought none back with them from India; yet he had seen seasoned men cry at the destruction of a trooper not weeks in their charge. And, he was bound to concede, it made mockery of his petition to the Horse Guards that shipping troopers was good economy *and* sound practice, for now there would be both the expense of remounting *and* delay in the troop's readiness for the field.

Hervey made his way back to the castle, but without the spring in his step with which he had left the rifle range. When he reached his quarters he found Johnson attending to the lees of their time at the frontier.

'What's up, sir?'

Hervey made no pretence about it. 'Sixty-odd horses from the troop have got some wretched sickness that will destroy all but a dozen of them. And there's nothing to be done.'

'*Porca Maria!*'

Hervey glowered at him. 'You picked up a little Italian, then, in Stepney?'

Johnson shuffled uncomfortably.

'Is there coffee?'

Johnson scuttled off, returning but a minute later with a tin mug. 'Will this do for now, sir?'

Hervey nodded. There was doubtless good reason why they were using camp stores still.

'Has there been any word from the lieutenant-governor? I'm dining with him this evening, and Lady Somervile.'

'Who's Lady Somervile?' asked Johnson, forehead creased.

Hervey looked at him, shaking his head. 'His wife!'

'Ah never knew she were a Lady.'

Hervey's eyes narrowed, uncertain whether Johnson was playing a game. 'Of course she's "Lady" now he's "Sir"!'

Johnson's brow remained furrowed. 'You mean they made 'er a "Lady" when they made 'im a "Sir"?'

Hervey shook his head again, disbelieving. 'Johnson, how long have you moved in what is called good society? Don't you yet know that the wife of a knight is always styled "Lady"?'

'No.'

'Astonishing. So, you imagined that when a knight – or a baronet, or whatever he is – married, his wife was made "Lady" by the King?'

'No.'

'*What* then?'

'Ah just thought somebody wi' a title married someone else wi' a title.'

Hervey was lost for words. And then he began to smile – but to himself, for he would not have given offence for all the world: happy the man for whom dignities and styles were of such little consequence! 'Well, now you know different' (he would not say 'better'). 'And while we're about the subject . . .'

'Ay, sir?'

'No matter.'

'Ah'd like t'know.'

'Really, Johnson, it is of such little consequence.'

'But it's been botherin' thee.'

'It has not been "bothering" me.' Hervey found himself sighing. 'But since we speak of it, there is a very little thing you might try to recall: if a lady is the daughter of a duke, or a marquess, or an earl, she is called "Lady" and then her name and then her husband's name. If she is the wife of a baronet or a knight she is "Lady" and then just her husband's name.'

'Nobody ever told me that.'

'And you never thought to ask?'

'Ah never thought there were owt *to* ask!'

The logic was without flaw. 'Truly, it is of no consequence.' He took a long sip of coffee.

Johnson was coming to the end of his huswifery. He stood holding a torn shirt. 'There were *one* thing ah al'a's couldn't fathom.

271

Why were Mrs 'Ervey called Lady 'Enrietta 'Ervey, cos tha weren't "Sir" to other people?'

Hervey saw his explanation had been incomplete. Nor could he suppress a warm smile. 'As I recall it, Johnson, *you* were the only one who ever called her "Mrs Hervey". It was because her father had been an earl, and even if I had been *Sir* Matthew Hervey, she would still have used her own name first. Is all now clear?'

'Ay, sir. An' so Lady Katherine Greville . . . ?'

Hervey stopped himself from clearing his throat. 'Is the daughter of an earl, married to a knight.'

'An' Lady Lankester?'

'The widow of a baronet.'

'An' so when she marries thee, sir, she'll be . . . not Lady 'Ervey?'

'No, because I am neither baronet nor knight. She will be plain "Mrs Hervey".'

Johnson put the shirt into a raffia box. 'Won't she mind that?'

If the question were impertinent, Hervey no longer recognized impertinence in his groom. Long years had convinced him of Johnson's heart, and the late trouble – the late *misunderstanding* – with Italians and coral had not altered his opinion in any degree. 'I must trust not.'

'Ah don't like that dog o' Lady Lankester's.'

'The dog is perfectly amenable if you don't startle her.'

'An' ah don't think she likes me.'

'She hasn't bitten you?'

Johnson looked puzzled.

'The dog, she hasn't bitten you has she?'

'Ah meant Lady Lankester.'

Hervey began hearing the same doubting tone with which Emma had pressed him in Gloucestershire. He tried to be cheery. 'She's only met you but two or three times!'

'Ah reckon she won't want me abaht after yer both wed, sir.'

So that was it! He had never imagined . . . 'Johnson, I may safely

272

assure you – and you must believe it – that I shall never dispense with your services until you yourself wish it.' A smile came to his lips. 'Or Bow-street requires it!'

Hervey went to the Somerviles that evening a happier man. There was nothing he could do about the 'epidemic disorder', as Sam Kirwan was officially describing it: the horses were in the best of hands, and Serjeant-major Armstrong could be relied on to enforce the quarantine. There was evidently a supply of remounts – though he doubted fifty would be to hand at once – and if other duties detained him, he could certainly rely on Lieutenant Fearnley to make sound purchases. As to the money – the War Office must be only too aware of the contingencies of campaigning. There had been no negligence, no neglect, and but for the inevitable and perfectly proper enquiries by some clerk in Downing Street he need have no disquiet in that direction. Above all, the business at the frontier had been both exhilarating and gainful: he had, by his own reckoning and Eyre Somervile's preliminary reading of his report (a brief interview in the late afternoon had been all that could be managed in the lieutenant-governor's day of inspections), accomplished what he had been sent there to do. Moreover, he had helped instigate certain measures to ease the immediate Xhosa nuisance. All this he could take the greatest satisfaction in, the more so for its standing in sharp contrast with events of the year before (Portugal, he trusted, would ever be his lowest ebb). He felt in large measure restored. And the gains had not all been His Majesty's. The country, the Xhosa and above all Edward Fairbrother had taught him a great deal more about the soldier's art. He had never once thought that he possessed all the art there was to have, but long years in the Peninsula and the tumultuous days of Waterloo, and then the extraordinary campaigns in the East, had given him a certainty in his own proficiency which, in truth, the late unhappy business in Portugal had not diminished. The affair with the Xhosa had been but a scrape, albeit a deadly one; he had observed how it must be done here – and above all how it must *not* be.

He arrived at the lieutenant-governor's residence as the sun was rapidly disappearing. He paused a moment outside to watch its descent, still a sight of wonder in these latitudes for all his six weeks in the colony:

> *The Star that bids the Shepherd fold,*
> *Now the top of Heav'n doth hold,*
> *And the gilded car of day,*
> *His glowing Axle doth allay*
> *In the steep Atlantick stream*

He nodded contentedly. This was a beautiful country, for all its frontier savagery – and its horse sickness. He thought he might be reluctant to leave it when the time came. But thinking of Milton made him think also of Joseph Edmonds: he owed that officer so much – his example, his encouragement; above all the forbearance and unswerving support whenever he overstepped the mark in rash cornet-judgement. Or *was* it merely *cornet*-judgement? Was he not so disposed still? Yes, he knew it; and that much was good, for he could not guard against what he did not recognize. And with Edmonds long gone, and now Daniel Coates, he was without such counsel:

> *And Advice with scrupulous head,*
> *Strict Age, and sowre Severity,*
> *With their grave Saws in slumber ly.*
> *We that are of purer fire Imitate the Starry Quire . . .*

Hervey nodded. He moved in the military firmament, periodically, but he did not – could not – imitate its 'Starry Quire'. Except, perhaps, that Kat had begun to show him how he might.

He felt a sudden twinge of guilt. He had treated Kat abominably, by any reckoning; and she had only returned his ill news with kindness and painful understanding – painful both for him *and* for her. He wondered what she would do now: perhaps return to Alderney, if she could think of Alderney as home to return to, and be reconciled in every way with her husband? No, in truth what he had seen of Sir Peregrine Greville made the notion fanciful. And so there would be other lovers. How could there not be, for Kat was a beautiful woman? *Why* should there not be? Only that he hated the idea.

He shivered suddenly. Such thoughts were now wholly improper (if they had ever indeed been even partially proper). He turned from the sun as it touched the horizon, and took the steps to the door of the residence. So much had 'sacred Milton' kept his thoughts from 'Riot, and ill manag'd Merriment'. He could not understand himself: the exhilaration of but two months in this place!

At the door of the residence Hervey found familiar faces: Jaswant, the khansamah, and several other of the Somerviles' Indian servants – and black faces too, got up very smartly in reds and blues.

'Good evening, Colonel Sahib!'

Hervey smiled and returned the greeting more fully than he needed to: a familiar *and* a friendly face so far from home was a welcome thing. And 'Colonel Sahib' sounded so fine! No matter that in all probability it was temporary, he was indeed 'Colonel'. And in a colony of a single general, a colonel was of consequence.

He began wondering when he would actually meet General Bourke. Not that it mattered greatly in the ordinary course of things: he had carried out his reconnaissance of the frontier under the lieutenant-governor's orders, and his commission with the Mounted Rifles came directly from the Horse Guards; but he would like nevertheless to make a proper beginning with the General Officer Commanding. 'Am I the only guest this evening, Jaswant?'

In deliberately well modulated Bengali, the khansamah replied,

275

'Colonel Somerset-sahib will be dining, Colonel Sahib, but he will not arrive until later.'

Hervey's heart fell a good way.

He followed Jaswant along a limed corridor, brilliantly lit, to where Somervile stood at the open French doors of a small reception room contemplating the last of the sun.

' "Now Phoebus sinketh in the west"!'

Hervey raised his eyebrows. 'Quite remarkable. I was observing only the same myself outside.'

' "And the slope sun his upward beam Shoots against the dusky pole." I confess I've quite forgotten the rest.'

'So have I.'

Emma came into the room. '*Colonel* Hervey!'

Hervey greeted her with a smile and an embrace. 'I had not thought your drawing rooms such formal affairs, Lady Somervile.'

'We are ever at the lieutenant-governor's command.'

'Just so, madam.'

Eyre Somervile remained at the window. 'You know, I do think Phoebus shows a different face depending on where he is: quite a different appearance from India, quite different.'

Emma looked at her guest.

Hervey glanced at his host, who remained intent on the setting sun. 'Indeed, I believe it so,' he tried, determined that the sun should not regulate the conversation. 'I have lately been in the eastern part of the colony. The country there is different in every degree from Madras and Bengal. It is savage, and yet at the same time not so . . . fierce. The sun, of course, has much to do with it. It warms the country rather than burns; though they say that in summer not greatly further inland it can be quite as desert-hot as Rajpootana.'

Emma continued pointedly on the subject of the weather, or rather climate. 'I confess I find it agreeable in the extreme, though I have been here but a short time.' Then glancing at her husband, without response, she changed the subject very decidedly.

'Now, Matthew, I bear a letter for you.' She held out an envelope.

He did not recognize the hand.

'From your betrothed!'

He looked embarrassed. 'Oh, I . . .'

'Eyre and I shall retire for a little while.'

'That won't be necessary,' said Hervey hurriedly. 'I mean, you should not have to retire in order to let me read.'

Emma smiled. 'I think a man ought to be allowed a little privacy in communicating with his sweetheart, even at such a remove.'

Hervey coloured rather at 'his sweetheart'. Of course Kezia Lankester was just that, but he had never quite thought those words.

Before he could protest further, Emma removed herself and her husband from the room.

Hervey took a few steps closer to a candelabrum and broke the seal (he noted it was not Lankester's, and presumed it therefore to be her own). He had not expected a letter. He had written to her on arriving at Cape Town, and intended doing so again now he was returned, but she could not have received his letter before writing hers.

Hertfordshire,
17th June 1827

My dear Colonel,

I trust that this finds you in good health and happy circum-stances, and I send you congratulations and warm good wishes on your promotion, as does my father, who asks me to thank you for your hospitality of the two days prior to your departure. He particularly wished me to express again his pleasure on meeting you, and at our betrothal. For my part I must say once more how delightful it was to meet both Miss Hervey and Georgiana . . .

277

He read on. The polite expressions of pleasure and various causes for satisfaction continued, but in a cool and somewhat mechanical way, so that by the end he felt it might have been from Elizabeth herself on a matter of family business. But, he told himself, this was a first letter, their betrothal had been an unusual affair following so brief an acquaintance, and the time for expressions of endearment would follow. He did not mind the somewhat arch salutation (it was probably a relief to her, not having to initiate the intimacy of their correspondence) and after all, *he* had managed only 'My dear Kezia' and a few paragraphs hardly more amorous. It perhaps seemed strange in comparison with Kat's last letter, received just as he was leaving for his ship, which was full of unselfconscious sentiments of affection. He shuddered at the import – what he *thought* was the import – and then put it from his mind as a mere demonic qualm.

He folded the two sheets of vellum – he need not read them a second time for now – and replaced them in the envelope. Then he went to the window to distract himself with what remained of the sun's glow 'in the steep Atlantick stream'.

Emma returned, alone. 'Eyre has just received a despatch from General Bourke. He will join us shortly.' She sat down.

The khansamah entered.

'Matthew, I'm so sorry: we evidently left you to your charming diversion without a drink in your hand.'

Hervey looked at the khansamah. 'Chota peg, Jaswant; mehrbani,' he said without thinking. The Somerviles spoke a very proper form of Bengali, whereas his Urdu was merely serviceable. It was in truth the emergent vocabulary of the cantonments which, since Warren Hastings's day, the British – and the wives who increasingly accompanied them – preferred to the real vernacular. It was a compromise, easy enough for the sahibs and memsahibs to acquire, and easy enough for the little armies of servants – native speakers of any number of the languages of the sub-continent – to understand. Much as Hervey despised the practice, it had not been long before he had succumbed, so common was it in the garrison of Calcutta. If only he had spoken to Vaneeta in Bengali, instead of in the English that she spoke so well . . .

'Matthew?'

'I'm sorry?'

'Jaswant asks if you prefer whiskey or brandy.'

'Oh, I hadn't . . . whiskey, thank you.'

The khansamah bowed and left.

'You were thinking . . .'

Hervey sighed. 'I was thinking – at that moment, at that precise moment – of Vaneeta.'

'Is that a cause for sighing?'

Hervey shook his head a little. 'No, it should not be. I never asked you: did you see her before you left?'

Before he himself had left, he had asked Emma to keep watch. He had settled a good income on Vaneeta: it was the very least he believed he could do (though a very good deal more than others did in like circumstances), but he had asked Emma to let him know at once if his former bibi fell into any sort of difficulty. Indeed, he had asked her to make whatever financial provision she felt necessary as soon as possible, and he would reimburse her at once. He had settled more than enough on Vaneeta for her to live in respectable comfort. Even though her standing in Calcutta would ever be that of bibi of a *Feringhee*, he had hated the idea that she might pass from one pair of military hands to another. The thought that she might even return to the *haveli* had reduced him almost to tears. He had at one stage – in a moment he now saw as beyond reason – thought to bring her back with him to England. And in a fit of distinct madness he had even contemplated marriage, remaining in Bengal, throwing in with the Company's forces, perhaps even with Colonel Skinner's regiment of irregular cavalry. Emma, who disdained the growing 'respectability' and aloofness of the new memsahibs, had received Vaneeta in her own drawing room, albeit discreetly for her visitor's sake more than her own. She had liked Vaneeta, both for her wit, sensibility and charm, and for her evident restorative powers: Vaneeta had nursed Hervey back to health in every sense. Emma had never sought to persuade him of the unsuitability of marriage, or for that matter taking her to England as ayah to Georgiana. She had only wanted him to think in terms other than wholly of duty.

'I did see her before I left, yes. She was very well.'

'And . . .'

'And what?'

Jaswant came with his whiskey and soda water.

Hervey took it, nodding his thanks. 'She . . . she was happy?'

Emma looked a trifle frustrated. 'It was not so many months after you left that Eyre and I sailed.'

Hervey looked anxious. 'And so . . .'

'Matthew, it is very hard for me if you will not finish your sentences!'

'Was she appearing to . . . be recovered?'

Their parting – Hervey and Vaneeta – had indeed been a painful one. He had loved her as much as he was able; she had loved him completely.

Emma's look of frustration only increased. 'Matthew, I understand that you should be concerned for Vaneeta's situation – but at this time? I made careful arrangements for her, with a very reliable party, as I explained in the letter I sent you, and for the rest . . . only time can do its work.' Her brow furrowed. 'Is there something in the letter that has prompted this – Kezia Lankester's letter, I mean?'

Hervey shook his head. 'Nothing at all.'

'Then in the circumstances I believe we should drop the matter.'

Hervey nodded. 'It's just . . . there are times . . .'

Emma leaned forward and placed a hand on his. 'Of *course* there will be times, Matthew. You cannot help it. It does you credit, indeed. But to dwell on it is . . . imprudent. I dare say unseemly.'

Somervile returned, with a glass in his hand. 'Great Ganesh, but Bourke's oldwomanly about that place!'

280

Hervey and Emma looked at him, uncertain.

'St Helena! He's got a notion the French'll seize it one day – make it a shrine or some such. Does it matter one iota if they do? How in the name of Shiva can it be worth the cost of placing one bombardier there? And why so urgent a despatch, I can't imagine.'

Hervey shook his head and raised his eyebrows slightly.

'In all else I've found him a most sensible fellow.'

'I am very glad of it,' said Hervey. 'You think, therefore, he will approve of my own despatch?'

Somervile gestured with his glass. 'Ah, your despatch. Indeed – admirable, admirable. I have written this afternoon to Bathurst, in large measure your words, with a copy to the War Office – who, I trust, will send it to the Horse Guards. And I have written to the magistrates at Port Elizabeth and Graham's-town commending their actions.'

Hervey looked pleased. 'And you will commend Fairbrother?'

'I shall. But first I would meet him. I very much like the sound of him. Indeed, had it not been for Colonel Somerset I should have invited him this evening. But it would have been unfair on Somerset to interpose to all intents and purposes a stranger when there is colony business to be about.'

Hervey would have preferred that Colonel Henry Somerset had not been invited at all. He had hoped for a reunion of friends; but then he reminded himself that Eyre Somervile, undoubted friend that he was, was now primarily his sovereign's regent in the colony, to whom even General Bourke must answer in the first instance. There could probably be no occasion that was entirely – or even, he had to admit, and with regret, in any large measure – an affair of friends. He took comfort, however, in Fairbrother's delightful assertion that where one gentleman was the subordinate of another, the superior would never mention it, and the inferior would never forget it.

Emma tilted her head, resigned. Her drawing rooms, be they in Madras, Calcutta, London, and now here, had ever been conference halls, or else offices, and occasionally even head-quarters. 'May we not first have a little conversation, my dear? I would ask Colonel Hervey how was his visit to the frontier.'

Somervile looked puzzled. 'Did you not read the despatch?'

Emma lowered her head emphatically. 'A very little. If you recall, I only had opportunity to take it up this afternoon, and your secretary at once had need of it.'

'Mm.'

'So, Matthew, after you left these wonderful-sounding clay pits, did you encounter the fearsome and magnificent Xhosa?'

Hervey's eyes widened. 'I did, though I had no occasion to observe any magnificence. I must admit they very nearly worsted us in an ambuscade, and again the same day – in the middle of the night. They might have taken our camp had it not been for Mr Fairbrother.'

Emma quickened. 'Oh, I must have the particulars, Matthew!'

Hervey knew full well that Emma would want the particulars. She had smelled more powder than many a man in England. He let the khansamah take his glass, accepted another, and began recounting the affair at the headwaters of the Gwalana.

When he had come to the natural conclusion of the action, Emma, who had remained silent but very intent, shook her head. 'I, too, am full of admiration for your Mr Fairbrother. Such resolution as well as skill!' She turned to her husband. 'Eyre, he must come to the castle as soon as may be.'

Somervile, who had been listening almost as intently, though he knew the affair from the pages of the report, smiled and nodded, as if conceding to his wife a personal favour. Hervey was touched by the evident orientation of the lieutenant-governor's heart. He said nothing, allowing Emma and her husband their intimacy.

Emma turned back to him. 'But Matthew, your corporal: again he dashed to your rescue – no, not rescue, defence. I—'

Hervey inclined his head. 'I should happily admit to "rescue".

Had there been more men in that bush Fairbrother might have been shot from his horse, as might I.'

Emma shook her head. 'I mean that yet again he was there with you. In Rangoon, and then again in Spain, and now here.'

'That is his position: he *is* my covering corporal.'

Her eyes widened with astonishment.

Hervey smiled. 'I sport with you, Emma. He is the most admirable of NCOs. I am, you may imagine, inordinately attached to him – not least because of the circumstances of his joining. I listed him from the Warminster sink, and I have to say that – God be praised – he is not the only man of his kind in the Sixth. Nevertheless he is singular in what he has been obliged to do these past five years. I have today made him serjeant.'

Emma clapped her hands. 'I am delighted for it! When shall I see him? For besides prodigious courage and a devotion to you, he has very agreeable manners. As does, too, your serjeant-major.'

'The night affair, Hervey,' Somervile interrupted. 'The fleysome affair of the night!'

Hervey looked suitably chastened. 'Ah, yes, the night affair. I should say, Emma, that after the ambuscade we retired north towards one of the frontier posts, taking the wounded man with us, making camp a little before sunset. It was impossible to know if the Xhosa had followed, and just before midnight Mr Fairbrother, of his own, went out of the camp to discover what was the cause of some rustling noise, and found three of them poised to the attack. He killed two at once and came into the camp with a third.'

Emma gripped her glass tight. 'Was it *very* dark?'

'The whole country's very trappy, with a great deal of thorn, and it was as black as Hades. How Fairbrother found them, let alone did what he did, astonishes me still. But then, he called for one of the fires we had laid to be lit, so that he could show any Xhosa who were waiting to attack that we had a prisoner.'

'But would that not encourage them to his rescue?'

283

'I omitted to say he held a knife at the man's neck, and called out to them in Xhosa that he would slit his throat' (he paused and cleared his own slightly) 'and cut off his manhood if they attacked. We managed to get away, first on foot and then at a gallop, all the time with the Xhosa captive bound and with a pistol at his head, until we came on a patrol from Fort Willshire.'

Emma sat back in her chair. 'Great heavens; I do not think I ever heard its like in all the time I was in India. This Mr Fairbrother: he sounds half savage!'

'I told you of his lineage, my dear,' explained her husband. 'There's the blood of the natives there somewhere.'

Hervey took another sip of his whiskey. 'I have a notion that a half-bred fellow with the education of an Englishman – which is what Fairbrother would answer to – might be the beau ideal of a cavalryman in this place.'

'Well, I am all eager to make his acquaintance,' said Emma, very decided. 'And he is a poet too, you say?'

Hervey raised his hands. 'I confess he has read those I have never heard of.'

'You never heard of Wordsworth?' replied Emma, incredulous.

'Of course he's heard of Wordsworth,' said Somervile, helpfully. 'Wordsworth the soldier of the Westmoreland Militia!'

Hervey would not rise to the fly. 'I said I had never read the poem he had composed about the warrior.'

'Neither have I,' said Emma, contented.

'But you will like him very much. He is a little thin-skinned in respect of his origins, but that is easily overcome.'

They passed a further quarter of an hour in pleasant conversation, though all of it with a purpose, until the khansamah announced Colonel Somerset.

A man of middle height and patrician good looks, and several years Hervey's junior, entered the drawing room and bowed.

'Colonel, you are most welcome,' exclaimed Somervile in

exaggerated greeting, intending to roust the prickly scion of the Somersets from habitual ill humour.

Hervey rose, as did Emma, who advanced on her guest with hand held out. 'You are indeed, most welcome, Colonel.'

Colonel Somerset, though evidently a little surprised, took her hand nevertheless. 'Lady Somervile,' he said, bowing, then again to his fellow guest: 'Colonel Hervey.'

'Have you travelled far today, Colonel?' asked Emma, before Somerset could make any conversation of his own – or even her husband (she was determined to have just a few of the civilities of the presidencies observed in this, by comparison, unrefined outpost of the realm).

Somerset, his head already half turned to the lieutenant-governor, and his lips parted to form the first of his enquiries, was obliged to return to his hostess. He looked a shade abashed (which Emma took satisfaction in). 'Forgive me, ma'am ... yes, it has been a long day. I was obliged to go to Simon's-town early this morning on account of a frigate's putting in.'

'To advantage?' asked Somervile.

'Yes, she brought the Horse Guards' approval for the estimates respecting the Cape Corps, as well as private mail. There is, I observe, a substantial bag for you and your dragoons, Colonel Hervey.'

Hervey was pleased to hear it: the mails were ever the soldier's cheer, but he was especially hopeful that his bag contained the percussion cartridges he had ordered from Forsyth's in Piccadilly. But beyond the information of the mails, Colonel Somerset was not especially communicative, and certainly not warm. Hervey knew that the business of the Cape Corps estimates was of some family concern to him: Eyre Somervile had told him that General Donkin had left a quarter of a million pounds to the credit of the colony, whereas Lord Charles Somerset had left a deficit of almost a million. General Bourke had therefore set about the economies necessary for the restoration of the budget, including taking

285

down the signal towers communicating with the frontier, leaving only those to Simon's Town from the castle, and the re-organization of the Cape Corps into something more akin to Mr Peel's Irish constabulary.

'Colonel Hervey has had a most interesting time of it at the frontier,' said Somervile, in the pause during which Colonel Somerset took his glass from the khansamah. 'Quite a sharp encounter with the Xhosa indeed.'

Hervey had no desire to conceal it, and certainly not to deny it, though he would have wished for it not to have arisen so soon.

But it was a vain hope on both counts. 'So I heard,' replied Somerset, not at all approvingly. 'And with that planter's bastard from the Africans.'

Somervile remained blithe. 'Rather a useful planter's bastard, though: he appears to have saved Hervey's life here, and rendered rather valuable service in other directions too. He collared one of the Xhosa in the middle of the night, who turns out to be no less than one of Gaika's own sons – and a favoured one at that.'

'Ah,' said Emma, suddenly returned to the conversation. 'You did not tell me that, my dear. Was the man therefore held to ransom?'

Somervile looked at Hervey. 'I think *you* should have the pleasure of the story, for it was your enterprise that brought about the happy end.'

Hervey tried not to appear reluctant. 'It was Fairbrother's enterprise, in truth. I confess I know of no one in the army who would have been able to crawl about in the black of that night and do what he did. Plenty, perhaps, with the courage, and some with the skill; but to dispose of two and then bring in a third prisoner – *hostage* – shows a rare presence of mind.'

Emma had not the slightest doubt that in her very drawing room stood a man who could have accomplished the same. 'I am all admiration for you both, Colonel Hervey – and indeed for your corporal – but I would that you were not so unforthcoming about things and let us have all the intelligence!'

Somervile smiled. She saved him the trouble of expressing the same sentiments, and she did so more bluntly.

Hervey resolved to trouble himself no longer on Colonel Henry Somerset's behalf. 'We took the Xhosa to Gaika two days following, and Gaika put his son into confinement in his kraal, and called for the others of the party to be arrested, professing of course that he had no knowledge of the raid.'

He was about to say next what had been Gaika's sentiment, but Colonel Somerset was already agitated. 'Whose was the discourse with Gaika?'

'Mine, principally,' replied Hervey, not altogether concealing his irritation at the tone of the questioner. 'Fairbrother was interpreter, though he made a number of judicious remarks of his own. It was an altogether rather effectual method of parley.'

'Indeed it appears so,' said Eyre Somervile, seemingly oblivious of the signs of rancour. 'For I believe we have the makings of a little peace on the frontier, at least for the time being. But see, dinner is announced' (he nodded to the khansamah). 'Let us adjourn to the table.'

When they were seated, Somervile resumed the conversation but in a more emollient tone. 'Colonel Somerset, I do not wish to interfere with strictly military matters; those are the preserve of General Bourke, and in his absence you yourself, and I am well aware that command of the eastern frontier is devolved upon you, but in those matters which are not strictly military I do, of course, bear ultimate responsibility to His Majesty's ministers.'

Somerset did not reply; there could be no question but that it was so.

'I have been in the colony a mere two months, and have yet to leave Cape-town, but it seems to me – indeed it did seem to me before even I left England – that the future of the Cape Colony would be best secured by a vigorous but enlightened policy towards the native people. That was, I understand, what your own father believed.'

He tasted his wine, nodding with approval at the khansamah's choice. Hervey was never entirely certain whether Eyre Somervile was diverted naturally or by design on these occasions for there was by no means eccentricity in his ways.

The lieutenant-governor continued. 'The Dutch are ever of concern, of course, but they are not – or need not be – so violently opposed to our presence, since theirs was a colonial enterprise here too, and as long as they are allowed their own customs, and taxation is not burdensome, I see no cause for vexation out of the ordinary. Except, of course, in the business of slaves; and there we must proceed with great circumspection. The Cape is not India, however, though its . . . shall we say *raison d'être* is India. The Company in India has become, now, an enterprise of factoring as much as trade – some would say *more* than trade – because, like the crab, it moved sideways, this way and that, crawling sometimes, scuttling at others, with no apparent great purpose, merely as the wind or the tides dictated.'

Somervile accompanied his soliloquy with increasingly extravagant gestures, to the consternation of the khitmagars trying to serve at table while avoiding his flailing arms.

'And so now there is a Company army as large as the King's own, and the prospect of continual skirmishes, for we are not committed to the settlement of the continent, only its administration. Here, on the other hand, we wish to see a settled European population. First the Dutch and then we have dispossessed the native tribes, which we have not done in India – merely their rulers, and in some cases the predatory hordes that made misery of so much of the country. We are not resented there except by those we have usurped – and these are they whom we must fight. Their power is limited to the arms they can raise, but that will always be under good regulation by the Company's. Here in the colony we have sown the seeds of a different peril. We have destroyed, to all intents and purposes, the Hottentots and the Bushmen.'

Emma was distressed, as much by her husband's casual reference

288

to it as the destruction itself (she knew his true mind well enough).

Somervile noticed her discomfort and sought to make amends. 'Grievous as that may be, it is done, it cannot be undone, and we might therefore make the most of it. The Xhosa, however, are a different prospect. By dispossessing rather than destroying them we have created a hostile neighbouring power. How permanently hostile, it is difficult to say. We have taken from them what might appear to be indifferent farmland, but patently it was greatly prized by them. If, of course, their present settled territory proves fertile – in every sense – then in a generation or so there might be contentment and therefore peace. It occurs to me we should help them towards that happy condition by treating with them as if they were any other sovereign nation – in the free intercourse of trade, for one thing. I therefore intend issuing instructions and regulations for trade with the Xhosa, on a strictly businesslike and cordial foundation. Colonel Somerset, I know your own father to have favoured such a view of the Xhosa – of Gaika, at least – and although it was not successful in keeping tranquillity along the frontier, we do not know that the opposite policy would not have brought an infinitely greater peril.'

Hervey remained silent, as did Somerset, who was nodding gently as if weighing the words and finding them sure. It was Emma who began the scrutiny. 'Is there a danger that the Xhosa might combine in alliance with another? For then they might truly overwhelm the Crown's resources?'

Somervile had contemplated the question long, but he turned to his senior guest. 'What is your opinion, Colonel Somerset?'

Somerset thought for a moment. 'Sir Eyre, for all my years here I will admit to a very imperfect knowledge of native affairs, but it is better than most, including the Dutch, who are inclined to believe they know everything. There are a number of smaller tribes with whom the Xhosa are conversant, made easier by the closeness of their speech, but in truth if *all* these were to combine I do not believe we should find ourselves greatly threatened –

no more than at present, such is the situation of their territory.'

The lieutenant-governor nodded, though in a way that said he understood rather than agreed.

'The one alliance that should trouble us, were it ever to be made, is of the principal Kaffir tribes, the Xhosa and Zulu.'

Emma inclined her head. 'I have heard of the Zulu, Colonel, but are you able to enlighten me a little more?'

Somerset glanced at his host, finding the same enquiry in his expression. 'I have had no personal contact with the Zulu, you understand, Lady Somervile, but throughout my time here there has been a steady increase in their influence. Their chief – king, as they have it – is called Shaka, by all accounts an able but exceedingly cruel man. The Zulu were but a small tribe before Shaka became king, about ten years ago, their country confined on the far eastern coast. Shaka made an army out of them – terrified the neighbouring tribes, who one by one submitted. They now occupy extensive territory.'

Emma frowned. 'It sounds to me as if the Xhosa have more to fear from the Zulu than we have from the two combined.'

'Unless,' began her husband, in the manner of someone considering the proposition as he spoke it, 'the Xhosa believed that, in becoming Shaka's vassals, they would recover their former territory here in the Cape. Would they rather live independent but in reduced circumstances, so to speak, in their present territory, or as a tributary to Shaka in their old lands? Do we know what that answer might be, Colonel?'

Somerset shook his head. 'I for one do not, Sir Eyre.'

After dinner, while the lieutenant-governor was called to read a second 'Most Urgent' despatch (but which touched only on finance, and was urgent only as far as the sender in Whitehall was concerned), and while Emma spoke with her staff, Hervey and Somerset took their coffee into the garden, Somerset (Hervey sensed) rather reluctantly.

290

Between the two there was little to speak of in age, and but an inch in height, though Somerset's hair was thinning somewhat and receding notably at the temples. In other respects they had little in common. Colonel the Honourable Henry Somerset was grandson of the Duke of Beaufort; he had first held a commission with the 72nd Highlanders, seeing no service to speak of, and had obtained a troop in the Cape Regiment through the patronage of his father, the then governor of the Cape. He had seen a little skirmishing in the frontier war of 1819, he had advanced rapidly by purchase and further patronage to major, and was appointed Commandant of the Eastern Frontier by his father in 1825 in the rank of lieutenant-colonel. He and Hervey did share a willingness, perhaps even propensity, however, to disregard the opinion of superior (not to say senior) officers – perhaps even to disdain it. But while Hervey's occasional disagreements and sometimes more deleterious disputes were ever on matters of military expediency, Somerset's were of the nature of petulance, and self-serving. Edward Fairbrother had told Hervey that not half a dozen years before, Somerset had been placed in arrest for insubordination to General Donkin when the general had failed to appoint him landdrost of Graham's Town, and that his father had flown into a rage at Donkin's presumption, exacting considerable revenge by placing both his sons in superior positions. Fairbrother had said he did not know all the particulars, but that it was well known throughout the Cape: Colonel Henry Somerset was a man to be wary of, not least because his ambition and experience were ill-matched.

But Hervey also knew that for the time being he must get on with the Commandant of the Eastern Frontier. Neither did he want ill-favoured reports reaching London, for he must presume that any letter of Somerset's would, via his father, reach the hand of Uncle Lord FitzRoy Somerset, now secretary at the Horse Guards. 'Colonel, may I say to you at once that I am entirely at your disposal,' he began, though in a tone far from submissive. 'My commission is to the raising of the Mounted Rifles, but I have

291

known the lieutenant-governor for many years, and it is only natural that he uses me in a rather more ranging capacity. I am conscious, however, of my inexperience here at the Cape, and by contrast your very great knowledge of this place. I will speak plainly: I do not wish to be your enemy in this or any other thing. Besides ought else, I have the greatest respect for Lord FitzRoy, whom I had the privilege to meet before Waterloo.'

Hervey had calculated carefully. The word 'Waterloo' excited admiration and resentment in equal measure in those who had not themselves been there. He had no idea of Somerset's opinion of 'Indiamen' (Somerset's own service in the Cape Colony indicated, however, that he might not share that of a Brighton fashionable), and he did not want to be thought of as a mere dust and heat soldier.

Somerset gave little away by reply. 'I imagine your work with the riflemen will be taxing enough. A year, your commission?'

Hervey took a sip of his coffee expressly to display a measure of insouciance. 'That is the expectation, as much to do with the detachment of the troop from my own regiment as with the requirements of the Rifles.'

'Mm. Your troop – their horses in a bad way.'

There seemed something just a shade censorious in the manner that Somerset expressed himself, but Hervey chose not to take offence. 'I have a most excellent veterinary surgeon.'

Somerset did not at once reply. When he did, his tone was almost icy. 'Colonel Hervey, let me be rightly understood. I do not take kindly to officers ranging at the frontier as you did, and I do not approve the conversion of the Cape Corps into a bunch of English burghers in green coats. Raise your Mounted Rifles as you will; it will be *regular* discipline that checks these savages.'

PART THREE
THE WOLF ON THE FOLD

The Assyrian came down like the wolf on the fold,
And his cohorts were gleaming in purple and gold;
And the sheen of their spears was like stars on the sea,
When the blue wave rolls nightly on deep Galilee.

Lord Byron, 'The Destruction of Sennacherib'

CHAPTER TWENTY

TO GLORY WE STEER

Gibraltar

Captain Sir Laughton Peto was not a dressy man. If the officers and crew of His Majesty's Ship *Prince Rupert* (120 guns) did not know of his character and capability then that was their look-out: no amount of gold braid could make up for reputation.

Peto's time with Admiral Hoste, not least in the action at Lissa, his command of *Nisus* with the East India Squadron, then commodore of the frigate squadron in the Mediterranean, and lately command of *Liffey* while commodore of the flotilla for the Burmese war – these things were warranty enough of his fitness for command of a first-rate. Not that it was any business of the officers and crew: he, Captain Sir Laughton Peto, held his commission from the Lord High Admiral himself. These things were not to be questioned, on pain of flogging or the yard-arm. Except that he considered himself to be an enlightened captain, convinced that having a man do his bidding willingly meant the man did it twice as well as he would if he were merely driven to it. Threatening to start the last man down a sheet might increase the speed of the watch's descent, but men fell in their dread of the knotted rope-end. Threatening to start the slowest team in gunnery practice risked the sponging done ill: a 'premature' could kill or maim every last one of them. Except, of course, it was one thing to have a crew follow willingly a captain who was everywhere, as he might be able to be on a frigate, but quite another when his station was the quarterdeck, as it must be with a line-of-battle ship. *Nisus* had but one gundeck. In action the captain might see all. *Prince Rupert* had three, of which the two that hurled the greatest weight of shot were the lower ones, where the guncrews worked in semi-darkness and for whom in action the captain was as remote a figure as the Almighty Himself. The art of such a command, Peto knew full well, was in all that went before, so that the men had as perfect a fear of their captain's wrath – and even better a desire for his love – as indeed they had for their Heavenly Maker. If that truly required the lash, he would not shrink from it, but at heart he was one with Hervey: more men were flattered into virtue than bullied out of vice.

Rupert had a fair reputation herself. Like the Admiralty's other first-rates she had not seen action in a long time – Peto thought it probably in the West Indies – but being later built she had been kept in full commission for longer after the peace of 1815. He knew her first lieutenant just a little, and what little he knew he approved of. *Rupert* looked in good trim, handsome even, as she rode at anchor in Gibraltar Bay against the background of the towering Rock.

Any ship would look handsome at Gibraltar, reckoned Peto, as hands pulled smartly for their wooden world – *his* wooden world. The barge cut through the modest swell with scarcely any motion but headway: not a degree of observable roll, nor more than ten of pitch – testament to the power with which hands were bending oars.

Peto saw nothing but his ship, his eyes fixed on her from the moment of stepping into his barge. In part it was because he would take the one opportunity to study her as an enemy might see her, before he had her under weigh, for with a freshening westerly and such a sky it would not be long before she could make sail. Those indeed were his orders, to proceed without delay to join Vice-Admiral Codrington's squadron in the Ionian, there to compel the Ottoman Porte to give up its repression of the valiant Greeks. He might have taken command sooner, but the incapacity of the prime minister, Lord Liverpool, had for some weeks thrown doubt on the enterprise. A year before, the Duke of Wellington, under Mr Canning's instructions, had signed a protocol in St Petersburg by which Russia, France and Great Britain would mediate in what to all intents and purposes had become war between the Greeks and the Ottoman Turks. The prospect of a new government had brought the future of the protocol into question; until in the middle of April the King had sent for Mr Canning and asked him to assemble a new administration. This had cheered the more active of the occupants of both the Admiralty and the Horse Guards, for although Mr Canning's manners were to the liking of few of them, his vigorous policies called for strong naval and land forces, welcome counterweight to the mood of retrenchment which had settled on Whitehall since Waterloo. The only problem seemed to be that hardly a man of repute would agree to serve under him: no fewer than seven members of the cabinet had resigned, including the duke himself, as well as Mr Peel and Lord Bathurst. However, through the accommodation of the Whigs, Canning had been able to form his government, and instructions followed for the protocol to be ratified by formal treaty – on which news the Admiralty restored its plans for the reinforcement of Sir Edward Codrington's squadron.

And so Captain Sir Laughton Peto R.N., in undress uniform – closed double-breasted coat with fall-down collar, and double epaulettes denoting his post seniority – with his India sword hanging short on his left side in black-leather scabbard, and furnished

297

with his letter of appointment, was now within a cable's length of another great milestone of his life. He had wondered long when it would come, or *if*; at their dinner at the United Service Club he had told Hervey he was certain it would not. 'There will *be* no more commissions,' he had predicted. 'I shan't get another ship. They're being laid up as we speak in every creek between Yarmouth and the Isle of Wight. I shan't even make the "yellow squadron". Certainly not now that Clarence is Lord High Admiral.' For yes, he had been commodore of a flotilla that had overpowered Rangoon (he could not – nor ever would – claim it a great victory, but it had served), and he had subsequently helped the wretched armies of Bengal and Madras struggle up the Irrawaddy, eventually to subdue Ava and its bestial king; but it had seemed to bring him not a very great deal of reward. The prize money had been next to nothing (the Burmans had no ships to speak of, and the land-booty had not amounted to much by the time it came to the navy), and *K.C.B.* did not change his place on the seniority list. The Admiralty not so many months before had told him they doubted they could give him any further active command, and would he not consider having the hospital at Greenwich?

But having been, in words that his old friend Hervey might have used, 'in the ditch', he was up again and seeing the road cocked atop a good horse. The milestones would now come in altogether quicker succession.

What a sight was *Rupert*! Even with all her sail furled she was the picture of admiralty: yellow-sided – 'Nelson-style' – gunports open (he much approved of that, letting fresh air circulate below deck), the crew assembling for his coming aboard (he could hear the bosun's mates quite plainly). What could make a man more content than such a thing? He breathed to himself the noble words: *gentlemen in England, now abed, will think themselves accurs'd they were not here.*

There was *one* thing, of course, that could make a man so

content: the love, the companionship at least, of a good woman (the love of the other sort of woman was all too easy to be had, and the contentment very transitory). And now he had that too! For in his pocket was Elizabeth Hervey's letter.

Why had he not asked for her hand years ago? That was his only regret. He felt a sudden – and most unusual – impulse: he wished Elizabeth Hervey were with him now. Yes, this very place, this very moment, to see his ship as he did, to appreciate her beauty and her possibilities – *their* possibilities! Oh, happy thought! Happy, happy thought!

'Boat your oars!' came the reedy voice of the young midshipman as the barge neared the lowered gangway on *Rupert*'s leeside, calling Peto back to the lonely state of captain of a first-rate.

Peto glanced at him, studied him for the first time – a mere boy still, not sixteen perhaps, but confident in his words of command and boat handling. He had blond curls and fine features – so different from the Norfolk lad of fourteen that he himself had been as midshipman in the early years of the 'never-ending war'. He had never possessed such looks as would delight both fellow officers and females alike nor earn the seaman's habitual esteem of the patrician. Big-boned he was: 'hardy-handsome' his mother had called him, which was not handsome at all in her reckoning (or so he had supposed). But Elizabeth Hervey had not rejected him. *No*; not at all. Indeed he thought that Miss Hervey had once actually made eyes at him – in Rome, many years ago. Oh, how he wished he had recognized that look (if look it had been – preposterous notion!).

He snapped to. *Belay* the thought! For he could hear the bosun's call.

The piping aboard, the shaking hands with officers and warrant officers – he had done the same before, several times; but never on a first-rate. To be sure, he had hardly set foot on a three-decker since he was a young lieutenant. He would not address the crew, as he had when taking command of *Nisus*, for whereas his frigate's complement had been but two hundred (and he could know every man by name and character), *Rupert*'s was in excess of eight – far too many to assemble decently for the sort of thing he would wish to say. Command of a first-rate was perforce a rather more distant business. Strictly speaking, command even of *Nisus* was properly exercised through his executive officer, the first lieutenant, and to some degree by the master, but in a ship of two hundred souls the captain's face was daily – at times hourly – known to all. His own quarters were on the upper deck: he had to climb the ladder to the quarterdeck, and in doing so he might routinely see half the crew. On *Rupert* he would merely step from his cabin: descending to any of the gundecks was therefore an 'occasion'. His world was changing even if he were not. He could no longer be the frigate-thruster. But his nature was by no means aloof, and he must find some happy middle channel between his own inclination and the customs of the service. He did not expect it to take long, or even to try him; but meanwhile – as any prudent captain – he would take up the command firmly yet judiciously. In an hour or so His Majesty's governor of Gibraltar would pay a call on him, and then, if the westerly continued to freshen, *Rupert* would make sail for Syracuse to take on the pure water of the Artemis springs, just as Nelson had before the Nile. And from there he would set course for Codrington's squadron in the Ionian. For the time being, however, he would withdraw to his quarters, hear the reports, read the signals, sign the returns.

Flowerdew, his steward of a dozen years and more, was waiting. The sentry presented arms – sharper, thought Peto, than even the well-drilled Marines on *Nisus*. The red coat, the black lacquered hat, the white breeches and pipeclay – Peto suddenly felt himself a little shabby by comparison in his sea coat. But that, he reminded himself, was how it should be: a Marines sentry was by his very turnout a powerful aid to discipline, whereas a captain's attire must be weather-seasoned. He might put on his best coat for the governor (his dunnage Flowerdew had brought aboard earlier in the day); there again he might not.

He took his first, portentous steps aft of the sentry, followed by his executive officer and Flowerdew. At once he saw how much bigger were his quarters – bigger, appreciably, than any he had occupied before. He saw the little oil landscapes on the bulkheads which he had had on *Nisus*, and the furniture, over and above what their lordships provided, which he had bought from the previous captain (who, transferring to half pay, had been only too happy to strike a bargain and thus save himself the expense of shipping home). He could be confident, too, that his cherished silver, china and glass would be safely stowed.

'Coffee, sir?'

'Thank you, yes, Flowerdew.'

'With your leave, sir,' said the first lieutenant.

Peto took off his hat and placed it on the dining table (Cuban mahogany reflecting the sun through the stern gallery like a mirror). 'By all means, Mr Lambe. A half-hour's recollection, and then, if you please, you may give me the ship's states.'

'Ay, ay, sir.' The executive officer replaced his hat, touched the point and withdrew.

When Flowerdew came with coffee he found his captain sitting in his favourite leather camp chair. Peto had had it made many years before in Minorca, with pouches fixed on each arm: the left side for his clerk to place papers for attention, and the other for Peto himself to place the papers after his attention. But rather than attending to his clerk's paper, Peto was staring out of the stern window, and with a look of considerable contentment. Flowerdew could not be surprised at this: if his captain mayn't have a moment or two's satisfaction in his new command then what did it profit a man to be in the King's service? 'Coffee, sir.'

Peto nodded, and raised his hand in thanks.

Flowerdew had no wish to intrude on the moment; there would

301

be time enough to get back into the old routine. He placed the cup in Peto's hand, and left the cabin quietly.

Peto reached inside his coat and took out Elizabeth's letter. He had placed it between the leather binding of an old copy of Steel's *Mastmaking, Sailmaking and Rigging*, from which he had removed the pages, and wrapped it in an oilskin. Even thus preserved, the letter bore the signs of much consultation.

Horningsham,
28th March 1827

My dear Captain Peto,

Let me at once say that I accept your offer of marriage with the very greatest delight. I perfectly understand that you were not able to travel to Wiltshire, and I am only content that you did not delay until you were able to do so. For my part, I should have wished at once to accept, but you will understand that I felt a certain obligation to my brother, though I could never have doubted his approval.

I am so very happy too at your news of command, though I shall confess also that my happiness is tempered considerably by the thought that H.M.S. Prince Rupert is taking you so very distant. But that is the way of things, and you may be assured that I shall never be a jealous wife where your ship is concerned!

I am so very proud, too, that your command is to be in the Mediterranean, not only for its healthiness and beauty but because I believe it a very noble thing that we should assist the Greeks in their endeavours to shake off the Ottoman yoke. You will, of course, be now daily in my prayers – I think I may say constantly *– and they will be for your safe and speedy return.*

My father will make the usual arrangements for the notice of our betrothal, which I must trust shall be to your liking.

I hasten to close this, though I would write so very much more were there the time, for the express boy is come even now, and trust that you shall receive it before you sail.

Your ever affectionate
Elizabeth Hervey.

Peto read it a second time, and then a third. It was the first letter in a female hand that he had ever received. He had no certainty of the tone or convention, but he considered it the warmest expression of esteem. How different it felt – strangely different – taking to sea with a wife awaiting his return (he already imagined her in the Norfolk drawing room): his world was no longer wholly wooden, sea-girt and male.

He folded the letter, replaced it between the bindings, wrapped it in the oilskin and put it back in his pocket. As he did so he thought again of Elizabeth's sisterly duty – so admirable a thing – and then the object of that duty, and wondered how was his friend in southern waters. Perhaps – his new command notwithstanding – he might even envy him a little, for would not Hervey have more prospects of the smell of black powder than would he himself in the Ionian? The native tribes of the Cape Colony would know no better than to chance against His Majesty's land forces; but the Turk must know that he could have no fight at sea with a first-class naval power. And certainly not *three* such powers, now that it was Russia and France bound in by formal treaty. The Ionian mission would indeed be a noble one, but it would in essence be an affair of display – a show of force, a demonstration. It would be his old friend who heard the sound of the guns, not he.

CHAPTER TWENTY-ONE

REPORTS AND RETURNS

Cape Town, 23 November

The onset of summer at the Cape, with fine weather for shooting and drill, was on the one hand most welcome: the Rifles were becoming the handiest of troops. Yet Hervey chafed at the enforced inactivity of his dragoons, whose days were spent breaking remounts. It was true that in drill the Rifles were by no means in advance of them, but as regular cavalry shipped with their own horses, E Troop should have been at duty already for the best part of three months.

When the time came – two months after returning from the frontier – for Hervey to submit his first report as detachment commander to Lord Holderness in Hounslow, he was at least relieved that the end of the Troop's incapacity was at hand.

23rd November 1827

To The Rt. Hon. The Earl of Holderness,
Commanding Officer,
H.M. 6th Light Dragoons,
Hounslow.

Sir,

*I have the honour to submit this my report for the first three
months of the detachment's duty at the Cape, as required by
Standing Orders. Returns and accounts are attached herewith.*

*Shortly upon disembarking, the troop's horses were afflicted
with a most virulent disease thought to be habitually present in
these parts, which no quarantine was able to prevent since its
nature is not properly understood. I regret to have to inform
Your Lordship that in spite of the best efforts of Veterinary
Surgeon Kirwan fifty-three horses succumbed to the fever.
Goodish remounts have been obtained locally, however, and these
are now fully trained, but the troop has been unable to take part
in the active operations foreseen by General Bourke when he
requested a reinforcement. These shall begin shortly and take the
form of patrols along the eastern frontier of the Cape, which is
called Kaffraria, and some punitory expeditions into the territory
of the Xhosa, who are the native people of this part of the
colony. I must observe, however, that the country is not entirely
advantageous to cavalry, where it is frequently impossible to form
line and to maintain it, and I have given it as my opinion to
General Bourke that the Corps of Mounted Riflemen, which are
now formed and ready to take to the field under their own*

officers, shall likely be a better force to employ in this work. This we may soon observe, and General Bourke has expressed himself entirely content that if the Rifles are steady and capable then he will release the Troop Detachment to return to England, for it is ever a draw on his resources, which accounts are already in deficit.

I regret to have to inform Your Lordship also that five men have died of disease or injury since our arriving. I have, with Your Lordship's presumed permission, authorized promotion in acting rank, of Corporal Wainwright to serjeant, and others, minor, as detailed in the attachments . . .

The report continued for three more sheets of foolscap, with a further four of attachments. Hervey hoped it would be deemed adequate. Not knowing his commanding officer, he found it difficult to be sure what matters might be regarded as trifling. Lord Holderness would know none of the detachment by name and perhaps next to nothing about the Cape and its condition. Of future dispositions and manoeuvres Hervey could, in truth, say very little, for these were to be of a speculative nature – patrolling, and the recovery of cattle. There was, still, no very clear understanding of what the Xhosa intended (if they intended anything at all). Despite what Gaika had promised when his son had been returned to him, his tribesmen had continued almost without let to cross the Keiskama to hunt, and of late had begun crossing the Fish again, so that the frontier settlers were once more reporting cattle losses. Fort Willshire had had to request reinforcements, and twice Colonel Somerset had travelled to Graham's Town to judge the situation for himself. Hervey found he could bear the absence easily.

General Bourke on the other hand, when he returned from St Helena in the middle of October, Hervey found to be a straightforward man, but much preoccupied with administration and the business of accounts. Hervey was sorry for him. It was clear that the War Office had set him the most stringent economies, and that his future depended on them. Hervey wished never for general rank if it meant being an actuary in a red coat.

Colonel Somerset had no difficulty persuading General Bourke that the Xhosa would soon make war on the colony. Or rather, he had no difficulty persuading him of the possibility – and, as the frontier defences stood, of the unfavourable outcome. So persuaded, it was the general's duty to alert the lieutenant-governor to the danger, and to set in hand the appropriate measures.

Hervey was not persuaded, however. Or rather, Edward Fairbrother was not, and it was Fairbrother's opinion for which he had the greater regard. They had indeed become firm friends, and Hervey had arranged for him to exchange onto full pay as super-numerary captain in the Mounted Rifles.

Throughout November memoranda had travelled backwards and forwards like petitions in the Court of Chancery: Hervey to Bourke, Bourke to Somerset, Somerset to Bourke, Bourke to Somervile, Somervile to Hervey, Hervey to Somervile, Somervile to Bourke. Until in the end the lieutenant-governor felt himself thoroughly apprised of both the arguments and the plaintiffs, and that a colonial council was the appropriate means of resolving the dispute.

'I thought it better to hold the council here rather than in chancellery,' he said as General Bourke took the coffee cup from the tray which the khitmagar held ready at the door of the residence's library. 'I have asked Colonel Hervey to attend, and I beg you would forgive me if it is amiss, for if the troop of cavalry is to return to England not so very long from now, and he with it, I would have him give as much an account there of our deliberations as possible.'

'Eminently reasonable, Sir Eyre,' said Bourke, unperturbed. 'As I informed you, there will be no need of a lieutenant-colonel in the Rifles once they are formed into independent companies. I myself

would not have wished it, but the state of the military accounts . . .'
He shook his head.

'And I have asked, too, Captain Fairbrother. I believe it would
be apt if he were to hear our deliberations, since I might wish him
for an interpreter at a later date.'

The general's countenance remained the same: if the lieutenant-
governor could be accommodating in the matter of military
economies, then he himself could overlook an irregularity of
military protocol. 'It is your prerogative, Lieutenant-Governor.
You will not, I imagine, be asking for their opinion on
military matters on which I should be obliged to give mine on a
par.'

'No, indeed, certainly not! Only their opinion of the peril we
face. Yours is the military opinion on which I must act.'

The show of mild dismay was effective: the general nodded. 'Of
course.' He drained his cup and took another.

Somervile now sought to be confidential. 'You are aware, are
you not, of all the changes in government?' (On the sudden death
of the prime minister in August there had been comings and
goings.)

'I may not be. Huskisson has War and the Colonies, as I
understand.'

'You understand right.' The former President of the Board of
Trade was now Secretary of State for the War and Colonial
Department. 'Palmerston remains at the War Office, and Anglesey
at the Ordnance.'

'And has Peel returned?'

'No. It is Lansdowne who has the Home department.'

'Capital.' General Bourke was of the opinion that no good
would come of things as long as Peel and those like him were
opposed to giving the Catholics their relief. 'He'd stand in the last
ditch outside Dublin.'

Somervile half smiled. 'Ah yes, Catholic Emancipation. Which
reminds me, the amendment to the Slave Ordnance . . .'

General Bourke looked at him intently, and not a little suspiciously.

'I take note of your memorandum,' said the lieutenant-governor.

'You mean you will delay its promulgation?'

'If we conclude this morning that action is necessary then I fear I have no alternative.'

Bourke looked satisfied. 'It is, of course, a civil judgement, but the military consequences are of concern to me. We should have to call out the burghers of Graaff Reinet and Uitenhage first, and they're among the biggest slave owners. It wouldn't do to embitter them now.'

Somervile nodded, reluctantly: it was a damnable thing to play with men's liberty like this – and, for that matter, to play false with the burghers so.

The khansamah appeared. 'The council is assembled, sahib.'

Somervile smiled his thank-you. 'Well, General, shall we to our council of . . . *war*, I am tempted to say?'

An hour they sat in council. They heard the reports from the frontier landdrosts, which the colonial secretary had collected, all of which spoke of intolerable levels of predation. Colonel Somerset, as commandant of the frontier, gave his military assessment: without calling out the auxiliaries there was nothing more that could be done with the forces at his disposal.

'A good deal of the present trouble is undoubtedly brought upon by the character of the settlers come from England and Ireland in recent years. They have no very great disposition to industry and no inclination to exert themselves. Indeed, at times it appears their chief object is to oppose or render odious all authority of any kind, to magnify all their difficulties, and even to sow the seeds of their discontent further afield.'

There was much nodding among the dozen or so officials round the table.

'Does anyone wish to add anything in this regard?' asked Somervile, glancing about the assembly.

Fairbrother, sitting not at the table itself but behind Hervey, rose.

Colonel Somerset looked astonished. His mouth opened in protest.

But he was too slow. 'Proceed, sir,' said Somervile.

'Sir Eyre, gentlemen,' began Fairbrother, nodding to the seniors with an exemplary show of respect. 'All that we have heard – even this ill disposition and magnification on the part of the settlers – cannot account for what is perfectly clearly a significant irruption by the Xhosa. I remain of the opinion that the Zulu are the true cause of the turbulence. They press in from the north-east of the Xhosa's territory, and the Xhosa in their turn are displaced towards the south-west and over the frontier. In other words the trespassing and the reiving is to all intents and purposes a Zulu peril.'

Colonel Somerset struck the table. 'Sir Eyre, we have heard all this before, in Colonel Hervey's memoranda. It is most improper for this . . . officer' (he appeared to force himself to say it) 'to address the council in this way.'

Somervile looked at General Bourke. He had a mind that since this was not a matter of *military* opinion the general would have no objection to hearing it (or at least would not declare so).

The general shook his head.

Somervile replied with considerable balm. 'Colonel, I do agree with you that we have read extensively of these views, but the benefit of hearing them in council is that all may hear equally, and a proper record of deliberations may be made. *Littera scripta manet?*'

With a bow, Colonel Somerset – for the time being at least – conceded.

'Carry on, if you please, Captain Fairbrother,' said Eyre Somervile, concealing a smile of satisfaction.

'Thank you, Sir Eyre. I know the following to have been placed before you already, but while Captain Hervey was received by Gaika I was able to speak with some of the Xhosa elders. I believe that Gaika and the other Xhosa chiefs could be persuaded to resist the Zulu if they are given military assistance. By all I know, this King Shaka will not give up his predations. At best he will push the Xhosa from their land, and they will come across the frontier and make war with the colony. But at worst Shaka will defeat them, or persuade them to an alliance, and then we shall be obliged to fight both Xhosa and Zulu.'

Somervile nodded. He had indeed heard it before – it was the stuff of many memoranda – but he wanted the words to be heard in council, and time for them to be weighed. He said nothing for a full minute, appearing to contemplate the paper in front of him.

At length he looked at General Bourke, who remained silent. 'Very well. The inescapable conclusion, gentlemen – unless there is something I have overlooked – is that it were greatly better to fight this Shaka now, and at a remove on the north-east of Kaffraria with the Xhosa in alliance, than face the prospect in not many more years of fighting the Zulu on the Fish River, with the Xhosa on Shaka's side.'

No one spoke.

Somervile looked at the colonial secretary (later Hervey would conclude that it was rehearsed). 'Colonel Bird, what are the reports of Shaka?'

Colonel Bird opened a portfolio. 'Sir Eyre, the reports to hand on the activity of the Zulu are – I trust that *I* do not magnify them – of an alarming tendency. The Zulu have already raided deep into the land of the Tambooka, and not two weeks ago, when the Natal report was sent, they had marched several days into Xhosa land and taken many cattle.'

Heads were lowered studying the maps on the table.

'It is far from clear that they have withdrawn from either territory, and it seems likely that raiding on this insolent scale has

311

been occurring for many months. I am of the opinion, too, Sir Eyre, that the present trouble on the eastern frontier is due indirectly to Shaka's predation. It would test our strength sorely to subdue the Xhosa, even with the auxiliaries called out, and if the Zulu then overrun the Xhosa territory – which would be in effect with our assistance – we should face a greatly more rapacious opponent. I submit, gentlemen, that Shaka is our more dangerous enemy, not Gaika.'

There was hubbub. Somervile, certain as he was that a consensus could only be reached by so palpably 'democratic' a fashion, let it continue while he appeared to gather his papers and his thoughts.

General Bourke looked contemptuous of the disorder, but said nothing (Hervey surmised that it was all the better to maintain his dignity thereby).

When the noise began to die down, Somervile tapped the table with the ends of his fingers. 'Thank you, gentlemen, for your admirably succinct and unequivocal opinion. General Bourke?'

Somervile played his cards well, thought Hervey (as he had always known him to do): to have asked for any other's opinion now would have been a discourtesy at the very least.

General Bourke looked thoughtful. 'I should like to hear Colonel Somerset's estimation.'

Somervile glanced at the commandant of the frontier.

The commandant gave it at once. 'Sir Eyre, General, I do not agree with Colonel Bird's opinion' (Hervey noted the omission of Fairbrother's name) 'that Shaka and his Zulus are the cause of the trouble along the frontier. He shouts "Eureka!" like Archimedes in his bath: the Zulu displace the Xhosa, who then wash over the border. It is not science here. The Xhosa are an indolent people; they wish for easy prey. That is why they trespass in the colony!'

General Bourke's expression was of mild surprise.

Somerset held up a hand. 'However, I do believe Colonel Bird is correct in saying that if the Zulu overwhelm the Xhosa – whose true fighting prowess I have never held in high regard – then we shall indeed have a more rapacious, and greatly more capable, enemy on the Fish River. From what I have heard of the Zulu under Shaka, I should not be content to let them rest there without two brigades of regular cavalry and three of infantry at the frontier. To that end, therefore, I believe that the defeat of Shaka should be our object as prelude to dealing with Gaika. Indeed, it may well be that the destruction of Shaka is a powerful enough signal to every Xhosa chief.'

Somervile could not hide his satisfaction. He now looked to General Bourke for his conclusion.

The general gave it decidedly. 'I concur. I believe we must send word to Shaka informing him that the colony supports the Kaffir tribes. It might have some moderating effect, though I doubt it. We might gain a little time, however. I would propose meanwhile to assemble a field force and call out the burghers.'

The lieutenant-governor sat silent with his hands together, as if in prayer. He had read the reports, listened to opinions, and received his general's advice. He could not – in council at least – decently consult more. Besides, he had heard beforehand the opinion of the officer he trusted above all others. 'Very well, General. The embassy to Shaka, if I may call it that, is to proceed at once, and I leave it to your discretion who shall constitute it, for although it is a matter of polity, yet I believe it best carried out by the military. Be pleased to assemble a field force such that could, in concert with the Xhosa, eject the Zulu from the tribal territory. I will today issue instructions for the call-out of the burghers. What is the earliest that you would be able to take to the field?'

'Three weeks.'

'Very well. For the purposes of the necessary authority and expenditure, Colonel Bird will enter that date, three weeks hence, as the commencement of active operations.' He bowed. 'Thank you, General, gentlemen, for your counsel. We may adjourn.'

*

313

Outside, in the warm summer sun, Colonel Somerset had words with Hervey. 'Do not suppose that I did not know what game was afoot in there, Hervey. You and your half-caste friend may have the ear of the governor – and for the time being of General Bourke – but let it be rightly understood: I shall command the field force, and you shall carry out my orders!'

Hervey bowed. 'I understand perfectly.'

CHAPTER TWENTY-TWO

THE KAFFRARIA FIELD FORCE

Graham's Town, 19 December

Instructions to the Commander of the Kaffraria Field Force
By Major-General Richard Bourke C.B.

In accordance with a directive received from Sir Eyre Somervile
K.H., C.B., Lieutenant-Governor of the Cape Colony, you are to
proceed at once to the frontier of the Kaffir tribes and the
territory of the Zulu and, in concert with the Xhosa and others,
take what measures you deem expedient for the ejection of the
Zulu from the country west of the Bashee River. Your object
shall be the utmost demonstration to the Zulu Chief Shaka that
His Majesty will not permit of the intrusion into the country west
of the Bashee River, for whatever purposes. The Lieutenant-
Governor does not consider that it shall be expedient to cross to
the East of the Umtata River, but he does not absolutely forbid
it if in your judgement it is necessary for the accomplishment of

315

the object. The Lieutenant-Governor does not consider that causing for Shaka to be killed, or his taking prisoner, shall be expedient.

The following shall comprise the Kaffraria Field Force (Lt. Col. The Honbl. H. Somerset).

H.M. 55th Regmt, Lt. Col. Mill
Det. H.M. 6th Lt. Dgns, A/Lt. Col. Hervey
Coy. Mtd. Rifles, Capt. Welsh
Two commandos (Durand and van Wyk), Albany district
    (all mtd. troops to be under orders Col. Hervey)

Det. R. Artillery, Capt. Baker
Trp. Civil Hottentots, Lt. Sinclair

(sgnd.) R. Bourke,
Maj-Genl,
Commander of the Forces of H.M. Cape Colony,
The Castle, Cape-town,
7th December 1827

Hervey contemplated his command. It was drawn up for final inspection before they would cross the frontier into the Xhosa territory, two wings of a bird, as it were, each very differently feathered but in its own way looking entirely serviceable. On his left – the right of the parade, as befitted their seniority – stood eighty-eight horses and men of E Troop, His Majesty's 6th Light Dragoons, the blue of their tunics already faded slightly by the Cape sun, the shako covers bleached perfectly white. The troop stood a hand or so lower than at the final parade before embarkation in England: the remounts were hardy enough, but short in the leg. Hervey had no great concern about this: in action against cavalry the difference of a hand might tell, for height gave a man the advantage in a contest of sabres; against infantry it mattered less, especially men for whom a horse of any height brought terror. On his right were ranked the Mounted Rifles, two hundred of them, true dragoons – men for whom the horse was the means of swift movement between one fighting position, dismounted, and another. They wore green rather than blue, as the riflemen of the English Line, their shakos were almost identical to the Sixth's, and they wore loose, strapped trousers not unlike the Sixth's overalls. Unlike the Sixth, however, what they called swords were in fact bayonets, although some of the riflemen had in addition curved or straight sabres attached to the saddle. Their horses were compact too. For the Cape Corps of Mounted Riflemen, however, a horse that stood 14.3 hands was something of an advantage: easy to mount, and to dismount from, easier to hold, easier to conceal.

One troop of light dragoons, one company of mounted rifles: the combined strength was that of a squadron, not much more. And yet Hervey had ideas for his command (which included the burghers, although he had his doubts about their reliability in a pitched battle) that made them more of a brigade. The Rifles had drilled with growing confidence in the past month, so that he was certain of their usefulness *en masse* rather than as mere mobile skirmishers or *patrouilleurs*. And their captain was a good fellow – Welsh, another Shorncliffe man, late of the Forty-third, who had come to the Cape five years ago when his young wife had died in childbirth.

'Hammer and anvil,' he said as he watched them – the blue and the green. Their serjeant-majors were satisfying themselves that all was well, each in his own way. Hervey marked the difference: the Rifles' man scurried and harried like a terrier; Armstrong stalked along the front rank like an old hound, snarling occasionally, and once or twice barking.

'Hammer and anvil?' asked Fairbrother, sitting astride a little chestnut entire that looked as if it could leap the Fish River in one bound.

Hervey wore Rifle green (as did Fairbrother): he had handed command of the troop to his lieutenant. And with the Rifles company under the able orders of its own captain he was able to sit at a remove and take in the scene. The last of the stores were being broken out at the wharves and loaded onto the sprung waggons – a dozen of them, real fliers compared with the groaning old carts they had had in India. He was looking forward keenly to the fight, and hammer and anvil was how he saw the blue and the green: 'You fix the shoe in place upon the anvil, then strike with the hammer. You fix the Zulu in place upon the Rifles and then strike with the troop.'

Fairbrother nodded.

'Or perhaps the analogy is better made with beaters and guns.'

'Each might be apt,' replied Fairbrother, his eyes still on the parade. 'Depending on who was to deal the fatal blow, rifles or cavalry.'

Hervey turned to him, with the suggestion of a smile. 'You should never have wasted a moment on half pay. That green suits you.'

'Black buttons, black face?'

'Do *not* begin on that again!'

'It is a little difficult not to when Colonel Somerset appears to consider me but a native scout!'

'Tush!'

Fairbrother returned his eyes to the parade. ' "Who is the happy Warrior? Who is he that every man in arms should wish to be?" '

' "It is the generous Spirit". That is what the poet said, is it not? Be generous then!'

'I am at your service.'

He was. Captain Edward Fairbrother – the rank now properly constituted – was appointed aidant to the Officer Commanding Mounted Detachments, Kaffraria Field Force. It was a fine title, he had observed; and, more sardonically, one that would look fine on a gravestone.

One of Colonel Somerset's gallopers came bowling along the line in a growing cloud of dust.

'Why do you suppose he thinks that necessary?' said Hervey, shaking his head. 'We have sat a good hour.'

Fairbrother shrugged. 'Somerset will be impatient for the off. That, or he confounds celerity and celebrity.'

Hervey laughed, then returned the galloper's salute.

'Colonel Hervey, sir: the column's to advance at ten o'clock.'

Hervey took out his watch. It was fifteen minutes before the hour. 'Very well.'

He turned to the two gallopers from the Sixth and the Rifles, who had closed with him on seeing Somerset's man approaching. He nodded to them; he need say nothing.

They relayed the order at the trot, the drill for muster parades. Hervey was pleased as he watched the lines form column of route with but a very few words of command. He glanced left and right. In the distance were the burghers. He need give them no orders. Their instructions were to guard the flanks during the march; they would conform by their own initiative. Hervey may have had his doubts, but in this sort of ranging the burghers were practised enough.

At ten o'clock Lieutenant-Colonel the Honourable Henry Somerset gave his bugler the order to sound the advance, and the Kaffraria Field Force began its march to the frontier. The fifes and drums of the 55th (Westmoreland) Regiment of Foot struck up 'The Lass o' Gowrie', and the battalion stepped off at attention as one, arms sloped, heads high. Hervey watched them with admiration: these were the men – the infantry of the Line – who had prised the French out of Spain and stood astride Bonaparte's arrogant march on Brussels. They could volley like no others, and they could charge with the bayonet. They could prise the French out of Spain again and out of Belgium if it came to it. But were these close-drilled ranks what was needed here? He did not know. Colonel Somerset was sure of it: breasts of red to affright the

319

savage, and cavalry to terrify him! And perhaps it would be so, for who knew how these Zulu fought? Hervey simply inclined his head: in a month or so they would have their answer.

CHAPTER TWENTY-THREE

THE HAPPY WARRIOR

Gaika's kraal, ten days later

Hervey reckoned that Chief Gaika's kraal covered the same area as what his father called the *cursus* of the Great Henge on Salisbury Plain. It lay on an east-facing slope in open country ninety miles beyond the Keiskama River, within sight of many smaller ones. This was Gaika's principal kraal (the one nearer the frontier afforded better grazing for his *iinkomo* – his cattle – in winter). The outer perimeter was a stockade of thorn about seven feet high, with an inner palisade fifty yards beyond. Grass-made huts like beehives occupied the space between the two, in which lived the tribal chosen. Inside the palisade Gaika's cattle were herded at night, and in the middle was the chief's own hut encircled by a smaller thorn thicket. Hervey and Fairbrother had not been invited into the sanctum when they visited the winter kraal three months before, but now they stood in Gaika's clay-floored courtyard with Colonel Somerset and his staff, welcome-mead in hand and with the unquestionable authority that a regiment of redcoats and several hundred horse conferred.

Gaika spoke freely and with animation. Colonel Somerset's interpreters – one Dutch, the other Hottentot – struggled to keep up with him.

'He's not saying that,' whispered Fairbrother. 'That's not what he means.'

Hervey leaned closer to him. 'What *is* he saying?'

'He speaks the *conditional*: they are translating as if he spoke an intention.'

Hervey was resolved not to stand on ceremony. He edged forward from the back of the party to where he might have Somerset's ear.

'A word, Colonel, if I may?'

Somerset heard but did not move a muscle. Hervey knew well enough the courtesies in front of a man such as Gaika; he would just have to wait.

After ten minutes, as Gaika sat down and motioned for more mead to be brought, Somerset turned to him. 'Colonel Hervey, your intrusion is not apt.'

Hervey bit his lip. 'Fairbrother says you are not being served faithfully by the interpreters. They give the impression of Gaika's concurrence with what you ask of them, whereas he speaks conditionally.'

Somerset checked his instincts to curse Fairbrother for his impudence: if what 'the half-caste' said were so then it changed the conclusions he was coming to. He bowed to Gaika, turned and beckoned Fairbrother to him.

'What is all this?'

'Colonel, Gaika is not saying that he *will* not cross into the colony, and that he *will* oppose the Zulu, he is saying that he *would* if he were able to persuade the elders of the Xhosa to muster their warriors, and *if* the men in red and the horses fight alongside him.'

Colonel Somerset looked dismayed. 'You are sure?'

'I am. And he implies he had already taken an unfortunate decision – I suspect to throw in with Shaka. He said *Ngebe silahlekile ukuba ubungasibonisanga indlela*: "we would have got lost if you had not shown us the way."'

Somerset thought for a moment. 'Come with me.'

Hervey followed too.

Gaika smiled, and invited them to sit on hides next to him. They drank more mead, and he revealed that he recognized Hervey, and Fairbrother (whom he called *njengomXhosa* – 'like a Xhosa').

'*Ndisafunda, mhlekazi*,' replied Fairbrother, raising his palms.

Colonel Somerset looked at him.

'I said that I was still learning.'

But Gaika smiled. He liked *mhlekazi* – 'big handsome one'. He turned to Somerset. 'This man we shall speak through,' he said, decidedly.

Fairbrother relayed the sentiment to Somerset, who nodded.

He did not wait to be asked by either party. '*Mhlekazi*, if you are able to muster all the warriors, how many will they be?'

Colonel Somerset looked affronted. But he did not speak.

Gaika told him twenty thousand, though Fairbrother told Somerset he thought he exaggerated. And Gaika spoke with increasing warmth. He and Fairbrother talked as if equals for a quarter of an hour, during which Somerset – with unexpected patience, thought Hervey – remained content to listen without understanding.

At length Fairbrother turned to Somerset. 'I believe I now have it. Gaika can muster seven thousand warriors at his own call, and his two vassal chiefs a further ten. He speaks of the Zulu in most measured terms, however. He says it had first been his intention in the event that they invade the Xhosa territory to hide all his corn and drive the cattle, of which he has twenty thousand head, towards the Keiskama. He says the Tambooka tribe, whose territory is nearest the Zulu, have already lost much of their cattle

323

and are powerless to resist. When I told him he would have the immediate support of a thousand of the King's troops, and artillery, he expressed himself willing to meet the Zulu in battle, and not to cross the Keiskama.'

Somerset's mouth fell open. 'You told him we would support his warriors?'

'I did. But it was a mere matter of pride. He would do precisely what you wanted him to do were we to confront the Zulu. He puts on a brave face, but he is terrified for his life.'

Somerset said nothing.

Fairbrother waited. He had said all there was to say to Gaika; if Somerset wished to repudiate the offer . . .

The commander of the Kaffraria Field Force braced himself. 'Very well. Please ask Chief Gaika when we may march.'

Hervey's head swam as he sat down in a camp chair in the welcome shade of his tent. The Xhosa mead had been strong, and the sun had seemed twice its usual power. Johnson brought him the blackest coffee, and he opened his journal and picked up his pen, as he had intended to do before Gaika had invited – summoned – the officers to feast.

29th December 1827

The country is so very like the Wiltshire plain that at times I almost imagined to see Dan Coates riding to his sheep. The march from Grahams-town, nine days, has been uncommonly tiring though, two hundred and thirty miles is the reckoning. Not so great a distance, perhaps, compared with marches in India, and the Peninsula, but the going has not been easy for the men of the 55th, and the waggons have frequently fallen behind. The artillery is six guns: four 9-pdrs and two 6-pdrs, drawn by oxen, and are a day's march to our rear. I cannot but think that a pair of galloper guns would be of better service, and were the troop to

remain long in the Cape I should have a pair made. Our horses
are good doers, perhaps better so than would have been the
troopers brought from England, and our sick have been few.
Private Attewell was left with an orderly two days ago at the Kei
River, very sick of a sting.

E.F. has been sent to find Dundas – the excellent fellow from
Graham's-town who is sent to speak with Shaka Zulu – to tell
him what Somerset has decided. We are now to rest here a day
while the artillery rejoins and Gaika sends word to his other
chiefs . . .

''Ow'd tha like thi steak, then, sir?' Johnson had left Hervey in
peace with his journal for half an hour. He considered that to be
more than enough time spent on a book of any description, even
the Bible (on which he spent no time at all; but the Bible he knew
to be special).

Hervey looked at him, puzzled. 'I *said* that I have eaten enough
for three men already.'

Johnson was equally puzzled. 'That's what ah said, sir: were it
good?'

Hervey's brow furrowed deeper. It was a trivial matter, but he
was not going to let it pass. 'No, Johnson, you said, "How would
I like my steak?"'

'Ah didn't! I asked 'ow'd tha like thi steak!'

Hervey's mouth fell open. 'Precisely!'

'What, sir?'

Hervey sighed, thinking. 'A moment. How would you ask,
"How did you like your steak"?'

''Ow'd tha like thi steak.'

'And how would you ask, "How *would* you like your steak"?'

''Ow'd tha like thi steak.'

Hervey raised his hands, smiling. 'As tricky as translating
Xhosa. You see my difficulty.'

'No.'

325

'The words are exactly the same.'

'Ay, sir, but ah wouldn't ask thee 'ow'd tha like thi steak doin when ah knew th'd 'ad plenty already!'

Hervey shook his head with mock gravity. 'How could I have made such a mistake?'

'Because tha's tired, an' that mead.'

Hervey looked long at him. 'Johnson, is there any of the India ale left?'

'Couple o' bottles.'

'Then fetch two, and I'll tell you about Gaika's hut, and what I think we'll do next.'

Not long before dusk Fairbrother returned unexpectedly – and urgently. Hervey was first alerted by a trail of dust which he observed through his telescope a full ten minutes before making out the rider. The lathered flanks of Fairbrother's Caper testified to their hard gallop: he had left his escorts far behind. He looked more purposeful than troubled, however, as he dismounted in the Sixth's lines. But all knew that a man did not ride as hard as he had for no good reason.

One of the dragoons took the reins. The horse was blown but by no means finished, Hervey noted: Fairbrother had judged it well. There were some who believed it necessary to ride a horse into the ground when carrying an urgent despatch, but Hervey had always been of the opinion that the precise moment of collapse was never predictable, and therefore that it was too hazardous a principle to follow. 'What's the alarm?'

Fairbrother took off his shako and wiped his brow with his fore-arm. 'Dundas,' he began, shaking his head, and taking a long drink from a flask of Cape wine which Johnson had produced from nowhere. 'Done the deucedest thing. I ought to report to Somerset straight away.'

'He's still at Gaika's hut. I'll send word.' He turned to find Serjeant Wainwright already standing at attention. 'We need to alert Colonel Somerset. Will you present my compliments, tell him that Captain Fairbrother is returned, and ask if he will come here or if he wishes us to attend on him.'

'Sir!' Wainwright saluted and spun round, setting off towards the kraal in a brisk march that would have matched a Xhosa's lope.

'Now,' said Hervey when there was no one within earshot, and sitting down in one of the camp chairs that Johnson had brought. 'What's the business with Dundas?'

Fairbrother settled heavily, and blew out his breath. 'He got up to the hills in the Tambooka country the day before yesterday, about thirty miles north and east of here. He had a report of a force of Zulu advancing towards the Bashee. The Tambooka were to make a stand east of the river.' He took another draw on the flask. 'So he crossed the river a few hours before dusk and met Voosani, the Tambooka chief, who told him the Zulu had already taken several thousand head of cattle. Dundas said he would assist him recovering them. Why he believed that recovering the cattle was a more effective means of conveying the message to Shaka I have no notion.' He took yet another long draw.

'And?'

Fairbrother shook his head. 'It might have passed with no great harm, for it seems Dundas's original intention was to block the ford through which the Zulu intended driving off the cattle. But as they approached, apparently with just a few drovers, he decided he'd attack. The drovers were seen off easily, but then he ran into the Zulu rear guard, and it was a desperate business for a while, until powder began to tell. He reckons to have killed fifty of them, but then came word that several *thousand* were moving on the ford, and so Dundas got the Tambooka to recover what cattle they could, but even these had to be abandoned as the Zulu began pressing them. So Dundas decided to escort Voosani to his kraal to try to rally more warriors, which is where I found him, and he at once sent me back to alert Somerset.'

327

Hervey began unfolding his map. 'How long do you think it will take us to get up to the Bashee? What is the country?'

'The infantry won't manage in less than a day. But why exhaust ourselves? Why not wait for the Zulu to come to us? They'll burn the kraals and take the cattle and the corn, but it might have to be the price if we're to be certain of stopping them. The Tambooka will flee this way. We could rally them and have another five thousand or so.'

'Do the Zulu have muskets?'

'The scouts didn't speak of them.'

Hervey was trying to calculate time, distance and relative strengths. 'Do you not think we might overawe them with a show of force – the troop and Rifles, I mean – while the infantry and the rest march up?'

'Divide one's force?'

Hervey raised his eyebrows. 'In ordinary, of course, it's folly; but in an exigency . . . I wish I had some better idea of how the Zulu fight.'

He and Fairbrother had talked a good deal of Shaka's system, such as they knew it. However, the accounts came either from (as Somerset called them) rascals, freebooting Englishmen, or else from the defeated tribes, and were hardly reliable therefore, given as they usually were in wide-eyed terror or with nefarious intent. It was evident that the Zulu did not simply overwhelm their opponents by sheer numbers – a great host of savages bearing down on their peaceable neighbours like the wolf on the fold. There were, it seemed, well-formed regiments – *impi* – who moved quickly and under strict discipline. Their weapon was the short spear, the *iklwa*, which was not thrown but thrust, like the jabbing sword of the Roman legions. And there was no doubt that a Zulu warrior was possessed of singular courage. But as to what this amounted to in the field neither Hervey nor Fairbrother could tell. Of one thing, however, Hervey was sure: *dash*, the bold offensive action which in India could turn the tables so spectacularly when the situation looked desperate, might not serve here. For if, as the stories went, the warriors were more afraid of Shaka's vengeance than of death at the hands of the enemy, they would not be so easily scattered as the bandits who passed for soldiers in India.

'We have lost the element of surprise, of course,' said Hervey, rising as he saw Somerset approaching. 'They know there are white faces with the Xhosa now, and guns. The only thing left to dismay them is numbers or some clever manoeuvre.'

Fairbrother said nothing. What he knew of his friend's capacity for audaciousness was considerable. From all he had read, and even more from those he had spoken to, he judged this measured response to be uncharacteristic – as well as intriguing.

Somerset was a shade unsteady and his speech not entirely even. Hervey felt only sympathy, and nodded to Johnson, who knew what was required.

Fairbrother made his report.

Somerset, sitting low in a camp chair, sipping repeatedly at his strong black coffee, began to look uncertain. His fighting, such as it was, had been on interior lines, east of the Fish River, with a number of strongpoints around which to rally. Here in open country, a thorn-fenced kraal the only feature, and his force not yet even united, he saw the possibilities of defeat only too clearly. His distaste for Fairbrother was now all but gone. 'I am grateful for your timely intelligence, Captain Fairbrother. Admirable. And Dundas?'

'As I said, Colonel, I believe he may be able yet to bring over Voosani and his men.'

Somerset nodded slowly. 'That is what Gaika said – that Voosani will fight if we support them.' He looked at Hervey. 'Colonel, what is your opinion?'

Hervey was surprised to be asked; Somerset had scarcely spoken half a dozen civil words to him since Cape Town. He sensed he was not being asked the best course of fighting the Zulu, however; rather whether they should fight at all. 'Well, Colonel, General

Bourke's orders are clear enough, and we know what is the lieutenant-governor's intention behind them. We have not been able to deliver an ultimatum to Shaka, but if we don't make a stand against these Zulu here then an ultimatum would have no effect. I see no occasion to withdraw.'

Somerset looked disconcerted. 'You do not consider it my overwhelming duty to preserve my force? We should be hard pressed to find another.'

Hervey saw no profit in debating the principle. 'I don't think we need consider it in those terms, Colonel. May I propose that I take the mounted detachments forward to make contact with the Zulu? It might still be possible to parley with them, especially since they have not yet seen troops under discipline. But if not, at least I should be able to ascertain something of their numbers and condition, and perhaps intention. Meanwhile, if Voosani's men can be rallied, and Gaika can muster all the Xhosa . . .' He tried to make his suggestion as unemphatic as possible: he had to leave the commander of the field force with an opening to take up the proposal as his own.

Somerset turned to the commanding officer of the 55th (Westmoreland) Foot, who had come in from the pickets on seeing the galloper. 'Colonel Mill, what do you consider is the capability of your battalion?'

Lieutenant-Colonel John Mill was a veteran of much fighting – the West Indies, the Peninsula, Waterloo – and his face bore the battle honours. Whatever he thought of Lieutenant-Colonel Henry Somerset, a man considerably younger than he and with a complexion as fresh as the schoolboy's, he kept an impassive countenance. 'In square my battalion could not be broken, and in line it could not be resisted, Colonel.'

That seemed to do the trick. With such resolution at hand, how could he, Somerset, do other than offer battle here, between the Kei and the Bashee? 'Very well, gentlemen. Colonel Hervey, you may take the mounted detachments as you propose and make contact with the Zulu. As soon as the artillery comes up, and Gaika's men are mustered, I shall march towards the Bashee – unless you report that the Zulu are in too great strength. I shall keep the burghers with me. They're not so steady, yet they will afford me some protection if – I mean *when* – we advance.'

No one spoke. Each man saluted and took his leave, knowing without need of elaboration what their business was to be about.

Somerset, alone, in his camp chair, lapsed into a gloomy, distant stare. His orderly brought him a bottle, which he took with resignation rather than relish. This was not how he had imagined it would be.

They broke camp at midnight. Four or five hours in the saddle, by Hervey's reckoning, and they would be in the more undulating country west of the Bashee. This would give a horseman the advantage, for with videttes on half a dozen high points they would soon be able to estimate the size of the Zulu force, and there would be less chance of being encircled. His one concern was colliding with the Tambooka if they were falling back towards Gaika's kraal; but they met no one. Hervey imagined that scarcely an owl could have been witness to their night march – a cold affair too, wanting capes, whereas by day it was shirtsleeves, and too hot at that.

How he wished he could have more confidence in Somerset, both his capacity for decision and for resolution! Yet he supposed, at bottom, that if the blood of the Beauforts coursed through Somerset's veins there could not be too much amiss. Proud he was, yes; and that verged on the perilously disdainful. But Hervey was certain that Somerset had the capacity to fight sword in hand (and he had a suspicion that when it came to fighting these Zulu it would be the will to take the blade to the enemy that counted). He quickened at the thought. He felt his hand twitch for the sabre hilt. Who *were* these Zulu that they should discompose one of the King's officers? He would not dismiss them as savages, as others might, but he would not invest them with supernatural prowess. Did that mean he might defeat five thousand of them with his three hundred dragoons and riflemen? Hammer and anvil, beaters and guns, whatever was the proper analogy, his force was the superior in fire and in manoeuvre. His rifles could bring down a warrior at a furlong, and he had yet to see men afoot and who did not form square resist the charge of cavalry. How did this Shaka suppose he could defeat even so much as a troop and a company of the King's men?

CHAPTER TWENTY-FOUR

FIRST BLOOD

Next morning

Just before dawn it began to rain. Not heavy, but a steady down-pour which was soon soaking tunics and overalls. The night had been starry, with a good moon, and then a half-hour before first light, cloud had rolled in from the south-east, out of the Indian Ocean, relict of the south-west monsoon. Hervey's spirits sank with the rain as he realized the fault in his appreciation. Rain had the potential to render the musket and the rifle no more than a pike. He cursed. He cursed doubly, for it need not be so. A man did not have to empty powder down a wet barrel, or into a wet firing pan for the wet flint to fail to spark. There were cartridges that could be placed into the barrel whole, and rifles which permitted loading at the breech, so that powder did not have to come into contact with damp air, let alone wet metal; and there were percussion caps – clever little things filled with fulminate of mercury – which could be inserted into the firing pan, so that when struck by the hammer

333

that had formerly held the flint, the cap would give off the necessary spark to ignite the cartridge. Neither was this new science: a percussion cap had saved his life at Waterloo, provenance of Daniel Coates. The Ordnance, however, had no time for the novelty. And so here, now, in the chill drizzle of the veld, the only firearm he could rely on was his own percussion carbine, and Fairbrother's revolver: two hundred rifles stood hostage to the rain and the new-acquired skill of their handlers. His own troop's carbines he might rely on a little more, for his dragoons were certainly more practised than the riflemen; yet he knew it was possible that a hundred carbines might misfire in the face of a Zulu attack. And what message of capability might that send to Shaka?

As the sun came up, not as fast as in India, but quickly nevertheless, the rain eased and then stopped altogether. Hervey's disquiet eased with it. They could begin to dry the firelocks – which dragoon and rifleman alike had wrapped with oilskin – and mop the barrels. It would be good to prove each weapon, he thought, though it was a practice he normally abhorred (for why give away anything to the enemy?). He was sure the Zulu would be within earshot, however: he would lose any element of surprise.

He almost lost it before he knew. The scouts stopped suddenly. They had ridden ahead as dawn broke, five hundred yards to the next rise along the line of advance. Moments later one of them began cantering fast in a circle, anti-clockwise.

Hervey lowered his telescope and turned to Lieutenant Fearnley and Captain Welsh riding alongside him. His voice compelled urgency. 'Into line, two ranks, dragoons front – as we drilled. Then wait my orders.'

They saluted, and reined about hard.

Hervey nodded to Fairbrother and took off in a hand-gallop towards the scouts, trying to keep low the dust which even the rain had not quite suppressed.

334

'Forgive me, Hervey,' called Fairbrother above the drumming of hooves, 'but has something decidedly cavalry happened?'

'Infantry – Zulu – in large numbers.'

'That much you can tell by a scout galloping in a circle?'

'Yes. If he'd circled clockwise it would have meant cavalry. The pace he circles gives an indication of numbers.'

It was three hundred yards to the rise where the scouts stood: a minute and a half's work for charging warriors – enough time to reload carbines and at least one barrel of the rifles. Hervey calculated these things as a matter of course; any cavalryman would – *must*. The range was too great for a bullet, though, let alone a carbine ball. If they were to check the Zulu as they came over the rise he would have to advance the line at least a hundred yards to rifle range.

But the scouts were now motionless. Evidently the Zulu were at a safe distance still.

Hervey slowed to a trot as he came up behind the ridge, Fairbrother at his side, coverman and trumpeter a few lengths behind. He snatched his telescope from the saddle holster, reining to a halt beside Corporal Wick. And he stifled a gasp. On the parching plain beyond was a sight that set rats racing in his gut and stirred the darkest corners of his mind. It was as if twelve monstrous black snakes were making straight for the ridge, any one of them with venom enough to kill an entire troop, or else to coil and crush the life out of them. There were warriors in single file for as far as the eye could see – and see through the telescope – spears and shields in hand, loping across the dry, green veld at the pace of trotting cavalry. He had not seen killing-columns come on like this since Waterloo.

He was shaken as much by his own shock as the sight itself. He breathed deeply so as not to falter or gabble when he spoke; he prayed the cold sweat was invisible. 'How many, Corporal Wick?'

'I reckon on two thousand, sir. And then that dust yonder must mean there's as many more.'

Hervey peered through his telescope again at the distant cloud. No matter how green the country there was always dust. How distant it was difficult to tell – the featureless veld, the sun in their eyes – but it must be far enough not to have caught the rain of the pre-dawn. Perhaps, then, they had a little more time than he supposed: these advance guards, as they must be, would probe rather than commit themselves to a fight if they were not sure of overwhelming their opponents. That, at least, was the received wisdom in His Majesty's army. But it was perfectly possible that in Shaka's they did things differently.

But where were the Zulu's scouting parties? 'Have you seen ought else, Corporal Wick? Scouts, men moving independently?'

'No I haven't, sir. Not a bird or nothing.'

Hervey was calculating as he spoke. The ground had no features by which to judge the distance perfectly, but since to the naked eye the Zulu were clearly afoot rather than mounted, by the usual yardstick it meant they were no more than seven furlongs off – say *five* since it was possible to make out their gait. And at their loping jog-trot (say five miles in the hour) – that would make seven or eight minutes at most before they closed.

'Corporal Dilke, silent-signal for the troop and Rifles to advance at the trot.'

His trumpeter turned and began raising and lowering both fists (left for the Rifles, right for the troop) as if he were pulling a beam-pump.

In seconds the line of blue began advancing, then the green.

Meanwhile Hervey scanned the plain through his telescope. 'Not exactly Chobham Common, is it, Corporal Wick?' he said in a manner convincingly cool.

'Sir?'

'The last time I seem to recall you were scouting in similar circumstances.'

Wick looked at Hervey, astounded. ''Ow'd you remember that, sir? It were years ago!'

The strange Shrewsbury vowels always reminded Hervey of school, where Wick's father had been gatekeeper. 'All of ten, I think. We did rather well in those manoeuvres, as I recall.'

'Well we did, sir!' But Wick had been an eighteen-year-old recruit; in ten years he had seen enough to know the difference between a field day and real fight. Nevertheless, if Colonel Hervey was conducting himself now as if he were at a field day, then who was *he* to worry?

Hervey checked the flanker scouts through his telescope. They were probing a furlong or so behind the ridge, left and right, keeping an eye on any little fold in the ground which crafty Zulu might use to outflank them. He took satisfaction in that: it was exactly as they had drilled at Hounslow. Things were working.

He glanced back at the advancing line of blue, and behind it the green. Two hundred yards, and a little more: it would do. 'Corporal Dilke, signal "Halt".'

The trumpeter stood in his stirrups again and raised his hand. The lines quickly came back to the walk and then halt.

Hervey observed the Zulu's progress. Five more minutes, he reckoned. 'Very well. Remain posted till I return, Corporal Wick.' He reined Gilbert about and spurred into a gallop back down the slope, Fairbrother, coverman and trumpeter following hard.

Fearnley, and Welsh at his side, saluted as he approached. 'Rifles loaded, but not carbines, Colonel,' said the lieutenant.

'Very good. Firelocks dry enough?'

'I trust so, Colonel,' replied Captain Welsh.

'Very well. The Zulu are advancing in twelve columns, without skirmishers so far as I can see. I estimate perhaps two thousand in the mile hence, and as many more at least beyond them. I intend to try parley. Mr Fearnley, bring up the troop to just below the crest and then onto it when I go forward.'

'Colonel.'

'If parley fails, I reckon I can gain a minute at most on them back to the ridge. When you see that, I want you to take the troop

337

to the left flank – the ground looks a fraction better that way – and stand ready in line in dead ground to take any advantage once they broach the crest. But listen hard for the trumpet for recall. No running on!'

'Colonel.'

'Captain Welsh, your company to check them as they broach the crest. Is the range to your liking?'

'Two hundred and fifty yards, and Zulus tight-packed? Admirable, Colonel.'

Hervey was sure of it. He had watched the riflemen put bullet after bullet into the target at two hundred. 'How many rounds can you get off from crest to here?'

Welsh had already calculated. He could fire two rounds a minute at least, and all his riflemen carried spare balls and powder flasks as well as the prepared cartridges; a charging Zulu might cover the ground in . . . a minute? 'Five, perhaps six. Better we snipe them at the crest, though, and open a general fire as they come down the slope.'

And then they would have to remount in good time, Hervey knew: they could not take on an unending swarm of Zulu with the bayonet. He nodded. 'Very well. Three rounds, then withdraw as they get to a hundred yards. Rally on that last ridge we crossed.'

'Three rounds it will be, Colonel. One hundred and forty rifles: four hundred and twenty corpses.'

Hervey smiled. A happy warrior indeed, Captain Welsh. He supposed that if all his riflemen were of the same spirit, the horse-holders would be prodigiously frustrated.

A different voice now hailed him: 'May I ride with you, Hervey? I should so very much like to see how these things are done.'

Hervey turned to see Sam Kirwan in his fore-and-aft, as incongruous a hat in the field now as once it had been commonplace. He smiled again: a happy warrior-veterinary. 'Have you ever unsheathed that sword, Sam?'

The veterinary surgeon judged the question rhetorical.

But Hervey did not forbid it. Sam Kirwan reined up alongside Serjeant Wainwright, and opened his notebook.

Hervey at once took off back to where Corporal Wick stood resolutely observing the Zulu.

'Still coming on, Colonel,' said Wick as Gilbert almost stumbled to a halt next to him.

Hervey took out his telescope for one last look before the parley.

Sam Kirwan closed with him and slipped from the saddle. 'Gilbert's running uneven, Hervey. Let me take a look.'

Hervey had noticed nothing: any horse could stumble, and they were none of them too fresh. 'What—'

'Breathing's very irregular, and the pupils are like saucers. Hervey, you'd better change horses. He looks as though he could drop at any moment.'

Hervey jammed the telescope back in its holster. 'Very well, but after I've had the parley. This isn't the time to be changing horses.' He glanced behind.

The troop was beginning to come up the slope.

'Time to introduce ourselves to the Zulu, I believe.' He squeezed Gilbert's flanks – just a touch with the lower leg – and the gelding stepped off at once.

There was no white flag. Hervey was sure it would mean nothing to the Zulu, and in any case he disliked the practice since it restricted his freedom of action. Instead the little party advanced towards what he presumed was the leading column, where he supposed he would find either the commander of this host or else an officer who would know where the commander was. Fairbrother rode at his side, and to the rear of them Wainwright and Corporal Dilke, and behind them Sam Kirwan.

They began to trot. Hervey felt at once that Gilbert had lost his spring. The horse was indeed tired; perhaps he would change to his second as soon as he got back to the ridge (Johnson, for sure, would be there waiting for him). But this slope was kind; they could take it in an easy canter down to the Zulu, and it would not tax them greatly to regain the crest afterwards – even if they had to make a run for it.

He glanced over his shoulder again. There was the troop in impressive line along the ridge, motionless, two hundred yards of blue and yellow, and white-topped. But, strangely, he found himself wishing it were a furlong of red: there were times (very few, but this was one) when he knew that Nature's own colour of danger magnified the effect.

The black columns stopped suddenly, and then came a blood-chilling moan which almost knocked him back in the saddle. He had never heard its like – not the shouting on the battlefields of the Peninsula, nor the cheering at Waterloo, nor even the fiendish cries at Bhurtpore. It was inhuman, one voice prodigiously loud rather than many thousands, as if they somehow spoke – *thought* – with one mind. It was eerie; indeed it was unsettling. He prayed it would not be unnerving.

He pressed on without checking, however, or without looking behind, the canter and the slope taking him voluntarily or otherwise towards the snake-like columns. At a hundred yards the columns became things of glistening, feathered warriors, of spears and shields. Hervey knew he had seen nothing of its like. Never before, no matter how savage the enemy, had he perceived Creation so . . . primitive; as if from the earliest days of the Fall. He wondered how he might speak with such a people – if these primitives could be dignified by the word 'people'. Not just speak but communicate, convey an understanding.

He slowed to a trot and then a walk, and came to a halt fifty yards from the head of the centre column. There he would wait for a propitious sign.

He waited for what felt a long age. And while he waited he began to see the remarkable uniformity of these warriors. At first he had observed merely shield upon shield; now he saw shield upon identical shield, the *exact* same. And they were evidently of animal hide, which uniformity spoke to him of Shaka's powerful dominion

340

over 'every living thing that moveth upon the earth'. Each warrior wore an apron of bunched hide and feathers (every one the same) and a headband of spotted fur (leopardskin, perhaps?) and white streamers just above the elbow on each arm – oxtail hair probably. Hervey wondered if they fought as regularly as they looked, in close formation; or if they attacked in loose, open order, as skirmishers did. He studied the short, stabbing spear – not *assegai*, as he had once thought it called, but *iklwa*. It appeared to be their sole weapon. The blade was about a foot long, a few inches at its widest, tapering to a rounded tip, unlike the pronounced point of the bayonet or the sabre. He reckoned it would need strength to stab home with it. But such a point, driven into the gut with force, would do such damage as to confound the best surgeon's art. The warriors held the short shafts to stab underarm. Hervey could picture the method – the shield not merely to parry, but to mask the coming thrust. He did not think it would do to face such a weapon with a sabre, dismounted.

One of the Zulu stepped forward, a thick-set, older man with a slight stoop. Hervey had not noticed him before, for he was dressed the same as the rest – except that he wore a necklace of claws.

'*Molo mhlob'am!*' said Fairbrother, saluting.

The tribesman eyed him cautiously.

Fairbrother supposed he recognized the friendly Xhosa greeting, even if the Zulu were different.

'*Yebo, sawubona!*'

The words were unfamiliar, but Fairbrother fancied the raised spear was greeting enough. He would try the simplest Xhosa by return. 'Colonel Hervey, here, commands a detachment of King George's army.' He indicated the royal representative.

The Zulu put the point of the spear to his chest. '*Igama lami nguMatiwane!*'

Fairbrother saluted again. '*Ndiyavuya ukukwazi, Matiwane.*' He had learned the Zulu's name (Matiwane); was he the cohort's

341

chief? He would press to know the reason for their advance. 'You come to see your brothers the Xhosa?'

While Fairbrother continued his halting exchange, Hervey took in all that he could of the extraordinary scene. He marked that the Zulu could see the troop on the ridge, a quarter of a mile away. They watched warily, like some animal when a distant predator appeared. Perhaps the horses did indeed make them uneasy? For all Hervey knew, this Matiwane might believe the horses could leap at him in seconds, like the leopard, with many thousands more of them waiting to pounce, all hidden the other side of the hill. But even as he watched them parley he became aware that the columns were not absolutely motionless. He glanced left and right. He could not actually see the Zulu moving, only somehow that there had been movement. He glanced left and right again. The progress was now evident, as must be the purpose: the Zulu were moving to encircle them. And they would not need to complete the circle: it would only take a rush before long and their line of withdrawal would be closed. He must act at once.

He held up a hand. 'Sharply, about turn and away!'

Fairbrother made to protest, but Hervey gave him no chance. They turned and galloped like the devil, Sam Kirwan leading.

The same blood-chilling moan followed them, like a thousand angry wasps in an echo-chamber. Hervey did not turn. He pressed Gilbert as hard as he could, but feeling with every stride that something was amiss. As they got within hailing distance of the crest at a struggling canter, the gelding stumbled once, and then again, and then tumbled onto the forearm, throwing Hervey clean from the saddle.

At once Wainwright faced about, the only man between the Zulu now and his commanding officer. Corporal Dilke circled, Fairbrother turned and jumped down beside his friend, and Sam Kirwan sprang from his nappy little mare to do what he could for the fallen gelding.

'No good, Hervey. An aneurism. He might recover, but—'

342

Hervey knew. The Zulu were not a furlong away, loping towards them as if the ground were as flat as a cricket field. He looked at Gilbert, his companion of many an affair. The gelding's nostrils flared, and his eyes stared crazily. Hervey reached for one of the pistols in the saddle holsters. It was loaded, tamped, ready. He took the other, pushed it into his belt, knelt by Gilbert's neck, lifted his head in his left arm and put the pistol into the fossa above the right eye.

'Goodbye, old man,' he said, softly but quite audibly. Then he pulled back the hammer and squeezed the trigger.

Before the smoke began to clear, Johnson was holding Hervey's second horse not ten feet away. 'Molly, sir.'

Hervey watched the last twitch of Gilbert's shoulder, then rose and vaulted into the mare's saddle. The Zulu were now but fifty yards away and the moan had become a deep-throated, menacing roar.

They galloped for their lives.

As they reached the temporary safety of the troop line, Fearnley gave the order to present carbines: if the Zulu did not recognize the danger in five-dozen muzzles, they would soon receive a lesson.

'Capital, Mr Fearnley,' gasped Hervey, still winded, but perfectly calm. 'One volley, and then to the flank. Clear the line of the Rifles' fire quick as you can.'

Fearnley saluted as Hervey spurred his mare between two dragoons, both of whom looked eager to practise their musketry.

He heard the volley as he galloped on to the Rifles.

'All ready, Captain Welsh?' he called as he pulled up beside him.

'All ready, Colonel,' replied Welsh, equally composed.

Hervey could not be surprised. It was the baptism of fire for the company as a whole, but enough of the riflemen had seen some sort of action. 'Capital. They come on in single file, a dozen or so. I hope Fearnley will be able to break them up for you a little.'

'We'll do a little of that for ourselves too,' said Welsh, mysteriously.

Hervey looked at him, curious.

'Did you not see the skirmishers as you galloped past?'

Hervey had not, and even when Welsh pointed them out he had difficulty seeing them. He smiled. 'I should have known. Exactly as the Ninety-fifth would have done it.'

'No. *Better* than would the Ninety-fifth. These are picked men – sharpshooters, snipers. And they have two rifles apiece.'

Hervey nodded approvingly. The black-powder smoke would too soon give away their position, but four well-aimed shots in rapid succession would surely tell. 'How many?'

'A dozen.'

They would serve very well. Hervey nodded again but said nothing.

And then came the most decided lump in his throat. Gilbert was not Jessye, but they'd been together a good many years . . . and now that handsome grey's carcase would be defiled by a swarm of savages, hacking off that fine mane and flowing tail . . .

He came to. The troop had gone threes-about and were trotting down the slope towards them. He watched with the keen satisfaction of a man who had drilled his command in the peace of Hounslow Heath and who was now seeing the profit of that exertion. Many a dragoon who had cursed him behind his back would now be seeing the method in those long field days. Not that he should ever concern himself too greatly with what the canteen was saying. All the same . . .

They broke into a steady canter and began changing direction right. Hervey continued to watch with approval, and not merely for a drill-book evolution smartly executed, for it was not to be found in the drill book: they used a 'non-pivot' movement to bring about changes of direction in line faster and with fewer words of command. It had been his doing: the usual wheeling required the left or right flanker to turn slowly on the spot while the rest of the line swung round, like a door on its hinge, each man at a slightly different speed. It was a movement that looked fine when performed well on the parade ground but which was painfully slow and inactive in the face of the enemy. If they tried to wheel here, now, there was every chance the Zulu would fall on the right of the line before the evolution was complete.

What effect had their volley had though? Hervey wished he could have seen for himself, for it would have told him a deal about the way the Zulu would now fight. But he would have obstructed the Rifles' line of fire had he remained with the troop and then tried to gallop back here.

It was not long – a minute perhaps – before he had his answer; in some part at least. The Zulu broached the crest more or less in line. This was what he had wanted: although Welsh's snipers would not now be able to pick off the column leaders, the Rifles would have many more targets than if the Zulu had remained in single file.

Atop the ridge the black host suddenly halted. Perhaps they caught their breath, he thought. Perhaps they surveyed the veld to their front. Either way it was a sight that he – *all* of them – would not forget, for this was the first clash of arms with Shaka's army. The Zulu were an unknown enemy; they had terrified the tribes of the far-eastern Cape for ten years and more. It was inevitable that the greatest native power would in due course fight the King's men. And this was the moment. Hervey marvelled at it – before wondering if he would live to tell.

Every officer's telescope was now trained on the black line.

'Not quite a thousand,' said Captain Welsh, matter-of-factly. 'But not many short of it.'

Quicker than had Hervey, he had calculated the length of the ridge, and the part of it the Zulu occupied: twelve hundred yards of warriors close-packed.

Hervey had no reason to dispute it, but he had hoped the frontage would be far less, for there was now a considerable over-lap (the Rifles fronted no more than two hundred yards).

There again, he had no intention of letting the Zulu close with them. 'Three rounds then, Captain Welsh – in your own time.'

As the captain touched the peak of his shako to acknowledge, the first of the snipers' shots rang out. One of the warriors in the centre of the line fell face down, dead. A great, painful moan swelled the length of the line, as if the death of one was the wounding of all.

Hervey felt a strange shiver in his spine. The battlefield was never so silent a place as here: no artillery, no musketry from opposing clouds of skirmishers; just a single shot, and a thousand voices – not so very different from the battles of the Old Testament on which he had feasted as a boy.

And then another shot, and another, and then several more. And every time a warrior falling. Hervey could not help but think that this was the way to give battle: sniping at the enemy from a distance, perhaps even picking out the men who would direct the fighting. He wished he had a troop of horse artillery with him. They would soon have the range, and shrapnel would fell these men in droves.

Why did the Zulu stand instead of advancing? Or withdraw behind the crest? Did they not comprehend what powder and ball was? Was it possible that so successful a tribe did not know of firearms? How he wished (did not the Duke of Wellington himself always say?) he were able to see over the other side of the hill. Were they waiting for the rest of the *impi*? Would the attack, when it came, be not this single line of a thousand warriors, but several?

That, however, made no difference to his intention here: three rounds and then withdrawal. And in any event he could rely on Fearnley to judge keenly how to wield the troop to advantage. No, he was curious only in what the attack would tell him about the wiliness of the Zulu in battle – and therefore how he might play them as his little command fell back towards Somerset's main force.

'Here they come!' said Welsh purposefully.

Hervey quit his thoughts and pushed his telescope back in its holster; and then almost at once he took it out again, for as the Zulu swarmed down the slope he observed that they left behind a knot of men on the ridge, which he supposed at once to be Matiwane (he now wore a great feathered headdress) and his staff. He recalled how at one point during the battle at Waterloo a horse gunner had told the Duke of Wellington that he had Bonaparte within range, and asked leave to open fire. The duke had refused him, saying that it was not the business of one commander-in-chief to fire upon another. Hervey had never quite believed it – even less understood it. Yet now he had a curious sense of why the duke might have been moved to say so, for he felt as if he would be shooting a magnificent perching bird if he fired on Matiwane. Ignoble deed! And yet he approved – *cheered* – the sniping of mere legionary warriors. It was not to be fathomed.

'Captain Welsh, see yonder, in the middle of the ridge – the plumes. Might one of your men try his hand?'

Captain Welsh arranged it at once. 'Serjeant-major! Corporal Cloete!'

They doubled to the company commander. He gave them the order.

The two sharpshooters doubled forward ten yards, and lay prone. Each took careful aim and fired.

The two rounds struck home, though the feathered target remained upright. It was extreme range, and the two riflemen calmly corrected their point of aim for the second barrel.

But before they could fire, other warriors surrounded the chief: a shield of flesh.

The serjeant-major fired; a warrior-shield fell dead.

Corporal Cloete fired an instant later but another Zulu had already taken his place.

The serjeant-major was reloading furiously. 'We can do it, Cloete, even if it takes a dozen apiece!'

But before they could, more Zulu swarmed onto the crest to shield Matiwane.

347

'As you were!' called Hervey. This was a diversion they could ill afford.

Horse-holders now galloped forward to where the other sharp-shooters lay. The picked riflemen sprang up and into the saddle, and spurred back to the line in a display that Hervey was sure would have delighted the duke himself.

'Smart work, Captain Welsh; smart work.'

'Thank you, Colonel. I will pass on your approbation at the first opportunity,' said the rifles captain, as if he were being dismissed at the end of a field day.

The Zulu came on steadily in the same loping gait. Hervey felt his stomach tightening again. The range was now two hundred yards: it was time for the Rifles to do their *real* work.

He did not have to say anything. Captain Welsh had primed his men well: 'In your own time, three rounds: *Fire!*'

The first round was a near-perfect volley. Every man had taken and held his aim, waiting the order, so that as soon as it came twelve-dozen trigger-fingers squeezed as one. The powder-smoke hung low in the still air, but not as thick as it would have been with a company of muskets (the rifles were in open order). The fire-effect was visible at once. Hervey was astonished. Every round seemed to have found its mark.

But the Zulu line did not falter. The second volley came not five seconds later, more ragged this time, but just as accurate, so that a quarter of the Zulu host now lay dead or writhing at the bottom of the slope. It would be half a minute before the third, final, round, while the riflemen reloaded. Hervey cursed that they could not have another two volleys as quick: the French for sure would have reeled in the face of such fire; the Burmans and the Jhauts would have taken to their heels.

The volley made him start. It had come in seconds only, along the entire line . . . He looked at Welsh, amazed.

'The horse-holders' rifles. Better used than in a saddle bucket.'

He wished he had thought of it himself.

348

'Now for the final round!' said the captain keenly.

But the Zulu would not face it. On the crest of the ridge Matiwane's spear was raised.

How the order was communicated to that blood-hotted host Hervey had no idea, but they turned as one. They had not run twenty yards, however, when the third volley caught them, a ripple of fire as the new-loaded rifles found a fleeing target.

'Now, Fearnley, *now!*' cried Hervey, as if his lieutenant might hear.

Lieutenant Fearnley was of the same mind, however. The troop surged forward, quick to the canter and then gallop.

'Stand fast, Rifles!' shouted Hervey as he pressed his mare forward.

The troop galloped into the left flank of the struggling Zulu, taking them by utter surprise. Hervey saw the sabres lowered – the point for infantry (the edge for cavalry) – and then the opportunity cuts as the dragoons drove through the ragged line. As he closed with the mêlée he picked out a crouching Zulu, shield up and *iklwa* menacing. He took him with a neat Cut Two from behind, severing the shield arm, before turning and taking another with the same cut, using his reach to slice the spear arm at the wrist without coming in range of the point. He galloped on towards the crest while the troop continued to sweep it left to right, Fairbrother, Sam Kirwan, Wainwright and Dilke hard on his heels. There was but one sure way to discover what lay on the other side of the hill.

The sight from the crest set the rats racing in his stomach faster than ever. Not a hundred yards off and coming fast up the slope was a line at least as long as the one they had just faced. And beyond was another, and beyond that another, and then another: five lines in all – perhaps four thousand warriors; perhaps even more.

'Christ!' he spat, and turned hard. 'Sound "rally", Corporal Dilke!'

Dilke pulled up to blow. He could do it at the gallop right

enough – at a field day. But the price of blowing ill here was too great. And it was not an easy call: semi-quavers and octave leaps. He would blow till he saw the troop rallying.

He did not see the Zulu playing dead twenty yards away. He did not see him coming flat like the leopard when it runs in for its prey. Nor the fast, furious sprint to the kill. Nor the *iklwa*, as it stabbed at his side, under his rib cage, deep into his vitals: eight whole inches when four would have been fatal.

He let out no cry, but the 'rally' ceased abruptly on the long, final C.

CHAPTER TWENTY-FIVE

THE COLOUR OF DANGER

Next morning

'Very well, Mr Fearnley: exactly as before!'

Lieutenant Fearnley squinted into the low, eastern sun and touched his shako in acknowledgement.

They had been in the saddle all night. The Zulu had swept over the ridge *i'mpondo zankhomo*: in the 'beast's horns' formation. Hervey had never seen such an envelopment before. And if he had obliged them and held his ground longer, the tips of the horns would have met and his force would have been trapped in a killing-circle. By some instinct he had sensed the danger in time, recalled the troop, remounted the Rifles and withdrawn in good order to the next piece of high ground. There he had recovered his balance, so to speak. He concluded that Matiwane had used his first cohort (*ivyo*, as later he would know it) to probe the strength of his unexpected adversary. He had used brave men's breasts to discover the awful power of the rifle, and it looked as if he were prepared to use many more to overcome it. Hervey knew it would not be possible to stand again in the way he had, for Matiwane could be no fool. He was certainly not without resolve. Even with the speed of the horse in his favour, Hervey could not be sure he could afford a close action when the Zulu were so practised in enveloping.

And so his three hundred had kept watch in the moonlight, the Rifles firing the occasional harassing volley, dragoons and riflemen retiring steadily along their former line of advance, never giving the Zulu a chance to rush them or work round a flank. Sometime after midnight Matiwane had discontinued the advance in line, reverting to the single file of the *ivyo*, easier to control and direct. And now, at the break of the new day and the veld coming to life, as the raptors began seeking out the first columns of warm air on which to rise to their own posts of observation (how Hervey envied them their elevation), they must begin the game again, and continue until Colonel Somerset and his red-coated battalion, with the artillery, the burghers and the legions of Xhosa, came up and delivered the decisive blow.

As soon as they had broken off the first engagement, Hervey had sent back a cornet to report to Somerset, and with orders to return as soon as possible after first light with Somerset's intentions, for he wanted as good an idea as possible how long 'the game' must continue. He was surprised, however, to see him galloping back now.

'Mr Beauchamp, you were up with the larks, I perceive.'

'Colonel,' replied Cornet Beauchamp, saluting and trying not to appear too eager. Yesterday was his first time in action, and his mission to Colonel Somerset his first as a galloper.

Hervey, sitting at ease astride his mare, a canteen of Johnson's best tea in his sword hand, touched his shako peak by return.

'Colonel Somerset's compliments, sir, and would you see the

Zulu to the Ox River one league to our rear. He will give battle there.'

Hervey sat up. 'One league? Only one league? Are you sure? Then they marched prodigiously quick!'

'Colonel. I came on them just before midnight not five miles from the river. I would have made them earlier but my mare went lame.'

Hervey wondered why Beauchamp had not at once taken his coverman's horse; but that could wait.

'After I had given Colonel Somerset your report he said they would continue the march and asked me to lead – he said he was uncertain of his guides – and we reached the river at about four o'clock. The moon was gone by then but we carried out a reconnaissance of the fords, and the colonel decided that he would stand on the defensive there on the west bank. I considered that it was proper to remain with the colonel during the reconnaissance since I would then be able to inform you precisely of the situation. I set out as soon as it was expedient. Colonel.'

Hervey nodded. 'I don't doubt it. You did right. How many Xhosa, by the way?'

'Colonel Somerset said seven thousand.'

Hervey sighed – to himself, but with considerable relief. 'Very well, Mr Beauchamp; you may rejoin your troop. Smart work.'

Johnson gave the cornet tea as he reined away.

Hervey turned to Fairbrother, who was observing the flight of distant vultures. 'You heard that? Somerset at the river but a league back!'

Fairbrother kept his telescope to his eye. 'I did indeed. Very gratifying. Colonel Somerset has vigour; I'll grant you that.'

'You might sound more convinced – or convincing.'

With no Zulu in sight, Hervey now dismounted and signalled for the troop to stand down.

'What do you look at so intently?'

'Yon birds. I've observed in the past that they can be useful.'

Hervey was well enough acquainted with vultures. In India there were so many, and carrion so plentiful, it was their absence only that was remarked. 'How so?'

'They're scavengers, but I've long observed that it is the living which first attracts them, not the dead – which they might not always see, though they must have a hawk-eye like their cousins. It is the natural order of things on the veld: the living continually become the dead.'

Hervey was unfastening the bit to give his mare a peck of corn. 'Fairbrother, neither of us has had any sleep, so I beg you to be brief.'

Fairbrother lowered his telescope. 'I thought at first the Zulu might have killed a bull – the sort of thing I believe they do to fortify themselves – but observe the distribution of the birds. They're not circling with apparent intent to come down on a particular spot; they're patrolling a wide area. Which I presume is that occupied by the Zulu bivouac.'

'Why aren't they all at yesterday's feast?' asked Hervey as he took out his own telescope again.

'You have your answer: it was yesterday's feast.'

'*So* quick?'

Fairbrother nodded.

Hervey peered at them for a good while. Their line of patrol was a full mile to the troop's front, and the same in length: much as he imagined the *impi* to occupy in bivouac – or else in the advance. 'If it is so – their watching the Zulu, I mean – then they're worth a couple of dozen scouts. I wonder shall they tell us when they advance?'

'I shall endeavour to read the signs,' said Fairbrother airily.

Hervey nodded, and smiled. He put back the telescope in its holster and took a handful of corn from the feedbag on the saddle. His mare ate it greedily.

'May I make a suggestion?' asked Fairbrother.

'By all means.'

'You'll send out scouts?'

'They're making ready this moment. It is the usual drill.'

'I should like to ride to that little hill yonder.' He pointed out what appeared to be the merest anthill on the green veld. 'I've a notion I might see things better.'

'I have no objection,' said Hervey, but warily. 'Take with you Corporal Byrne.'

'If I may, I'd rather go unaccompanied.'

Hervey was reluctant to accede; it took only his horse to lame itself and Fairbrother would be at the mercy of the spear. But then, he had crawled about the bush at night and dealt singly with three Xhosa . . . 'Very well.'

With the scouts forward, Hervey was able to stand down both troop and company to make a proper feed for the horses and breakfast for themselves. For over forty hours neither dragoon nor rifleman had eaten but what they carried in their haversacks: corn cakes, and dried meat which without slaking was like chewing bridle leather. Hervey sat on the ground holding his mare's reins, letting her pull at the rough veld grass. It would have no goodness in it (except, he supposed, for the game – the antelope and such) but a little bulk inside would do her no harm.

He looked up at the vultures. Had they picked clean Gilbert's bones yet? He hated the death of a horse without ceremony, without proper disposal, leaving it to the pecking and tearing of crows and ravening dogs, and then to the ants and maggots and worms . . . He grieved separately for Corporal Dilke.

'All well, sir?' came a voice of the Tyne.

'*Passing* well, Sarn't-major,' he replied, without looking up.

'A close shave wi' Gilbert, I understand.'

'Ay. How's the troop?'

It was not rightly 'procedure' for the troop serjeant-major to speak above the head of the troop leader (and Hervey had placed his lieutenant squarely in command); but with Armstrong 'right procedure' was an aid, like spurs or a whip, not an end in itself. Hervey would ever welcome his counsel, or even, as now, simply his company.

'They're in good fettle. Them greenheads did all right yesterday. Not one unseated. And not a horse lame this morning.'

Hervey had had the parade states already, but Armstrong's assurance was welcome nonetheless. As it had been for a dozen years and more. Indeed, he had almost begun to think of Armstrong and the army – certainly the regiment – as one and the same. 'We made a deal of vulture meat yesterday.'

'We did an' all, sir. But I doubt they'll be caught like that again. Not the way they kept coming on when the rifles began dropping 'em. An' if they can learn to form square with them spears . . .'

Hervey agreed. They had fought men under discipline yesterday, strict discipline; well-trained men, and brave too.

Suddenly Armstrong braced. 'Cap'n Fairbrother's coming in at a fair lick, sir!'

Hervey got to his feet. Fairbrother was a furlong off, his horse flattening. 'Stand to, Sarn't-major. Trumpeter!'

Armstrong was gone in an instant, barking words of command like a jack-corporal at his first picket. Trumpeter Roddis came running, bugle in hand, ready. He halted at attention and saluted. 'Sir?'

'Stand to your horses.'

'Sir!'

It was a simple call: triplets and a minim repeated, all on C. As well, since Roddis was still unpractised.

Fairbrother galloped straight at them, reining back only in the last few yards. 'Call in your scouts, Hervey: there're Zulu on both flanks!'

Hervey didn't hesitate. 'Skirmishers in, Roddis!'

It took a second or so for the trumpeter to recollect the call, and then he began blowing for all he was worth.

'Zulu on both flanks?'

'Ay,' said Fairbrother, slipping from the saddle and catching his breath. 'Crawling so flat you'd have to run into them to see. That's why the scouts didn't.'

'How—'

'That hillock yonder's bigger than you think. I thought as much from the length of the shadow at first light. And then the vultures started taking a look this way, as if they'd seen something. That's when I saw them, running like monkeys on all fours, so flat as to be hid by the grass.'

Hervey rattled through his options. They were few. He could throw out a flank – *two* flanks – but that would avail him nothing if the Zulu were behind him . . . 'How many do you suppose there are?'

Fairbrother shook his head. 'No way of knowing. But it would make sense for Matiwane to send a column round each flank: a couple of hundred or more to each, I mean.'

Hervey was astounded. 'You mean there might be five hundred Zulu, unseen?'

'I do.'

That settled it. His force was too weak to deal with an encirclement in such strength. And the rest of the *impi* would no doubt be readying to hurl itself in a frontal attack. 'Hammer on anvil,' he said ruefully.

Lieutenant Fearnley and Captain Welsh were soon come up. Hervey was emphatic: 'We retire at the trot, Rifles leading!'

Colonel Somerset was waiting at the ford of the Ox River as they approached. Hervey had led with the Rifles since he judged it too risky to dismount for rearguard action, the sabre handier therefore than the firearm. Once they had put a mile of veld behind them, the furthest distance he calculated a Zulu could have advanced unseen, he threw out skirmishers in a wide arc behind, sent Cornet Beauchamp back to the river to inform Somerset, and continued the retirement at the walk. From time to time a dragoon took a shot with his carbine and sent back word of a Zulu – or else some wild animal – in the long grass, but besides the advancing vultures there was no definite sign that Matiwane was following in strength.

Half a mile from the river Hervey ordered Lieutenant Fearnley to post a picket line and to mark his routes of withdrawal to the ford, and told the Rifles to prepare to cross to the far bank. Then he galloped for the ford to speak in person with the commander of the Kaffraria Field Force.

'Mounted detachment returned to your disposal, Colonel,' he reported, saluting with due ceremony.

Somerset touched the peak of his forage cap. 'Where are the Zulu?'

Hervey did not like the peremptory tone. 'By my best estimate, the main force is half a league off, but their scouts may be a good deal nearer. The troop is in picket line yonder' (he indicated the distant trees beyond the scrub of the flood plain) 'with orders to send patrols forward if there is no sign of the Zulu within the hour.'

Somerset was indignant. 'But my orders were for you to see in the Zulu. You appear to have let them bustle *you* in.'

Hervey was even more indignant. 'Don't be an ass! We'll see them in all right. But I won't lose men when there's no need. These Zulu are damned clever; they know how to use ground. We need to take careful measure of them.'

'I seem to recall some great captain of your arm saying that a cavalryman, properly mounted, ought never to be taken captive.'

Hervey was determined not to anger further; Somerset had marched all night, as he had. 'Colonel, you will do me the honour of allowing me to know my business, and judging me on the results. So far, I have delayed the advance of the Zulu sufficiently for you to be able to take a stand here, where at least the chances of being outflanked are so much the less. There's not another river in ten miles.'

Somerset made no reply. There was truth in what Hervey said, and very evidently his intention was to be of support.

'Shall you give me orders?' asked Hervey, quietly. 'How is the force disposed? Where are the Xhosa?'

Somerset nodded, as if resolving on amity. Then he told him the plan of defence. The Xhosa were clearing the cover on each bank – not nearly as thick here, mercifully, as on the Fish – the artillery were posted on the rising ground fifty yards back from the river, able to command both the ford and its approaches, and the 55th Regiment would take post covering the ford itself. The burghers were to range up-stream and down, and the Rifles, dismounted, would skirmish on the eastern bank before crossing and reinforcing the Fifty-fifth.

Hervey could not disapprove; it was a sound plan. Except, perhaps, in one detail. 'I should say, with respect, that the Rifles – and the troop – are very tired. They have had no sleep to speak of in three days. They'll need more time to get back than supposed. Although the cover is good for their purpose this side, the field of fire, as you perceive, is not great.'

Somerset looked irritated again.

Hervey knew the look well enough. He had seen it many a time in his twenty years' service: the look of the officer who is apprised of some piece of information which interferes with his otherwise perfectly laid plans, and whose instinct is to dismiss the intelligence by dismissing its bearer.

'Do you say your dragoons and these half-baked riflemen have no more stomach for the fight?'

Hervey, so tired that his patience was near the end, but by long years persuaded that such men as Somerset could only be dealt with through flattery, spoke calmly. 'They do indeed have stomach, Colonel. They will fight for you to the last. It is only that . . . their stomachs may be a little *empty*, so to speak.'

The emollience worked. 'I see. Yes, of course they will be tired. I will take careful note of it. Perhaps, now, you will ride with me as we post the Rifles, and I will point out the lie of things.'

'By all means,' replied Hervey. And then, imagining he would not likely have a better – or perhaps any – chance to say it, added: 'I must commend to you, Colonel, in the strongest possible terms, the valuable service of Captain Fairbrother these past two days. Without his address I do believe we should have suffered many casualties; and, I venture to admit, perhaps even a reverse.'

Somerset was not entirely dismissive of the notion, though his 'surprise' was unconcealed.

The first reports came within an hour: the black host advanced as before, a dozen columns, single file. Hervey at once alerted Somerset, who was siting each field-piece in detail. Somerset declared he would see for himself. Hervey did not discourage him.

In minutes they were with Fearnley at the picket line, and with just enough elevation to see what they faced. The sight shook Somerset, as it first had Hervey – the order, the discipline of it, not at all the horde of savages he had imagined.

'We must suppose they know we are here,' said Hervey. 'They'll likely make a probing attack at once, or else try again to encircle us, though the river will confound them in that. May I recall the outposts?'

Somerset was less confident than an hour ago. 'Yes . . . by all means . . . do.'

Trumpeter Roddis repeated the call until Hervey saw the outposts acknowledging, and then bid him cease.

The Rifles were trained to the bugle too, but Captain Welsh had decided instead on signals by whistle in order to avoid confusion. Hearing the recall of the picket line he gave three long blasts – the order to stand to arms.

'It will now depend on each rifleman's initiative,' said Hervey, and to Somerset's evident discomfort.

*

The outposts came in at the trot, tall in the saddle though the horses looked weary. Each dragoon saluted as he passed the two colonels, eyes on Hervey but Somerset acknowledging with a finger to the peak of his cap. They had done their work, they had done it well, and they knew it. Once across the river they could dismount and take a little ease before it was their turn again. For it *would* be their turn again; it always was. When the men with the rifle and the musket had done their work it would be theirs to turn defeat into rout – to make vulture meat of the fleeing enemy so that they might not turn again. It was a grim business sabring those who no longer wanted to fight, but it had to be done lest the next day these fleeing men became resolute once more. To think otherwise was nothing but sentiment – *dangerous* sentiment.

Rifle fire began on both far flanks almost at the same time. Hervey marvelled at the evident ability of the Zulu to coordinate the movement of the two horns of the crescent formation. And then the firing spread along the entire front as the main columns began approaching, still hidden by the prodigious grass.

But not, apparently, hidden to the gunners. A shell buzzed high over him and to the left, bursting twenty feet above the ground three hundred yards in front. Hervey smiled to himself. Never had he known an artilleryman to miss his opportunity. How he was able to place his fire so accurately, and have the shrapnel shell explode at the precise height, was quite beyond him. He was only grateful for it; vastly grateful. It was, in truth, how war should be made.

'Colonel Hervey?'

He turned to see his lieutenant, and detached himself from Somerset's party to confer with him. 'All eager, Mr Fearnley?'

'Indeed, Colonel. Minnie has wind aplenty left.'

Hervey glanced approvingly at Fearnley's second charger. Minnie – *Minerva* – had won one of the regimental races at Hounslow that year. She looked in as hale condition now as then. 'The intention for you now is clear?'

'Exactly clear. I think I shall be well pleased to see that ford.'

A cry like hounds breaking covert turned every head. The staunchest heart faltered for a moment as Zulu rose up from the ground like corpses on the Day of Judgement, swarming, stabbing, grunting like rutting pig.

Hervey saw two of Somerset's staff tumble from the saddle, and then Somerset's own horse fall to its knees, and Somerset himself half under it, his escorts desperately lashing out with sword and pistol.

Hervey spurred for him at once, sabre drawn, Fairbrother and the others close on his heels. He cut left and right, taking a passing spear in the thigh though not feeling a thing.

Fairbrother sprang from the saddle beside Somerset like a tumbler at a fair, drawing his revolver and firing three shots in quick and lethal succession at the nearest Zulu.

Wainwright and Roddis circled, keeping a dozen others at bay while Hervey and Fairbrother pulled Somerset from beneath his charger and heaved him astride Hervey's mare.

Fairbrother emptied his revolver as Hervey vaulted on her quarters to support the winded colonel.

Hervey turned his mare on her hocks and dug in his spurs, fending off a Zulu and losing grip of his sabre in the process.

Fairbrother managed to clamber into his own saddle, draw his second pistol and shoot the Zulu before he could take advantage.

But the horde was already reluctant to follow: every rifle within range was now turned on them.

As he glanced back, Hervey could see but a handful of black shapes haring for the cover whence they'd sprung. He heard Welsh's whistle repeated along the front, the desperate recalling of his riflemen. They had done their work. They had stood their ground, shot well, broken up a surprise attack that would have prevailed against all but the most resolute.

As his mare splashed into the ford, and yet another artillery round whistled overhead, Hervey saw the Fifty-fifth standing like a red stone wall. Not for the first time he blessed the legionary infantry who would now bear the brunt of the fight. And he cursed himself for doubting them, as he cursed Somerset for doubting his Rifles.

CHAPTER TWENTY-SIX

BATTLE HONOURS

Cape Town, six weeks later

Hervey sat with a blanket about his shoulders in a cane chair by the window while his Hottentot bearer changed the bed linen for only the second time that day. He was getting better, no doubt of it: for the best part of a week the bearer had changed the linen *three* times daily.

''Ave a bit o' this, then, sir,' coaxed Johnson.

Hervey took the enamel cup in both hands. He no longer trembled, but he felt strangely weak still, and he did not wish to spill Johnson's precious brew.

'Good God!' he spat, his face contorted as he swallowed. 'What infernal sort of tea's this?'

'It's not tea, it's whistlejacket.'

Hervey shook his head. 'Johnson, I feel wretched enough without guessing games.'

'Whistlejacket: gin 'n' treacle.'

'One of your orphanage purgatives, was it?'

'It's right good for thee. None o' t'stuff t'surgeon give thee did owt.'

Hervey was not inclined to dispute the latter, and thought it best to oblige his groom – for all his doubt as to the whistlejacket's efficacy and all his certainty as to its ill taste.

Unquestionably he was feeling better, however. He had not yet regained his appetite, but at least he now cared. It had been a longer than usual attack of the fever, though several days had passed without his having any knowledge of them. At least there was no more pain from the wound in his leg. He would soon see two scars, a dozen years, but only inches, apart, and each made not with bullet or shrapnel, or even sabre, but with the thrusting point, as primitive a thing as any of the ancients'. There was no weapon too short in the hand for a brave man.

He sighed, but with some contentment. He had done well; he knew it. Everyone from General Bourke to the rudest burgher had told him. He had blooded the Rifles, and ably, and proved their worth. And in the fight at the river, the red and the blue and the green had worked with such mutual and effective support that the Zulu had never been able to close with them and test the power of their short spears. Matiwane had left so many men dead at the ford that it would be many months, if not years, before they would have the temerity to challenge the King's army again. Kaffraria could expect a little peace; and wise counsel in Cape Town ought to be able to make good use of it. That was what Somervile had said to him before this fever had taken hold.

He drained the cup. Almost at once his head began to swim. 'Is there a very lot of gin in this, Johnson?'

Johnson shrugged.

Hervey looked at the pile of letters on the table beside his bed: from home, from Hounslow, from the Horse Guards, from Kezia Lankester – all unanswered. Tomorrow he would make a beginning, perhaps, if he continued well; and if Johnson didn't poison him with his cures.

'Have you seen Serjeant Wainwright?'

'I 'ave, sir. We 'ad a wet in t'canteen last night on account o' 'is new stripe.'

Hervey nodded. 'And you, Johnson?'

'Ah'm all right, sir. Al'a's am.'

He nodded again. Yes, Johnson was always 'all right'. Except for the unfathomable business of the coral; or rather, his refusing to confide in him about it. It was good to have him back, and the same Johnson as in the best of times.

'I mean that you did fine service. Never more so than when you brought up Molly when Gilbert fell. I'm excessively grateful.'

Johnson shifted awkwardly. He didn't much like things singled out like that. And he had been as fond of Gilbert as had Hervey himself. It was the very devil of a thing to have to leave an old friend to the savages and the vultures – old *friends*, indeed, for Corporal Dilke had been a decent messing-mate. 'It were nowt, sir,' he muttered, turning to the bearer for distraction. 'Come on, Inky! Tha's quicker than that as a rule!'

The bearer beamed happily as he tucked in the last of the corners.

'*Enkosi*,' said Hervey, trying to be cheery. '*Enkosi*.'

The bearer picked up the sweated linen, bowed several times while still smiling broadly, and trotted out of the room.

''E's a good'n, sir, is Thandi. Reckon we should take 'im back wi' us.'

'Perhaps we should.'

The door opened.

Johnson braced. 'Sir!'

Hervey looked round to discover the cause of Johnson's sudden soldiery. 'Somervile! I am glad to see you.'

'And I you,' said his old friend, advancing on him with hand outstretched.

Hervey took it, though the vigour with which Somervile shook it reminded him he had a way to go before being back to hale condition. 'Shall you stay? Will you have tea, or something stronger?'

'I will have tea with you, gladly. Emma has forbidden me anything stronger in the afternoon.'

Johnson left for his tea-making duties.

'Is there news from the frontier?'

'Nothing but tranquillity. No reports of reiving in weeks.'

Hervey let the blanket slip from his shoulders: he was getting hotter and he was certain it did not help. 'That is gratifying.'

Somervile pulled up a chair. 'It most positively is. I have just been reading Somerset's report to General Bourke. Admirable, Hervey; quite admirable.'

Hervey was unclear as to quite what was admirable. 'I should like to see it.'

'Oh, you will, you will. Admirable – a most handsome acknowledgement. Your Captain Fairbrother is evidently a man of resource and sensibility. I wonder the castle had never sought to employ him before. And most commending it is of you too – in the fullest terms imaginable. I declare I thought Somerset a tricky man when first I met him, but he has shown himself of a very true disposition.'

'I am pleased for it. It would not have served without Fairbrother.'

'You saved Somerset's life.'

'We were several. Believe me: no single man could have done anything for Somerset at that moment. I confess I thought him lost.'

'He says he has written to his uncle FitzRoy; *that* shall do you no harm! And Bourke too has written to the Horse Guards. I very much hope there's a promotion in it, else I myself shall have to write to Huskisson.'

Hervey tried a self-deprecating smile. He thought the praise overblown. But he would certainly not gainsay it.

'I have approved your home leave.'

Hervey blinked. 'But I have not requested it.'

'You will not decline it?'

'I cannot leave my command like that!'

'Your command – both Rifles and dragoons – is well found. Thanks to you. And there are things I would have you advance on my behalf in Whitehall. We have a peace for now in Kaffraria, but I am certain it will not hold indefinitely. *Si vis pacem, preparate bellum?*'

Hervey nodded.

'Besides, you have obligations under the law,' added Somervile, with something of a smile.

'Law? What law?' asked Hervey, rallying at the challenge.

'Mosaic: *When thou goest out to battle against thine enemies.*'

Hervey shook his head. 'I confess I haven't an idea what you're speaking of. The fever must be addling me.'

Somervile picked up the bible from the table beside Hervey's bed. 'Deuteronomy,' he said, turning the pages confidently. 'I'm astonished you need reminding. Here, chapter twenty ... verse seven: "And what man is there that hath betrothed a wife ..."' He handed it to him. 'Read on. And none of your churchy primness! A wise bird, Moses.'

Hervey read. And he smiled (a shade lickerish, thought Somervile) as he tried to imagine complying with the injunction. 'Oh yes, wisdom indeed!'

'I fear, though, that our Nation may think the business here but a skirmish compared with the Greek war.'

Hervey quickened. 'Oh? How so?'

'Nothing worth your regrets: no work for cavalry, as far as I can make out; nor even for foot,' he began airily. 'The whole thing appears to have been decided at sea. We had first news of it this morning, a considerable battle in the Ionian: a combined fleet – English, French, Russian – with Codrington commanding. Appears they sent the Turkish fleet to the bottom of Navarino Bay.'

'Navarino Bay?'

'You will know it better as Pylos, perhaps, if you recall Thucydides.'

'I'm afraid I recall nothing. A considerable affair, you say?'

'Indeed, a hundred ships and more. Bigger than Trafalgar.'

Hervey sat upright, the blanket quite falling away. 'Have you the casualty lists?'

Somervile shook his head. 'I expect they'll come with the official papers. This is news from *The Times* only. But it was a desperate affair, I think. The report said perhaps four or five thousand.'

Hervey said not a word. His mind was wholly occupied by thoughts of Peto: had he not been under orders to join Codrington's squadron? His fevered face began losing the remains of its colour.

Somervile leaned forward to steady him. 'Hervey, my dear fellow, are you quite well?'

AFTERNOTE

The extraordinary 'Indian' gardens at Sezincote, with the statuary that so engaged Hervey and Kezia Lankester, are open to the public. So too is the 'Moghul' house.

Private Johnson's brush with the Bow Street investigators was not without foundation. At the Court of Exchequer on 29 April 1827, *The King v. Giuseppe Guecco* (on various counts of importing coral without payment of duty), the jury, after retiring for about twenty minutes, returned a verdict for the Crown, with an earnest recommendation of leniency. It was agreed by counsel on both sides to compound for the offence by the payment of £400.

Students of early Zulu history may dispute my account of the first contact with Shaka's army. They would be right to do so. Chief Matiwane owed no allegiance to Shaka. His clan, the Ngwanes, although one of the Nguni people like the 'pure' Zulu, had for a decade resisted incorporation into Shaka's greater Zulu kingdom. In the course of evasion, however, they became a marauding tribe as troublesome as the Zulu to the Xhosa and others of Kaffraria. But at the time of Hervey's brush with them the precise status of Matiwane's warriors was unknown, and their depredations were lumped together with those of Shaka in the reports reaching Cape Town. Scholars also disagree: while published sources have tended to make Matiwane *non*-Zulu, later academic research has not been so certain. For instance, John Burridge Scott in a thorough doctoral thesis (*The British Soldier on the Eastern Cape frontier 1800–1850*, University of Port Elizabeth, 1973) calls Matiwane's tribesmen unequivocally Zulu. And, indeed, after Shaka's death Matiwane declared his allegiance to the new king, Dingane, Shaka's half-brother.

It is more than likely that Matthew Hervey will find himself involved in the coming tumult on the Eastern Cape frontier, and perhaps even further afield – in Natal, the very territory of the Zulu nation.

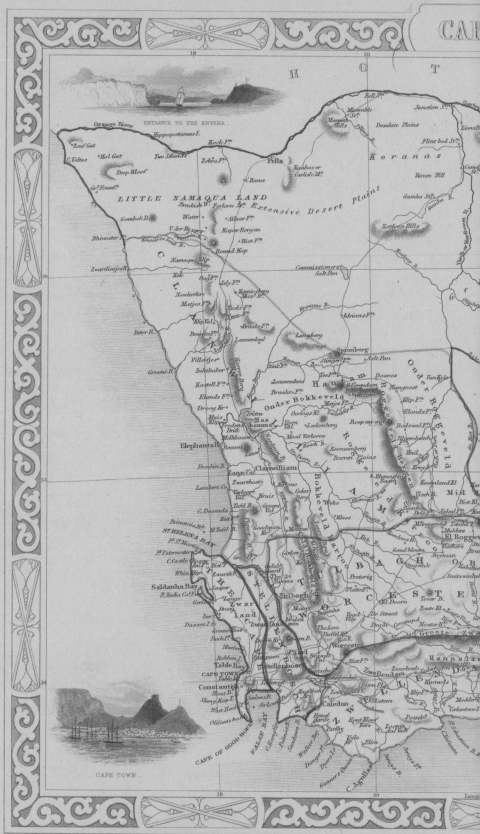